The Vexations

The Vexations

Caitlin Horrocks

Little, Brown and Company
New York Boston London

Copyright © 2019 by Caitlin Horrocks

Hachette Book Group supports the right to free expression and the value of copyright. The purpose of copyright is to encourage writers and artists to produce the creative works that enrich our culture.

The scanning, uploading, and distribution of this book without permission is a theft of the author's intellectual property. If you would like permission to use material from the book (other than for review purposes), please contact permissions@hbgusa.com. Thank you for your support of the author's rights.

Little, Brown and Company
Hachette Book Group
1290 Avenue of the Americas, New York, NY 10104
littlebrown.com

First Edition: July 2019

Little, Brown and Company is a division of Hachette Book Group, Inc. The Little, Brown name and logo are trademarks of Hachette Book Group, Inc.

The publisher is not responsible for websites (or their content) that are not owned by the publisher.

The Hachette Speakers Bureau provides a wide range of authors for speaking events. To find out more, go to hachettespeakersbureau.com or call (866) 376-6591.

ISBN 978-0-316-31691-0
LCCN 2019930467

10 9 8 7 6 5 4 3 2 1

LSC-C

Printed in the United States of America

for Leo

A Simple Question
Which do you prefer:
Music or Ham?

—*Erik Satie*

Conrad

— 1 —

Like a door opening

CONRAD DOESN'T HAVE THE KEY. HE STANDS AT HIS BROTHER Erik's apartment door, waiting for one of Erik's friends to pull it from a trouser or jacket pocket. It is 1925, and all the men are wearing suit jackets despite the July heat, despite the fact that everyone except Conrad is a composer or a musician, and Conrad had always supposed them to be a breed apart, unconcerned with propriety. The only composer he's ever known personally was his brother, and how well did Conrad even know him? Not well enough for a key.

Erik's friend Roger unlocks the door but does not open it. He steps aside, gesturing for Conrad to do the honors. No one has entered Erik's apartment in the days since his death, and nearly no one in all the twenty-seven years he lived here. Conrad pauses to feel and then set aside the guilt of violation. With both dread and anticipation, he pushes the door ajar.

Dusty light filters in from the hallway, and slowly the contents of the apartment become visible: a great profusion of umbrellas and walking sticks; stacks of handkerchiefs (eighty-six, it will turn out); mountains of yellowed newspapers; a small table with a single chair; a battered piano. A wardrobe that, when they open it, will contain only six identical gray velvet suits. In the front hall sits a baffling gymnastic machine, like an insect of

3

cracked rubber belts and leggy metal bars. Conrad steps in a pile of dog shit whose provenance is a mystery, since Erik never owned a dog. The waste is scentless, dried and crumbling. There is no stink, nothing on Conrad's shoes except a light chalky powder.

The men move farther into the apartment, but there is no easy way to catalog Erik's possessions under the filth. After some discussion, a couple of the friends leave to ask the building concierge for the loan of a broom, a dustpan, whatever else might be spared in memory of the neighborhood celebrity. Along with Roger, Conrad stays, searching in vain for some evidence as to how his brother could have emerged from this place every Sunday with his beard trimmed and collar white, standing on Conrad's doorstep to be let in for dinner. He sits on a piano bench that groans under him, the joints gone so loose he stands again. Roger turns, frowning, even indignant, perhaps because Conrad knows nothing about music. Ignoring him, Conrad wonders if it should have been Philippe here with him instead. Or maybe not, because Philippe never knew anything about music, either. Conrad does not arrange his hand to make any particular sound, simply settles his fingers onto the white keys at the far right end of the keyboard. Roger winces, perhaps expecting a shrill, tinkling catcall, but no sound comes. Conrad taps, then pounds, his way up and down the keys. Silence.

Wordlessly, the two men lift the lid of the piano. Inside they find a morass of cut wires and scattered wooden hammers, the unstrung guts of the instrument mixed with drifts of paper, letters and unopened bills, notebooks and telegrams and pneumatiques. Conrad pulls the papers out by the handful, arranges them into piles on the piano bench, then gives up and allows them to scatter across the floor: empty, doodled-upon envelopes; drawings of tiny, elaborate castles; self-portraits of Erik wearing enormous spectacles; patent applications for inventions that never existed; a declaration of excommunication from a pretend church for a music critic; and hundreds of newspaper clippings, some so small they look like confetti, two-line notices of group shows or prizes, only some of them about Erik. Most of the names are unfamiliar to Conrad. They aren't household names, although the men are all young enough to be aiming for it, and some of them may yet succeed. These are Roger's friends, and he handles the scraps like relics, as if he sees in them proof that Erik cared about his acolytes, that surely he didn't mean those things he'd said to them toward the end.

He did, Conrad thinks. *He meant every word.* And he is almost cruel enough to say it, to claw his brother back for himself. Ever since he was picked up this morning by Erik's friends in Roger's ludicrously bright yellow car, Conrad has been plagued by what he is only slowly allowing himself to acknowledge is jealousy. *Erik would have dropped you soon enough*, he thinks of the friends. But how could he possibly wish his brother any more alone than Erik already was? He doesn't. He never did. Conrad has always wanted to believe that blood weighs more than music, but he knows that the metaphor, besides being off-kilter, is also probably untrue. Erik's music, while light as laughter, was heavy enough to break even him in the end.

The piano keeps vomiting: steady letters from their sister, Louise. Earnest notes from Philippe: *How are you, old friend? Tell me you're well.* Nothing from Suzanne, though why would there be? Even Erik didn't expect to hear from her after she married someone else, and expectation was Erik's constant state. No one could measure up. Not Suzanne, nor Philippe, nor Conrad, although he'd tried hardest and longest. The apartment is an accusation, but what more, really, could he have done?

Roger marvels over an exercise book that appears to contain some manuscript long since thought lost. "He said he left it on a bus," Roger remarks, and neither of them knows whether Erik thought that was the truth, or whether he invented the bus so that everyone would stop asking him about an opera he didn't know how to finish. Many of the pieces in the composition notebooks are only a few lines long, and Conrad can't tell if they're deliberate sketches—Erik often worked in miniature—or abandoned efforts. One loose-leaf page contains two lines of music and a note about how to prepare oneself to play the piece 840 times in succession, as if Erik would ever in a thousand years have had the patience to do such a thing.

The air, tight with dust and soot, is full of smells Conrad does not want to think too long about. He forces a window, nearly sealed shut with old paint and dirt. On hot days in Arcueil-Cachan, this industrial suburb south of Paris, the smog is so thick that sunlight tumbles down through it like a bird with its wings wrenched back. A fly careers in as soon as the window squeaks open, as if it has been waiting politely for an invitation. Conrad sneezes and searches his pockets for a handkerchief, then reluctantly takes one from what he hopes is a freshly laundered pile on the gymnastic device. When he blows his nose the mucus is grimy. He examines it, both giddy and guilty; he is alive, full of warm, gray snot, sneezing the sneezes of the living. But when he imagines Erik's innards, his drink-sick liver and smog-choked lungs, his gratitude feels unseemly.

Conrad resumes his place on the piano bench and the two men listen to the silence, which is really the sound of their own breathing. They listen to the children shrieking in the street outside, the factory whistles and the scrabble of pigeons on the windowsills, the single loud fly buzzing near the ceiling. Roger joins Conrad at the piano and curls his fingers over the disconnected keys as if he's holding something priceless, the only precious thing in the room. What notes are the right ones to fill this miserable space, to say hello and goodbye? Both men grope for some music that can fill death's mute wake, as if a life is anything other than noise.

Eric

— 2 —

Looking at yourself from afar

TODAY THE BOY IS ORDINARY. NOT YET EXTRAORDINARY IN ANY way, not someone you might one day care to read about. The accomplishment he is most proud of is winning a neighborhood farting competition back in Paris, and he was the favorite in an upcoming belching contest. He is missing it right now, he realizes, as he calculates the hours eaten by the train carrying his newly diminished family north. There have been so many sadnesses it seemed there was not room for more. But now they all squeeze together in Eric's heart to admit another: this lost chance at glory. He confides in his sister about the contest, a plea for sympathy.

"Mother would be ashamed of you," Louise hisses.

Eric is a boy magnificently without shame, but Louise's statement at least makes him think. Their mother wouldn't exactly be *pleased*, he decides, but she would not be ashamed. He would still be her little monkey, and he hears his name the way she said it, the *R* at the top of her mouth, the sounds of her language soft like raindrops on a muddy yard. He sticks his hand in his armpit, directs farting noises at his sister. Louise rolls her eyes, asks their father to tell him to stop. Conrad ignores them both, pulling his hat on and off his head with single-minded determination. He is nearly four years younger than Eric, his hair still toddler-fine and sparse, floating in a staticky corona around his face. Louise is the middle child, but her gestures are a disapproving old woman's, all wagging fingers and pursed lips. Eric loves her anyway. When she bossed the neighborhood children, he would always persuade them to take her back, let her play again. The neighborhood parents liked Louise because she could always be trusted to tattle when something risky was afoot. Little Mother, the woman in the next apartment called her, and Eric cringes when he thinks of this, as if the word has been said aloud, as if their father could hear him hearing it.

Their father, Alfred, is a lightning-struck tree. It is November of 1872. In September, the family contained a fourth child, Eric's infant sister, and now it doesn't. In October, the family had a mother, and now it doesn't. Alfred slumps in a corner of the train compartment, staring out the window at the black-and-white cows in the endless yellowing fields. "I grew up here," he says, his palm against the glass, and the children glare. They were supposed to grow up in Paris. They feel kidnapped, not by fate or by their mother's death, but by the only person present enough to blame. "Do you remember your grandmother?" their father asks them. He licks his fingers and tries to smooth down Conrad's hair. Conrad twists away, removes his left shoe and puts it on his hand. Louise shakes her head.

Eric announces he's hungry and Alfred sighs and takes a red apple from his satchel. Eric has already bitten into it when Conrad squeals in protest, and their father orders the children to share, opening up his pocketknife and holding out the handle. Eric doesn't move. He's never sliced an apple before, and if his father wants it done on a moving train, surely he can do it himself.

"That's all right," Louise says. "I'm not hungry."

For once Eric wants her to go back to her bossing ways, to explain to their father that children shouldn't be cutting fruit on their own laps.

"Take it," Alfred says sharply, his fingers pinched around the flat of the blade. Eric does, gingerly, and Alfred settles back into his seat. "You mustn't act this way at your grandmother's house," he says. "She won't have it."

Eric follows his father's gaze as it returns to the window. Nothing but bare fields, bled of color in early November, stolid cows, stark stone houses and barns. The train curves and water appears below an indentation in the fields.

"The Seine," his father says. "All the way out here."

Louise slips the knife from Eric's hand, folds the blade away, and tucks it in her skirt. Eric imagines wrenching the window open and flinging the apple into the river, flinging himself alongside it, and bobbing all the winding way home. He imagines a note in a corked bottle: *Please help. Kidnapped to Normandy. Cows everywhere.* He stands and moves close to the window.

His father puts a hand on his shoulder, leans into his ear. "It's flowing westward," he says gently, almost a whisper. "To Honfleur, then out to sea."

"Oh," Eric says. Has his father guessed his plan? Eric looks down at his tooth marks in the apple, whose white flesh is already browning, and gives the rest to Conrad, who takes the apple with both hands, presses his face to it, and gnaws. Eric thinks of his imaginary note moving helplessly into the great nothing of the Atlantic: *Please help. Cows.*

In Honfleur, his grandmother Agnès assigns Eric and Conrad a single lumpy horsehair mattress in the attic. The garret windows rattle in the sea wind, salty air eating at their wooden frames. Everything about this town feels wrong, blown raw and new each morning. There is no warm smell of sewage on the river, no coal dust collecting over the sills and doorstep. Even the milk is grotesquely fresh, with a grassy, fleshy sort of taste. The butter is of a color and sweetness like fruit. It makes Eric gag.

"Too fresh?" his grandmother says scathingly. "How about

that. And the wind? You're half Scottish, you know, so you should be all right with the cold."

This quickly becomes the retort for everything. Eric can't complain about the draft in his room because of his mother's Scottish blood. He can't complain about the scratchiness of the linens, or Conrad's sharp, jabbing toenails, because Scots wear rough tartans. He can't complain about the food, because Scots eat oats and sheep stomachs. Since Normans are supposedly of hardy Viking stock themselves, the children are effectively never allowed to complain about anything.

Eric cuts triangles of newspaper, rolls them into horns, and pins them to Conrad's knit sleeping cap. "Conrad the Pillager," he announces, but Conrad just cries. The boy asks, incessantly, for his mother, and the sound pierces them all, a knife in apples. "I'll smother you," Eric says. "I will."

For the first few days Alfred seems to be pretending they're on holiday. He gives them tours, pointing out where Champlain set sail for the New World, but also the home where Jane, their mother, was visiting when they met; the ship brokerage where Alfred was employed; the hotel where Jane's parents stayed to meet him before the wedding; the Anglican church where Eric was baptized, whereupon the devoutly Catholic Agnès shrieked that neither she nor God would forgive Jane for this. Agnès never did, and while God's opinion could not be known for certain, no doubt Agnès considered Jane's death a kind of proof.

The church Agnès would have preferred was St. Catherine's. As the largest wooden church in France, it is also on the tour. The old stone one burned many centuries ago, in the Hundred Years' War, their father explains, praising the local shipbuilders who, rather than wait for the war to be over, for the Church to allocate funds and masons and craftsmen for a new one, built with what they knew. It was all ax work, he says, the beams and the thousands of wooden shingles covering the roof and walls. Towering straight oaks, trees of a sort that can no longer be found in Normandy, were used for the nave, the oldest part of the church. There is an obvious lesson here, says Alfred, about *resourcefulness*, about *initiative*. "They didn't wait for someone else to help," he insists. "They made the best of things."

"Well," Eric says dismissively, "a hundred years is a long time to wait."

"They didn't know it would be a hundred years. And the war wasn't really like that. It kept stopping and starting." Eric senses his father's impatience, as if Alfred knows he is not getting through. "They might have thought the war would be over in days, and they'd have all the stonemasons they wanted. No one knows these things when they're living inside them. Wars only have their names put to them later."

Eric can make no sense of a war lasting a century, of how long that might be. He can make no sense of a war fought with England, a place the family vacationed once, at the seaside in Brighton. A voice whispers in his head that his mother will be dead for a century, and a century after that, and all the centuries after.

That Eric's own name will last a century after his death, a century at least, does not enter his mind. He does not feel born to fame, nor entitled to it. Greatness sounds like a lot of work, frankly, and he is not given to study, or to practicing his piano. But however long Eric's name lasts, it will be longer than his mother's, longer than his sister's or his grandmother's or his father's. Conrad will one day publish a chemistry manual, so that his name will molder, if not in people's consciousnesses, then indefinitely in the catalogs of the Bibliothèque nationale de France. But none of this has happened yet. Lives, like wars, carry names assigned to them only once they're over.

St. Catherine's sits on a slope overlooking the harbor, separated from its bell tower by a stone courtyard. The height of the tower invites lightning, and the largest wooden church in France is also the most vulnerable to fire. The family climbs the steps of the tower up to the small belfry. The roof shingling is green with moss, and there is a moist, rotting smell. Alfred lifts the children so they can see through the wooden window slats: the harbor, the town, the city of Le Havre across the narrow channel, all divided into dim narrow slices. In an effort to share a joke, their father tells Eric that the townspeople here call Le Havre "the city on the other coast." But to Eric the distance looks vast enough for the name to be entirely appropriate. On the way back to his grandmother's house, he whispers words of his mother's English: "House, house, house," he says, and does not think to say "home." He traces the letters on his leg, his finger moving through the fabric of his pocket, an anxious charm against forgetting.

Their uncle, Alfred's younger brother, insists on being called Osprey, in English, by everybody: the children, his parents, friends and business associates, and the passersby who wave at him in the Old Basin. He owns a boat there that never leaves its mooring, although he pays a sailor to look after it, keep the sails mended, ropes coiled, railings freshly varnished. On weekends and evenings, after he leaves his stationer's shop, Osprey sits on the boat smoking his pipe. Alfred and the children occasionally join him, and Osprey teaches Eric how to tie knots while Louise and Conrad pretend to fish over the side with sticks and string. Osprey has a wife and three children of his own, but his wife bitterly resents the expense of the boat and rarely brings her children to see their cousins. Agnès and Alfred grouse about Osprey's finances over dinner, their disapproval couched as concern for his family. This is the only thing that seems to console Agnès about her influx of Parisian grandchildren; there are now new people to whom she can complain.

When Osprey comes to Sunday dinner, Alfred rattles off old grievances, how Osprey used to short-sheet their bed, how he planted dead mice under the coverlet. And there was the time he placed under the covers a baked potato so hot that Alfred burned the bottom of his foot and limped for a week. Eric supposes he should feel loyal to his father, but mostly he feels embarrassed at his father's feebleness at pranks. Alfred complains about misplacing his pocketknife, eyeing Osprey as if he might be somehow responsible for that, too. The main course is a briny lamb, raised on salt marshes near the coast, a local specialty Agnès prizes and the children loathe, and before it's even finished Osprey retreats to the garden to smoke. Agnès soldiers on with dessert, an apple tart drenched in eggy custard. Eric tries extracting the apple slices, but his father makes him eat the entire quivering yellow square.

When Agnès finally excuses Eric from the table he finds Osprey sitting on a wooden bench in the back garden, tapping his pipe out and rubbing ash into the gravel with his shoe. "You're still here," the boy says, surprised.

Osprey asks him if he gets along with his brother and sister.

"Mostly."

"Well, good for you."

Eric feels that he's disappointed his uncle. Both stare at their shoes. Osprey's feet, Eric notices, are exceptionally large.

"Have you found the mermaid?" Osprey finally asks.

Eric shakes his head.

"Come for a walk."

They leave by the back gate and circle around the block, passing the front of his grandmother's house and turning left up a pedestrian stairway, one of many shortcuts that mount the steep slope rising from the harbor. The sides of the staircase are the ivy-covered walls of private gardens.

Halfway up Osprey pauses, looks around as if to mark his bearings, then pulls at the ivy, searching for something. "Here it is," he finally says, and holds the vines aside.

Inlaid in the brickwork is a large brass plaque without words, just the relief of a mermaid, her tail curled into a J and her hair streaming down around it. She is topless, with rounded breasts

15

and tiny nubs of nipples. The plaque is a weathered, greenish color, except for the golden breasts.

"Boys used to rub her for luck," Osprey says. "They would pass her every day on the way to school, and there were little spells people would say, for extra luck, or to conjure the mermaid in real life."

Eric isn't sure if he's allowed to rub the breasts. Is his uncle inviting him to carry on the game, or to mock the gullibility of the village boys?

"Go ahead," Osprey says. "Make a wish."

Eric thinks at the mermaid, harder and harder, until his brain feels the way his eyes do when he pushes on the lids. He strokes the mermaid's hair, dabs the tip of his finger to the two fins at the end of her tail.

"Now you know the secret of the mermaid," Osprey says. "You must be a good steward."

That night Eric worries over what it means to be the steward of the secret of the mermaid. Should he share it with Conrad, or Louise? There are those bright scandalous breasts. There's the risk that Louise might tell Agnès, and that Agnès will find some way to ruin it for everybody. Eric decides that he can wish hard enough for everyone. He'll keep the secret to himself. *Is that all right?* he thinks into the air, imagining the darkness of a sea at night, the moonlight catching on the silver streaks of fish, a pale woman with a finned tail. He presses his hands to his eyes until she flickers into movement. *Of course,* she says. *That's fine.*

The next morning their father is gone. "On the first train," Agnès tells them at the breakfast table. "He's . . . traveling."

Eric sets aside a part of himself to be especially angry that his grandmother has rehearsed no better explanation than this. He does not really expect adults to be truthful with him, but surely they could take their lies more seriously.

"It's impossible," Agnès says. "A man trying to mother three children. That's why I told him to bring you here."

That afternoon she walks Eric to the shops in the town center. From a crisp envelope she unfolds a list of everything the school will require him to have: one mirror, two combs, a brush, a shoehorn, a prayer book, a glass and set of silverware, bed linens, twelve handkerchiefs, eight shirts, twelve cloth napkins, twelve small towels, six pairs of summer stockings and six winter. Three pairs of plain leather shoes. At the shoemaker Agnès orders three different sizes, the largest so big Eric needs two pairs of stockings and crumpled paper in the toe to keep his feet in them.

"So they won't get outgrown before they get outworn," she says.

For the shirts and towels and sheets, she buys yards of fabric. She does not buy the finest of anything, nor does she buy the cheapest. This, Eric thinks, is as much love as she has shown him.

"You can take flatware from the house," she says. "And a glass."

"Take it where?" Eric says.

She ignores him, but at the cabinetmaker she reads off precise dimensions for a box, absolutely no more than a quarter meter high. "I don't know why," his grandmother says, "but those are the instructions."

"So they fit under the beds," the cabinetmaker says. "Dormitory size. I'm sure we've got one ready-made. Do you want it delivered to the house or the school?"

"The house, for now," Agnès says. "He'll start next week."

Agnès walks him home past the Collège de Honfleur, the same one his father attended as a day student. It is one street over and one above his grandmother's house, a five-minute walk.

"It's so close," Eric says. But he doesn't say, "Don't send me away." He doesn't say, "Please."

Agnès says nothing. She hems the towels and sheets, begins work on the shirts, poking Eric with pins by lamplight. After she's cut and joined the pieces, Louise counts out the buttons.

"Will I go to school, too?" she asks.

"One at a time," Agnès says. "I have to figure out what to do with you children one at a time."

There has been no word from their father. As the shirts are finished Agnès folds them into the wooden box delivered from the cabinetmaker's. Eric slides it in and out under his bed to be sure that it fits. He dreams entire nightmares of arriving at school with a box too big to fit under the bed. One night he opens the box and finds a packet of licorice, tied with a ribbon, tucked inside one of his new shoes. When Agnès suggests on Sunday morning that he leave for school early, to settle in before Monday's classes, he is prepared. He begs for one more day; he loves the salt-marsh lamb, he claims, the eggy apple tart. Agnès twitches an eyebrow in victory.

While he's still here, she says, he should see if he can do something about Conrad's toenails. The boy hasn't let anyone touch them since leaving Paris, has bitten and scratched Agnès whenever she tried. She hands Eric a small silver pair of nail scissors and shoos them upstairs. Conrad pulls his stockings up past his knees, grips them as high on his thighs as he can make them stretch.

"They're so long you'll trip on them," Eric says, "and then you won't be able to run away with us."

Conrad blinks.

"We're going to leave together," Eric says. "On Osprey's boat."

All afternoon the children plan their escape, divide Eric's school bounty into neat piles, although Louise is dismayed at the thought of dressing like a boy. Eric announces that they will sail all the way to Argentina.

"That's too far," Louise says, sensible even in play.

At least, Eric assumes they're only playing, until Louise runs to her bedroom and returns with their father's pocketknife. She's kept it secret since the train, she says, hidden from Agnès.

Eric thinks that he could have told Louise about the mermaid, after all, that she would have kept that secret safe, too. "Where should we go?" he asks, sincerely.

"To Paris, down the river," Louise suggests, and Conrad agrees.

Eric gives Louise and Conrad his licorice, draws maps and makes provision lists until it's a game again, just a game, until the daylight runs out and their bellies are podgy with custard and Louise and Conrad are yawning. Agnès sends them all to bed and Eric follows his sister, watches as she tucks the pocketknife between mattress and bed frame. They wish each other good night, sweet dreams. He returns to the horsehair mattress, where Conrad tries to wind himself around his brother like an octopus. With Conrad's toenails now safely shorn, Eric lets him. He doesn't tell his brother or sister what their father told him, that the river flows north, to the sea, and that there will be no going back the way they came.

From the school office, where he sits with his grandmother and the headmaster, Eric can hear the full-time boarders clattering in the rectory. The hallway gets rowdier as his fellow Monday-through-Saturday boarders and the day students arrive. While the headmaster chats interminably with Agnès, Eric pushes his head through the open office door. In the white hallway a herd of dark-uniformed boys mills about. They remind him of the cows out the train window, black spots against white flanks. Then he remembers that he is wearing the same dark uniform jacket, that he'll soon be a splotch of the same cow. A boy turns and makes eye contact and Eric pulls back, embarrassed, and scratches his temple on the brass edge of the strike plate.

"Your father was a student here too," the headmaster says.

Eric presses his left palm against his temple. The office is a cavern of bloodred wallpaper and mahogany furniture, with a heavy leather blotter and silver coffee service on a side table. His grandmother looks so at home in the visitor's chair, her dress nearly matching the upholstery. He thinks this is probably the velvety sort of space she once hoped to live in but never had quite enough money for, even before four grief-ragged people fell into her starched lap. A dangerous empathy begins to uncurl inside him and he tamps it down.

"He knows," Agnès says. "About his father and uncle attending here."

Eric pictures his adult father walking among the children outside, his legs hairy above his stockings as he leans down to make fun of the boy with his face stuck through the headmaster's office door. No bell has rung, but there is the sound of classroom doors being unlatched, students filing in.

"I've kept you too long," the headmaster says to Agnès, then turns to Eric. "Let's get your things upstairs, and then to class with you."

Agnès stands and trains her eyes on Eric. He wonders if she's going to embrace him to say goodbye, the way a mother would. He wonders if he wants her to.

"Behave yourself," she says. "I'll see you Saturday. We'll have apple tart, now that I know you like it."

The headmaster hefts Eric's school box into the air and balances it on one shoulder like the men offloading boats in the harbor. Eric tries to pick up the rolled mattress, bound with twine and wrapped around the bedsheets like a pork roulade, but it's heavy for him, and awkward, so the headmaster lifts that, too. The walk down the hallway is excruciating. The boys in the classrooms they pass have only notebooks and pencils in front of them, at most a small satchel hanging off their chairs. To have his box paraded down the hallway on the headmaster's shoulder, filled with everything he owns, is hideous. His rolled mattress might as well be a flag made of underpants. He follows the headmaster up three flights of stairs to a long attic room with rows of iron beds. There are several bare metal frames, but the headmaster seems to know which is meant for Eric.

"You'll be on this end," he says. "With the younger children."

The box slides easily under the bed, and Eric sighs, relinquishing some small corner of a larger fear he's been holding. The headmaster puts the mattress roll on top of the metal frame. The nearest bed is neatly made and beside it stands a shared dresser. A window looks down upon his bed, but Eric doesn't know if this is a desirable spot, because of the view, or a bad one, because of the cold. The gray water stretches outside the window, with the gray hump of Le Havre across the channel and the gray sky above it. The houses too are gray in their march down toward the harbor, and by counting the streets and chimneys, he can pick out his grandmother's roof.

Nailed to the wall above the neighboring bed are a small wooden cross and a photograph, a family portrait: mother, father, two tall sisters, a boy of about Eric's age. Eric's family never sat for a portrait together. It was expensive, and there was always a reason to delay—until his father's business took off, or until his mother said she felt slim again, no longer big with Louise, then big with Conrad, then—

"I'm sorry about your mother," the headmaster says, and Eric's breathing grows jagged. He lunges at the basin on the dresser to splash his face with water. "Why don't you skip penmanship?" the headmaster says. "Just for today. Here, on your schedule— you can see where to go after the bell for second lesson."

Eric nods gratefully, his face still turned away. The headmaster puts his hand on Eric's shoulder, then leaves. When he's gone Eric drags his box from under the bed and opens it. He needs his notebook and pencils, and a handkerchief. A folded paper slips from the notebook, a drawing Louise has snuck in. Eric is glad she's labeled the figures—*Eric, Louise, Conrad*—because the sketch isn't any good. All three children are composed of sticks and circles, Louise's dress a black triangle. They stand close together in the center of the page, although Eric's eyes are placed strangely, staring not at the viewer but somewhere beyond the edge of the paper. Louise's eyes stare forward in accusation. He

21

wonders if the drawing is the kind of thing he might tack above his bed, or if he would be made fun of.

Do I put it up? he thinks toward the mermaid.

How in the world would I know? she answers. *You've seen where I live. Paper gets wet. We keep no pictures.*

So how do you remember the people you love?

We don't. Sea creatures are very forgetful.

What did my uncle ask for, when he talked to you?

I don't remember.

With no regular school classes on Wednesday afternoons, Agnès schedules music lessons. Eric is sent to a house in the Rue Bourdet where the only decoration is a black-and-white print of a piano hanging directly above the actual piano, as if without it Monsieur Vinot, the teacher, would not seem sufficiently musical.

"Play something," Vinot says. "Show me what you know so far."

Dark, curly hair crawls down Vinot's face and wraps around his chin and mouth into side whiskers so fecund they remind Eric of the ivy over the mermaid. He'll play a new piece, he thinks. Vinot will be so impressed he'll tell Agnès and she'll tell his father. His father will come back to Honfleur to hear it. Not a little minuet or gavotte, but something big like the ocean, with beautiful things floating inside it. Sweet arpeggios like mermaids, a melody like a mother. Eric builds the song in his head, how grand, how beautiful it will be, how the footsteps in the street outside will stop to listen.

He holds his hands over the instrument, but the yellowed keys seem somehow unfamiliar. Vinot clears his throat, and Eric plunges his hands down—too loud, the piano has a lighter touch than the one in Paris. And the notes are wrong, too low, but when he moves up the keyboard, the higher notes are dissonant. The more he tries to recapture the music he heard in his head, the worse it becomes.

"What game are you playing?" Vinot says, and it becomes even more important that Eric somehow rescue the song. He plows ahead until Vinot grabs his wrists and lifts his hands off the instrument. Eric is breathing hard. "I expect you to take your lessons seriously," Vinot hisses.

I was absolutely serious, Eric wants to explain. He had such plans, but they all went wrong. From outside the room come snorts of laughter, probably other boys waiting for their own lessons, and he imagines them imitating his playing. How much worse if they knew it was supposed to be a song about the ocean, about the endless things it gobbles up.

"It was just a joke, sir," Eric says. "I won't do it again."

After Saturday-morning school lessons the weekly boarders are allowed home. Eric has stolen a piece of chalk from a classroom and stops at the mermaid to outline her form, her curved fin, her curved chest. Once it's done, she just looks dusty, sullied. "I'm sorry," he whispers, rubbing at the chalk lines with his hands, then his handkerchief. He arrives home with chalk dust on his cuffs and trousers and tells Agnès he was invited to model his letters on the board for the whole class. She seems almost to believe him, penmanship being one of his few discernible talents.

Sunday morning at St. Cathcrine's they're joined by a man Agnès introduces as her brother, the children's great-uncle, in from Le Havre with his wife. Agnès tells them that Monsieur Fortin will serve as their godfather and Eric shrugs, fidgets through Mass. Conrad falls asleep. At the end of the service Eric scurries off the pew and toward the back doors. Agnès catches him by his jacket and leads the three children to the nave, where by prior arrangement with the priest they are rebaptized as Catholics. Eric lets it all happen around him with bemusement. Conrad whimpers when the water hits his forehead, but is otherwise untroubled. For once Louise is the one who misbehaves, squirming out of the priest's grip until Fortin holds her in place. On the way home Eric tries to take her hand, but she waves him off so that she can use both hands to hold her dress away from her neck where water has run down the collar.

The weather has grown cold now in December, although there is no ice in the Old Basin, and the ships still come and go easily. Fortin escorts his wife to the ferry dock and comes to Agnès's house alone for Sunday dinner.

He quizzes Louise relentlessly. What is the Incarnation? What is the Redemption? What is the Blessed Trinity, and what do we mean by the quality and distinction of the divine Persons? From religion Fortin moves on to plants and animals and the capitals of Europe. Louise fields the questions with increasing despair.

"She doesn't know that, nobody knows that," Eric says when Fortin asks something about Belgium.

"*I* know that. Do you want to grow up to be the kind of man who knows nothing about Belgium?"

"Yes," Eric says emphatically. "And Louise doesn't want to know anything about Belgium either."

"I'm trying to see what she's been taught," Fortin says.

"She's reasonably clever," Agnès offers. "She'll learn whatever you want her to."

At dinner Fortin says grace, adding a special thanks for the opportunity to meet his great-nephews and niece, and guide them in their religious education. The children eat in silence until they are excused to play.

Eric offers—generously, he thinks—to play paper dolls with Louise. "It'll be all right," he says, though he doesn't know what he's referring to.

"Don't you understand?" Louise says. "We'll never see her again now. Not ever."

That night Eric dreams that both heaven and hell, Catholic and Anglican, are nothing but ocean, infinite and gray. He can swim, and even breathe underwater, but he is alone. He looks all night for his sister, his mother, his father, for Conrad, bobbing at the surface like a fat pale cork. He can't even find the mermaid, although he swears he hears her singing.

The next weekend Louise is gone. She's to live with Uncle Fortin, who has agreed to look after her, Agnès explains. "Three children! I'm not young anymore."

Eric has more pilfered chalk, and that night he sneaks into Louise's bedroom with a candle and draws a picture of her on the wall, but it doesn't come out. He tries a picture of the mermaid too—also a failure. He gives up, chalks a white splotch onto the floor until the pieces shrink down to nothing, until the tips of his fingers are bleeding from running them across the wood. The splotch is nothing more than a pond, but Eric pretends it's the ocean. He drags a blanket off Louise's bed and sleeps there in the sea.

The next morning there's chalk all over the blanket and Agnès takes him to church without breakfast. When some of Agnès's friends ask after Louise, Eric says she's been kidnapped, and then Agnès doesn't feed him lunch, either. She packs his bag with a note for the school's night chaperone and a few coins so Eric can join the late meal with the full-time boarders. Before he leaves, however, she makes him scrub the floor in Louise's room, and he thinks to check the bed frame. He reaches under the mattress and touches the pocketknife, feels sure Louise has left it for him on purpose. *So I can rescue her,* Eric thinks. He finishes his scrubbing, takes his satchel from Agnès without protest, and slips the knife out of his pocket and into the bag as soon as she shuts the front door behind him. He walks down the street toward the stairs, and then he walks past them.

His reflection flickers along the front windows of Osprey's shop, then the cobbler's and clockmaker's and joiner's. It's dark, but this time of year it grows dark early, and there are still plenty of people about. Eric attracts no special notice. He circles the Old Basin, to where Osprey's boat is tied. Eric thought perhaps Osprey might take it out of the water for winter, but tonight it sits close against the wall in the still water. Snow has begun to fall, collecting on the deck, the top of the railing, the spokes of the steering wheel, with little white hillocks on the tie posts on the shore.

Clove hitch, Eric remembers, seeing the knot and following the rope back up to a cleat on deck. He even remembers his uncle showing him how to undo them, taking the working end under and around. When he heaves the untied rope toward the deck of the boat, it smacks the side and slides down the hull into the water, but Eric is still able to jump easily onto the deck and pull the rope up after him. He coils it near the jam cleat, although the fiber is wet now, and his coil is sloppy. He is so focused on the rope he doesn't realize at first that he isn't going anywhere. The boat hasn't moved.

Le Havre. Just on the other coast. Alfred laughed when he said it. It mustn't take long to get there. The ferryboats aren't terribly big. Eric has not thought about how a man raises a sail, has not observed which way the wind is blowing. He hopes that his Viking heritage will simply awaken in his blood, that this is something all Norman boys, even ones raised in Paris, can do, or at least something they can do when their sisters are in peril.

With the boat still refusing to move, he searches for an oar, a pole, a fishing gaff, something he can use to push off from the wall, but he can't find anything long enough. Frustrated near the point of tears, he shoves himself against the railing on the opposite side, wondering if he can somehow rock the entire boat to freedom. The lights in the building across the street have gone out. The square is emptier. The temperature is dropping and Eric's bare hands are stiff—he tries to wiggle his fingers, and they move slowly, brokenly. He could hop back over the railing and walk up to the school. Rumor has it that the full-time boarders get hot chocolate Sunday nights. But if he can hop over so easily, that means he should also be able to push the boat while standing on the wall.

In his new shoes, still not quite broken in, he braces his feet on the slippery, snow-covered stone. This works, well enough that Eric is startled by how quickly the boat rocks away from him. His weight pitches forward, and for a moment, in reaction, he throws himself backward, off the wall. He is so afraid the boat will float off without him, though, that he climbs back up on the wall and leaps for the boat, aiming for the railing, to grab it and pull himself over. But with his hands too frozen to close around the railing the way they should, he slips straight down the side of the boat with a splash.

The cold is shocking and black and silent. There is no clatter of feet on the stones, no lantern raised over the wall. He thinks his thoughts toward the mermaid, but there is no answer. He thinks, *Help*. He tries to say it aloud, and water rushes in. The boat is right there on one side, the shore on the other, but there is nothing to grab onto. His body won't answer. He wonders which afterlife he'll go to—if Louise is right, or his mother, or the mermaid.

Then his jacket rises up around him, pinching under his arms, the fabric bunched up at his ears. "Eric? Eric!" He allows himself to hope that the miraculous voice is his father's. But when he opens his eyes he sees Osprey.

His uncle leans over him, dripping onto the stones, grabs an end of the rope that Eric left piled on the deck, and reties the boat. Eric watches the long stretch of Osprey's body and wishes he were grown, wishes he were a man able to simply reach out and bring two things together. He feels angry that his father is grown but can't seem to do the same. Another man comes with a lantern, and in the light Eric can see there's a woman with Osprey who isn't his wife. Osprey takes off his jacket, wraps it around Eric. The woman whispers something and disappears into the dark. Osprey takes Eric into his arms, thanks the man with the lantern.

"My school bag," Eric says, when he can breathe. "It's still on the boat."

"Later," Osprey says.

Eric sees the street sign for the Rue Haute above Osprey's shoulder, and realizes he's being carried back to his grandmother's house. His skin hurts. "I'm supposed to be at school," he says. "She sent me back early." Then, after a pause, "She stole Louise. She sent her away."

Osprey comes to a stop and sighs. "I need to get you warm."

"I'll never see her again," Eric says.

"Don't be silly," Osprey says, but Eric can feel them change direction, feel Osprey walk even more swiftly back the way they came, through the town and then away from it, down a country road that looks to Eric like the end of the earth. Without apartment buildings rising up on either side, without even the little houses and shops of Honfleur, the fields spread in a menacing silence around them.

At Osprey's home his wife builds the fire back up, wraps Eric in blankets, rinses his clothes in fresh water and spreads them to dry. Because Osprey's children are all girls, there are no boys' clothes in the house, and Eric stays wrapped in the blankets. Osprey's wife says nothing about why her husband might have been out so late. Eric falls asleep on the floor with Osprey's arms around him, the fire roaring.

Eric tries to remember later what he dreamed that night, whether he was late to school the next morning, whether he had his satchel. He remembers Osprey telling him, as they lay curled on the floor together, that they would take the boat out some weekend soon and sail to Le Havre. He would make Eric wear a cork vest for safety, but they'd wave to the ferries as the wind sped them past. He would teach Eric more knots, and Eric and Louise and Conrad could spend their Sundays together. But the boat stays moored, and because Osprey gets along so poorly with Agnès, he seldom comes to the house. There is some trouble with his wife, and then Osprey emigrates, alone, selling the boat in secret to help pay for his passage. Agnès tries to learn where he's gone, but after an Atlantic crossing the trail goes cold, so that he might be anywhere from the Canadian Arctic to the southern tip of Argentina. Or dead, of course, and somewhere else altogether.

Fortin, meanwhile, almost never leaves Le Havre, and on the rare occasions when the children see each other Eric can feel Louise's anger, her loneliness. To share the story of his attempt to rescue her—the boat, the lantern, the bone-dissolving cold of the water—would seem like a plea for sympathy, and he knows Louise has none to spare. He tells himself that the next time they see each other, or the next, she will be easier to speak with, or he will feel braver. He begs the mermaid to soften his sister's heart. Louise speaks mostly to Agnès, requesting instruction on how to achieve custard's proper gelatinous quality.

Whenever Eric reaches the mermaid on the stairs now he curses her, pinches her nipples. He hears her voice less often with each passing month, each passing year, but sometimes, although he feels too old for pretend, a voice nudges him, an echo that must be the mermaid. *Tell her,* the voice says. *How you tried to sail to her. How you ended up half-drowned and frozen.*

She'll only be angry that I didn't try again, he answers.

Then send her something other than words.

I've been writing her songs.

Not music, the voice urges. *Send her the knife.*

He still has it, wrapped in a sock and tucked inside one of the hollow metal legs of his dormitory bedstead. But what good would it do Louise now? It has started to rust, its spring stiff from disuse. A poor steward, then, of both mermaid and knife.

When he pictures the vast, empty gray ocean of his dream, he knows that although he might try to explain it for the rest of his life, in every note on every page, there is no music like the maw of the sea, no sound to replicate its limitless hunger. There are no songs that bring people back. Not his mother, not his father, not Louise. He has known this, he realizes, since he was very small.

Louise

— 3 —

At the top of your voice, don't you think?

I HAD TO BE TAKEN OFF THE FERRY LIKE A SACK OF POTATOES tossed over Uncle Fortin's shoulder, pounding my fists into his back. I managed to kick both my shoes off in my thrashing, one onto land, the other, with a satisfying *plunk*, into the sea. A sailor fetched the land-bound one, brushed off the dust, and tried to hand it to Fortin.

"What good does the one do?" he said, then apologized. An orphan I was, he said, overcome by grief. Out of my mind with it. Still, one tries to do one's Christian duty.

"I'm not an orphan!" I remember screaming into the black wool of his coat. Or maybe I only wanted to say it, shouted it only into the dark of my own head.

That is where so many of my words seem to end up, guttering like a lamp nearly out of oil. A lamp—what a ridiculous image! None of my students today would even know what I meant. Fire at their bedsides, a glass globe of oil? Their parents would shiver at the thought. How flammable the last century must have been. How full of little children burned to cinders in their blankets. How like one long Grimms' tale, the unelectrified past, all witches and woods.

There were few woods in Le Havre, or in Honfleur. Or in Paris, of course. There are few in Buenos Aires, and no ginger-

33

bread houses, although we do have armies of tipa trees lining the streets and brilliant purple jacarandas in the parks. In the plaza where I wait for the bus there is also an enormous ombú tree that would make a perfect witch's house. Though if there is any witch here, I fear it may be me. Louise of 46 Chacabuco, the gimlet-eyed old lady in room 12. I keep an eye on the neighbor-hood children, and I am too old now to worry about the politics of tattling. I tattle freely. Little Mother, Little Mother, same as ever. There are few women who live alone in Monserrat, and none my age, which when the children are ill-mannered enough to ask I give variously between one hundred and two hundred or sometimes the truth, which is seventy-six, and sounds perfectly ancient and witchlike to them. In truth I make a poor witch, with little magic. My one talent, if indeed it is one, is this bend-ing backward and forward of the years.

In any case, I would never have been allowed to take an entire lamp to bed at Uncle Fortin's. Light was not to be wasted, and little girls were not to read books behind closed doors, where one could not see what they might be learning. Or perhaps that was just Uncle Fortin's rule.

During my first weeks in Le Havre, with him and his wife, Estelle, my dreams were practical. Always in the dream Agnès would send a letter, a ferry ticket, an apology. I would arrive back at her house in time for supper, be installed on the same horse-hair mattress, and go to bed within the dream, buried by sleep twice over—only to wake, in reality, on another lumpy mattress, in another narrow room by the sea, so that many mornings I felt like I did not quite know where I was, or who.

In every place but the harbor, Le Havre was dust in dry weather and mud in wet. Three rings of earthworks were being torn down, walls flattened and ditches filled, the city allowed to outgrow its old fortifications. The demolition had taken twenty years already, and no one seemed to have any particular hope of it ever ending. The largest bulwarks had all faced England. Now everyone's fear was in the other direction, toward Prussia, but I couldn't help noticing that I was living in a city which had girded itself thrice over against my mother's people. I felt like a spy. As if I should be collecting information, though I had no one to report to, and worried about coming to grief among my enemies.

Uncle Fortin was a keen photographer, and had chronicled, in painstaking detail, the building works. His earliest images were daguerreotypes, and people showed up only as ghosts, blurry smudges like ash piles left in the streets. Uncle Fortin described the photographic processes involved in such exhausting detail that I once went literally to sleep and a glass plate negative slipped from my hands and shattered on the wood floor. I don't remember what the image was, but I remember the whipping I took for it. It would have been some wall or moat or maybe one of the equally abundant pictures of his dead daughter, Berthe.

Uncle Fortin was not all Christian duty, after all. For him and his wife I was a replacement, like a new pet, though not quite as loved, not quite as clever or purring as loudly—the wrong color, with coarse fur, inferior all around but better than nothing. I'm surprised Uncle Fortin didn't put a ribbon around my neck when he presented me to Estelle. And maybe a bell, so they could hear me coming. At first I crept about the house; then I tried to make as much noise as possible, so that I would interrupt fewer conversations about how generally dissatisfying they found me. Uncle Fortin suggested at first that I call Estelle "Maman," but none of us could bear it.

He had been a rich man when they married, Estelle told me. "Wood and charcoal," she said, like that was an occupation, and I suppose it was. Especially there, at the edge of the country, where things came in and out, occupations could be objects—the acquiring and dispersal of them, anyway. Wood and charcoal had gone sour, and now he was in copper. "In copper" was the only description anyone ever gave me of what he did, and as a child I pictured him encased, a statue standing in a busy square with seagulls landing on his head. I did not question how this might bring an income. It made as much sense as anything else that had happened to me that year.

The longer no one came for me, the more impractical my dreams became. I dreamed of Eric trotting up on horseback, or swooping in on feathered wings, peering through the small window with his toes curled around the windowsill. His toenails were little pink oyster shells, sharpened to kick Uncle Fortin away if he woke and staggered after me, creaking and armored, his skin the greening shine of copper. Eric was my angel, my nightingale, my last best chance. I sometimes imagined him arriving in Osprey's boat, the white sail a wing. The wood was so polished we could see our faces, could feel the oil when we put our hands on the railing. It made the boat feel like something alive, an animal we could tame and ride through the woods, past all the witches. In my dreams we caught and ate fish: Conrad ate the flesh, Eric the scales, I the bones, and we were all somehow satisfied. Occasionally I knew the dream for the fantasy it was even as it was happening, and spent all night trying to convince Eric that he wasn't really there, that none of this was real, that he had to make our father come back and rescue me properly. More often I believed in every moment, and wept frantically at waking. Either way, I awoke blaming Eric, and the longer the dream didn't come true, the more I blamed him. I know, of course, how unreasonable this is. I know that children have no power. I think I have learned this every day of my life.

Berthe had been twenty when she died of typhus. At the time she was engaged to a man I heard still lived in Le Havre, so that I looked for him everywhere, wondering if I would somehow recognize him—wondering if I was meant to take Berthe's place in that way, too. Estelle had already done all the hard work of mothering, had rejoiced at seeing her daughter on the threshold of being safely packed off into matrimony. She met the prospect of starting over not with pleasure but exhaustion. I wondered if she had been consulted as to this plan of Uncle Fortin's, or if I really was like a kitten, picked up for free from an unwelcome litter and brought home as a surprise. Would Agnès have drowned me in a burlap sack if I hadn't been claimed?

My father eventually returned to France, though not to the north. He settled back in Paris, looked again for a wife. Older and more encumbered than when he'd courted my mother, he understood that his choices had narrowed. No longer young herself, Eugénie worried that she'd missed her chance at marriage and children. She'd spent all those hours at the piano instead, and nothing had come of them except crow's-feet from squinting and a permanent ache in her wrists. Then along came Alfred, flush with a modest inheritance—his mother had recently drowned while out walking, either a fall or a freak wave, he'd been told. No one had quite seen how it happened. It was cruel, capricious luck, especially for a woman who strove to spend as much of her life as possible indoors, but after the deaths of his wife and infant daughter years earlier, Alfred had concluded that the world was indeed capricious and cruel, and his mother's drowning simply provided further proof.

His mother had been caring for his sons when she died, he told Eugénie during their courtship. The boys were with him now. Would that be all right with her?

Eugénie had no reason to suspect that there was also a daughter. When she learned much later of the omission, Alfred explained that I had been in the care of his uncle since I was small. After Agnès's death, the boys were the more pressing problem. I had been taken into the bosom of my great-uncle's family, he told her, and to uproot me would have been no kindness, the two of them decided.

At least, this is the story I told myself. It might even be true. I clung to an image of Eugénie and Alfred putting their heads together—for some reason their heads were literally pressed together in the vision I had of this moment, forehead to forehead—and determining that I was loved and happy where I was, and that my father might continue best loving me from afar. They could be excused for thinking this. I could excuse them for thinking this, or try to, anyway.

I knew the truth might be far colder. Perhaps without regular bills from a boarding school to remind him, my father simply forgot I existed. So far as I could tell, Uncle Fortin never asked for money, never asked for help. Never even asked to be thanked. One does one's Christian duty. Those were the habits I was raised with, dutiful silences piled to the ceiling. Sometimes walking in that house felt like swimming, and one does not speak underwater. If you open your mouth to ask why you weren't sent for—why them but not me?—too much else might rush in.

It took fifteen years, but my father finally sent for me. Eric was absolutely *not* dying, he insisted. There was no chance of it—none! he'd make a complete recovery!—but still, perhaps a trip to Paris was in order. Perhaps a train ticket should be purchased, arrangements made, so I could see my older brother. Just in case.

In case of what? I wrote back. An ornery question. Why did I want to make him say it? Why would I want the possibility committed to paper?

Conrad will meet you at the station, my father wrote, ignoring me. It was a great talent of his, ignoring, and it seemed that Eric's illness had created no disruption.

At the Gare Saint-Lazare, steam and smoke from the locomotives hung in clouds under the glass roof, dimming the light. I'd been in Paris for three minutes and already felt like a moth asphyxiating in a glass jar. What memories I had of my life here were a jumble of objects and interiors, like my mother's best dress and the loudly ticking clock with brass feet that had sat on our mantel. The city itself was utterly alien. Since leaving I'd been in no place larger than Le Havre—Fortin traveled seldom for business, and Estelle and I not at all.

Conrad and I had failed to make a code, no indication that he would be, say, holding a black cap, or that I would be wearing a red shawl. We had not wanted to admit that we would need such a code. But as I scanned the crowd I was forced to acknowledge I had no real idea whom I was searching for. We found each other eventually, though only because the platform emptied of other young people. When we met each other's eyes, the only recognition was a shared mathematics, the calculation of years and ages. He walked toward me but made no greeting.

"Conrad?" I said, quick to speak first, because his lips seemed perilously close to forming the word *Mademoiselle,* just in case he was wrong, and I did not think I could bear to hear my little brother call me by anything other than my name.

We did not look alike, even when we searched for a family resemblance, or for traces of the children we'd once been together. Conrad was gangly and awkward, swinging helplessly between childhood and adulthood as if he'd had a chair kicked out from under him. There was no trace of the tidy, compact roundness of the toddler I'd last seen. A toddler, I thought, just a toddler. Did he even recall ever having had a sister?

Conrad took my luggage and walked us to the cabstand, where the driver misinterpreted our shyness and asked if we wanted to drive the short way or the long way. "A detour, with the curtains down," the driver said, when Conrad expressed confusion. "Give you two sweethearts a little private time."

"The short way!" Conrad yelped, his voice breaking.

I pulled the curtains back violently, letting in as much of the April light as I could, and the cab lurched as the driver whipped the horse forward.

"How is he?" I asked.

"He'll be fine. He didn't want Mother to send for you," Conrad said, realizing a beat too late how that sounded. "Not that he didn't want to see you, of course. He does. It's just that he said it would make more sense for you to come when he was feeling better. So you could go out and do things."

"Mother?" Another ornery question. I knew whom he meant.

"Eugénie," Conrad said, more apologetically than he needed to, and I was sorry for needling him.

None of this was his fault. Not Eric's illness, or our father's brief, clumsy letters, or the fact that Eugénie was the only mother Conrad would ever remember. It was not his fault that he had been loved every day of his life.

Eric had gotten sick in February, up in Pas-de-Calais, where he was stationed with his regiment. He'd enlisted only a few months before that, and at twenty was a bit old to be starting his mandatory service. He'd been hoping to stay in school long enough to cut the required five years down to one, but when he left the Conservatory early, the army scooped him up. The army doctor had pronounced an all clear on his illness weeks earlier, only to put his patient on a train south, gray-faced and gasping, when the fever returned. Far from departing, the fever kept easing and surging in turns, and it was almost as if my invitation had also been an invitation to the illness to make up its mind one way or the other.

He would recover, of course—of course!—and they'd all been doing a very good job of believing this until Eugénie insisted I be sent for.

When I arrived at the family apartment, Eugénie was putting dinner on the table, although with such clattering that I imagined a maid must usually do the cooking, or at least that Eugénie preferred it when a maid did the cooking. As if she knew what I was thinking, she explained that she usually scheduled piano lessons at this hour, but that she'd canceled them all so the noise wouldn't disturb Eric. She handed a fistful of silverware to Conrad, and he obediently began to lay the place settings.

"Your father's going over proofs at the printers', but he'll be home any minute," she said.

I asked the time and she pointed to what I recognized as the brass-footed clock from my childhood, ticking away loudly as ever. "Proofs of what?" I said.

"A four-hand piano duet, which is probably why it's taking forever, making sure everything lines up."

"He works for a music publisher?"

"He *is* a music publisher. We are. He didn't tell you?"

The front door opened then, and I went into the hallway to greet my father. His face was younger than I'd braced myself to see, although hollowed out somehow. He'd lost something, the way Conrad had lost his toddler's fluffy hair, and it wasn't coming back.

"Louise. You look just like your mother." Instead of grief or joy his expression held gentle curiosity, as if my face were the answer to the idle, half-asked question of how I had turned out, after all these years.

He stepped forward and embraced me, a plain, warm, fatherly embrace. I was nearly his height, and part of me wanted to lay my head on his shoulder, but a greater part was stiff and angry. I realized I'd wanted him to approach me warily, with an apology held on his flat palm like I was a wild animal to be lured. But he didn't seem to think there was anything to apologize for.

In novels, people who are terribly ill are always terribly honest, full of deathbed confessions, revelations of the heart. But Eric mostly sweated and slept. For the first day, I had to introduce myself at every waking, though the sting of doing so was lessened by the smile he gave me afterward. Then he'd tell me his dream, always the same dream, in which he was being chased by enormous asparagus stalks. As the days wore on, however, his sleep was easier, his periods of wakefulness longer. I read to him or listened to him complain about the invalid soups and broths

Eugénie prepared. Otherwise I sat vigil and sewed, all the little repairs—buttons and hems and holes—that Eugénie didn't have time for, what with giving piano lessons and running the music-publishing business she and Alfred had started. My father was at work during the day, and in the evenings he disappeared behind a newspaper or a music manuscript or Eric's bedroom door. One evening I watched him holding Eric's hand in both of his own, brushing each finger joint, as if making sure every piece of his child was accounted for. In that moment I hoped I'd catch what Eric had, so that my father might hold my hand like that. But mostly we avoided any conversation other than pleasantries. At least that way I could pretend there was something more beneath and beyond the pleasantries, whether we ever spoke of it or not.

Eugénie played piano mornings and evenings. Evenings were for new compositions, her own or those submitted for consideration to the publishing concern, which as far as I could tell was little more than a desk that a kindhearted music-shop owner had allowed my father to set up in the back of his store. Most of the family's money came instead from a string of office jobs my father held, and from the inheritance he'd received after Agnès died and her house in Honfleur was sold. The marginal publishing concern specialized in light music, chansons and café-concert novelties and dance tunes, love songs and songs about spring. Eugénie would play and warble along with herself. Eric groaned whenever he was awake enough to notice the lyrics, all those *dresses* and *caresses*, rhymes of *rose* with *knows* or *little toes*. In the mornings, however, Eugénie played a ferocious classical repertoire. I was impressed at first, until I realized she always played the same seven pieces, a different one each day. It turned out they were the most difficult things she'd learned by the time she left formal instruction, each piece neatly preserved, like sealed jars of summer vegetables.

"Good Christ," Eric said, and rolled onto his side, making a show of pulling the pillow up over his ear. "The Hiller again. Tuesday, is it?"

"She's good, though," I said. "Better than she is at singing."

"You'd hope so, the number of years she's been playing it."

"Would you say she's good generally? Is she musical?"

"Why are you asking me?"

"You were at the Conservatory."

"I got kicked out."

"I thought you quit." I poured him a glass of water and waited for him to explain. When he felt well enough he liked to talk, especially about himself. This had been true when we were small and I was pleased, mostly, that it still was, that his self-regard was something I could recognize.

He'd quit practicing, he said. Had toddled his way through his examination piece and then flubbed the sight-reading. He needed to win at least an honorable mention every few years to stay enrolled, and it wasn't going to happen. "It's a shithole anyway," he said. "They all play like she does, mechanical Turks. Listening in on each other in the practice rooms. Whenever I try to play here she's always shouting corrections from the next room. There's no getting away from it."

"You think she plays mechanically?"

"I think she's awful. That's my expert opinion. She plays like a windup toy."

More silence, more sewing.

"You don't think she's good, do you?" he said.

"No, of course not." But in truth I'd been learning the Hiller with my teacher in Le Havre, and I thought Eugénie played it a little like me. I knew we weren't magnificent, but it would have been nice to hear that we sounded all right.

Eugénie boiled pots of water in the kitchen and when Eric was strong enough she made him come in and sit with his face over them, a towel on his head, to clear his lungs with the steam. She boiled so much water she steamed the wallpaper right off the hallway leading to the kitchen. It wrinkled and pulled away from the plaster in long sheets. When these sheets fell in the night, I woke to the sound of what I thought were birds rustling down the chimney. One morning, the first to awake, I found a panel of paper slumped on the floor like something dead. I rolled it up and leaned it in a corner to get it out of the way. But the glue was still soft and tacky, and when Eugénie tried to pull the roll apart again later, it ruined the floral pattern. She yelled at me, then demonstrated how she was storing the panels to let the glue dry so they could be rehung. Once all this was over, one way or another, the paper would be going back on the walls. No sense in losing one's décor as well as one's stepson.

"Did you change something in here?" Eric asked groggily, as Eugénie shepherded him down the now-bare hallway, its walls a dull white smeared with old glue. "It was nicer before."

"It was," we agreed.

"I follow the doctor's recommendations," Eugénie said later that night, after Eric was back in bed, the water boiled to nothing, the kitchen muggy, with only the two of us awake. "But it feels like there should be something else. It always feels like there's something else one ought to be doing."

"I know," I said, then stiffened like a cornered animal when she started to cry.

"I'm not a nurse," she insisted. "I don't know what I'm doing. Like being a mother," she added. "It's better if it doesn't just happen all at once."

But that was the way everyone became a mother, I thought, and still think now.

"When I married Alfred—a husband and two boys, like *that*." She snapped her fingers. "I suspect Eric and I both handled it rather badly. I think I did better by Conrad, but then Conrad's so agreeable. One feels he could have been raised by gypsies and come out all right."

44

"I'm sure you did better than gypsies."

She smiled, but only at the corners of her lips. A thank-you note rather than an actual expression.

"I like hearing you play," I said, trying for kindness, comfort. "The piano. At home, Fortin reads aloud to us in the evenings, but there's no music unless I make it."

"I didn't realize you played."

This struck me as odd, since I'd written about my lessons in all my letters. I would have had little enough news to report otherwise. Although I addressed the letters to my father, I intended them for the whole family. *Love to Eric,* I always wrote, *and to Conrad, and also to Eugénie, whom I hope someday to meet.*

"I need to feel good at *something,*" Eugénie continued. "I always feel competent when I play those pieces. I've got them all by memory. I always know just where I am and I can feel what's ahead. Not like nursing. Or mothering. Do you understand?"

I did.

"I play them and daydream I'm a concert pianist. Breathless audience, furious applause, the whole bit. It's so silly."

It wasn't.

"I was going to be great, you know. By the time I stopped playing seriously, I knew it wouldn't happen. But as a little girl, I was sure I was going to be so extraordinary."

I didn't know if this was a moment when a kinder person would tell her that she truly was extraordinary, or that she might yet prove so. But I didn't see how, and moreover I understood that she was confiding in me because she didn't think I was extraordinary either. Both of us ordinary, I would understand how it felt to play and pretend to be otherwise.

The next day Eugénie asked me to help wash Eric, who was too addled to protest. We left his drawers on, but there was still so much skin, the waxy white of cheddar, bony legs and arms shrunken by sickness, his middle still soft. I knew little enough of men's bodies, but I knew this was not the body of a soldier, and never would be. Only his hands seemed strong, with their sprawling, square-ended fingers, and I was jealous of them, jealous of the intervals and chords they must be capable of.

"I'm never ill," I said out loud.

"That's lucky," Eugénie said.

"Almost never. Never like this."

She wrung a washcloth out into a bowl, the sound of the water her only response.

This is the one you wanted? I raged silently. Sick and pale and too dumb even to know he's dying?

I stood and left, not so much with anger but with shame, worried that Eric could somehow hear my thoughts. I stood on the balcony to breathe, although even in spring the air in Paris was no relief from the sickroom. The smells wafting up from the street to the third floor were of cracked leather, coal dust, and dung. Nothing had ever made me miss Le Havre so much, though all I was really missing was the wind that came over the water, on its way to and from someplace else.

A sound heart is the life of the flesh: but envy the rottenness of the bones, I imagined Uncle Fortin quoting to me. *Proverbs 14:30.* I bought a notebook that afternoon and copied the verse out for two full pages. Conrad saw and teased me. At first I thought it was for the repeated lines, a sort of schoolchild's rosary, but it turned out he meant religion in general. Maybe boys who have been loved each day of their lives have no need of it. Maybe children with mothers need less of God.

Later he apologized and offered to accompany me to Mass on Sunday, since both my father and Eugénie preferred to spend the morning reading the newspaper in their dressing gowns. After Mass we wandered. The weather was fine, the sun strong enough to warm my hair beneath my hat. It was April in Paris. April in Le Havre, too—April everywhere—but spring had come to a firmer decision about itself here than it had in the north. The trees were flaring green, the pushcarts laden with flowers. We bought daffodils for Eric.

Once Conrad and I acknowledged the impossibility of shading in the last decade of our lives, our conversations were freed for his many enthusiasms. Beneath his adolescent self-consciousness was a little boy's volubility. He taught me about fireworks, about enormous lizard bones being excavated from the sea cliffs in England, about the orbits of passing comets.

One afternoon he asked me if I was planning to stay with the family in Paris after Eric was better, and I told him I didn't know.

"I'd think it's more exciting here," he said, "but I suppose it's noisy and dirty and all that. That's what people say. And I'm sure you've got friends in Le Havre." He thought I was trying to decide, I realized—weighing a life in Paris against a life in Le Havre. He didn't know I hadn't been asked to stay. "I suppose it's nice to live by the sea," he added, after I was silent too long.

"I would miss the sea," I said, truthfully. "Besides, where would you sleep?"

Eugénie had put me in Conrad's bedroom, Conrad on a sofa in the living room, where more and more of his clothes had been accumulating, since he was so afraid he might discover me in a state of undress in his room that he couldn't even bring himself to knock on the door to get into his dresser.

I could have Eric's room, Conrad said, after Eric recovered and left again for the army. Or I could stay where I was and he would take Eric's room. It was my choice, he said, gallantly.

"The army will want him back?"

"He's not discharged. It's only a medical leave. Unless the doctor says he's unfit. But he'll be fine," Conrad added, after a pause.

"Of course he will be. But I imagine he'd probably sneak away from his regiment so often he'd still need his room."

"Eugénie would turn him in straightaway. She and Eric don't get on." Conrad said this quietly, as if confiding a secret rather than a state of affairs I'd thought was evident to all. "If he deserts," Conrad continued, "he'll have to hide elsewhere." I could tell he didn't like the word "desert," even as a joke. Some duties, he thought, should not be taken lightly.

"I suppose we'll see," I said, and both of us let that hang there like it was an answer to all our problems.

"I'm indestructible," Eric announced. He'd woken me with his coughing: a sloshing, choking cough full of all the fluids that Eugénie's pots of water hadn't been able to dissolve. "Couldn't even drown," he said. "Winter in the harbor and it didn't get me. Or maybe it was lying in wait. Maybe that's what this is, years on. It's been living in my lungs like a worm."

"I don't understand."

"That time I tried to rescue you. I was going to sail to you, on Uncle Osprey's boat."

"Really? You never told me this."

"Really. I fell into the harbor instead. Osprey fished me out."

I took his hand in mine, not trusting my mouth to know what to say.

"But it's just as well. You're lucky, you know."

Oh, Eric. O! as they'd say in an opera. O Eric! Why did you have to ruin it? We were having such a good conversation. "Name me how," I said. "Name me one way I've been lucky."

"You've had a family, all the way through. You weren't sent off to school. You haven't had a wicked stepmother fussing at you since you were shipped back to Paris like a parcel."

"She's not wicked. She means well."

"You've just met her, and you're on her side?"

"That's right, I've just met her. They've been married for years, and I've just met her. So tell me again how I've been lucky."

"She sent in the conscription papers herself, you know. Fished them out of the rubbish bin and filled them in! I'm not a coward. If the Prussians come back, I'll fight. But nothing was happening in Calais. It was all so boring. I was going to be old and boring by the time I finished."

"You would have been twenty-five," I said, and Eric gave me a look as if I clearly did not understand how very decrepit twenty-five was.

"I didn't fancy shooting off my toes, so I soaked my uniform and stood outside the first good snow we got."

"You did this on purpose?"

"It didn't work the first time, so I did it again without a shirt on. I lay down and made snow angels."

No doubt a proper nurse, unwilling to dishearten a fragile patient with bad news, would have withheld the next thing I said. But on hearing this admission—that he'd done it on purpose!—I was too angry to lie. "You're not discharged," I told him. "You're only on medical leave. You'll be sent back when you're better. That's how it works."

It took a moment for this assertion to penetrate, but then Eric shook himself, his whole body jerking, and I worried at first that he was having some kind of fit. But he was just flinging off the words, like a dog shaking itself dry. "I won't go. I just won't."

"You'll do what instead? Keep making yourself sick until you kill yourself?"

"Something will come up. It will all work itself out. It always does."

"Does it?"

"Yes," he said, and I thought that for him, perhaps it always had. Perhaps it always would. Who was I to say otherwise? If God really did go around closing doors and opening windows, then each life was a giant house full of blowing curtains and broken locks, all of us wandering from room to room to room. "There's so much still," Eric said. "I haven't even started."

"You're an idiot" is what I said aloud. But under the surface of the remark something else heaved and spun. Fear and anger, yes, but also love. *Don't ever lose this,* I thought. *Please. Even if you're wrong. Somebody has to be extraordinary. Why not you?*

Then: *Why not me?* The thought quiet as a puff of steam from a boiling pot. But I put a lid over it, because that was something else Uncle Fortin had taught me—how not to be foolish.

"What kind of husband do you want?" Eugénie asked me. "Tell me one thing you're looking for."

"Do you have somebody in mind?"

"No, no, just making conversation."

Eric was back in his room after a final kitchen steam bath. His breathing sounded nearly normal, his lungs clear and hungry. In celebration, Eugénie put a little lemon in the last of the boiling water, poured two cups, and set them on a tray. With Conrad on an overnight school excursion, we moved to the parlor and sat side by side on the lumpy sofa that had been serving as his bed. The only light came from the windows, gray starlight trickling across the floor. Alfred was in bed already.

I thought about what Eugénie might be expecting to hear. The truest things—that he be kind, and honest, and hardworking—seemed dull. I wondered if she wanted us to be women who would speak freely, even scandalously, to each other, if she wanted to be a confidante to whom I should say I admired a certain build or breadth. "One who lets me have a handbag," I finally said. Uncle Fortin forbade it—he thought carrying a bag was a manly thing to do, like a hunter with a pouch of powder, or a lawyer with a leather folio of papers. It suggested I had some destination or trade that required me to equip myself; perhaps Uncle Fortin thought it would look like he hadn't taken suffi-cient care of me. Estelle carried things the old-fashioned way, in fabric pockets that hung from a string tied round her waist, ac-cessible through slits in her skirts. If I was sent out on an errand, I carried the money in my fist.

If Eugénie thought my criterion strange, she did not inquire about my reasons for it. She simply took the comment in stride. "Alfred doesn't mind a handbag," she said. "Sometimes when I walk to the music shop I'm juggling so many things I might as well carry a suitcase."

"But does he really even notice—what sort of bag you leave the house with?"

"Probably not," she conceded.

"Then it doesn't count."

"Of course it counts."

"Not caring isn't letting."

"Not caring is exactly like letting." She paused. "In a marriage, anyway."

"Then Alfred was a lucky find."

"I wish you wouldn't call him that. He's your father." Eugénie sighed and clinked her cup back down onto the tray. "If you're missing your lessons, you're certainly welcome to play the piano here," she said, her dress rustling as she gestured into the dark at the instrument. "If there's anything in particular you're working on, I might have the music somewhere. Or Alfred could find it in the shop."

I thanked her and meant it sincerely.

"I suppose you won't be here much longer," she said, "if Eric keeps improving. Still, you probably don't want to return to your teacher entirely out of practice." So here was the answer to Conrad's question. There was no hint of disinvitation in her voice, no sign I had displeased her. It was simply that I had my place, and that place was not here. "I could even listen to you," she said. "Give some corrections. We could have a little lesson."

"I'm not sure you have anything to teach me," I told her, and ruined whatever might have lived between us. I stepped on it like a glass and listened to it break.

"Did you share them?" I asked my father several days later. "My letters?"

He was smoking on the balcony. It was a warm evening, late sun blazing in the windows across the street. Birds darted past, taunting cats in the windows on either side of us. Eric was well enough that Eugénie had tried to resume hosting afternoon lessons. At the first set of scales, Eric yelled from his bedroom, threatening a relapse if the racket continued. Eugénie was giddy that his lungs had the strength to yell.

"Your letters?"

"My letters to the family."

"You were always so good about writing to me. Did you send others to the family?"

"Those *were* to the family. They were written to everybody."

"Were they?"

It was hard to be angry with the dying, and useless to be angry at the dead. My father had been gone, in his own way, as long as my mother had. He'd floated out of his own life years ago, and never quite floated back in.

"I'd tell the boys you were well," my father said, as if to reassure me. "You always seemed to be doing very well."

"You think Uncle Fortin would have posted the letters for me if I'd said I wasn't? I wasn't supposed to worry you."

"Should I have been? Worried?"

I'd been fed and clothed. Warm enough, safe enough. Uncle Fortin had brought me up with God, whom I could tell now I wouldn't have known here in any shape, Catholic or otherwise, and whom I would have missed. Uncle Fortin had made it easy to understand what he wanted me to be, which was a good and ordinary girl. And he'd given me a good and ordinary life.

"I suppose not," I said. I explained that he needed to have the doctor write a letter to the army, saying Eric's lungs were too weak to return to active service. It was probably true.

"Probably?"

"There's no point in it, for him. Eric a soldier? Unless you *want* France falling to Prussia."

"We thought he might learn some discipline."

"He won't. Not in the army. He'll refuse to learn anything."

"You think so?"

"I'm sure of it."

My father looked pensively into nothing, or maybe at the balconies across the street, the other men smoking and pretending they were alone. "It's useful to have your opinion," he said. "A sort of outside perspective. Eugénie seems to think like you, but I haven't been sure what to want for him."

An outside perspective? Oh, Alfred. O Alfred! Uncle Fortin had been right, all those years ago—I was an orphan after all. "Let's keep our fingers crossed," I said. "Let's hope he's as special as he thinks he is."

"I'm grateful I don't have to worry about you," he said. "You'll make some man a very good wife, you know. You'll make a wonderful mother."

I thought about the unspoken qualities he'd think a good wife and mother should have—kindness, devotion, resourcefulness—and basked in the compliments he'd more or less given me, words you could fold up and place in a handbag (should you be allowed to have one), carrying them with you wherever you went. Should I have wanted something more from him? *You'll make a wonderful concert pianist!* Or a painter? Or a scientist? But I wouldn't. That wasn't the way my life was ever going to turn out, and as little as my father knew me, we both knew that.

The following week my father and Eugénie went out for the evening. They hadn't offered many details, but I gleaned that it was a meeting related to financing for the publishing concern, that they needed it to go well, and that it was not expected to go well. They'd left us with a supper of cold fish and potatoes. Eric harassed Conrad and me into buying a bottle of white wine. Eugénie hadn't allowed him any alcohol since he'd become ill. We made a toast to Eric's health, to my safe travels back to Le

Havre. I'd bought the ticket myself, written to Uncle Fortin with my travel plans: "I promise not to kick off my shoes this time. You won't have to carry me."

We even toasted the conscription office, which had received that afternoon a doctor's letter describing Eric as permanently unfit for service. Conrad didn't think the ruination of our brother's lungs was an appropriate thing to be toasting, but Eric waved off his concern.

We hadn't told Conrad—scholarly, rule-abiding Conrad— that I myself had been the one to persuade the doctor to write the letter. On his last visit, the doctor had been dangerously optimistic. "With a little more recuperation time," he began, and I elbowed my father to make his case. Men squirmed out of service all the time—it wouldn't be unacceptable to hint, maybe even to ask outright. But my father hemmed and hawed so badly the doctor couldn't understand what he was getting at. Finally I burst into tears, wailing at how close I'd come to losing my brother, how he still coughed all the night long, how after losing our mother I couldn't bear this, too.

"Hush now," the doctor said. "If he's still as ill as all that..."

I let myself be placed on the sofa, a cold cloth on my forehead, my top buttons undone. The doctor told Eugénie to unlace me once he left, see that I got some rest to recover from the strain of nursing my dear elder brother. The two of us were clearly so close. Eugénie gave me a long, skeptical look. The doctor thought me a hysteric. But he wrote and signed a letter.

"To Louise," Eric added now to our celebratory toast.

"Hear, hear!" Conrad said, without asking why, and I was flattered to be found so generally worthy of toasting.

"Did you really—" I wasn't sure how to put it, though, and wasn't sure Eric would even remember most of our night-fevered, cough-spattered conversations. I took a gulp of the wine. "You said you tried to fetch me once. From Le Havre. With Osprey's boat. That you fell into the harbor instead."

Eric and Conrad both tilted their heads like dogs—like brothers.

"Was that true?" I said. "It's all right if it isn't."

"It's true," Eric said. "Why would you think it wasn't?"

"You really did that?" Conrad asked, but Eric was looking only at me.

"It seemed like something you might just say. But I believe you," I said, and stuffed a forkful of potatoes into my mouth and chewed.

"Do you?" Eric said, every furrow of his illness plowed across his face. He looked much older than the twenty-five he was so afraid of turning.

"Please don't fight," Conrad said, and I felt, for a moment, like we were real siblings.

"Thank you," I said. "For trying." Even if it was a fantasy, he'd been dreaming about me. My rescue was a story he'd told himself for years. I owed him that doctor's letter: for the attempted rescue, for my jealousy and bitter anger. "And now I've saved you. I've given you back five years. Maybe more, since you might've ended up with jail time for desertion. What are you going to do with the time?"

"I'll be king of France," he said. "No, emperor."

"Do *something*," I told him. "Do something, and we'll be even."

"I'm not sure yet what I'm good at," he confessed.

The statement seemed miraculous to me, implying as it did that he was so sure he was good at *something*, without any evidence as to what.

"You're good at lots of things," Conrad offered. "You're terribly good at music."

"Not really," Eric said.

Conrad shook his head. "You too, Louise. You're good at lots of things."

But how would he have known? We both understood it wasn't really true. I was and always had been dutiful and ordinary. Little Mother, perhaps one day Little Wife. But there are many, many worse things to be. Had Le Havre been a door or a window? It had felt at the beginning like an oubliette. But there had always been a view across the water, a window from which I might someday fly. If not noticing was a form of permission, as Eugénie claimed, who might my father's uncaring allow me to become?

"I missed you," Eric said. "I missed you a lot, after she sent us away."

"Me too," Conrad said, unwilling to be left out.

"You don't even remember me," I told him. "You were too young." In truth I wasn't sure how much I remembered him and Eric. My memories of them were hopelessly intertwined with the brothers I'd imagined later, the ones I'd dreamed, the ones I'd wanted.

"I know I missed you. I must have," Conrad said.

"I missed you both, too," I said.

This, at least, we could know was true. We'd all missed each other, and now those child selves had disappeared forever, devoured by these awkward giants: erratic Eric and clever Conrad and livid Louise, like the stars of an unpopular novelty song that Alfred might try to sell, one where all the jokes were a little too bitter. In the final verse the elder prince slays death itself and rides his own ambition into the sunset. The younger prince proves kind of heart and voracious of mind. The princess returns to her tower in the city on the other coast, and it will feel both farther and nearer than it did before. That they all lived happily ever after I cannot attest to, but they did all live after.

Philippe

— 4 —

Like a nightingale with a toothache

WHEN PHILIPPE LATER TELLS THE TALE—THE STARVING, SHABBY years of his youth—he can't help telling it wrong. He starts out correctly, all nostalgia and self-deprecation. He imitates his younger self's shuffling walk in broken-soled shoes, every pebble in Paris bruising his feet. His audience usually laughs. Not his children, because although Philippe will turn out to be a fortunate man in that he has children, he is also an ordinary man in that they rarely find him (intentionally) funny. But guests, they laugh. They want to know what the city was like then, and Philippe answers in the only way he knows how—by explaining who he was when he wanted so badly to live there. He mocks the teenager who stepped from the train already asking directions to the Chat Noir, before he'd asked after boardinghouses or cafeterias or jobs or Spanish aid societies. And what did he know of the place? A sleek cat on a poster. Rumors of Sodom, Gomorrah, a Garden of Earthly Delights. All the cleverest people in the cleverest city in the world, talking over one another in conversations like sea waves—the crash, the pull, the effervescence.

Philippe knows his older self should acknowledge that of course the Chat Noir was never quite like that. No place in the world could ever really have been like that. Yet everyone knows exactly the sly black-cat logo that Philippe remembers, the arched whiskers slicing across a dark-yellow background. That this cat means anything to anyone, so many years later, is a miracle. There are religions that have not lasted so long. The indelible figure is like a church, a shrine, an altar to his younger self, to all those younger selves, all those eager pilgrims.

A fool, he is supposed to say, and does, "I was a fool," but he says it with befuddled respect. Who was that boy with the wrong accent, the wrong currency in his pockets, and so terrifyingly little of it? Every letter home for years was a lie: *Yes, I am warm enough. No, I am not hungry. Yes, everything is as beautiful as you've heard.* His bad shoes nearly cost him three toes his first winter. He had never felt cold like that, didn't realize it could gnaw off whole pieces of a man. He was an idiot, but so *brave.* So confident he could throw himself into Paris and that the very air, like water, would bear him up. He has never been that brave, or trusting, since. And maddest of all, wasn't that boy right? His toes stayed attached. His belly got filled, one way or another. And everything he's loved in his whole life since then started over drinks at the Chat Noir.

He was desperately thirsty, that first afternoon. Exhausted by the journey, he had a headache so severe he could feel his heartbeat at the back of his eyeballs. He set off for the Chat Noir on foot from the train station, asking directions every few blocks. Like going to see the local lord, in a feudal age. "Or in Spain five minutes ago," French listeners sometimes joke, and Philippe pretends to find it funny, his country's distress, the way he walked away from it and never looked back.

The café's front was narrow and half-timbered, its wooden shutters splayed, though nothing was visible in the squares of darkness save a stray elbow or a cigarette ashing over the sill. From the open door crawled a smell of beer spilled so deeply into the floorboards there was no point in ever trying to mop it up. Something golden glinted in the rank-smelling doorway, and as his eyes adjusted Philippe realized it was a man in a metallic medieval costume. When this man asked for his name, Philippe froze in terror. Was there a list? For the first (and what would turn out to be nearly the last) time in Paris, he sputtered out his full real name, all ten words of it.

The doorman asked for the long string of foreign sounds to be repeated. Finally he recited it to Philippe ceremoniously, knocked the base of his halberd against the floor three times, and bowed. "Your Lordship," he said, and gestured Philippe inside.

It was a slow hour, midafternoon, but eventually enough patrons entered for Philippe to overhear that the doorman's greeting to him was the one used for everybody. The solemn inquiry, the pounding of the halberd, the courtly words—all ritual. He felt reprieve more than disappointment. There'd been no misunderstanding; he wasn't in danger of being kicked out as an imposter. They'd known he was a nobody and still they let him in. Some of the arrivals, clearly used to the routine, gave professions as well as names, either real or imagined—sculptors, beekeepers, kings of Tahiti. There were two separate popes. Philippe rued his missed opportunity to call himself a poet, to be announced as such to these people he was sure held his future in their hands. Or would they have mistaken it for a joke? How did one communicate the desperate seriousness of Art?

Philippe was relieved that the barman didn't pressure him into ordering a second beer, but was dismayed that there was no food to be ordered, for any price. His hunger passed from desire to discomfort to real pain, until his stomach began to clench desperately. Still he lingered, waiting for his future to present itself. He curled his toes over the canvas bag at his feet like a mother bird with an egg. Everything he owned was in there—every item of clothing, every word he'd ever written. What money he had, in a mix of pesetas and francs, was distributed across trouser and jacket pockets, tucked into his shoes, and sewn into his hems. His mother had even pinned a few bills in the waistband of his

61

underwear, but the pin had come undone, jabbing him, and the bills had migrated uncomfortably downward.

He pulled a notebook from the bag and a pencil from his pocket. Now a moment of paralysis, because what were the correct words to note on the first page of the first afternoon of the next, best part of his life? The date and place he recorded with a frisson of terrified delight, but what next? He could describe the room, that would be easy enough—the medieval bric-a-brac, the grimy portraits, the fake coats of arms, a wooden throne suspended by wires from the ceiling, spinning slowly in the slim breeze from the doorway. The doorman's ridiculous plumage. But Philippe already suspected that if he looked too hard, by daylight, the charm of this place would fall apart in his hands. Instead, he tried to describe the sensation of his hunger—scissors, stoning, a tiger's teeth. He made a parade of words down the page, in French, then crossed them all out. They weren't any good, and he wanted anyone who might be watching—the barman? God? Rodolphe Salis, the café's famed founder, somehow peering over his shoulder?—to know that he knew they were no good, that he had the discernment to be capable of better.

He was loath to abandon his vigil in favor of a meal, but he eventually stood, promising himself he could come right back. As he approached the front door he overheard a conversation between the doorman and a manager about the night's impending cover charge. When he learned how much it would be, he realized he was effectively trapped inside the Chat Noir for the night.

At sundown, finally, the crowds came. Men wearing peasant smocks on top, but with thin city shoes and store-bought trousers underneath, like confusing centaurs. Painters, he understood as he eavesdropped, their smocks left on as laziness or fashion, so they might know each other, so others might know them by sight, so that they might be excused from the door charge levied on the bourgeoisie gathering on the sidewalk outside. He had never dreamed of seeing so many painters in one place, flocking as common as sparrows. He'd known just one back home in Tarragona, an old man still eking out a living on portrait commissions. It was only the very ugliest or most narcissistic rich people, Philippe had thought then, who would bother with portraits in an age of photographs. Only people who needed to be lied to, and who would want to paint for them? He was not sure whom he wrote his poems for, but surely not people like that. Not, he had to admit, that people like that had ever offered to pay him. Nobody had ever offered to pay him, for anything he'd ever written, but he hoped that was about to change.

"You a writer?" a man asked, glancing at Philippe's notebook. The man was wearing a jacket, not a smock, and his collar was gray and crooked. He made a strange tinkling sound as he leaned over the bar, as if he were strung with wind chimes. His nose was a nearly bloody-looking red, and his eyes were already glazed.

Still, Philippe thought this was possibly the best single thing anyone had ever said to him in his life. "Yes," he said. "Yes. I'm a writer. What are you?"

"A drunk," the barman said, refusing to serve the man the absinthe he'd requested. "Salis's orders, Tinchant. You know that."

Tinchant didn't seem angry at either the description or the refusal, just shrugged in agreement and drifted away. But Philippe wanted to come to his aid. He ordered an absinthe himself and, when it arrived, stood to deliver it.

"Bad idea," the barman said. "If he's too drunk to play tonight, it's on your head, not mine."

"Play?"

"He's the house pianist. For the cabaret." Both men looked across the room to where Tinchant was producing stoppered vials of liquor from his pockets and hems, stashed clinking all over his person as if he were some mad scientist. The barman sighed. "Looks like it may be a lost cause tonight. I'd say one more won't kill him"—he gestured at the drink in Philippe's hand—"but someday one more's going to. You probably don't want it to be tonight, and you probably don't want it to be yours. You seem like a nice kid."

In a moment, Philippe had been demoted from "writer" to "nice kid." He knew instantly where his loyalties lay. He walked across the room to deliver the drink. Behind him, the bartender yelled for the errand boy to go find someone named Eric and tell him he'd almost definitely need to play the second half, maybe the first too, and that he ought to get here by the top of the show.

The bar was packed by the time Eric showed up, but Tinchant had managed to keep an empty chair at their table, growling like a dog at anyone who'd tried to take it. The guests filtering in now were not wearing smocks. They were finely, even elegantly dressed, and they didn't play games with the doorman, who'd since been joined by a knight in chain mail collecting a hefty cover charge. The guests' names and titles were ordinary, and if they had given their occupations, Philippe imagined, they would be a string of bankers and shopkeepers. Not his people, he thought. Amazing how clear the lines were between the bourgeoisie and the artistes, so stark that even a foreigner could see them snaking through the room, glowing like the tracery that hung in the dark behind the doorman's torch.

Eric, when he arrived, muddled the lines. He looked slightly older than Philippe, with shaggy hair and an unremarkable face. His clothes were the puzzlement. Suit, linen, shoes, all looked as if they had been well made, even expensive, before being caught in some mysterious natural disaster—there was no sign of wear in the normal places, at the elbows or cuffs, but one breast pocket was nearly ripped off, dangling by threads, and one of the lapels had been neatly slashed. He carried a rolled towel under one arm, tucked beside him as he sat next to Tinchant. Eric gave the older man a complicated stare. Pitying and contemptuous, envious and sad, all at once. An expression almost too complicated for a poem, Philippe thought. He'd need a whole novel.

"This is my understudy," Tinchant said, leaning hard against Eric.

"I'm really a gymnopédiste," Eric said. "But yes: I take over when he gets too drunk to play."

Philippe assumed *gymnopédiste* was a French word he didn't know but should, and wondered whether to admit his ignorance or hope the meaning eventually became clear. His mother had grown up in a border village in the Pyrenees where the people spoke French and Catalan and Spanish, all flawlessly, or so she claimed. She'd told her children she was raising them to be fluent in three languages, and Philippe had believed her. His poetry was in French—he prided himself on his command—but conversation at the Chat Noir hovered at the edge of his comprehension. He could keep up, but barely, guessing at all the fast, slick slang, and only with an effort that had sent his headache surging.

When a waiter came by the table, Philippe ordered an absinthe, this time for himself, willing to dull his comprehension if it meant also dulling the pain. He'd thought absinthe was a popular choice, an artist's drink, but Eric raised an eyebrow. "Starting early?" the gymnopédiste said.

Was it early? It felt so, so late. He hadn't slept on the train, except for a few accidental minutes against a stranger's shoulder that had lulled him with its smell of dirt and sunlight. When the farmer eventually shook Philippe off, it was with such violence that he fell from the hard bench onto the floor of the fourth-class carriage. At least the farmer gave him a hunk of bread and cheese in gruff apology. It was the only food he'd had since the border, when he'd finished the paper packet of olives his mother had sent him away with.

He asked Eric if there was anywhere nearby to get a meal.

"Of course. Lots of places. Are you visiting?"

"I think I've moved here," Philippe said. "But that was only four hours ago."

"Then if you don't mind the advice, I'd keep to wine or beer, especially here. The weekend prices are extortionate. If you can wait to eat until after the show I'll take you somewhere for supper."

"Why are you so sure you'll be paid tonight?" Tinchant said. "I'm fine. I'm feeling fine."

"If you're still able to walk to the Auberge later," Eric said, "I'll buy your meal too."

"Actually, he doesn't even need money," Tinchant confided to Philippe. "He's got it from his father. But that doesn't keep him from coming here every night like a vulture, circling, just waiting for me to play a wrong note."

"No one minds a wrong note," Eric said. "Salis only minds when you piss the piano bench in the middle of a show."

"And then you sit in it," Tinchant hissed. "You may think you're better than me but you sit in it all the same."

Eric held up the towel. "Salis keeps one for me in the Institute." He gestured at a low door nearly behind the bar, which, he explained, led to a special, invitation-only room for regulars, the closest thing the place had to an employee lounge or greenroom. Eric's welcome at the Institute was meant to flatter him into overlooking the fact that he earned nothing for whole nights spent on standby, when Tinchant successfully finished the show.

"He thinks he's going to be a composer," Tinchant said. "But he flunked out of the Conservatory."

"What are you?" Eric asked Philippe.

"A poet," Philippe said, having screwed up his courage to say it.

"That's fantastic," Eric said.

Philippe tested the words in his head, searching for sarcasm. He couldn't hear any.

"Twice, he flunked out *twice*," Tinchant said, throwing an arm around Eric's shoulders.

Eric reared up and out from the embrace like a skittish horse. He'd been looking for new poems to set to music, he told Philippe, because he couldn't afford the rights to anything published. Would Philippe want to collaborate? he asked.

"But you don't know my work at all," Philippe said, trying to check Eric's enthusiasm for him, if the would-be composer didn't have the sense to do it himself.

"His family begged his way back in after the first time," Tinchant said, "and then he played just as badly."

"What's your name? I'm Erik, spelled with a *K*. I'm descended from Vikings."

Philippe gave a shortened, more French version of his real name, and Erik-with-a-K explained to him that his father owned a music-publishing business and that there would be money in it for them if they could give him something he could use.

"He mentions the Conservatory whenever he advertises for private piano students," Tinchant griped. "Says he 'attended,' leaves out that he never finished. It's false advertising!"

Ignoring Tinchant, Erik acknowledged to Philippe that he hadn't read his work, but no matter: Philippe could do his part first, then Erik would compose to suit the words.

"What sorts of poems did you have in mind?" Philippe asked.

"Plus it doesn't even work!" Tinchant said. "Salis told me he's only got two students."

"We should start with love," Erik said. "Or flowers. But probably love."

"Love!" Tinchant howled.

But Philippe was filled with love at that moment. He loved Tinchant, for introducing him to Erik. He loved the Chat Noir, for being everything he'd hoped it would be. He loved Paris even more than he had dreamed he would, and he had dreamed long and hard and eagerly.

"Love," Philippe said. "Yes. Love."

*　　*　　*

Tarragona, Spain, had once been a Roman capital, before the Visigoths and the Moors and the Reconquista. There'd been an amphitheater and a circus and a forum and temples, aqueducts and good roads and formidable walls. That had been thirteen hundred years before Philippe was born, and the general agreement was that Tarragona had been declining ever since. More than a millennium ago, Philippe's hometown had been as great and important and populous, as beautiful and civilized and entertaining, as it was ever going to be. Even as a child, Philippe found this crushingly depressing. Many of the town's modern buildings were made of stones harvested from Roman ruins, with Latin inscriptions peeking out from cornerstones and lintels, or scuffed into nothingness on front stoops. The ruins within the old medieval walls had been pillaged centuries ago, but when Philippe was small, the town fathers, in a burst of unfounded enthusiasm, decided to expand the modern street grid westward. Philippe's father was employed on the building works, clearing ruins previously left unmolested, and occasionally carrying home to his children fragments of inscriptions or statuary, disembodied numerals and toes. Philippe thought he would rather have been born in his mother's village, where there had never been any great monuments, where people built and repaired the same plain houses and stables and sheds, with no reminders of another, better world.

Philippe had one close friend, a fair boy who burned so easily in the sun that he crept along the shady side of every street. Miguel's parents were generous with spending money, which allowed Miguel to subscribe to slim French publications full of cartoons and humor columns, dirty poems and event listings that might have been weeks or months out of date by the time they reached Spain but were nonetheless miraculous for their evidence that such events existed. Miguel's subscriptions were mostly for in-house publications from music halls and cafés whose rivalries threaded through their newspapers in dizzying, baffling detail. The boys formed loyalties, decided which cabarets were worth the admission fees, which cafés they would be regulars in when (not if) they moved to Paris. They studied the newspapers more diligently than their textbooks, and their marks began to suffer. This did not dampen their obsessive research, their plans for future glory.

Not sure which poems Erik might want, Philippe swept into his bag the whole row of notebooks on the single shelf in the room he'd rented at an address Erik had suggested, near the top of the Montmartre Butte, the highest point in the city. The pricier, flatter part of the neighborhood lay at the bottom of streets so steep that Philippe had to throw his weight backward from his hips as he walked, wary of his slick, worn shoes on the cobblestones. Happily, he'd had no heavy luggage to bring up the hill, where horse-drawn cabs refused to go. Like all the other men and women who filled the streets around the Place du Tertre, he lived lightly, with what he could carry on his back.

He met Erik at the Auberge du Clou, the same place he'd eventually been taken to eat the night he arrived in Paris, two days earlier. The Auberge was a quieter café than the Chat Noir, decorated like an alpine farmhouse with farrier's nails for coat hooks and horseshoes hung over the bar. After pleasantries, Erik began flipping through the notebooks, but Philippe couldn't stand to watch him. When Miguel had read his poems, Philippe used to wander the apartment into the living room or kitchen, where Miguel's mother usually gave him a sweet as consolation against the admirable but problematic honesty that the boy she'd raised was sure to mete out. Most of the time Philippe could steel himself to acknowledge the accuracy of Miguel's disapproving critiques. Most of the time he could even manage to be grateful.

Now he left Erik reading at the cramped table and wandered to a front window covered by cheerful, red-checked curtains, and from there to the bar, then to the back wall and its framed pictures of cows. There was nothing else to look at, though, without intruding on the handful of other occupied tables. Philippe was homesick, he realized, for the first time since leaving Tarragona. He felt guilty that it was Miguel's mother he was missing and not his own, who'd had no sweets to spare. Back at the table, he blanched to see Erik poring over forgotten schoolboy rhymes on the earliest pages of the earliest notebook, festooned with doodles and dirty Catalan insults, free of Miguel's editorial interventions.

"Never mind those," Philippe said, resisting the urge to yank the notebook away.

"I rather like this one," Erik said.

"Really? Which?"

Erik turned the book sideways and Philippe leaned in and pushed their beer glasses to the edge of the table to make room. It was a love poem to a woman with a mouth made of rubies, a voice sweeter than honey, smile like a rainbow, hair dark as . . . darkness. So beautiful she made the angels jealous. Philippe imagined what Miguel would say. Maybe that the only possible object of jealousy in this poem was the rhymes—very neat and regular, if unoriginal.

" 'Sylvie,' " Erik read the title aloud. "Was she a real person?"

"Based on one," Philippe lied. "She died," he added, thinking to avoid further questions on the fictional Sylvie.

"I'm sorry," Erik said, sincerely.

Philippe tried to look bereaved.

"It will inspire me," Erik said. "Her loss." He was clearly struggling not to ask more—how she'd died, or how far she and Philippe had gone down the road of love before she expired.

"Not my best work," Philippe said. "I can't say I did her justice."

It was a love poem, though, Erik said. It would do.

Philippe had assumed there would be some kind of ongoing collaboration, but Erik disappeared with his notebook, leaving him sitting like a fool by himself with beer he couldn't afford. For three days he heard nothing. He still didn't even know Erik's last name, or where he lived. Philippe thought about all the cafés he hadn't seen yet because he was stuck at the Auberge, too new for Miguel to have subscribed to its paper, much less for either of them to have developed any affinity for it. Philippe started to detest the clean curtains, the pictures of cows, the stupid woven baskets of fabric wildflowers taking up space on the tables. He detested the regulars, who came here to get away from the dank, boozy glitz of the other cafés and didn't trouble themselves to be friendly to a stranger. Philippe hadn't experienced nearly enough dank, boozy glitz to grow sick of it. He thought of all the sights he and Miguel had planned to visit, and how little he'd seen so far.

On the fourth day without any sign of Erik, he gave up on the Auberge and ordered lunch at the Rat Mort, where everything from the décor to the names on the menu had a theme of dead rats. Miguel had never been quite sure from the newspapers whether this was an actual place or a joke, and Philippe was both charmed and unsettled to find that it was quite real. The café sold postcards, pictures of the dead-rat-festooned interior, and he bought one for Miguel. He ordered something called rodent piss and, after two more glasses of it, asked the first person who sat down beside him if he knew where Erik-with-a-K, understudy pianist and gymnopédiste, lying composer and thief of notebooks, might live.

"He's at the Auberge du Clou right now, if you're looking for him."

Armed with this information, Philippe tried to decide whether he was, in fact, looking for Erik. He'd wanted only to learn where Erik lived, so he could steal his notebook back from an empty apartment. He'd been imagining the most embarrassing of his old poems showing up in the café papers, plastered all over the neighborhood, read aloud as comedy acts at the cabarets.

"He might have been looking for you, actually," the man beside Philippe said. "A Spanish poet, he told me. Bad shoes and big hair?"

"That's me," Philippe said, reaching up to touch the dark mane he should perhaps have had tamed before he left Tarragona. Haircuts, like everything else in Paris, were expensive.

At the Auberge, Erik showed off the rough draft of his composition, the staves furry with notes. He was giddy about the opening. "A striking thirteenth!" he said. He didn't want the root-position tonic stated clearly until the very end, he said. He also preferred not to do a strophic piece, if that was all right with Philippe. "It should be through-composed instead. What do you think?"

"That's fine," Philippe said, terrified, now that the rodent piss was wearing off, of revealing his ignorance. Was he supposed to know what any of that meant? He pressed his hair down with a sweaty hand. At least, Philippe thought, cheering himself, Erik had turned out to be a real composer. He had no idea what a thirteenth might sound like, but the name of it alone was intimidating.

Erik announced that he'd begun more songs based on poems in the notebook: one about angels, one about flowers, one about death, and one just called "Song." Miguel had made comments so scathing about three of the four that Philippe had abandoned them without revision. The poem about death, Philippe remembered, had eventually met with Miguel's grudging approval. Erik showed off the drafts to Philippe. "Sylvie" was fully harmonized, he said, but "Song" was so far nothing more than a few musical phrases in the treble clef. Not that Philippe understood what "treble clef" meant until Erik pointed at the handful of dots on the top set of lines running across the page like fence rails. Erik seemed to think Philippe could translate the black dots, that they all resolved into sounds in his head the same way they did in Erik's. But Philippe might as well have been looking at a page of Chinese characters.

Finally Erik realized that his written drafts were not having the desired effect. "Sorry," he said. "I assume everyone reads music. Everyone I grew up with did. It was the only thing we had in common."

"Makes sense, I suppose, if your father's a music publisher."

"A recent development," Erik said. "My stepmother put him up to it so she'd have someone to publish her own compositions. Then she finally realized she was awful, but they're still at it." When Philippe asked if he'd sold them things before, Erik said he'd never been interested enough in popular music to try. His usual work was more ambitious, he said with a sniff, but he needed the money.

Was this a clue as to what a gymnopédiste did? Philippe wondered. But if gymnopédistes didn't usually write popular music, what did they aim for instead? Unpopular? Unpleasing?

"Here," Erik said, and rose abruptly from the table. "Let me show you what your poems sound like."

The Auberge didn't mount a regular cabaret and Philippe followed Erik to the freezing basement, where huge puddles of rank water pooled on the stone floor and the café piano sat on a low wooden platform serving as a stage. Philippe leaped from the bottom of the stairs to a wooden bench and pulled his feet to safety, sitting cross-legged, an expectant audience of one.

The songs were meandering, in a pretty way, the tempo at times excruciatingly slow. The rhythm of the accompaniment was mechanical, the notes spare but full of eerie, almost abrasive harmonies. A thirteenth, Philippe learned, sounded like a songbird dipped in lye. The arrangements didn't highlight his poetry so much as make it strange. He was startled at first, even a bit offended, but the odder the songs were, the more he began to appreciate them. In Tarragona, he had been strange without meaning to be, without aspiring to it. In Montmartre, where a concentrated number of people were all trying very hard to be very strange at one time, the result was that nothing was very strange at all. Philippe had heard no songs like these, with their square, solid rhymes and gaunt melodies. He wasn't sure what Erik's parents would think, whether these could be money-makers, but he decided he liked the songs regardless, liked them more and more as they unfurled, lovely and strangled.

When Erik finished playing the last one, or rather told Philippe he was finished, because the piece was incomplete and it wasn't clear it was over, Philippe applauded loudly.

"Thoughts? Suggestions?" Erik said.

Philippe wasn't sure what to do. It seemed lazy to say no, arrogant to say yes. "One or two of them might work better a little faster?" he tried. "Not the death one, of course, but the flowers one, perhaps?"

Erik's face instantly closed, and he balled his hands and pressed them against the sides of his thighs. Philippe understood then that he wasn't to critique but to praise, and tried to repair the damage with a flood of compliments—What did *he* know about technique? He couldn't even read music! At first Erik seemed mollified, but when he proposed they work through the pieces phrase by phrase, Philippe suspected a trap. "Wonderful," he said at every pause. "I can't hear anything I'd change." But Erik kept playing the same lines over and over, demanding advice.

Rescue came from the day manager, who clomped downstairs and told Erik to shut the hell up—people came to the Auberge to get *away* from self-indulgence like that. "If you want to play something fun, you can play, but you can't just noodle around. We can hear it upstairs and it's driving everyone mad."

"For free? You want me to play for free?" Erik asked, choosing to ignore the insults.

The manager didn't particularly *want* him to play anything, he said. But if Erik insisted, he ought to play something that actually sounded like something.

Erik flipped to a blank page in his staff notebook and titled it in block letters so large the manager could read it from the bottom of the stairs: *SOMETHING*. The piece, when Erik played it, sounded much like "Chopsticks." He banged through a reprise until the manager asked him to leave. Philippe followed his friend two blocks into exile, until Erik plopped down on a bench in the Place d'Anvers.

"They never mean it," Erik said. "I've been thrown out of loads of places." He kicked lazily at a bustle of pigeons that barely scattered in response. "Say, did you ever find a room to rent?"

What would Erik say if the answer were no, and Philippe had been sleeping rough? Philippe thought about lying, just to find out. Then he weighed the prospective humiliation of Erik's indifference against the odds of guilt or apology, and told the truth.

"Good," Erik said. Nothing more.

In Tarragona, Miguel had cut out pictures and headlines from the Paris café papers and pasted them into collages. He propped up the cardboard panels in a triptych on his bedroom dresser. The central panel, where a crucifixion would have been, or a Madonna and Child, was instead a drawing of a jaunty rabbit leaping out of a frying pan. Mostly Miguel chose animals, or music notes and disembodied words—*Refreshing! Shocking! Delicious!*—but on the left panel there was a small cartoon of a priest peering up the skirts of a cancan girl. Philippe had never been especially devout, but the cartoon troubled him. He cringed when Miguel began lighting candles in front of the triptych like a real altar, praying for deliverance from their stolid hometown. After Miguel mentioned that he was pocketing the candles from the cathedral, Philippe began to fear in earnest for their souls. Miguel's only fear was what his parents might think, and he began closing the door when the candle was lit. With the window shutters pulled against the afternoon heat, the room was stifling, and Philippe didn't understand why the altar was worth it. Did Miguel really think there was another god, some giant Parisian rabbit in the sky, that would answer their prayers with train tickets? That would spirit them off to Paris and then lie down in its frying pan and let the boys eat their fill of its crackling flesh? Offer its body and blood? Philippe cringed at his own blasphemy.

The longer the door was closed each day, the more suspicious Miguel's mother seemed whenever Philippe emerged. If he roamed the apartment while Miguel read his poems, she sometimes shamed him into helping with chores, rather than offering him sweets. He steeled himself to stay in the bedroom as Miguel's narrow fingers ran down the pages, tapping out all the clichés and sentimentality, the unearned wisdom about age, or manhood, or romance.

"Is this even *accurate*?" Miguel asked one afternoon, of a couplet about what it felt like to kiss a woman's lips.

A poem wasn't about "accuracy," Philippe tried to argue.

"This poem isn't 'about' anything except maybe the fact that you've never gotten laid," Miguel retorted.

Though Philippe knew for a fact that Miguel had never gotten laid either, this was a critique too far. He left furious, and avoided Miguel for days.

Finally Miguel dragged him into an alley near their school. He pressed a nectarine into Philippe's hand, the fruit so soft and nearly overripe he could have crushed it by accident. "He said it's like this," Miguel said. "My father. Kissing a girl."

"You asked your *father* what it's like to kiss a girl?"

"Who else would I ask?" Miguel said matter-of-factly. Both boys were reminded, yet again, that they had no other friends. "Kiss it."

"I'm not going to kiss a piece of fruit."

"You're supposed to kiss it, then bite into it."

"I think your father's confused about some things."

Miguel rolled his eyes. "I thought you could wrap your head around a metaphor. But maybe not."

Philippe sank his teeth into the fruit spitefully and tore away a bite, then another, barely taking time to chew. Juice runneled down his chin so fast it dripped onto his clothes before he could catch it. The nectarine was delicious, intensely sweet. When he'd swallowed the last of the flesh and skin he sucked the pit clean, then took it out of his mouth and threw it hard at Miguel's head. The pit struck him smack between the eyes and ricocheted audibly.

Miguel yelped, but a moment later both boys were laughing. The pit was too ridiculous, rolling away down the alley. The rift between them too ridiculous, when there was no one else in town who understood them a fraction as well as they understood each other. Miguel took a clean white handkerchief out of his pocket. Philippe held out his hand for it, but Miguel reached up to clean Philippe's face himself. The juice was sticky, and Miguel spit on a corner of the cloth. He held Philippe's jaw steady with his other hand and scrubbed. Philippe stared up at the strip of sky above the alley, so bright it looked white instead of blue. He felt the white scalloped ends of Miguel's fingernails against his jawbone, running across the margins of him like a poem. Finding something to like, something to correct. Reading, always, with rapt sincerity.

Despite Erik's help, Philippe landed more meetings with editors who were interested in publishing his poems for free than for cash. He hadn't understood that the bulk of a café paper was written by a single café employee using multiple pseudonyms, and much of the rest by drunks, who churned out pornographic cartoons for free. Even Erik contributed occasional articles under the byline Virginie LeBeau, who hated Prussians and custard apple tart, but particularly loathed the work of the Chat Noir's second pianist, that talentless Viking upstart Erik. A huge portion of the Chat Noir paper turned out to be written by Albert Tinchant, who accepted payment exclusively in liquor. Philippe couldn't quite believe that the first person he'd spoken to in Paris turned out to be the author of so many of the articles and dirty poems that had consoled his adolescent self. No, it was more than consolation, he thought—Tinchant had authored his actual adolescence, his whole idea of what he wanted his life to be.

"That's terrifying," Tinchant said.

"I'm trying to thank you," Philippe protested, describing the articles as polestars, or the lantern of a lighthouse, beckoning him into harbor.

"Lighthouses warn people away, pissant."

"Ignore him," Erik said. "He's drunk." Which was of course the reason Erik was there in the first place, all three of them back at the Chat Noir, waiting for the cabaret to start, waiting to see how far into it Tinchant would last. He was fading out earlier and earlier as the weeks passed, until Erik was covering the majority of every show. Salis had hinted that he would grant Erik a promotion to first pianist if Erik would simply ask. But not only did he not ask, Philippe had even seen him tuck some of his earnings into Tinchant's pocket while the man slept, slumped in a corner of the Institute using a discarded cabaret costume as a blanket, a mock royal robe with ermine trim made of towel strips dotted with black ink.

"You're one of the reasons I came to Paris," Philippe told Tinchant, wanting him to believe it.

"And now you're trying to take away my job. I've only got two and you're each trying to take one."

"I don't know what you're talking about."

"Salis told me. He told me you think you can fill the whole bloody paper."

"That's not true," Philippe said, although it was in fact a little true. The betrayal was that Salis had revealed it, no doubt knowing how Tinchant would react.

"This place doesn't work like that. No one comes here and gets what they want," Tinchant said, then paused. "I mean, not right away. You have to work for it."

"I want to work," Philippe said. "I'm trying to work."

The most accomplished poet he'd met so far, a man who had won serious literary prizes in Lyon, was making a living selling olives for two francs a kilo, wrapping them in pamphlets of his own poems, hoping someone would read them after eating. That discovery had depressed Philippe for two whole weeks: the first week at how low the poet had stooped; the second, that Philippe had no capital with which to import his own olives. The writing business was his only business, and it was a bad one.

"If you're so hard up you're begging Salis for work, have *him* bail you out," Tinchant said, waving his hand toward Erik, who had sat by silently during Philippe's paean to Tinchant. "He's got family money. So much he doesn't want anyone to know where he lives. But Salis sent me one day to drop off some songs he didn't trust me to learn. And I went. Like an errand boy," he added, with an air of astonishment. "I really went."

Philippe stared at Erik, waiting for a joke or protest, a story about squatting in a rich widow's apartment, maintaining his vows of artistic poverty. Literal vows, which Philippe had seen him make one night during the Chat Noir cabaret. One of the singers had been dressed in rags for a skit, and Erik borrowed a wedding veil from a pile of costumes in the Institute. He played his own wedding march, put a twist of paper round the woman's finger, and kissed her on the lips. It was the only time Philippe had ever seen Erik touch a woman, much less kiss one. "My bride," Erik yelled, then looked dismayed at the crowd's joyful roar. "Not *her*. An *idea*. I'm marrying an idea. She's simply a representation." It was the only night that Philippe had ever seen Tinchant, after several cups of black coffee, swapped back in for Erik.

79

"Maybe I did mean it the first way," Tinchant said, looking back and forth at the two of them: Philippe's wounded expression of betrayal, Erik's of guilty discomfort. "Maybe no one gets what they want. Maybe that's the way this place works after all."

One afternoon when Miguel had run out of new café articles to decode and Philippe had no new poems for him to praise or disparage, Miguel pulled out a battered guidebook to Paris, nearly thirty years old, and the boys tried yet again to plan their futures. But that day the conversation felt threadbare, ridiculous. They'd been doing this for years, Philippe thought, playing children's games, but they weren't children anymore. He asked if they could do something else instead.

Miguel looked surprised. When he offered a pack of playing cards, Philippe didn't have any better ideas. They played Truc into the evening, until they could barely see the numbers and suits, tilting their hands toward the orange glow that seeped through the wooden shutters closed against the heat. Finally Philippe stood, unlatched the window, and leaned out to feel if the air had cooled. On the street below a fruit vendor's horse stamped and flung its tail across its hindquarters, sweeping off flies that settled again immediately. A faint breeze reached the window, and Philippe felt how his hair and shirt refused to move, stiff with dried sweat. He heard the squeak of the bed behind him as Miguel rose and placed a hand on Philippe's shoulder, urging him backward. Miguel reached past him to pull the shutters closed again, and snicked the metal latch into place.

"It's dark," Philippe said.

Then Miguel kissed him. Of course Philippe should have realized this was coming. Their own parents had known, he understood later, and Philippe wondered which would humiliate his father more—thinking that his son was a sodomite, or that his son was so naïve he hadn't even recognized the possibility. How had he convinced himself he would thrive in Paris when

80

he didn't even understand what was happening in Miguel's bedroom? He was a fool, and he was going to live and die a fool, in
this forsaken town in Catalonia.

He pushed his embarrassment away. At least, this is what he
told himself later about that moment. What he really pushed
was Miguel, who staggered backward into the dresser and jostled
the altar. The central cardboard panel, with the cheerful rabbit,
fell forward over the candle flame. The candle went out, and the
room was barely light enough for Philippe to register Miguel's
expression of abject hurt. Then the cardboard caught in a puff of
smoke and flame. Miguel snatched it up and blew on it, which
only made the flame leap higher, whereupon he unlatched the
window and flung it outside. While Miguel had his back turned,
Philippe grabbed his schoolbag and ran. He nearly collided with
the fruit vendor in the street. The horse was nudging a hoof at
the burned triptych, the scandalous pictures still unburned, and
Philippe darted under the horse's legs to grab it. The vendor
shouted at him—was he trying to get his head kicked in? But
Philippe emerged safely from beneath the horse with the cardboard. He burned the rest of it in the stove at home, destroying
the evidence. But of what? he wondered. He was unsure what
to call it. Miguel was going to hell, he decided. But Philippe
couldn't go to hell with him. Philippe needed to get to Paris.

Erik invited Philippe to join him for long collaborative work ses-
sions at the Auberge or other cafés, hours spent sketching out
musical plays or ballets or full-length operas. They ordered drink
after drink to hold their table, and staggered when they rose at
the end of the day. They were often interrupted by friends of
Erik's doing the exact same thing, drinking so they had a place to
work, and drinking too much ever to finish the work. These were
invariably men with grand ambitions and terrible apartments.
Stoveless, waterless, lightless rooms, cold enough in the winter to
kill. The men gathered wherever they could and paid whatever

it cost for the privilege. They ordered cheaply, sipped slowly, and tried to be so entertaining that the proprietors wouldn't notice how little they drank. This was one reason, Philippe learned, that Montmartre had developed its international reputation for charm: everyone was afraid of being thrown out and having to go home.

The ideas that came out of these café days felt to Philippe like vegetables—good only until they wilted or browned, sometimes all at once, sometimes over days or weeks, until even a sniff of his own work revolted him. We're trying for a potato, he thought, or an apple—something that could last a long time, if properly stored. Something firm and fleshy and satisfying. Something people would pay for.

At least, Philippe assumed they were trying for a potato. When he shared this metaphor, Erik looked nonplussed. "A potato? Really?"

Erik never suggested they work at his apartment, which, if Tinchant was to be believed, would have offered plenty of room. Tinchant had given Philippe the address in an effort to enlist him as co-conspirator for a break-in. Erik went out every Sunday to eat a home-cooked dinner at his father's apartment, Tinchant explained. "We won't take anything, we'll just cut all the piano strings. He'll think it's funny." Philippe was pretty sure he wouldn't.

Philippe thought of his own father, who one evening had walked Philippe and his brothers to the harbor and asked them what was different. A stub of a Roman lighthouse had held vigil over Tarragona's bay for more than a thousand years, until its final stones had collapsed into the water that afternoon. Philippe was the first to see the empty water and sky where the crumbling tower had once stood. His father told him with grudging approval that he was a boy who noticed things, and he went on to list for his son lucrative occupations where this talent for observation might be of use, poetry not included. In Paris, Philippe tried sometimes to conjure his father's voice for comfort, for confidence: "You are a boy who notices things." *Boy*, Philippe thought despairingly. Hopeless, helpless *boy*.

A mutual friend, Alphonse, invited them both to an exhibition of "Incoherent Art," to which Alphonse had contributed two paintings: *First Communion of Young Chlorotic Girls in a Snowstorm* (a blank piece of white paper stuck to a wall), and *Tomato Harvest on the Shore of the Red Sea, by Apoplectic Cardinals* (a solid red rectangle). On a nearby pedestal, beside a small label crediting Erik, sat a single baked potato. Philippe couldn't decide how he felt. Angry? Foolish? Disappointed not to be given credit? Hungry, at the waste of a perfectly good potato, when he hadn't eaten since yesterday?

He glared at Erik, who was still standing in front of the red rectangle, chatting with Alphonse and another mutual friend, Narcisse, also an artist. Alphonse and Erik had attended the same school in Honfleur, although Alphonse had been several years ahead, and they'd rediscovered each other in Paris quite by accident. Philippe was terribly curious as to what Erik had been like as a boy, but hadn't bothered asking; he assumed Alphonse would omit anything particularly revealing out of loyalty. This was an ongoing problem for Philippe—he'd made friends other than Erik, but they'd all been Erik's friends first, which made them feel like they didn't quite belong to him.

"That was my idea," Philippe protested, pointing at the potato when Erik finally turned around.

"Not exactly," Erik said.

Philippe wondered if either Alphonse or Narcisse would acknowledge his claim, but neither had been present for the original conversation. Fair enough, he thought grudgingly. By *potato*, he had not meant an actual potato. He had not dreamed of an actual potato, baked or otherwise, being in any kind of art exhibition, incoherent or otherwise. Philippe was missing something, some instinct that Erik had in spades. He sometimes doubted Erik as a composer, but he never doubted his genius for incoherence.

Philippe excused himself, gulping down a last glass of the gallery wine. On his way home he ducked into an alley to piss. As he opened his trousers, worn thread gave way and the top button popped off and skittered away into the dark. He crept after the sound, searching with his soles in the hope he might be able to feel the button beneath his disintegrating shoes. Not wanting to crawl—his trouser knees were nearly worn through already—he bent at the waist and pressed his palms to the ground, an awkward elephant walk. His right hand made contact with something wet and slimy he was glad he couldn't see. A rat squeaked to ward off his groping left. He searched until his bent back was shrieking, his shoes and hands fouled. The alley had devoured his button. He tried to decide if there was a café-paper article in this, but he didn't know how to make it funny. If it had happened to someone else, someone who had another pair of trousers, or sufficient remaining buttons on the fly to re-arrange, a mother or sister or wife to do the mending, it might be funny. But this was happening to him, and he wanted to cry. He was hungry and exhausted and a failure, and now his trousers wouldn't even stay up.

He nearly greeted Erik with this litany—*hungrytiredfail-uretrousers*—when Erik arrived home from the gallery to find him on the front stoop. Pride overrode misery, and Philippe man-aged to keep it simple: "Tinchant gave me your address. Do you have any buttons?"

"Buttons?"

"For my trousers. I need a button. I don't have needle or thread either."

"I do," Erik said, after a pause. "I've got all those things." He gestured Philippe inside and let the way upstairs to his apart-ment.

Philippe waited just inside the door, his waistband gathered in his fist, until Erik, sure-footed in his own home, could make his way to a lamp and light it. The windows were heavily curtained, the room pitch-dark until the lamp flared. Light fell first on the piano Tinchant was so eager to sabotage, a walnut-colored upright with a bright, toothy keyboard, then on a plain wooden stool and a balding velvet armchair pulled up alongside, for a teacher or page-turner. The top of the piano was covered not just in folios of music but in teacups and plates and newspapers. As Philippe's eyes adjusted, he saw that it was the only flat surface in the room. There was no other furniture.

"Some trouble with my creditors," Erik said. "I'll be joining you on the Butte soon enough, but this address is better for attracting piano students. At least, that was the intention. As it turns out, the address doesn't accomplish much. Plus the neighbors hate the noise."

"How are you going to get a piano up the Butte?"

"No idea. Have a seat." He gestured at the piano stool. "I need to take the light to the other room to find a button."

"They look like this," Philippe said, lifting his shirttail to show his fly. "I mean, any button will do. But if you happened to have different kinds. Or just a pin. If you can lend me a pin, I'll be fine."

After Erik disappeared with the lamp, the sudden dark felt vertiginous. Philippe groped for some mooring and accidentally struck the piano keys, an ugly yowl of notes.

"The *neighbors*," Erik hissed from the next room.

"Sorry. I didn't mean to." He felt above the keys to grip the open fallboard and concentrated on breathing until Erik's footsteps returned.

"Which of us is likely to be less hopeless at this?" Erik said, needle and thread in hand. The button was a tarnished metal that Philippe suspected Erik had clipped off his own clothing. He was too grateful to protest.

"I've never mended a thing," Philippe said truthfully. "My mother did it."

"Me, then," Erik said with a sigh. "Trousers off."

Philippe winced, but of course sitting in his drawers would be preferable to Erik jabbing into his crotch with a needle. He stood and let his trousers drop before he remembered to remove his shoes. Then he folded to untangle himself.

"Your socks are appalling," Erik said idly, as he arranged Philippe's trousers in his lap. He removed a small notebook from a pocket and handed it to Philippe.

"How was the rest of the exhibition?"

"I didn't know you'd left. I was looking for you."

"Why?"

"Just looking."

"The army?" Philippe asked, taking in Erik's unexpected competence with the needle.

"And boarding school. My grandmother would have mended things on the weekends, but I didn't want to have to thank her for anything. The other buttons are loose as well. Should I reinforce them while I'm at it?"

"If you don't mind," Philippe said. He curled his hand and ran his fingernails across the tops of the keys, so gently the only sound was a light clicking. "You know I've never played a note?"

"Don't. It's late."

"I didn't mean I would. Just saying I hadn't."

Erik shrugged, sewed.

"May I read you something?" Without waiting for an answer, Philippe flipped through the notebook to the last page. It was an apology poem he'd written for Miguel, not for the shove, or for running, although he was humiliated by those now, too. But for the weeks of silence afterward, the way he'd treated Miguel like a ghost he would no longer allow himself to believe in, the way Miguel's school life had become unbearable once he was a solitary target. "What happened between you two?" one of their nemeses had asked him, and Philippe sealed Miguel's misery by telling an uglier version of the truth. He thought that once they finished school, once he had saved enough money clearing the ruins to take the train to Paris, it would all be behind him. But he'd been seeing Miguel on every street corner since his arrival.

The poem was the best work he'd managed: regret as heavy as a marble statue, a city choked in its own ruins, trying to clear and build on top of its mistakes. It was the first time Philippe had read the words to an audience, and he delivered them slowly. "Could you do something with it, do you think?"

"Again," Erik said, and Philippe read it through twice more. Erik looked thoughtful, then finally shook his head. "I can't hear it. I'm sorry."

"Would you want to try later, with the piano?"

"There's an awful lot of *feelings* in it," Erik said. "I wouldn't know what to do with them. Maybe I'm not ready."

"What does that mean?"

"It means what it means."

"You've written plenty of songs about love."

"That's different."

"How is love not a feeling?"

"It's not a feeling when it's in a cabaret song, rhymed with 'dove' and 'heaven above' and all the rest. Ruby lips and hair dark as darkness. Then it's only cliché."

The quote from "Sylvie" was a low blow, but Erik wasn't wrong.

"I don't know what you want from me," Philippe said. "I don't mean just the writing. I mean—are we even friends?"

"Of course we're friends."

"Truly?"

"You're trouserless in my living room in the middle of the night while I do your sewing. We might as well be married."

If you want to kiss me I'll let you, Philippe thought, but did not say. What about himself? Was it let or want? His imagination failed him. Not when it came to the act—he could imagine the kiss itself, but nothing beyond it. Erik's whiskers would be scratchy, he supposed. The prospect confused more than excited him. But confusion was not repulsion, which was the way he'd been raised to think of such a kiss, between two men. When he thought of Miguel, it was with wonder. Miguel had been able to imagine the two of them as something other, something more, than what they already were. His friend had had more vision that day in the bedroom than all the artists at the Incoherent Art exhibition put together. Philippe always considered invention one of his shortcomings as a writer, but he also wondered if it was his larger failing as a person. Miguel had looked at him and seen someone different than who Philippe understood himself to be. Erik had looked at a potato and seen a piece of art.

"I want to give you what you want," Philippe said at last, "but I can't figure out what that is."

"A fool's errand, since I never know myself."

Erik was breezy as he said it, and Philippe didn't know how to respond. Then his stomach, embarrassingly, spoke for him, a growl that seemed earsplitting in the silent room.

Erik invited him to eat the leftovers on the windowsill, the dregs of Erik's stepmother's Sunday dinner.

Philippe couldn't prevent wild fantasies from taking root, even in the few seconds it took to reach the window. But the food was a quarter of baguette and a cold bowl of potatoes. "Do you have a fork?" Philippe asked, trying not to sound disappointed.

"Somewhere," Erik said, but made no move to unearth one.

Philippe decided he could eat with his fingers.

"They agreed to buy a song," Erik said. "At dinner. Just 'Sylvie' for now, to see how it sells. A flat fee up front and then royalties, depending."

Philippe was so shocked he spoke with his mouth full. "That's fantastic. You didn't even tell me the songs were finished."

"My father said they all sounded rather similar. He worried about trying to bring them out at once."

"Makes sense to be cautious. Not that I think they sound alike, of course."

Erik bit the thread, and wound the tail around the last of the buttons. "There. These are still about the saddest pair of trousers in Paris, but they won't fall off. Let me get you your share of the money." He laid the pants over the back of the armchair, and disappeared again with the lamp.

Philippe stood eating in the dark, then licked the bowl clean. The potatoes sat lumpy in his otherwise empty stomach, and a suspicion about whether the song had really sold clumped there, too.

"It's not much," Erik said, returning. First he tossed Philippe a rolled-up pair of socks, worn but clean. Then he placed a fistful of money directly into the pocket of Philippe's trousers where they hung on the chair. Not the neat stack of bills Philippe had imagined, but a wad of crumpled francs and coins.

"I don't need charity," Philippe said, although he did. He needed it desperately.

"The socks are so I don't have to look at your feet, and this is your half of the advance. We'll split the royalties down the middle too, if there are any."

"Then tell your parents thank you from me."

"She's not my mother. My mother's dead."

"I'm sorry," Philippe said, and stupidly held out the bowl, rather than putting it back by the window.

"Keep it," Erik said. "A gift. Eugénie has a hundred of them at least."

"Another gift? Tell me the truth. Did they really buy one of our songs?"

"They did," Erik said. "I'm telling the truth."

Philippe let himself believe it. But instead of the warmth, the triumph that he had expected to flow through him, he felt the same plunging fear that had come when Erik took the lamp away. He thought he'd been longing for darkness. Paris was so maddeningly bright he'd become nostalgic for nights in Tarragona. Paris was a thousand moons suspended over a thousand street corners, galaxies of illuminated signs and windows. There was always enough light to write a poem by. But whereas the painters and sculptors and musicians had stopping points, 365 of them, when there was too little light to paint, or exasperated neighbors insisting on a halt to the noise, Philippe never did. For everyone else, it seemed, there was a moment every day when the world told you to knock off and have a rest, raise a glass and pretend you'd accomplished all that day that you'd meant to. Factory workers had a whistle. Farmers got winter, bricklayers got dusk. Night-soil men and grave robbers had the dawn. But there was nothing in Philippe's life that could tell him when it was time to stop.

And without the small pauses, how should he recognize the bigger ones? The moment when he gave up on writing altogether, either his ability to do it well or its ability to feed him? The moment he tried to get hired on at a factory outside Paris, or put his tail between his legs and begged his parents for money to return to Spain? If no one, not even Erik's parents, could be persuaded to pay money for his work, then Philippe had his answer. Not the one he wanted, but an answer all the same. But if they bought one of five? If they bought a poem he'd written when he was fourteen years old, set to music by someone who wouldn't know a good poem if it sank its teeth into his ass, what kind of answer was that? If the song had never even been finished and Erik was lying, he had no answer at all. Except that Erik cared enough for him to lie. Philippe supposed that was something. It wasn't an answer to any of the questions he'd brought with him to Paris, but it was an answer to something.

Louise

— 5 —

Without your fingers blushing

I MEANT TO GO TO MASS THIS MORNING, BUT IT WAS POURING rain, and a chilly dampness pried its fingernails under the window frames and into my knees and hips. The day felt more like February in France than the usual February in Argentina, which I would once have compared to August but is now only itself, *febrero*, a summer month. Buenos Aires on even its coldest mornings is rarely as cold as France, but I am much older than when I last lived there, and so feel it more. By this I mean both that the cold worms more easily into my joints and that my patience for enduring it has thinned. But then, my patience for many things has thinned.

I could just stay in bed, I thought, *and no one would care.* I had no lessons, no arrangements with friends. No classes to teach at the resettlement center or the French Institute. Only God to greet, and I thought He would understand. We have been through worse, He and I, and if He is willing to forgive the things I have thought or said of Him, then He will forgive me a morning spent in bed. It was a delicious morning, the decadence of sleep and warmth and not bothering. Occasionally I reached for a book, pulled it under the covers with me, drifted off again after a few pages. When I got hungry I ate a small bag of alfajores that the mother of one of my students had given me. I rose occasionally to use the hall toilet. I did not bathe.

My only regret was that the day made me think with admiration of Estelle and even Agnès, my substitute mothers, rising every morning in their sea-chewed houses. Yes, perhaps Agnès's maid—the country girl working for little more than board in the closet off the kitchen—already had the fire lit. But if her mistress didn't rise, what would the girl think? And what would she tell the other maids, when they saw one another at the market, and what would those girls tell their mistresses? No doubt it was Agnès's presence that indirectly kept all the sinks in Honfleur scrubbed.

If people stopped caring what others thought? Well, it would be too easy to stop doing everything else, too. To pry apart the last of the alfajores, eat both sweet halves, and never venture out for more. But Monday always comes, and my piano students, and the classes at the resettlement center or the Institute. My life is full enough to keep me in it.

Besides, in a boardinghouse one's absence from meals is noted quickly. I've lived at this address long enough for all the residents to have formed their opinion of me: I am an independent-minded eccentric or a sad spinster or a glutton. "You have a big appetite for an old lady," I'm told. "How are you so thin?" People are much blunter in Spanish than in French, which troubled me until it didn't any longer. After forty years I think in Spanish. Occasionally I still dream in French.

An Italian girl has moved into the neighboring room with her beau, an Argentine boy from the wine country near Mendoza. "We're going to be married soon," she assured me at breakfast her first morning, when all I'd done was advise her that Señora Rodríguez made better maté than coffee.

"I don't care," I told her, meaning that I was not scandalized, but it came out coldly.

"People mind their own business here," she said. "I like it." The

General Immigration Office was slow because of the war, she said, plus the latest Argentine coup d'état, but once she had the proper papers, there'd be a wedding and a better job, something more than cleaning houses in Recoleta. She referred to it as "the war in Europe," even though by February 1944 the war seemed to be happening everywhere but here.

Several of my piano students lived in Recoleta, I offered.

"Rich stiffs," she said conspiratorially, assuming that I too had never been in such houses as anything other than hired help.

I did not correct her. I prefer the light sort of friendship that takes place over meals and makes no greater demands. Comments on the weather and complaints about the food, although in truth the proprietor and his wife cook plentifully and well enough.

"But so much meat! There's nothing like home-cooked," the Italian girl says with a sigh during dinners, and I understand that she is refusing to think of this as a home. She's sure that 46 Chacabuco is only a way station before her beau takes her somewhere better. Maybe to the big houses in Recoleta or Retiro, even a country house in Temperley.

That this is the only home I have and that I am barely able to afford it, that I pile high my plate with medialunas at breakfast and asado at dinner because I am trying not to need lunch: I do not tell anyone these things. Why embarrass us both?

After I returned from Paris to Le Havre, I set myself a goal of practicing rigorous realism. I thought of this as a skill to cultivate, the custom of seeing the world as nearly as possible for what it was, for seeing myself as close as possible to the way that others saw me. No more dreams of rescue, of heroic brothers. Conrad wrote me that this was an admirably scientific habit of mind. *I don't know anything about science*, I wrote back. *But I am trusting in its power to reduce disappointment.*

Fortin and Estelle had begun discussing my marriageability at great length. They often started conversations while I was playing piano, assuming I couldn't hear, and I asked my teacher if we could work on some very quiet pieces, saying I wished to hone my skill at playing pianissimo.

Fortin had continued to pay for lessons uncomplainingly. He'd even bought a better piano. "This is for me," he said, "not for you. You've gotten good enough that it isn't unpleasant to listen to you." He asked for music after dinner, as he read the evening newspapers. He liked the Germans—Brahms, Bach, Beethoven—and was a little ashamed of this. "Surely even the Boches can get a few things right," he said.

"The devil makes seductive music," I said, to tease him.

He asked for our countryman Saint-Saëns, but I could tell his heart was not in it. He seemed relieved when I told him Saint-Saëns wrote mostly for the opera, not for piano.

Fortin was an orderly man, and he enjoyed orderly music. Likewise, he wished me to be married in an orderly way, and he made an orderly appraisal of my prospects: I was not a great beauty, but not unpleasant to look at. I read books, but not too many. I had ideas enough for companionable conversation, but not so many I might think them worth writing down. I had done well at the convent school, but was not inconveniently or self-importantly pious. In the column of my deficits, though, my lack of assets or income counted heavily. Trying to look on the bright side, Fortin—who believed he had instilled in me an excellent foundation for a life of sensible moderation—praised my lack of expensive tastes, never mind that I had of course been given no opportunity to develop any.

Does it make me sound like the dullest creature imaginable to confess that Fortin and Estelle's appraisal pleased me, that I felt myself higher in their esteem than I would have guessed? Well, then, in the spirit of realism, perhaps I was that dull. And if I am less boring now, is it something I have tried to cultivate, like pearls, or merely a product of circumstance? Sometimes I suspect that the most interesting things about me are the things that have been done to me or the choices that have been made for me—the irritants themselves—for I have made no pearl.

Ever since I'd finished school Fortin sometimes invented tasks for me to do at his office. I understood that he was displaying me to the clerks. This was mildly humiliating, but worse was that nothing came of it. My cheeks burned every time I so much as walked past his office, so that the men of the port district must have thought I was the color of a cooked lobster.

Without school, the hours were long, although the hours had also stretched long with it, beset as they were by the sisters' lessons in domestic economy and moral science, such that languages and mathematics and natural history were squeezed into the small corners of the day. I could not make sense of whole swaths of Conrad's letters about his studies. The mayor had proposed a girls' lycée for Le Havre, but there had been years of argument over what location would best shield its pupils from unsavory influences, and by the time it finally opened I was too old to enroll. Not that Fortin was likely to have allowed a secular school. Nor that I was likely to have had the brains to make a success of it, he said, when I rued aloud the mayor's slowness.

Fortin began to cast his net farther afield, to past associates or fellow photography hobbyists. We entertained more often, single men for weekday dinners or weekend lunches. It was a burden on Estelle, given that Fortin had fired the maid when I finished school. He said because I was home all day I could help more, but Estelle was the one who rose every morning before dawn to light the stove and start the coffee, grumbling about having been made a charwoman at her age. I was not privy enough to the household finances to know whether this was an essential economy or one of Fortin's petty privations.

Whenever I tried to rise before her she chased me back to bed. "You need your beauty rest," she said, not teasingly. She was the closest thing I had to a mother, and I was the closest thing she had left to a daughter, and she had solemnly shouldered the responsibility of securing me a future.

One night we hosted a Monsieur Auguste Cannu, visiting from Cherbourg. A pharmacist and a fellow amateur photographer, which is how Fortin knew him. I'd worried their friendship meant Cannu was closer in age to Fortin than to me, but he was young. He had a sharp nose, very thin lips, and slightly thinning hair. None of this I held against him, but his conversation was indescribably boring. Once he had exhausted photographic plates and exposures and lenses, he cataloged the important people he'd prepared medicine for while they vacationed in Cherbourg.

I was already well practiced in listening sympathetically to Estelle's and Fortin's various ailments. I had looked with anticipation to a future in which dinner conversation no longer revolved around backaches and boils. I could not imagine smiling forever through the dyspepsia of France's largest silk importer or the yellow toenails of Countess F____. Worse, none of the stories had endings: after he delivered the medicine, the patients returned home or resumed their travels, and we never learned whether their condition had improved or worsened, although of course we were meant to assume they'd been cured by Monsieur Cannu's expertise.

After dinner Fortin gestured for the customary decampment to the living room, and my turn at the piano. This was the part of the evening where I generally made my best impression. I knew I was playing for my future, and sometimes during easy passages my mind wandered to Eugénie, performing for her past self, her past ambitions. I didn't know if it was sympathy or scorn I felt in those moments, and before I could figure it out, the difficulty of the music would claw my attention back.

"Might we just have a drink?" Cannu said, gesturing at the calvados Fortin was pouring. Estelle had already settled into a chair with her needlework and looked up in surprise.

"Without any music?" Fortin asked.

"I don't really care for it," Cannu said.

"You mean all music?" I asked, surprised into speaking. "Music in general?"

"Yes," Cannu said.

"The man needn't defend his opinions," Fortin said.

"I'm just trying to understand," I said. "'Music' is...rather sweeping."

"I prefer silence," Cannu said. "Is that a problem?"

"Of course not," I said automatically, though of course it was.

We had a strained game of cards, Estelle recruited from her needlework and Cannu and Fortin talking about the Universal Exhibition opening in Paris. Their opinions were in accord: the Eiffel Tower sounded uninteresting beyond its height, but both the Machinery Hall and the Human Zoo might be worth a visit. I said very little.

Two days later Fortin opened his mail and said, "A bite at last. Our little fish. Monsieur Cannu wants to see you again."

I tried to conceal my dismay. Tried to conceal it all the way through another dinner and a tea with Cannu, followed by a photography exhibition at the city museum. Arranging the first visit, Cannu had claimed to have other business in Le Havre, but the second was made specifically to see me. This was as close as I had come to a proposal, and I was twenty-one. I'd heard girls only a few years older than me described as old maids, unmarriageable even with advantages—money, family, great beauty—that I didn't have. Nor did I possess property or profession or any great talent that might earn me an income. If I ever hoped to have a roof over my head that was not my great-uncle's, it would need to be a husband's. I knew I should have found Cannu acceptable: he wasn't a drunkard or a profligate or a brute. But the prospect of being his wife felt like drowning. I wouldn't even have the piano to retreat to, to make music when I'd run out of polite words.

He wrote to suggest an excursion to Paris, with Estelle as

chaperone, to visit the Exhibition. As Fortin read the invitation aloud I started shaking my head. At first I didn't even realize I was doing it, but then I felt the motion of it, back and forth, the weight of my tightly pinned hair, the collar of my dress against my neck. I couldn't stop it, no no no no no no. I even started crying, which I couldn't recall ever having done in front of Estelle or Fortin. As a child I'd kept myself so guarded I wept only in bed or outdoors, where I could blame my watery eyes on the sea wind.

"What on earth?" Fortin said.

"Please don't make me."

"Make you what?"

"Go to Paris. With him." But it was clear enough that I meant more than Paris.

Fortin wanted a rational debate, a listing of positives and negatives. He allowed that Cannu's distaste for all forms of music was unfortunate. But unfortunate enough to let such a chance slip by? I did a poor job holding up my end. Some sentences dissolved into sobs, while others, even when I could get them out, expressed sentiments I knew he found vague and unconvincing. I was losing, which made me even more distraught and less able to argue.

Estelle finally cut in. "If she feels like this, whatever her reasons, are you really going to *make* her marry him?"

There was a long silence as Fortin eyed us both. "No. I suppose not. I think she's being *completely* irrational, but—I wouldn't force...the issue."

He wrote to Cannu, saying that he didn't think the Human Zoo would be fit entertainment for ladies, since the natives would be in states of undress. I don't know what else he said, to put off Cannu but still salvage their association, and I didn't care.

Fortin never meant to be cruel. His cruelty, when it came, stemmed from his trusting his own intentions more than he trusted me. I think he even wanted me to be happy, though his vision of happiness was so solemn and severe it could be hard to recognize.

A year later I was still unmarried, and Cannu sent us a matrimonial announcement, along with a picture he'd taken of his new home in Cherbourg, a spacious house with a pharmacy on the street level and two floors of living space above. He claimed this was so Fortin could admire some technical achievement in the photograph, but it was clear enough, even to Fortin, that he was showing off the building. Cannu had made a rather spectacular match, Fortin said, trying to convey the stupidity of my rejection. The daughter of a very old family, with an estate on the Cotentin Peninsula. Not as flush as they used to be, perhaps, but then few grand families were. This news didn't sting as much as Fortin thought it would—I didn't want Cannu any more than I had before—but I was curious as to what his appeal had been to the grand lady.

I would have been content for this to remain a permanent mystery, but Cannu wrote a few months later with an invitation: he and his wife had rented a villa in Deauville, he said, and there was plenty of room. He would be honored to welcome us as guests for a few days in July. The invitation put Fortin at war with himself. On one side was his miser's enthusiasm for any vacation that would cost nothing more than the fare to Deauville, a seaside town to the west. On the other was his general scorn for vacations and the lazy people who took them, as well as recognition that Cannu's motives were impure, the latter of which I preyed on.

"You know he's only showing off," I said. "It will be impossibly awkward."

Ultimately Estelle put her finger on the scale again, this time against me. She hadn't traveled since her wedding, she said, and she'd been working like a drudge. She wanted a holiday.

We began packing to join my spurned suitor and his new

bride. Deauville, though only forty kilometers away, was much more popular with Parisians than with locals. We already had as much sea and fresh air as we knew what to do with, although Le Havre had given too much of its shoreline to shipping and industry to be a truly pretty town. Deauville had beaches, and thermal spas where people went to take the waters for their health, and in the summer tourists lined the long terrace along the water to watch fireworks displays. Deauville had been purpose-built as a resort town, to profit from the popularity of neighboring Trouville-sur-Mer. Trouville had the same sandy beaches, snapping banners, and canvas bathing cabins, but it had once been a fishing village, and had the residual air of a real place, whereas Deauville felt like no place at all. This had made it very fashionable.

I assumed that the town's having become vogue was why Cannu and his wife had chosen it, but it still seemed odd. Cherbourg itself was already on the water, and what was the point of money if it couldn't carry you out of Normandy? Why not Marseilles or Nice, or even Belgium? I had never traveled, but I nevertheless had strong opinions about how it ought to be done.

The trip ended up costing Fortin more money than he'd planned, because Estelle and I didn't have any of the right clothes. We both needed canvas bathing slippers for walking on the beach, and I needed a flannel swimming costume. Estelle bought a sun hat with a brim the width of the rings of Saturn. She added a little bunch of mock grapes to the hat, and an extra red braid to my slippers, because she was determined for us not to be shamed in front of Cannu's bride, although I suspected the entire purpose of the invitation was to shame me.

The party when we arrived was small, only Cannu and three members of the Lafosse family: Cannu's wife, Albertine; Albertine's brother, Pierre; and their mother, Madeleine. Albertine was polite enough, though baffled by our presence. They'd been hosting a string of visitors, the goal apparently being for Cannu to extract as much social advantage out of the villa as he could, to be traded on later in Cherbourg. Albertine could see no advantage we would offer, nor was there one. Madeleine and Albertine offered perfunctory tours of the house and town, then left us to our own devices.

Fortin spent his mornings scrounging newspapers from hotel lobbies and dining rooms that other guests had left behind. He read Estelle and me every single obituary in a newspaper from Brittany, simply because it seemed far away to him, and here were all these poor dead Bretons, who'd lived and died in a place nobody ever thought about.

"*We* live in a place nobody ever thinks about," I said, and Fortin protested.

Each day, after luncheon, he and Cannu hauled their photography equipment around town. Fortin's pictures of the casinos and hotels and bath lobbies gave no sign as to whether he admired them or was assembling a vast documentary of human foolishness.

Nothing could entice Estelle to sea bathing, but she did not object to my going in the water. Albertine was free to walk straight into the sea in the women's section, but Fortin expected me to use the bathing machines, little wheeled sheds that squatted on the sand like tortoises. A bather climbed in the front door and changed clothes in private while the shed was dragged out into the water. Then she climbed out the back door, the shed between her and the shore, so that no one could see her in wet, clinging flannels.

I lied to the attendants that I could swim, so that they wouldn't tie a rope around my waist. I'd been told once that my mother had been a strong swimmer, and I hoped I might already have the knack. When strong waves knocked me off my feet and thumped my body into the sand, I learned I was wrong. The impact was terrifying and thrilling in equal measure. The first few times I lurched up immediately, panicked. But then I learned to pause for a moment on my knees, trusting that the sky would still be there above me. The sound of the waves underwater made a pure and obliterating music that I tried to imagine was my mother's voice, whispering that she would keep me from drowning.

The days were so pleasant that I even began to wonder if I'd made a mistake in rejecting Cannu, although I knew the money for the villa was Albertine's, not his. Fortunately the evenings were excruciating enough to fortify me. Albertine was a hypochondriac, which explained Cannu's appeal as a font of health advice and solicitous concern. He was also full of veiled slights for me, peppered through the awkward hours.

Albertine's brother, Pierre, seemed nice enough, though he took breakfast in his room and did not appear until dinner. He always had dark circles under his eyes, which I imagined meant he was up all hours in the casinos, slinking home late, but Albertine laughed at the thought. "My brother?" she said. "A choirboy."

A doctor at the central hospital in Le Havre, Pierre was the only member of the family who worked. His medical anecdotes were often the saving grace at dinner, much more entertaining than Cannu's, although they occasionally stopped abruptly when Pierre realized he had strayed into a degree of gore or anatomical detail unsuitable for the company.

After all of Fortin's economizing, the food was also a grace. "Pineapple! There's a treat," Estelle exclaimed one night. "I can't remember the last time I had pineapple."

"You've never asked for any," Fortin said defensively.

"Oh, I didn't mean it that way, not at all, dear."

"Is this one of your father's?" Madeleine asked, and Pierre snorted.

"A shame he couldn't join us," Fortin said, although the *us* sounded wrong, as if he was trying to force his way into the company.

"He couldn't leave his plants," Albertine said.

"He didn't want to," Pierre corrected.

I asked Pierre if his father really grew pineapples.

"He has a soft spot for exotics," Pierre said. "The more quixotic the better. But I doubt the plants will fruit."

"Your father's got the magic touch, though," Madeleine said. "Don't count him out."

"Of course not, Maman. If there's a man in La Manche who can grow the world's most expensive, pointless little weather-blasted runt of pineapple, it will undoubtedly be him."

"*Pierre.*"

Everyone except mother and son looked down at their plates and for a moment I was back in Paris, in the days right before I left, when Eric was recovered enough for gladiatorial arguments with Eugénie while Conrad read a book hidden beneath the edge of the tablecloth. Rich families were as squabbly as any other, I realized. I looked up, and among all the lowered heads Pierre's eyes met mine, and we smiled at each other.

It took me until the next morning to realize that Pierre's absence during the days was more than an idle mystery to me—I wished he would tell me where he went, and then I realized that I wished he would invite me with him. Was this what it felt like, a woman's wanting? Lord knew I'd done enough wanting of other kinds, but romance was so alien to me that I had trouble recognizing it. Why would my treacherous heart want me to feel something for Pierre? The match was impossible. Albertine and Cannu was improbable enough, and he brought a business to the partnership. I had nothing.

It grew late in my day of nothing, of sleep and hiding. The Italian girl and her beau started enjoying their afternoon very enthusiastically in the room next door. A hazard of boarding-house life. All in all, I was happy for them. They seemed very compatible. But it was awfully loud, and it went on for an aw-fully long time, and then after a pause it seemed as if it might start up again, and I thought a little fresh air might do me good after all.

I wrestled myself into stockings, into girdle and skirt and square-toed shoes and hat, and walked to the evening Mass at San Isidro Labrador. The new priest with the unplaceable accent performed the consecration, and in his odd Latin I heard neither French nor Spanish, but a lovely floating anywhere, a no-place in which I felt very much at home. I was glad I'd come. I even found myself humming as I walked the few blocks home, although as soon as I realized I was doing it, I lost the tune.

Dinner was on the table when I arrived home. *Home*, I thought, and didn't mind. It neither stung nor felt cozy. This was where I lived. This is where I live now. No one commented on my absence at breakfast, and I didn't know if I wanted them to or not. The Italian girl and her beau sat close. *He isn't going to marry you*, I thought. *But you might as well enjoy yourself. Hold him close, for as long as you can.*

Our last night in Deauville there were fireworks, but Albertine, Cannu, and Madeleine said they'd already seen them and didn't want to fight the crowds. Pierre had been in Deauville for several weeks by that point so must have seen them as well, but he said he'd accompany us anyway. We walked up and down the terrace, trying to find a place to sit. Estelle finally shamed a group of young people into vacating a public bench by limping exaggeratedly past them several times, sighing.

Fortin sat at one end, then Estelle and me and then Pierre. There wasn't really enough room for all four of us, and I could feel Pierre's leg alongside mine until he drew away to the very edge of the bench. Even so my skirt, squashed between us, fell against his thigh. It seemed very intimate for the fabrics to be touching, my cotton twill to his gray summer wool. When I finally glanced up he was looking at me. The sky was still more blue than black, but twilit enough that Pierre seemed a little ghostly, his gray face and narrow neck floating above his crisp collar. His suits all hung off him, and Albertine was constantly waving food in his face, trying to fatten him up. He crossed his legs and put his hands on his knee. His fingers were very long and very white, as pale as my own hands in their gloves. I arranged and rearranged my fingers in my lap. I wanted to say something, but more so I wanted there to be something to say. I couldn't think of any scenario in which I would ever see him again after tonight.

"Why are you here?" I asked, very quietly, although I had to assume Estelle at least could hear me.

"In Deauville?" he asked, and I let him think that was my question. "Doesn't everyone come here for the same reasons?" But the way he'd spoken of his work at the hospital made it seem far more important to him than the pleasures the town offered to vacationers, none of which I'd seen him partake in.

The crowd near the water stirred in anticipation. Then a crunch and a whistle and finally the flowery bang of an orange flare, and I put my hands over my ears, my arms as tight against my sides as I could keep them. The fireworks were famous for their colors, pink and red and green and white and violet, new and expensive like everything else in town. In the din and glitter, the clashing hues did not flatter Pierre. Rather they made a strange gleam in his eye, like fever. I wondered about my own coloring, and I hoped he would understand it was the fireworks and not my face.

During the finale—thunder all round and the sky a bouquet of burning flowers, with tendrils of smoke hanging like stems beneath them—he uncrossed his legs, and his thigh lay again near mine. After the flurry of noise, in the pool of silence as people waited to be sure the show was over before clapping, I lowered my hands from my ears just as he was raising his, and our arms banged together. He stood, then reached down and put his hand around my elbow, as if it might require medical attention.

"I would like to see you again," he said, without cleverness or artifice or any chance of his intention being mistaken.

"I would like that," I said, wishing to make myself similarly plain.

Back in Le Havre, a dinner was arranged. Pierre brought a pineapple—a sense of humor?—and we ate it sliced with cherries. He smiled at me three times, once when I passed him something at the table, once when I managed to say something amusing, and once for no particular reason.

"It's going well, don't you think?" Estelle whispered to me, when we stood to move to the parlor.

Fortin poured calvados for himself and our guest and gestured that I should play something.

"What would you like?" I asked, assuming he had the rest of the evening programmed.

"I suppose we should let our guest choose," he said.

"I couldn't," Pierre said. "I enjoy music—I'd like you to play—but I don't know enough to be qualified to tell you what." Fortin, who had never felt unqualified to tell me what to do, was opening his mouth when Pierre added, "*You* should choose. Play your favorite."

But I was scared of selecting the wrong thing. "That's too hard," I said. "Please, choose something." Here I'd thought I was fed up with being told what to do, but the moment disarmed me. I hadn't realized how safe it was to hide behind Fortin like a shield.

"I insist," Pierre said, and now if I tossed the question back again I'd be making a quarrel. It occurred to me that perhaps he couldn't think of a piece by name, and thought we were trying to embarrass or test him.

"All right." I swept my skirt against the back of my legs, sidestepped and angled myself onto the bench, and rotated my torso toward the keys, my right foot tipped up and ready for the pedal.

I'd made these gestures ten thousand times, but now I was terribly conscious of my body, how it moved, how it might look from behind.

With so much of my mind occupied, I didn't dare try to play by memory. I grabbed at the books nearest to hand, on top of the piano. Plenty of Chopin, but the études I'd been working on most recently I didn't know well enough to play with any polish, and the preludes I'd done before that were rusty. A polonaise, all jaunty and martial, would ruin the mood. Fortin cleared his throat. I couldn't dither any longer.

I picked a nocturne, by Ignace Leybach, No. 4, Op. 36. Nobody seems to play it anymore, but I liked it then and still do. I especially liked the way I sounded when I played it, which is a hazard of practicing music: admiration gets tangled with narcissism. Do I like a piece for how it's written, or for how neatly I can play it? But given the occasion, that seemed a more than-reasonable criterion. With Estelle's help I'd curled my bangs to their best effect, and now my job was to play something pretty and accomplished, something of a type that Pierre might want to hear regularly in the evenings, with a fire roaring and the children playing—oh Lord, I was ahead of myself! I erased our imaginary children and focused on the music in front of me, making sure the treble melody sang out above the low notes without the left hand going muddy. When played well, the piece was sweet and dramatic, but not too sugary.

I finished and Pierre applauded. This was not the usual custom in our house, but Estelle and then Fortin joined in, the latter only a little grudgingly.

"Another?" Estelle asked, but it was unclear to whom she was posing the question. It didn't seem to be me.

"Please," Pierre said. "That was lovely. You're very good."

It was a general rather than specific compliment, the kind that people make either when they've never thought enough about music to have opinions, or when they have opinions they aren't going to share and are choosing easy insincerity instead. But Pierre seemed sincere.

I kept on with Leybach, Nocturnes No. 1 and No. 5, and then Estelle dealt a hand of cards and gestured for me to trade places with her. She brought out a book of pieces simple enough for her, neatly tucked under my regular music, and I knew she'd stashed it there, ready.

Fortin started to complain that Estelle had mistakenly dealt only two hands for the game.

"You were going to fetch some of your photographs, dear, to show to our guest."

"Was I? Are you interested in photography?" he asked Pierre.

"You have never let the answer to that question sway you one way or the other," Estelle said. "Go upstairs now, and take your time."

Conversation with Pierre was awkward at first, but the cards gave us things to say, and eventually my questions about his work bore fruit when he mentioned he was planning to leave the hospital for private practice.

"Oh?" I had no idea what response he wanted, so I said as little as possible.

It wouldn't be in Le Havre, he said. He would establish himself back in Saint-Côme-du-Mont, where his parents lived.

But his parents didn't live in Saint-Côme-du-Mont by choice or chance—it was where the family estate was—and I didn't know what to make of his oblique phrasing. "You're close with your parents?" I said.

"Not particularly. But it's a lovely region. I'd like the slower pace. And I think I'll make a better country doctor than a city one. Healthy air and house calls."

Compared with Paris, I hadn't thought of Le Havre as a city so big a person might need to leave it, nor our air so polluted. But his reasons for leaving didn't matter to me, only his reasons for saying so. Was this an announcement that he was not looking for courtship before he left, or the opposite: an attempt to learn my feelings on country living?

"That does sound lovely," I said.

"Have you ever been there?"

"Saint-Côme-du-Mont? No."

"Then...?"

"I'm taking your word for it."

"That's very trusting of you."

"You've given me no reason to doubt."

"But you—do you wish to move back to Paris, eventually?"

I snorted, and it was not a ladylike snort, if such a thing exists, "It's too crowded. No room left for me."

"Then we agree," he said, and left it undefined as to what exactly we agreed on.

He admired Fortin's photographs and made his goodbyes at a savvy hour, not so early it might seem he'd had a poor time, and not so late as to risk imposing. Once the door had closed safely behind him, I collapsed into a chair. I felt like I'd run a footrace or performed the lead in a difficult opera, *Norma* or *Lucia di Lammermoor*, where I was onstage the entire time, singing my heart out.

"That was well done," Estelle said. "Whatever happens. You did well." She touched my hair gently, as if I were a little child. As if I were her daughter Berthe, I thought, and wondered how many evenings like this she'd already choreographed.

"Did Berthe play the piano?" I asked. I'd inherited her old exercise books, with fingerings penciled in, but I didn't know if she'd played beyond childhood, performing for a future she'd never have.

We almost never spoke of Berthe, but Estelle did not seem surprised at the question. "Yes." After a long pause, she added, "Though not so well as you do."

I reached up and touched her hand, still resting on my head, and hoped she could feel passing between us this sensation that was so nearly like love.

That night I finished a long letter to Conrad, about Deauville, and the sea bathing, and the fireworks, and about Pierre. He responded with a treatise on explosives: did I know, he wrote, that until the 1830s fireworks had come only in orange and white? Green came from barium, red from strontium, blue from copper.

Don't you understand? I wanted to write him. *I may have met the man I will marry.*

Conrad's letters were often hopeless, although of course I appreciated that he wrote. In the three years since I'd left Paris, my father generally didn't, beyond short postscripts added to notes from Eugénie. The letters sometimes had spots of tea or food, and I imagined them languishing on the table as she nagged him to add at least his name. Eric wrote rarely, though both Conrad and Eugénie provided updates, often differing in either fact or tone. He'd managed to reenroll at the Conservatory but wasn't there any longer: Eugénie said tossed out, Conrad said quit. Now he was living in his own apartment: Eugénie said seeing private piano pupils, Conrad said working as an accompanist at the cabarets in Montmartre. He was calling himself a composer, although Conrad shared this with pride and Eugénie with great skepticism. Eric's occasional letters were filled merely with doodles and cartoons, mock-epic poems or the lyrics to fake hymns, the bylaws of fictional societies or the minutes of their meetings. They were quite funny, but he said nothing at all about himself, and I wished for a sincere letter, because then I could write back one of my own. I felt foolish, answering doodles with confidences, yet if I tried to write back playfully, we could both tell I didn't have the knack.

I supposed I was doing the same to Conrad when I wrote very personal things. An adolescent boy, he couldn't find the right words to respond. He wrote about what he called "feminine chemistry," which was not a real field but simply topics on which he thought we might find common ground. He had a great deal to say, for instance, on the subject of fabric dyes. I learned from him that mauve was invented in 1856 by an Englishman, but that most of the later advances were made by Germans; Frenchmen had patented few shades apart from methyl green and diphenylamine blue, which Conrad seemed to consider a source of abiding national shame.

Pierre's first gift to me was a shawl, brilliantly green (methyl? malachite?—Conrad might have known, but I didn't). "I noticed you didn't have anything like it," Pierre said. "But I couldn't decide if that meant it would be a good gift or a bad one."

"A good one," I said.

After Deauville, Pierre's courtship was as precise as a piece of Baroque music, regular in its intervals, measured in its timing. He came regularly to the house, sent letters and flowers, and Estelle chaperoned a few walks around town. He proposed several months later. Estelle had cake and champagne ready, and I realized that I was the only one of the four of us who hadn't known. Pierre had visited Fortin at his office to arrive at the customary agreements. He'd been so certain I'd say yes that he'd already bought the corbeille, which he proudly announced he'd assembled himself—stuffed with gloves and fans and a hat and a little embroidered purse full of coins, to give to people outside the church after the ceremony—rather than merely picking a ready-made basket out of a department-store catalog. These were all very traditional engagement gifts, and custom dictated that they shouldn't change hands until the marriage contract was drawn up. But Pierre couldn't resist telling me how he'd packed them into a large, sturdy trunk, because he wanted the outside of the present to be as useful as the inside. It had a solid lock, he said, and I thought that was a good sign, both that I would own things worth keeping safe and that he would allow them to be mine alone.

After the champagne, I played piano both terribly and as well as I'd ever played in my life. Pierre stood at my shoulder, and I kept missing notes, but every so often I made a passage float. I got up after only one song, the Leybach nocturne I'd played the first time he visited.

Pierre peered down at the piano stool. "A pineapple!" he said. I tried to figure out what in the world he meant, and finally followed his pointing finger to the embroidery on the seat. "I never noticed," he said. "That's a neat coincidence. Fate."

"Is it? A pineapple?" I bent closer to examine. I'd been sitting on the stool every day for more than fifteen years and had always thought it was a hedgehog.

"A hedgehog!" Estelle protested, then explained, with some embarrassment, that it had started off as a tree but had gone a bit roundish. It was a beginner's effort, from before she and Fortin were married. He'd had the stool upholstered with it as a surprise for her. She hadn't realized they'd be using it for the next forty years.

"It's a tree?" I said. "It's been a tree all this time?"

We were all laughing, even Fortin, once he was sure that Estelle wasn't upset, and I felt a little wistful, wondering why we couldn't have been this kind of family all along. I liked this side of us. Of myself. The way it felt to give and receive affection, the warmer, sillier person I became.

All my Leybach sheet music is in tatters now, but there's nothing in print anymore except the fifth. You can't get No. 4 anywhere. Leybach's No. 5 is pretty enough, but I can't hear whatever supposedly sets it apart from his others. Every time I have a student I think would be suited to one of the first four nocturnes, and it to them, I have to take the risk of lending it out. Then I have to decide whether to mark it with notes, and whether to write over or around the notes from the last two students, which I didn't erase because I'd erased the last several before that and grew worried about erasing the paper into nothing. Why couldn't the students at least make the same mistakes, requiring the same corrections?

The music shop on Calle 25 de Mayo has my name on file in case any copies come through the doors or appear in the catalogs for a price I can afford. I've picked up extras of the first and third this way, but still own just one copy of the fourth, and none of the second. In Paris it would be easier to find them, but much like the people here, music arrives unpredictably. We disembark with whatever is in our baggage or on our backs, and sometimes the objects of our old world trickle in after us, and sometimes they don't. The fourth nocturne arrived in my trunk, the same one Pierre gave me. My current landlady offered to put the trunk in storage for me, but I use it in my room as a bedside table. I like keeping it near.

If I want that fourth Leybach nocturne to have a future, then which choice is the better part of valor: to keep lending it out, knowing that someday some student, even one of my best, will spill juice on it or drop it in a puddle? Or for me to keep it locked in that trunk, preserved?

I know the "correct" answer to this. I know there is no virtue or life in music left moldering. I know children are the future and so on and we must take our chances with them. But I don't *feel* it. Instead I want to hold the pages tightly, pressed close to my clenched heart. That way I can hold on to the person I was when I played them, giddy with champagne and good fortune. And with love. I can say now what I would not have allowed myself to say at the time, for fear of greed or jinxes: I would have accepted much less out of a match, but I loved Pierre, and I believe he loved me.

I can never play those pieces now the way I did then. Nor can I play them better—they're romantic pieces, and bitterness does not mix well with them. Sometimes I think I have kept the songs back from my students because I am trying to protect them—not the songs but the students. From heartbreak? From

115

disaster? From needing to learn how to live a life that is not the one they hope for?

But then, that's every piece of music. There's the way my students hope it will sound, and the way it actually sounds, banged out and lurching and full of mistakes. I throw them into that frustrating gap, over and over, and tell them this is how they learn. Some of them do. But many of them drown there, in that space between what they imagine and what they have.

Philippe

— 6 —

On the tips of your back teeth

THE CHAT NOIR SHADOW THEATER STARTED AS A CYNICAL puppet show, something to offer guests who couldn't be crammed into the main floor, or who had already seen those acts too often. Some of the sock puppets were plain socks, pulled directly off feet a few minutes before the sketch began, and smelled like it. Less malodorous were the shadow puppets, made of cut cardboard or zinc glued to sticks. The shadow plays cast an eerie but familiar magic, like telling ghost stories by firelight. Salis set the regulars to work making puppets, payment in beer, and the wooden tables became flecked with knife cuts. Philippe wrote pompous but sincere articles predicting for the shadow theater a long and monumental future.

In five years no one would care about the shadow theater. In ten years, after the turn of the new century, they would all be at the movies. But for now, the Chat Noir's shadow shows were so lucrative that Salis created a specially darkened theater upstairs, and Tomaschet, the owner of the Auberge, finally paid to have the cesspool regularly emptied and the cellar drained. Philippe and Erik were working on a show for Tomaschet called *Pierrot Pornographe,* which thus far consisted of fastening phalluses to the puppets from *The Temptation of Saint Anthony.* Philippe had suggested bent pins instead of glue, to make a hinge on which the phalluses could swing out and in. Philippe had been in Paris for almost four years now, and if *Pierrot Pornographe* ever launched, this would be his most visible contribution to the Parisian cultural scene: movable cocks on card-stock puppets in a cellar. If he thought about this too long his stomach lurched, as if he were running sickeningly late for an important appointment. As if he were running as fast as he could but might not make it.

Erik and Philippe had worked on biblical plays and novel adaptations and classic comedies. With only shadows at your disposal, it was difficult to tell a story other than one the audience already knew. They'd done political shows like *The King Disembarks*, Napoléon's campaign narrated in twenty elaborate tableaux accompanied by gunfire and screams of victory. The puppeteers practiced making cannon blasts with their mouths, and the ones who had never heard such a sound took notes from the ones who had. The youngest men, or the provincials, privately regretted that they had missed the siege of 1870.

Philippe suggested recycling the animal puppets made for a Noah's ark play into one about the siege, when Parisians ate horses, then dogs and cats, rats and pigeons, then the carp from the ponds in the Tuileries, then the exotic animals from the zoological gardens: yaks and buffalo and zebras, and finally the two beloved elephants, Castor and Pollux. By the end of the siege the only stocked butcher shop in town was on the Boulevard Hausmann, where Pollux's skinned trunk was nailed to the wall, available in razored slices, and the fancy glass cases were full of elephant-blood sausage and camel kidneys. The meat had been far too expensive for most people to afford, but the shop had become an attraction, and many of the men at the Auberge carried childhood memories of visiting. Despite all the human deaths in the weeks during and after the siege, it was that skinless trunk on the wall that brought death close.

The butcher shop seemed to Philippe the key tableau of the entire play, but Tomaschet demanded a heroic ending. Philippe pointed out that the siege had not ended in heroics but in sur-render, followed by the Communard uprising that had killed another ten thousand people in the two months after the siege ended. The Montmartre Butte had been central to the battle be-tween the Commune and the national army, the streets choked with barricades, then bodies.

"You can do a scenario on spec if you like, and I'll take a look," Tomaschet said, "but I think it's too soon for a play like this."

"It's been twenty years," Philippe said.

Tomaschet agreed. Apparently they had very different ideas about the length of twenty years. "Also, you're foreign," Tomaschet added. "People might not take it well."

But everyone here came from somewhere else, even the French people. Almost no one had been born in Montmartre. Tomaschet himself was from Switzerland. Who was he to lecture Philippe?

Erik meanwhile had moved to a cheaper apartment, 6 Rue Cortot, at the top of the Butte. "I've come up in the world," he said. Speaking vertically, this was true.

Philippe still rented the same lightless, heatless room whose bleakness was softened only by the bowl Erik had given him, which Philippe put on a shelf next to a marble toe he'd brought from Tarragona. They were the prettiest things in his room, the only pretty things in his room, the white toe and white bowl printed with small white flowers on pale green stems. The re-straint of the bowl had seemed silly at first (white on white?) but came to feel elegant, restful, a corrective to everything else around him. The bowl was the opposite of the cancan girls' glass jewelry, just as it was the opposite of the cabaret costumes so ruined that the girls posed only at certain angles, to hide what could no longer be mended, and of Tinchant, ruined from nearly every angle, so that people tried not to look at him anymore. The bowl had nothing to hide.

At first Philippe didn't trust his luck, and confirmed with

Erik repeatedly that Eugénie didn't need or want it back. "It's just a bowl," Erik finally said. "Take it and shut up." But to Philippe it wasn't just a bowl. He wrote odes to it, unembarrassed rhapsodies, his love for it exceeding that for the pretend girl Sylvie. The song had been published, though he still didn't know whether the sale had come before or after the night Erik had paid him. The printed sheet music carried a dedication to someone named Louise.

"Oh ho," Philippe said, thinking he was finally learning something about the heart Erik kept so closely guarded.

"She's my sister," Erik said, rolling his eyes.

"You have a sister?" Philippe reread the lyrics, even though he'd written them. Yes, definitely still a love song. "That's a little odd, then."

A dedication didn't mean the song was *about* the person, Erik said. His *Gnossiennes* and *Sarabandes* had dedications, too, and they weren't *about* anything.

Philippe didn't want to hear Erik's thoughts on about-ness. He wanted to hear about Erik's mysterious sister. If he counted those old conversations with Miguel, he'd been talking about about-ness for half his life and had come to no conclusions.

Alfred had bought a few more songs, here and there, and with each one Philippe tried not to hope too desperately that he might hear his words paired with those strange notes of Erik's wafting from café and apartment windows. When, inevitably, he didn't hear them, he told himself he might be in the wrong neighborhood. The songs were probably catching hold in places like Erik's old street, where the sidewalks filled up with round black hats every morning, neighborhoods in which Philippe was so ill dressed that people sometimes stepped aside to avoid him, or fingered the coins in their pockets, either protecting them or preparing to bestow a few upon him if he asked. He considered asking, but didn't. He was not yet a beggar. Whenever he walked back into Montmartre it was with relief, a sense of returning not so much to where he belonged but to the only place that would have him.

None of the songs earned enough for royalties, so there were only the advances. With the latest, Erik and Philippe decided they needed new clothes even more than they needed food. Erik's top hat had long since been crushed, and the velvet ribbon on his glasses was frayed. Philippe was down to only one complete outfit, which meant he had to use the Laundry for the Unforesighted, an establishment catering to a clientele who more often than foresight lacked any change of clothes. The windows were covered with old newspapers to conceal the waiting area full of half-naked men, smoking and scratching.

At a used clothing market Erik and Philippe rooted through enormous piles of wool popping with lice. The only purchases they could individually justify were barely nicer than the clothes they had. They decided that the money was best pooled for a single good outfit that could be traded between them. They were approximately the same size in the shoulders and chest, though Erik was rounder in the belly, and he sewed a second button onto the waistband to accommodate Philippe. The suit, they decided, would be awarded to whoever had the best place to go in it that day.

Now that they were neighbors, this could be decided in person, and Philippe showed up at Erik's apartment in the mornings to compare agendas. On many days neither of them could make a compelling case for the suit, and they either flipped a coin and headed out to the cafés or ended up on Erik's floor in their underwear, trying to make progress on a shadow play. Erik's apartment was spartan, though the building was still significantly nicer than Philippe's, with both a water spigot and a single toilet on the ground floor. Philippe took advantage of the indoor facilities until the concierge yelled at him for depositing his non-resident waste in the private cesspool.

"I don't know what you want from me," Philippe had said that night Erik sewed the button on his trousers and gave him the bowl. It had taken him a long time to realize that the last four years *were* the answer, Erik's only answer: he wanted someone with whom he could make and talk about art, and as little else as possible. In this way he differed from Miguel. Although Philippe had been afraid at first to write to Miguel, given all that had happened, he'd decided to send the Rat Mort postcard after all, and had spent an entire day on the message: *A real place after all, it turns out. It would have been nice to see it together. I know I ruined everything. I'm sorry.* As he'd expected, there was no reply, but he still mailed the occasional letter. Why not? No one had written back to tell him to stop. He mentioned the casual friends he'd made, the men he drank with or carved puppets alongside, often so drunk they didn't remember each other's confidences the next morning. He never wrote about Erik, for reasons he did not examine.

The messages were coins dropped down a dark well, rattles in the offering box, candles lit in penance.

Erik spoke rarely of his family. He pretended he had come into the world fully formed, as though spawned by Muses and sprung from Zeus's head. When they went out he was charming, with a talent for wordplay that no amount of alcohol ever blunted. In private he spoke of nonartists as irrelevant and of fellow members of their Montmartre circle with corrosive jealousy. Nearly the only person he admitted any particular admiration or affection for was a composer named Claude, whom Erik met at the Librairie de l'Art Indépendant to play duets on the piano in the back room. In his bleaker moments, Philippe suspected that his own friendship with Erik survived only because Erik didn't feel threatened by him and his spare portfolio of publications. Erik was not charismatic in the usual ways, not handsome, not reliably kind, and only spasmodically generous. But perhaps because he was so prickly, his approval was rare coin—a childish, total enthusiasm that warmed like sunlight. One wanted more and more of it.

Philippe thought of him sometimes as a soul mate and at other times as a broken stove into which he threw his best ideas and only occasionally received warmth in return. He'd made other friends, but no one else with whom he would share a pair of trousers, the buttons sewn beside each other on the waistband with an easy intimacy that their actual friendship only sometimes achieved. If Erik wanted to pretend he barely had a family, Philippe didn't feel he could talk about his own.

He'd nearly stopped writing home now that his pretense of prosperity had become too hard to maintain. One of his sisters was sick, and his parents had asked for help with the doctor's fees. He couldn't decide what would be worse: to tell them he simply didn't have it, which would demonstrate that he'd been lying all these years, or to let them think he was unwilling to share. He knew that he was a colossal disappointment either way: what had all his parents' years of scrimping for school fees and books been for, if not to launch him into a position that would benefit the whole family? Certainly they had not done it for poetry, a word his father wrote in outraged capital letters: *POETRY??? You are still making POETRY? What good is POETRY to us?*

Of romantic encounters, there was little news to furnish. In four years Philippe had managed to have sex with two women: one avoided him afterward, until he was forced to conclude that the experience had not been quite the poetry-inspiring encounter for her that it had been for him, and the other became the mistress of a wealthy man who did not wish to share. After the initial sting, Philippe was glad for her. He was painfully aware of how little he could offer: he was a man who owned a bowl, a marble toe, and now one half of a half-decent suit. "And words," he whispered to himself. But finding the girl who would value those more than a decent meal had been hard going. Montmartre's reputation for free affection was, he'd discovered, nearly as flashy and fake as its costume jewelry. Affection was never free.

There'd been men who promised otherwise, with looks or drinks or questions about him and Erik, which Philippe always answered truthfully: they were only friends; he had no idea what Erik liked. Philippe had been unsure enough of what he himself liked to let a man take him into his mouth once in the Saint Vincent Cemetery. The place was safe at night, the man had guaranteed him, hidden from passersby. But it was also directly behind the giant basilica being built on the Butte, and Philippe couldn't shake the feeling that he was sinning on God's very doorstep. There'd been pleasure, but also so much furtiveness and fear that he'd not wanted to do it again. The man had called him a coward later, and maybe it was true. Maybe Miguel had seen him correctly, and Philippe lacked the nerve to be that person. Maybe with Miguel he could have tried, or with Erik, if that was what Erik had wanted. But not in the Saint Vincent Cemetery, not with the damp stone tomb against his back and his body tensing at every sound, terrified of discovery. Women were hard enough, he decided. Coming to Paris, broke and staking his hopes on art, weathering his family's utter disappointment—surely he'd made the rest of his life sufficiently difficult already.

The division Erik maintained between their artistic collaborations and what Erik called the mundanities of life, a category into which he placed all women and most men, made the party invitation all the more surprising: a reception in honor of his sister's engagement, at Alfred and Eugénie's home.

"Did they invite me, or are you inviting me?" Philippe asked. He tried not to let his imagination run wild, but he was already envisioning soft chairs with upholstery, wallpapered walls, carpeted floors. Clean windows and forks and cups. A laden buffet table.

"They said I could bring someone. And Claude was busy."

Philippe felt slapped.

"I'm joking. And you can wear the suit."

"What will you wear?"

"I have hidden reserves," Erik said, although his hidden reserves turned out to be merely his father, who bought him new clothes for the occasion.

When he arrived the morning of the party to pick up Philippe, he was a freshly shaven, clean-scrubbed, well-dressed stranger. Which was the costume, Philippe wondered, this one or the top hat? Was Erik a bourgeois playing a bum or a bum playing a bourgeois? Or an artist playing a bourgeois playing a bum? An artist playing a bum playing an artist? Was that just an artist, full stop? Philippe's thought ate its own tail, swallowed, shook off the indigestion.

The sky threatened rain, but the family apartment wasn't far. The two of them never had any money for tram fare anyway. Down the Butte they walked, out of Montmartre and Pigalle, to the Rue de Maubeuge to the Rue d'Abbeville, to the Boulevard de Magenta, a wide avenue lined with shops and peopled by ladies in progressively more imposing hats. Philippe felt he was entering enemy territory.

"Who's she marrying? Your sister."

"I have no idea."

They passed several florist shops. Philippe, growing increasingly uneasy about their empty-handedness, asked if they should bring a gift.

"I am."

"Is it from both of us?"

"No. It's from me. It's personal. And it's really more for her birthday." Erik jammed his hand into his pocket and produced a small, dingy pocketknife, as if that was some kind of explanation. Surely it couldn't be the gift.

"It's her birthday, too? So I'll be doubly rude if I show up empty-handed."

"Not today. Next Wednesday. She'll be twenty-three."

Erik sounded rueful at the number, and Philippe remembered what a disaster Erik's own birthday celebration had been a month earlier. He'd been so unrelentingly maudlin about turning twenty-five that Tinchant, fed up, knocked Erik's hat off his head and it landed in a pile of horse manure in the Place d'Anvers. "A bad omen for your waning years," Tinchant said, sarcastically, but Erik merely nodded.

Now, at Philippe's urging, Erik veered into a florist's. The shopgirl talked them into roses—extravagant, but it was June, and roses wouldn't be this cheap again for another 358 days, she told them, with strange precision. "Depending on the weather, of course," she added. She wrapped the flowers, and Philippe was relieved to see Erik pull enough money out of his jacket.

At the party, a maid met them at the door and took the flowers to put in water. Since they hadn't written a card, there would be no easy way for her to announce whom they were from. Erik sighed, clearly ruing what he now considered an unnecessary expenditure.

Philippe had worried about how he would know who anyone was, but Louise, at least, was obvious, in an ostentatious white dress. Any white dress was ostentatious, since it was a color that dirtied so easily. The cut was already a bit out of fashion, rounder at the hips than the newest silhouettes, which were narrow except for the bustle. Provincial, Philippe thought, noting his own arrogance. This was as Parisian as he ever felt—when he was judging other people's clothes.

The groom, Monsieur Pierre Lafosse, was thin as a reed and pale as a mushroom. *Do better,* Philippe urged himself. *You can do better than reeds and mushrooms.* He tried to combine them into a single image. A tree root, or a white-painted flagpole. Or perhaps a single stick of dry, unboiled noodle, jaundiced and brittle.

"The roses," Erik said urgently, as soon as he'd kissed Louise on the cheek. "Those are from me."

Not *us*? Philippe thought.

"The pink ones," Erik said.

"All right," Louise said, and looked around the room. Erik and Philippe followed her eyes, taking in the profusion of pink roses clustered on side tables and the closed lid of the grand piano.

"Well," Erik recovered, "one of those is ours."

Now it was *ours*, Philippe observed, when the gift was worthless.

Louise smiled at him—genuinely, he thought. The groom, too, was polite, though reserved, and Philippe noted his unimpressive handshake. Noodle indeed.

Philippe had heard only slightly more about Conrad over the years than the mysterious Louise. Erik seemed fond of him, but everything he'd ever said of Conrad—the excellent grades, the admission into the finest chemistry program in the country, his easy good looks, his strength at swimming—associated Erik himself with bourgeois respectability. In person, Conrad was the star of the otherwise rather awkward party. He circumnavigated the room, having conversations about sports, then about chemistry, then politics (carefully: Carnot and Freycinet were safe, the clerical question was not), and then local municipal improvements. He charmed Eugénie's young pupils, then he charmed their tight-lipped mothers.

"A little gentleman," Erik said mockingly. Or jealously?

Erik made the rounds of Eugénie and Alfred's friends, neighbors, students, and business associates, talking of nothing but his supposed or impending fame, testing what he could get away with. To the gullible or to out-of-towners, he was already a sensation; to the Parisians, on the razor's edge of glory. In every formulation, Philippe was an afterthought. Often, Erik didn't bother to introduce him at all.

Philippe detached himself to wander the apartment alone. He perused all the containers the flowers were in, thinking to find pitchers or milk bottles pressed into service, hidden at the back of the piano. But all he saw were proper vases.

Some nicer than others—everything from cut crystal to thick, bubbled glass—but vases all the same. Surely even the most prepared homemaker couldn't have this many on hand. The apartment appeared to be as stocked as a florist shop for an occasion that couldn't happen more than once in nearly never, an only daughter's only engagement party at the very moment when roses were blooming in the countryside around Paris. Philippe couldn't decide if he was now more or less surprised that Eugénie had been willing to part with the little flowered bowl.

When the currents of the party finally brought them together, he explained who he was and thanked her for her hospitality. He tried to thank her as well for the song publications without implying that the transaction was anything other than a sound response to the merits of the work, but this became a verbal tangle, and in the thick of it his tact abandoned him and he asked outright, "How *are* they doing? Sales."

"Oh, well enough," she said, and smiled politely.

Philippe had disappointed his mother enough times to know this smile instantly. "Always time for them to catch on, I suppose," he said.

But he knew this wasn't true. Although songs were theoretically imperishable, just waiting for the right person to come along and love them, they were really more like hat ribbons. The fashion would spark or it wouldn't. The women would all be wearing bunches of Malaga grapes on straw and humming a certain tune, or they'd be wearing tulle roses and humming a different tune, and then next season they'd have discarded both for something else.

Philippe offered Eugénie a little shrug. He wanted her to understand that he was worldly enough to do business with. He wanted her to recognize, he supposed, that he was not like Erik. "Thank you, by the way, for the bowl," he said.

"A bowl?"

As Philippe described it, her face darkened, and he knew instantly that Erik had been meant to return it.

"I'll bring it back."

"No, you thought it was a gift."

"I insist."

"Well, normally I wouldn't—it's just that I tried to replace it, but the pattern isn't being made any longer. We don't often entertain, but when one does . . . it's nice to have a full set."

"Of course. I'll get it back to you. Straightaway."

"You know, I almost fired our girl over it," Eugénie said. "She didn't seem like one to steal, but I thought she'd broken it and wasn't willing to confess. Truthfulness is very important to me."

No wonder she and Erik had never gotten along, Philippe thought. He retreated to the balcony. It was raining, but there was another balcony above that shielded him. He put his hand into the chilly curtain, then drew it back. He was the only one visible on any of the balconies, all the floors of all the buildings, up and down the street. Nearly everything beneath him was black or gray: bobbing umbrellas and coats and damp hats, dark horses slicked with rain or sweat, and the black tops of swaying carriages. In all of it there was only a single bright umbrella, printed with pink peonies and bold green leaves. From the way the water was soaking into it, the silk appeared not to be waterproofed; it was a thin summer parasol, useless in the rain and soon to be ruined. Philippe tried to construct a metaphor about fleeting beauty, about butterflies or moths. All he knew of the bearer was the back of her dress, light purple going dark with rain. Others noticed the parasol, this frail little mystery, and the dour crowd rustled as it parted around her, though no one looked long. If this was a performance, she was in the wrong neighborhood. Here people pretended to ignore strangeness rather than striving to draw it or dance it or sing it or surpass it. Philippe watched faithfully, as if an audience of one.

There might still be a chance to catch her. He could knock the party guests over like tenpins and bolt up the street. What a good story it would make. If they fell in love and married, he could tell it for the rest of his life—the balcony, the rain, the parasol. But really he'd end up wet and cold, and in his dank room it would take the suit forever to dry. Let her go, foolish woman, whoever she was.

"What are you looking at?"

Philippe turned to see Erik standing beside him on the balcony. "Nothing," he said, and then noticed it was true—the parasol had disappeared for good around the corner of the Rue de Marseilles. "You promised a luncheon, but it's just cake and punch," he added sullenly.

"I was misinformed," Erik said, so mournfully that Philippe believed him. "You know what else no one told me?"

Philippe paused expectantly and, when that wasn't sufficient to prompt Erik to continue, asked, "What?"

"They're already married! I thought this was an engagement party. Turns out they married weeks ago in Le Havre." When Philippe expressed surprise that Louise hadn't told Erik, he said he'd written her about a premiere he was conducting that weekend in Belgium, and she claimed now that she didn't want to make him miss it. "She should have assumed I was lying!" Erik said.

This wasn't mock outrage, Philippe saw, not the sort of overheated offense he'd witnessed Erik take at hecklers in the audience or from critics in the café papers. He was genuinely hurt and declared that he was ready to leave. Philippe pointed out that it was still raining, but Erik said he didn't care.

"I do," Philippe protested.

"We should have brought umbrellas."

"I don't own an umbrella."

"Nor do I. But never again! I'll not be caught unawares. Not by rain, not by weddings. I'm going to buy a dozen. Umbrellas."

"With what funds?"

Erik waved a hand dismissively.

"There you are." Louise broke in with glee, like a little girl who'd just won at hide-and-seek. She squeezed onto the balcony, her white skirts lapping at their legs. "Sulking?" she asked Erik.

"I can't believe you didn't tell me."

"You were busy."

"I would have made myself unbusy!"

"It was just a little thing. City hall, then lunch at Uncle Fortin's house after the Mass."

"That doesn't sound quite grand enough for the Lafosse family." This was said with suspicion instead of spite, as if perhaps Pierre's parents hadn't done right by his sister.

"They aren't grand people."

"Aren't they? Grand enough that Eugénie sounded amazed that Pierre married you."

Louise raised an eyebrow.

"I didn't mean it like that. You know I never mean it like that."

Philippe felt like he was eavesdropping, but there was no exit unless Louise moved or he pitched himself over the railing. Then Lord Noodle stuck his pale face out on the balcony. He kissed Louise on the cheek but did not try to join the crowd.

Conrad appeared behind Pierre's shoulder, taller by a head than his new brother-in-law, to ask Erik what he was doing after the reception. When Erik shrugged, Conrad said he'd been telling Pierre that he ought to see more of Paris before he left.

They'd spent all morning on the Champs-Élysées, Louise said.

Well, yes, Conrad said, but it was a Saturday night. He thought Erik would know some good places.

Erik and Philippe exchanged looks. They knew many, many places, all of which were difficult to imagine bringing Erik's baby brother and Lord Noodle along to.

"All right," Louise said, inviting herself along. "Let's. Where do you suggest?"

"I don't think you'll like it," Erik said. "Any of it."

"How would you have any idea what I'll like?"

"They're not really for..."

"For what—girls? I'm a married woman now."

Philippe watched the two brothers' dawning realization that their sister had become a married woman. More specifically, that she had had sex, and that she'd had it with the bony man standing at the glass doors. They had been naked together, unless she'd kept on... or he'd kept on... or.... Both brothers shook off a vision they wished to pursue no further. This was a trip wire, the way respectable girls became respectable women all at once, with indisputably carnal knowledge. Disreputable girls could exist in shades of gray. Girls like Louise went from being one thing to another, all at once.

"Am I working tonight?" Erik asked Philippe.

"I'm supposed to remember your schedule?"

"Well, I don't. I thought you might."

Philippe realized with displeasure that he did, and informed Erik that he was substituting for Hervochon at the Mirliton. "You wouldn't shut up about it when Bruant asked you last week. Remember?"

"Aristide Bruant?" Conrad asked. "He's famous."

"Is he?" Philippe asked. Bruant was famous in Montmartre, but that didn't always or even often mean that someone was famous in the world beyond.

"Yes, he's famous," Conrad insisted. "He's genuinely famous."

"Then we must go," Louise said. "You can get us in, surely."

Erik looked as if he were facing a firing squad. "I think I may have missed a rehearsal."

"I doubt Bruant rehearses," Philippe said.

"I missed something, because I've got no idea what I'm playing tonight. I need to get to the Mirliton."

Couldn't they meet him there later? Louise asked.

The Mirliton was tiny, Erik demurred. Seats were full for the first show by four thirty.

But wasn't there a late show? she said.

"Well, but you'd need to get in line with everybody else. By seven, probably. Hervochon's been accompanist since the place opened, and he couldn't get his mother in for free. Not that he'd *want* his mother to go."

"What are the young people discussing?" Alfred asked, another head peering over Pierre's shoulder, as if summoned by Erik's last remark.

Conrad said they might go out later.

"After supper, I hope. You know Eugénie's planned a family meal."

"Of course," Conrad said. "I suppose you could join us, if you want?"

The invitation was painfully insincere, and Alfred just smiled. "Oh, we'll leave such things to the young and fashionable," he said, in a voice that suggested he had never been young or fashionable, not for a single minute of a single Saturday night.

"Perhaps we should stay in," Pierre suggested to Louise. "You see your father so rarely."

"I see my brother even less often. Shall we try for the Mirliton? I'll change now, and we can leave right after dinner."

Philippe looked through the thicket of heads at the balcony door and saw that the apartment had nearly emptied. The rain had stopped, and the remaining guests were collecting umbrellas and saying their farewells to Eugénie at the front door. "I should be going," he announced to the assembled group, but nobody moved.

"You're leaving?" Erik asked.

Well, yes, since nobody's invited me to stay for supper, Philippe tried to say with his eyes, but Erik wasn't following.

"If you don't have plans," Erik said, "you could get in line at the Mirliton, save a space for them."

Philippe did some quick calculations. It was too late for a seat at the early show, and lining up now for the late one would put him standing by himself, in between a bunch of well-heeled rubes, for several hours. His people, his real ones, would walk past laughing, wondering what he thought he was doing. And what if the siblings didn't show up on time, money in hand? He didn't have cash to buy drinks to hold a table, even if they reimbursed him. A small glass of beer at places like the Mirliton jumped from forty centimes on weeknights to five francs on weekends—as much as Erik made from an entire night of work. On nights he worked. Which was, Philippe had to admit, five francs more than he himself made on any night.

"I have plans," he said.

"Really?" Erik said. "With who?"

Philippe nearly said, "With your sister," a joking insult that their friends used so often it had lost all meaning. He was not used to being in the presence of people's actual sisters. "No one you know," he said instead.

"I need to speak to you for a moment," Erik said. "In private."

Alfred backed up, then Conrad and Pierre, then Louise, and finally Philippe was freed. Erik dragged him into the kitchen.

"I know I'm being awful," Erik said.

"Do you?"

"Yes. And I'll make it up to you. But you know Bruant won't let me reserve seats. I don't know how else to pull this off."

"You thought the whole show was going to be a disaster when I reminded you of it a few minutes ago."

"If they're at the late show I'll have a performance to work out the kinks." Erik said this as if he'd ever done the show before, as if there were a set list in which some kinks might remain, as opposed to an evening ahead of nothing but. "If you end up out any money, I'll get it to you. I promise. I *promise*."

This was such a different side to Erik, needy and urgent and sincere. Tonight he was acting not like a Brother-in-Art, but like the ordinary kind of brother. Philippe thought of how much he missed his brothers, how badly he'd disappointed his whole family. Here was at least one person who cared about him, and who needed something he could provide. "Fine. I'll do it."

"I'll be right behind you. Shove some food in my face and then head to the café early enough to talk to Bruant."

"No chance of food for my face?"

"I'm sorry. Eugénie thinks you stole some bowl from her. I told her you're an upstanding citizen, but she doesn't seem to believe me."

Philippe sighed and walked through the apartment to the front door, leaving Erik in the kitchen.

"Did you have a coat or umbrella?" Eugénie asked Philippe, so coldly that he knew Erik had been telling the truth: she was still, unfairly, holding the missing bowl against him.

No coat, he said, and since there was no relationship left to salvage, decided to satisfy his curiosity. "Where did all the vases come from? You have so many."

There was a long silence, so long the maid finally replied. "I borrowed them. From the neighbors."

Philippe nodded knowingly, as if this told him something important. Maybe it did. He hoped the maid wouldn't get in trouble for answering. How civilized, he thought, and as he walked downstairs he imagined all the doors opening onto friendly neighbors, everyone willing to share because everyone had enough. When he thought of his own apartment building, he pictured a barrel full of swarming rats.

My family thinks I'm a failure, he'd written in his most recent postcard to Miguel, needing to confess it to someone. Miraculously, there had come a response, written on the back of a hand-colored postcard of Tarragona's harbor, an old picture with the lighthouse still standing. *From your postcards it's sounded like you* are *a failure,* it read, Miguel's handwriting immediately, excruciatingly recognizable. That was the end of the message, but Miguel had also included a new address. The street name alone made Philippe homesick: it was part of the new grid, past the Rambla Nova, where his father had spent a decade moving rocks. The building number hadn't even existed when Philippe left, and he wondered what the new construction looked like, how many flush toilets it might have. Was it a new family apartment, or had Miguel moved out? Was he living on his own, or with someone? With whom might he be living? Philippe knew he'd lost the right to ask. But he took the address as an invitation to write back. *I think I may be doing it wrong*, he'd written. *Paris. Poetry.*

As he walked back into Montmartre, toward the Mirliton, it started again to rain.

Erik

— 7 —

Hard as the devil

THE OUTSIDE OF THE MIRLITON IS PLASTERED WITH POSTERS OF Aristide Bruant, the massive red sweep of his scarf, giant black hat, the face in between just a few penciled lines. Bruant in person always looks just like Bruant in the posters, because no one can tell from the posters what he really looks like. He's a scarf and a hat, black-topped villain and debonair hero at once, so stylish he does not need to advertise his face. It is a strong face, not handsome, with forbidding eyebrows and a cruel mouth. Part of the performance is just how cruel that mouth can be.

Bruant advertises Friday and Saturday nights as being exclusively for "the smart and elegant," which gives his insults a head start, since every guest can be found lacking in either quality. Bruant was the only performer at the Chat Noir more calculating than the owner, Rodolphe Salis; he hawked his own sheet music from the stage and, after deciding to open the Mirliton, guessed, correctly, that drink minimums and "donations" could bring in even more money than a cover charge, as long as he aggressively shamed the audience into donating.

When the Mirliton first opened, Erik went to a cheap midweek show and admired the rough bravado, the way Bruant didn't need the variety acts or dancing girls or professional farters. He could fill the stage all by himself. Each time he passed the hat Erik put in a scrap of paper with a single line of a musi-cal composition rolled tightly enough to be disguised as money. At the bottom of the last one he wrote, *Someday this song will be worth one hundred thousand francs.* He's glad now that he signed it only with his initials, which will offer deniability, if Bruant ever remembers the scraps. But no doubt he immediately tossed aside anything that wasn't cash.

The Mirliton is packed for the early show, and Erik hopes Philippe made it into the line outside in time to get seats for the later performance. Already onstage, Erik sits with his back toward the wall, the upright piano perpendicular to the front of the stage, which is only an empty wooden square at one end of the cramped room. Bruant swaggers on, a musketeer in top boots, velvet coat, scarf, and giant black sombrero. He doffs the hat, looks inside it. "Empty as my pockets," he says with a heavy sigh, then tosses the hat over the first rows of tables and into the back, where a man catches it before it can land on his wife.

"Thank you for your eagerness, sir," Bruant says, with false gratitude. "Glad to know we'll be getting off to a good start."

Although his sight line is partly blocked by the top of the pi-ano, Erik watches the man grope for money. No doubt he didn't expect to be on display in the far back of the room. Bruant is supposed to be on display. This is why the audience has come, because they've heard that Bruant is very amusing, stalking back and forth like a panther in the zoological gardens. But the pan-thers do not ask for money. There are no iron bars here at the Mirliton, and Bruant looks like he might bite.

Still watching the hat make its way through the audience, Erik doesn't notice Bruant gesturing for the first song. Bruant walks over and flicks him hard in the forehead, whispers "'Mirliton,' *now*," and it takes Erik another moment to remember that it's a song as well as the name of the café. He starts the thunder-ous chords of the opening and the audience jumps, so that the wooden chairs and the wooden room creak at once. Who needs lights, or a curtain? Part of Bruant's showmanship is how unadorned it is.

Just me, Erik thinks. *He needs me.* And he is both buoyed and terrified by his indispensability. The Conservatory was not the best preparation for this kind of work. While his classical training provided Erik with more than enough technical skill to play cabaret music, he never learned to play by ear, or improvise, or transpose well, moving the key up or down to suit a singer's voice. He has worked hard to compensate, spending hours of unpaid time copying out transpositions by hand. If he has something written in front of him, he's all right. His hands and eyes are quicker than his ear.

The first song goes well enough, a few wrong notes but nothing obvious. Erik's feeling all right until Bruant launches straight from the last chord of the opener into a patter song completely different from the one Hervochon has placed second in the folder. Erik scrambles through the pages for whatever Bruant is singing. He finally finds it, but there's nothing on the page save the key signature and a freckling of notes. He does the best he can, noodling up and down the keys until something sounds passable, then repeating it until Bruant glares at him.

The song, "Automatic Women: You Get What You Pay For," is about newfangled automatons: an actress, a barmaid, a dancer. The lyrics explain, in detail, just how many coins must be inserted in each, and exactly what actions result. "New accompanist tonight, folks," Bruant says in the fourth verse. "I put in the coins, but I am *not* getting what I paid for."

In truth Bruant hasn't paid him anything yet, and now Erik's afraid he won't. He shrugs his shoulders exaggeratedly up and down, makes apologetic eyebrows and a crumpled mouth. Sad clown.

"What's your name, boy?"

"Erik," he says—no point in lying. There are almost certainly people in the audience who have seen him onstage elsewhere.

He's known in Montmartre just enough to have lost his anonymity. It's the state he thought he was working toward, but right now he wishes he had it back.

"Try to keep up, Erik."

For the next few songs, he can. Bruant does them in the order in the folder, announcing the titles ahead of time so Erik can put them in the rack. When he first arrived this evening, it took forever to find the folder—no one at the Mirliton could remember Hervochon using written music. Here's one about a chimney sweep. Here's one about a coal carrier, how he starves all summer and breaks his back all winter hauling heavy loads up narrow staircases. He's so excited about the invention of elevators that he makes one his sweetheart. He leaves his wife and rides the elevator up and down all day long. Rides it, rides it, up and down. All—day—long.

The government censors usually guarantee at least some restraint from performers, but tonight Erik doesn't see any of the familiar faces, turnip-colored bureaucrats scribbling in the back row with a free drink in front of them and often a bribe in their pockets to edit the final report. Maybe they've been dispatched elsewhere—Montmartre has grown beyond the government's ability to police it—or maybe Bruant has paid them off in advance.

"Pass the hat," he says. "I saw you, sir, passing it along without even looking inside. So little intention of giving you don't even think about stealing! I see the cost of your gloves, fine leather, sir, and yet those gloves pass the hat without making a small donation?"

Bruant doesn't dance, just stalks and postures and grimaces expressively. His body manages to be both elastic and sharp, a rubber tiger. His voice is nothing special, an octave of gravel and an octave of sunlight, but he's learned how to drag the one through the other.

The sole reason Erik is getting by at all is that some of Bruant's material isn't original—Erik has played these songs for other singers. Bruant commences one about a luscious lady of the night, then stops himself.

"Who are we fooling?" he says. "We're all adults here, yes? The song's about a whore. Ladies and gentlemen, here's a song about a fucking whore. Maybe it'll sound familiar. Fucking whores, every one of you."

Two adventurous girls, unchaperoned by any male companion, have been exchanging glances since Bruant started, and at the mention of whores they rise to leave. The girls are heckled, of course, but they push their way steadfastly through the packed crowd.

"Can't wait any longer, can you?" Bruant asks them. "Can't wait to get your hands on each other. Unlace yourselves. Am I invited?"

One girl is frozen. The other shakes her head.

"Could Monsieur Erik come home with you?" Bruant tries.

Erik shakes his head as well. He doesn't want these poor girls to think he's part of their problem.

"No?" Bruant says to him in mock amazement. "Two flowers like that?" By now his hat has been returned to the stage. He empties it of francs and walks over to Erik. "Nothing here, or here, *or* here?" he says, touching his hat first to Erik's head, then to his hands on the keys, and finally to his crotch.

Now Bruant hurls himself into a parody whose vicious political lyrics are laid over the tune of an old waltz. He tells Erik to transpose it into a different key, but Erik can play it only as written. At first Bruant gives it a go. The high notes are too high, though, out of his range. He squeaks and cracks and whispers, then kicks the back of the piano and draws his finger across his throat.

This is one of those dreams, Erik thinks, like showing up to school in your underwear, except that this is happening. He's never been halted mid-performance, never heard a performer stop dead like this. He's watched people finish their songs and fall drunk off the stage. He accompanied one green-faced man who up and died the next night. But the show has always gone on, even if it skipped the last verse. Maybe, Erik thinks hopefully, this *could* be a dream. He pushes back from the piano and urges his body into the air, as if to take flight.

"What are you doing?" Bruant hisses.

"I can't transpose. I'm sorry. Not by sight."

Astonishment and loathing flicker across Bruant's face before he collects himself. "Where did you learn to play?" he thunders, speaking to the audience now rather than to Erik.

"The Conservatory."

"That explains so much. I need an accompanist, I get a little faggot from the Conservatory. Probably knows Mendelssohn but can't transpose a little song about our dear president."

Erik plays a line of Mendelssohn. The crowd laughs obligingly. Maybe, Erik hopes, they'll think this is all staged.

"Beethoven? Mozart? Chopin?"

This he can do. He collages the phrases into each other, famous passages the crowd will recognize.

"Bruant? Let's give him his place among the stars."

Erik plays an approximation of the first lines of "Le Mirliton." Bruant throws out a few more names, buying time, as he pages through the music in the folder atop the piano. He removes some pieces, shuffles them into order, and drops them into the rack. "Rest of the set," he whispers. He taps out the tempo for the next song with his tall boot, and Erik comes in cleanly. The wheels are back on, but however well Erik plays, Bruant keeps cracking jokes at his expense. Toward the end of the show a brave soul shouts out a request. "Better not," Bruant says. "I don't think Monsieur Erik would be up for that one." The audience boos Erik. His face goes hot.

Bruant performs the finale a cappella as Erik stumbles through the tables with the hat held out like a collection plate. "If you've enjoyed what you heard," Bruant calls out, "but especially if you haven't, please consider a donation so Monsieur Erik may get some piano lessons." As the audience files out, Bruant doesn't retreat to a back room. He waits on the stage, by the piano, for Erik to return with the hat. "You were shit. That was shit." Erik stays silent, eyes downcast, a kicked dog. Bruant snatches the hat, pours it out so that the money rattles like hail onto the keys. "Listen to that. I'd rather listen to that all day than to you."

Erik offers to try to find someone else for the second show.

"On half an hour's notice, on a Saturday night?" Bruant shakes his head. "We do it again this way. Actually, play even worse, if that's possible. That'll be the theme for the late show: hopeless. Since you already are."

"Let me try again for real. We've got—" Erik's not sure how much time remains before the second show, but maybe enough to write out the songs Bruant needs transposed.

Bruant shakes his head. "Since you didn't have the sense to turn down the job in the first place, this is our best option."

"Am I still getting paid?" If the answer's no, he'll walk out now.

Bruant gestures at the money on the piano, on the floor, under the pedals. "I said it was yours. For piano lessons."

It's no small amount. Much more than they'd agreed on, in fact. Even with the humiliation of scrambling on the ground to collect the money, Erik is giddy for a moment. Then he remembers who will be in the audience for the late show. He thinks he has time to run outside and tell Philippe to get out of line, to make up some excuse for Louise and Conrad and Pierre. After Bruant stalks offstage, Erik scoops up the money from the floor and keyboard and shoves it in his pockets, where it clinks against the pocketknife he's been carrying all day, waiting for his opportunity to give it to Louise. When he looks up, pockets stretched and full, Erik sees Philippe already pulling a chair away from one of the long communal tables. At Philippe's request, the young woman seated across from him lends him items of clothing—a hat, a scarf, gloves—to drape across chair backs to hold the seats.

Erik rushes to the table, strips the chair backs, and starts handing the clothing to the woman. "You can't stay," he says to Philippe. "The first show was a disaster."

"You got sacked already?"

"I'm playing but it's going to be terrible. You have to get them out of here."

"Your brother and sister? They were always going to hate it. I thought that was a mistake you were letting them make."

"*I'm* going to be terrible."

"Well, apparently Bruant thought you were good enough to manage the second show."

"Only because he's going to make fun of me the entire time." Drinks arrive and Erik reaches for Philippe's beer, takes down half of it in a succession of gulps. "I'm not Hervochon, I'm just *me*," he says, summing up the problem.

"Always," Louise says, arriving from behind him with Conrad and Pierre.

Since the party she has changed into a green dress and re-arranged her hair into elaborate loops falling over her ears. Maybe they'll interfere with her hearing, Erik thinks. "You should go," he tells her. "The show is terribly racy. I really don't think you'll enjoy it."

"I can handle racy," Louise says defensively.

Pierre sits down, assuring Erik that they're not expecting anything in particular and will be pleased with the show regardless. His gentle encouragement makes Erik want to spit. As if he cares what Pierre thinks. As if the opinion of some rich, spindly gentleman doctor means anything to Erik.

He cares, of course. He cares what everyone thinks.

Erik finishes Philippe's beer and walks back to the piano like a man headed to the guillotine. As the rest of the seats fill, he studies the folder of music as if it will help him. He wants to announce to the audience that he is really quite well liked at his regular gigs, at the Auberge and the Chat Noir, where the singers have learned to give him their music ahead of time. He's never too drunk to play. Perhaps because he's often operating at the edge of his own confidence, he's patient, quick to adjust his volume to a nervous voice or circle back for a missed entrance. If an audience member gets too nasty, Erik will shame him from the stage. He writes original songs and lets performers sing them for free. At first the songs were too odd and soft for anyone to bother. But they've been getting brassier, sassier. Most remarkably, Erik has never tried to sleep with any of the performers. Yet he knows Bruant would be unimpressed by this list of achievements.

Once the seats are full and the first round of drinks served, Bruant takes the stage and nods his head at Erik. Erik's fingers, positioned on the keys for the opening of "Le Mirliton," tremble slightly. The expectant silence is nearly complete. The only sounds are the rustlings of clothing, a few scattered coughs, glasses being set gently on the table.

Erik clatters in with the opening chords and Bruant, full of glorious contempt, screws up repeatedly so that he can blame Erik. The audience batters him with laughter. During the roll call of classics, Bruant throws in some extra names: Massenet and Liszt and Bach. It's Erik's one chance in the show to look competent, and he milks it for all it's worth. Louise has the musical skill to appreciate what he's doing, and he imagines he's playing his medley of classics for her.

He can tell Bruant is about to move on to the next bit, and Erik can't let this chance at the Mirliton go by: he yells out his own name. What he plays is the wrong song for the room, for the mood, the moment, but whatever he plays will enrage Bruant, and this is his favorite of his compositions. It's three years old and still his favorite, which sometimes frustrates him—why hasn't he surpassed himself by now?

The piece is serene, unashamedly pretty. The crowd is unsure how to react. If it were a cabaret song they would get the joke, but there is no hint of insincerity or showmanship. Bruant stands with his eyebrows nearly disappearing into his hair. Erik is prepared to be stopped at any moment but tries not to rush. If he doesn't make it to the end, then let whatever fragment the audience hears sound the way it's supposed to sound. He dares to hope Bruant will pretend to be in on the plan long enough to let him finish.

For the moment the notes drop into a pool of silence, one by one, ripples spreading outward. Both the melody and the quiet, mournful accompaniment of the left hand are delicate. It's a simple piece; unlike so much else of what Erik has been attempting, there is no sense of the reach exceeding his grasp. The piece is small and complete unto itself, a clear glass globe. It feels like that rarest of rare things, a creation that has come out exactly the way its creator wanted. It's a song you could weep to, deliciously, but also one so gentle and pretty that you could stop listening to it and just let it hang, draped against the background of your life.

He's written three of these pieces, all similarly simple, similarly lovely, similarly unheard. There wasn't really a market for them right now, Eugénie told him matter-of-factly when he played them for her and Alfred in the apartment. The name was baffling, Alfred added. It sounded a bit ridiculous—"Gymnopédies"—like made-up Greek. The intent was to evoke ancient statuary, Erik said, the quiet half-smile of a caryatid. He felt he'd done it, carved three elegant marble statues out of piano notes, but no one else seems to hear them the way he wishes they would.

All Bruant says when Erik finishes is "Pretty." Then he's silent so long Erik wonders if he should push his luck and start playing the second one. He's trying to feel the room, decipher what they thought. Do they even understand the piece is his?

"Pretty, like a girl," Bruant finally adds. "A little sylph."

Perhaps "sylph" isn't a bad descriptor? All Philippe said when he first heard it was "Nice." Philippe doesn't know anything about music anyway. He always says Erik's music is good, even when Erik knows it's shit.

"Do you have a little sylph, Monsieur Erik? A sweetheart?"

Erik shakes his head.

"Do you have a sister?"

He pauses, but nods.

"Is she pretty?"

He nods again—dangerous, but of course there's no other option.

"Then let's have a song about another pretty girl. A little more fun, eh? Since these people have come out for fun." Bruant flips through the folder on top of the piano, pulls out a song called "Aimée," and hands it to Erik. "What's her name, your sister?"

This whole turn is so unexpected that Erik wonders if Bruant knows his sister is in the audience. Is this some elaborate plot? He's afraid to lie. "Louise," he says.

He's soon accompanying a song about Lou-Lou-Louise, instead of Ai-Ai-Aimée, a cancan dancer who raises her legs just a bit higher than all the others and wears just a bit less underneath. But oh that bit, that little bit, it makes a big, big difference. With every Lou-Lou-Louise, Bruant grabs his crotch. At first Erik doesn't notice the gesture—Bruant's pushing the tempo faster than Erik's ever played it. Then the audience's laughter goes up a notch, but Erik knows there aren't any great lines in the third verse. He finally looks up, straight into Bruant's face. The man is nearly draped on the piano, rubbing against it. He puckers his lips obscenely around Louise's name.

Erik keeps playing. *Don't try to leave*, he thinks toward Louise, remembering the girls from the first show. *This could all get worse*. He thinks it toward her the same way he used to push his thoughts toward the mermaid. Maybe it's working, because Louise stays seated.

But he has forgotten about Pierre. He stands and reaches for

Louise's arm, and Erik can't tell what's happening, whether she wants to go or stay. Then Pierre starts to push his way out of the room, leading her by the elbow.

"You forgot your stick," Bruant shouts, which is true, a fashionable walking stick still hanging on the back of Pierre's chair. "Presumably it goes up your ass?" But this is too easy—so easy that Bruant's already losing interest as Conrad grabs the stick and holds it out to Pierre over the heads at the next table. "Why this one?" Bruant calls out. After all, there were racier songs earlier in the evening. Pierre doesn't bother to answer and Bruant just shrugs, then turns back to Erik, who remains the most rewarding prey on offer.

The rest of the set is a blur. "Good night!" Bruant finally yells. "Show's over! Don't come again!" The old hanging chair from the Chat Noir, a parting gift from Salis when Bruant struck out on his own, spins slightly in its wires as the crowd rises to leave.

Bruant picks through the final take from the hat, counts out Erik's wage. Instead of reaching for it, Erik sulks. "You already paid me."

"No, I insulted you. Here's what we agreed on. The rest is extra. Fun show, in the end. I don't ever want to see your face again, but I had some fun."

Reluctantly, Erik takes the money.

"What was that piece you played?" Bruant asks. "The slow one."

"A gymnopédie," Erik says, not without a little solemnity, as though trying to slip back into his dignity like it was a jacket he removed at the beginning of the evening. "What did you think of it?" he ventures, even as he's unsure he truly wants to know.

"I think you brought the room down so far I had to haul it back up with both hands. Melancholy is a dangerous mood. People like a wallow, but they don't open their pockets for it."

"Is money your only measure?"

"It's the most useful one I've found. What are you, really? You're barely an accompanist."

"I'm a composer."

Bruant looks at him for a long moment. "I got pieces of music in the hat once. Little fiddly bits of paper, all rolled up. Initialed *E.S.* Was that you?"

Erik swallows, tries to discern which answer is the least bad. "Yes," he admits.

"I tried to play it, out of curiosity. I couldn't even figure out what order the lines went in."

"It was just a joke."

"Was it?"

Erik says nothing.

"I don't know if you've got a hundred-thousand-franc piece in you, but those scraps of paper weren't it."

"I know," Erik says, truthfully.

"Good luck with your wallow," Bruant says.

Outside the Mirliton, Conrad is standing by himself. Erik didn't really expect Louise and Pierre to still be here, but where is Philippe? He's annoyed that Conrad's been left alone in this neighborhood, though Conrad is older now than Philippe was when he moved here. Why does Conrad, for all his competence, seem like he still needs looking after? Is it just because he'll always be Erik's kid brother? Conrad probably feels like *he* is the one who needs looking after, Erik thinks. Conrad's face as Erik approaches looks unusually like Alfred's, and Erik realizes it's because of the disappointed expression.

"That was awful," Conrad says.

"Believe me, I know. I told you it would be."

"Not the show. What you did to Louise."

"What I—what? You think I planned that? Does she think that?"

"How could she not? Didn't you?"

"I had no idea what Bruant was going to do!"

"Really?" Conrad seems skeptical.

"I have to talk to her. Where is she staying?"

"The Hôtel Continental. But it's late. You can't go there now."

Erik is always up at this hour. It doesn't feel late at all. And he hates the idea of Louise thinking for another minute, let alone all night, that he meant to humiliate her.

"I wouldn't risk it," Conrad counsels. "They could be in bed already."

"I assure you that waking them up won't be nearly the most obnoxious thing I've ever done."

"I mean . . . *in bed*. They're newlyweds, remember?"

"I suppose we shouldn't," Erik says grudgingly, then insists on walking Conrad home. "What did you think of it? The original composition I played?"

Conrad isn't at all musical, the only person in their family who isn't, but Erik will take any opinion to wash away the taste of Bruant's. "The slow one?" Conrad says. "It was really pretty."

Erik is silent for a couple of blocks.

"What else did you want me to say?" Conrad asks.

"I don't know," Erik says, and doesn't.

At the apartment's front door, Conrad points out that it doesn't make any sense for Erik to walk all the way back up the Butte, then down again in the early morning to the Hôtel Continental. "You've still got a bed here. Just stay the night."

It's the logical thing to do, but after Erik enters his old bedroom (which became his sickroom) and climbs into the bed he almost died in, he can't sleep, wondering instead whether he's truly accomplished anything since.

The two brothers arrive at the Hôtel Continental the next morning with pastries, bought with Bruant's hat money. But Pierre and Louise are already eating room service. Erik explains everything as he stands there holding the pastries, the paper going shiny with butter, and he can tell that Pierre and Louise don't quite believe what he's saying. Louise seems to want to, but she's already spent all night with a certain story in her head, a certain idea of him, and she can't write over it completely. Pierre resumes eating while Erik is still speaking, a clear dismissal.

Erik wants to give Louise their father's old pocketknife, which he's kept all these years, ever since those horrible early days of boarding school in Honfleur. He even went to the trouble days ago of chipping off the rust and oiling the hinge. But he can tell this isn't the time. He also wants to ask Louise what she thought of the gymnopédie, of course, but it isn't the right time for that either. He should have come last night, he thinks. Stupid Conrad, stupid caution.

"How long are you in town for?" Erik asks, wanting to arrange another meeting, to try again.

"A few days," Pierre answers, "but I'm afraid we're fully booked."

Louise looks down at her plate.

"Another time, then," Erik says. Leaving the hotel, pastries still in hand, knife still in his pocket, he feels very alone, even with Conrad walking along beside him.

Louise

— 8 —

Weep like a willow

PIERRE'S PLAN, HE'D EXPLAINED BEFORE OUR WEDDING, WAS FOR us to live at his family's château while he settled into his medical practice. Then I could choose: we might rent a house in Saint-Côme-du-Mont or stay at Château Bellenau. In our conversations I had a bad habit of following the word "château" with a nervous giggle, as if to acknowledge that no one like me had any business living in anything called a château.

"You need to stop laughing at yourself and enjoy it while you can," Pierre finally snapped at me.

"Do you plan to divorce me?"

"Of course not. You'll outlast the house by far. We'll outlast it."

"That's either a very strong marriage or a very shoddy house."

"The house will still be standing, but someone else will be living in it."

His family had been in the house since 1717, and I didn't understand why that would change. As it turned out, he'd already explained the whole matter to Fortin, wishing to be honest about his prospects, but Fortin—perhaps worried I'd throw away my chance with Pierre the way I'd irrationally thrown away Cannu—had decided the matter wasn't my concern. Pierre, to his credit, was horrified when he realized Fortin hadn't told me. The family estate was catastrophically indebted, he now explained, and the loans would come due upon his father's death. His family would have to start selling land to satisfy the creditors, and then there wouldn't be enough income to maintain the estate.

He told me I could still call the wedding off. His circumstances were not what I'd thought they were, he acknowledged, and he didn't want me to feel misled.

I was furious with Fortin, but not with Pierre. I wasn't marrying him for an inheritance, I said. I was marrying him because I wanted him, and he wanted me back. That alone seemed a better, more miraculous fairy tale than any castle.

I thought back to Deauville. What I had then imagined as very different personalities between Pierre and his sister now seemed like different understandings. She was living like someone who'd been raised in a château and couldn't imagine anything being different, and he'd already begun building a life that would survive its loss. Or was it a difference not in understanding or personality, but in sex? That men *could* build something, and Albertine would have to wait and walk through whatever doorway she could?

I asked him if his sister knew about this.

"Nobody 'knows' it," he said. "Not officially. My father's been insisting for thirty years that everything will be fine, and everyone except me has been choosing to believe him. Who knows—perhaps it will be."

"You seem very sure, though."

"The garden alone is enough to warn anyone who's seen it with his eyes open. Like you. You've got your eyes open. I couldn't marry anyone who would be expecting too much."

This was hardly romantic, but I felt more relief than disappointment or anger. Now I wouldn't have to spend the rest of my life wondering why in the world Pierre had chosen me. He needed a hardy weed rather than a hothouse pineapple, to prepare for the disaster he thought was around the corner. He was preparing for the wrong disaster, as it turned out, but a weed is a weed, and he proved right about me—I can take root far from where I was planted. I also liked that I wouldn't have to spend my life feeling as grateful to him as the world would think I should. Once the estate was gone, we'd be a housewife and a country doctor, a more comfortable match than an heir and an orphan.

After our visit to Paris, Pierre and I returned to Le Havre only long enough to pack our trunks for Château Bellenau. I wish now that I could have seen it just once without knowing what I did. What Pierre told me was a veil I couldn't lift, and after we arrived I saw everything at Bellenau through that shadow. Which was of course why Pierre had told me, but Bellenau's brightness would have had its own truth.

Behind a stone wall and iron gate, the front of the house was elegant in a very traditional way: a packed dirt courtyard encir cled a round central planting of neat shrubs and flowers girding a small fountain on a pedestal. The house comprised two stone stories plus a third row of windows in the mansard roof, two towers at the corners. Eight broad windows across, times the three floors, times a four-sided building, plus the little dormers in the tower roofs: I couldn't help calculating how much the house must cost in window tax alone. There was a stone balcony above the front door, where I briefly imagined myself being pre- sented as the new bride of the heir to the manor, but presented to whom? The only visions my imagination could supply were eighteenth-century images—either stolid, unwashed peasants or an unruly mob with pitchforks raised.

I had practiced for my arrival, hoping to banish from my face any hint of goggle-eyed intimidation, and I mostly succeeded, until I was whisked by my new father-in-law, Pierre-Joseph, through the house and out the back doors. Every generation had its own Pierre—my husband was number six, and the family resorted to the use of second or middle names to keep everyone straight. Madeleine followed us, fussing about offering refreshments first, but with the daylight fading, Pierre-Joseph insisted we see the garden before sundown.

At the time I thought my shock was in part my own naïveté. I had seen no place like the garden, but then I had not seen many places. Pierre-Joseph's garden was a tropical jungle crossbred with Venice, grafted to a fairy hollow and a botanical museum, then spliced with Hameau de la Reine, Marie Antoinette's pretend village at Versailles, where she dressed up like a milkmaid so she could wear another life. It remains the most impossible, most wondrous place I have ever seen, and I am someone now who has voyaged over an ocean. Now that I have seen at least a little of the world, I understand there are no other places like Bellenau, nor ever were, nor will be again. Not even Bellenau is Bellenau any longer.

I don't know how long it takes a garden to fall to ruin, but the tropical plants at Bellenau wouldn't have made it through their first winter uncared for—they had to be trimmed or bound and wrapped, tucked in blankets like children. In the spaces they left after freezing and dying, weeds squeezed out for half a century would have rioted the following spring. Could the palms survive without tending? The yuccas, or the Argentine pampas grasses in the meadow? If the big plantings failed, how soon until the marshy soil eroded from around their dead roots? Until the rivers, the whole system of man-made canals, slackened and silted up? Until the banks crumbled, leaving the tree roots to clutch at nothing, and the trees fell gasping into the water, splintering the footbridges? Until the hand-built grottoes flooded and birds nested in the little stone house perched on the Island of the Birds? Until the Island of the Birds itself dissolved, because it was not a real island but a hillock built on pilings? Until the little pleasure boats sank and the statues tipped off their pedestals? Until the inscriptions blurred and chipped away?

Now I'm getting carried away, because I doubt enough time has passed to erase the stones themselves. And the statues are likely just fine, or at least the serene Our Lady sheltered in its underground niche. (She was a gift from the villagers, ostensibly for Pierre-Joseph's support of renovations to the village church, but really I think for his several decades of employing their fathers and husbands and sons as gardeners and laborers.) At least some of the canal system must have held its shape, although the word "canal" suggests something squared off and industrial, locks and mule paths. These were purposefully crooked, sinuous, interlocking rivers that could be navigated with the little rowboats kept moored throughout the garden. Some of the oldest trees were probably well enough established to survive unscathed. The sequoias were already fifteen meters tall when I arrived, confirmed in their implacable mission to grow ever taller.

Pierre-Joseph could remember when each stand of each variety had been planted, down to what the weather had been like that season and where the seeds or cuttings or seedlings had been acquired from. Some trees' planting dated to a specific day, commemorating his wedding, or the visit from the Linnaean Society, which awarded him a medal for being the first person in France to successfully grow Chinese palms. He had even named some of the individual trees, like a *Wellingtonia* specimen he called The Patriarch.

Pierre-Joseph was an exhaustive tour guide, and it grew dark before we could return to the house. He led us into a small stone building to retrieve a lantern. I had assumed it was a potting shed until the lantern was lit and a dozen white skulls flashed out of the darkness, causing me to shriek.

"I should have warned you," Pierre said. "I didn't realize it would all still be here."

"I kept it for you," his father said.

"You didn't have to do that," Pierre said, and I already knew him well enough to hear something slightly different—an un-spoken *I wish you hadn't.*

"What is this place?" I asked.

"My father's effort to find something we'd have in common."

It was a naturalist's studio, Pierre-Joseph explained. He thought if his son insisted on medicine, and pigheadedly resisted botany, they might meet in the middle. Pierre would get practice with dissections, and Pierre-Joseph would end up with speci-mens of the garden life. So he built this. "The gardeners have been keeping tools in here," Pierre-Joseph said, "but now that you're back, it's yours again."

"None of this was ever mine," Pierre said.

That night, getting ready for bed, I could tell Pierre was annoyed. I had praised the garden too much, seen too much beauty in it. But how could I not? And how could I ignore what I'd seen? I wished to be polite to my new father-in-law and I wished to be honest, and by a miracle those two aims were not at odds. I regretted only that my comments were so shallow, the kinds of comments Pierre made about music: that a piece was *pretty*, or *fast*, or that it sounded *difficult*. Such words were sufficient for my level of playing, but insufficient to describe the garden.

"It's impossible," I had told Pierre-Joseph at dinner. "It's an im-possible place."

"It is," he said with satisfaction. "But I made it."

"It's a ridiculous place," Pierre said that night in our bedroom.

Parts of the house had been shut down to economize, but there was still plenty of distance between our rooms and Pierre-Joseph and Madeleine's. We could argue freely; we could do other things freely. A benefit to Pierre's anger was that he was too preoccupied to notice me staring as he changed out of his clothes into pajamas, something I was still too shy about to be brazen.

Before we were married I had pictured him in a nightshirt:

pajamas still seemed avant-garde to me. "You pictured me in my nightclothes?" he'd said, when I admitted it, and I blushed. Neither of us knew what we were doing, but apparently we did it well enough, because I was pregnant within a month of the wedding. Once it was clear that I was with child, Pierre was afraid of hurting the baby. I was vomiting too often to argue the point. Joy and regret were mingled that it had happened so soon—it would have been nice to enjoy each other as only husband and wife for longer. On the other hand, there was a satisfaction in knowing that our bodies worked as they ought. Also, my life at Bellenau still felt so strange and accidental that I couldn't help worrying one of the Lafosses might toss me out on my ear. But surely that wouldn't happen to the mother of Pierre-something the seventh. I hoped for a boy, for that reason, though I also already imagined other children after this one. I wanted at least one girl, if only because then the Lafosses might allow me to name her what I liked.

Bellenau was famous in the district, and people often showed up hoping for tours. Pierre-Joseph didn't care for the gawkers, but he loved serious guests, men in good boots and sensible hats who could speak intelligently about acclimatization and drainage. The horticulturists were sometimes asked to stay for a drink or a meal, which gave the days more liveliness than they would have had otherwise. The conversation might have been about invasive weeds or pest damage, but at least there was conversation. If they came with their wives, I asked the women questions about the places they were from or had traveled, and my world grew. Nights without company usually found us all reading together, separate books, in companionable silence. I played the piano sometimes, but I also plunged into the library, agog at the choices after Fortin's slim clutch of edifying books. It was a very easy life, and eventually I became comfortable enough in the house to stop being intimidated by it, to find the corners and rooms and paintings I liked best, and even to allow myself some dislikes.

I was not overly fond of the dining room, whose walls were covered in enormous equestrian paintings. Pierre's grandfather had been a keen horseman. He'd sponsored purses at the local racetrack and had run a stud farm nearby. Although he had kept the saddle and carriage horses, Pierre-Joseph had sold the race-horses off two decades earlier and still cited this as evidence of his fiscal responsibility. Even that sacrifice must have weighed on him, however, based on the quantity of horse memorabilia scattered throughout the house, rubbing shoulders with horticulture specimens and awards, and with the more ordinary decorative objects—vases, clocks, candelabras—that accumulate when a wealthy family has lived in one house for a very long time. Nothing went together except that it was all muffled in the same dust that collects when the wealthy lady of the house is worried for that wealth and retrenches the household staff. The scrollwork on the gold frames of the paintings had nearly disappeared under a fur of gray dust.

Happy to have Pierre back at home, his parents fussed over him inordinately. Pierre, though still kind and even-tempered with me, grew more and more snappish toward them. The doctor he was supposed to be replacing in the village had begun having second thoughts about retirement, and Pierre wasn't sure whether to wait him out or look for a job elsewhere. Then the old doctor proposed keeping his office hours, while Pierre, as the younger man, traveled to the house calls. There wasn't really sufficient work for both of them, but in an optimistic frame of mind Pierre informed his parents that he would need the use of a horse.

"Absolutely not," Madeleine said, with genuine shock. "Out *riding*? In all weather?"

"Just until the bicycle I've ordered arrives," Pierre said.

"A bicycle!" Madeleine yelped, at an operatic pitch.

They seemed to want Pierre to content himself with a sedentary, gentlemanly life. They were happiest when he spent all day in the library reading medical texts. The house-call plan disintegrated in large part because Pierre-Joseph threatened to sell all the saddle horses out from under Pierre if he borrowed one. Then the bicycle, a new and popular model, was on indefinite back order.

"This is a beautiful time of year in the garden," Pierre-Joseph said. "Why not just enjoy it for a little while? Spend time with your new bride? Someday it's all going to be yours."

"Someday it's going to belong to the bank, and someone in this family needs to establish an income."

"Calm yourself," Pierre-Joseph would say whenever he encountered such a protest. "Everything's going to be fine."

This was a very old argument between them, and Pierre felt his anger was righteous, not on his own behalf but on Albertine's, our child's, all the future generations of Lafosses, and the people in the village who depended on the estate for work. But I could understand the other side—why *should* the money be Pierre and Albertine's? Just because it had been Pierre I's through Pierre V's, what law said it had to be Pierre VI's? Natural law, Pierre would say, the natural concern of a father for his offspring. But Pierre-Joseph had three children: twice he had only planted the seeds and let his wife do the rest of the work. The other he had formed and raised himself, to his design and specifications. A human child, by comparison, was both ordinary and faulty.

The worst fights Pierre and I ever had were about the garden, about how he couldn't view it with anything other than resentment and I couldn't help loving it at least a little. For his father I felt both affection and deference. Pierre-Joseph was the first person I'd ever met who had done something truly extraordinary. Eric was full of talk, but Pierre-Joseph had done it.

"What do you expect of him, really?" I said. "At this point he could never just stop the work and let it die."

Is there any legacy so fragile? You cannot walk away from a garden like that for even a week. You cannot put it away in an attic and hope someone finds it fifty years after you die and makes you famous. If music had already seemed to me a vulnerable, unlikely way to fashion fame or greatness—dependent as it was upon other people to find it and to play it well and feelingly in front of a crowd who could tell other people about it, who would purchase the sheet music, teach it to their students, and schedule it for their concert seasons—then by comparison a garden was much, much worse.

I wanted to invite Eric to visit. He would see what I saw in the garden, and then some. I imagined it inspiring music as strange and singular as the place itself, the kind of music he said he wanted to write, the kind I'd glimpsed during the terrible show at the Mirliton. I would be doing them both a favor, Eric and Pierre-Joseph, although I couldn't tell either of them. How does one say *immortality* and not sound daft?

But after the "Lou-Lou-Louise" song, my husband wanted even less to do with Eric than he did with the garden. At first I found his chivalry charming, but it came to wear on me. If I could create a whole other being inside me, surely I could choose whether or when I ought to be offended. The embarrassment of the prank paled in light of the song Eric had played beforehand—it was the best thing he'd done, and how frightening it must have been to play it out like that, hoping it would be admired.

When I told Pierre, he said he doubted my brother had ever been frightened of anything in his life.

"You've got him completely wrong," I said. "I'd guess he's terrified at least one-third of the time. May we please invite him? It isn't as though there's any lack of room."

Pierre relented, and to follow etiquette asked Madeleine to write, since it wasn't our house to invite people to. I wished I knew what she'd written, or what Pierre had told her, because all Eric sent back was a very short letter to me: *Don't think I can fit it in. Working on my application for election to the Académie des Beaux-Arts. I'm spelling it Erik now, by the way.*

Annoyed and feeling cheeky, I wrote back an even shorter letter: *Why?*

He wrote back in turn: *Why which? Académie or spelling?*

—*Why either? You'd have better odds running for the National Assembly, and a K looks Scandinavian.*

—*The answer to both: because I want to.*

— *That's your only reason?*

—*You are wasting a lot of stamps.*

—*Well, so are you.*

No reply came. I'd gotten the last word, but it wasn't much of one, so I wrote once more: *I'm going to have a child.*

Instead of a letter I first received a telegram: DIDN'T THINK YOU WERE SERIOUS WHEN I WROTE BUT CONRAD SAYS YOU ARE STOP SORRY STOP CONGRATULATIONS! STOP ERI(C)K

His letter arrived shortly thereafter: *Do you think it will be as insufferable as you?*

Because Pierre wanted to share news of the baby with his family all at once, we waited until Albertine planned a weekend visit with Cannu. I had my doubts about this plan: Albertine was not expecting, as far as we knew, and I worried our announcement might be salt in a wound. Pierre thought there was no wound. That there were ways to prevent conception I understood only vaguely. There was no knowing which of us was right, though personally I would have been in no hurry to bring a tiny Cannu into the world.

When we finally told Pierre's family, they were ecstatic. If Albertine was anything other than pleased for us, she didn't show it. The intensity of their joy took me by surprise. Was this the way a family like theirs welcomed not just a child, but a prospective heir? Or had they worried I'd be somehow deficient? Pierre merely basked in their approval, with uncomplicated satisfaction. He was at odds with his father so often that this change was pleasant to see. *I did this*, I thought. My body was creating the person who was making this possible. What other miracles might I perform?

Albertine invited me out on a walk the next morning. "Just the two of us," she said. "Sisters."

She knew the winding paths through the garden much better than I did, and I was soon lost. She took us to a boat tie-up I couldn't remember having seen before, with a rowboat painted in red and green stripes like a toy.

"Let's row back to the house," she said.

"Is it... seaworthy?"

"I used it all the time as a girl."

This did not fill me confidence, but we managed to get in without soaking our skirts. We each faced toward the middle, our knees nearly touching. The boat rode low but didn't take on water.

"I'll row," Albertine said, grabbing the oars. She promptly rammed us into the bank. "Just give me a moment. I'll remember the hang of it."

I gripped the sides, but she caught on quickly enough, and the boat stopped rocking once she found her rhythm. She pulled us smoothly past stands of palms and a kind of fern that went nearly translucent in sunlight. Neither of us could remember the name of it. She slipped past the Island of the Birds, where the canal branched and narrowed, and the little stone chapel with its stained-glass windows. It was quiet except for the dip of the oars, fluted birdsong, and the whir of insects. The birds and insects were ordinary native species, and I wondered if Pierre-Joseph considered this a flaw in his Eden, that there were sparrows nesting in his tropical plants instead of parrots or macaws.

"We're so pleased Pierre has you," Albertine said. "Really." She added the *Really* after a pause, as if to acknowledge that there were reasons they might have felt differently and both of us were clever enough to know it. I too was a plain sparrow, building a nest in the sequoias.

As the boat passed beneath a low stone footbridge we both lowered our heads and leaned forward, nearly into each other's laps. Albertine brought the oars alongside and I reached up to touch the stone, damp and soft with moss. The mortar felt crumbly, and I wondered if I ought to tell Pierre-Joseph.

"We weren't sure he'd find someone at all, with his health. And then we didn't know if— We're just so excited, that he's doing so much better. Even starting a family."

"His health?"

"We were so worried, by the time he went on leave from the hospital to take the waters in Deauville. The doctors had recommended somewhere farther south, with drier air, but Pierre's so stubborn you take what you can get. As I'm sure you know!"

I lowered my right hand, let the water run through my fingers. I wanted to come up with some wild excuse and run from the conversation, but there was nowhere to go.

"It hardly seems fair. I was always the sickly one, as a child. He caught this on the ward, you know, at that awful hospital. Once he left, he started improving immediately. Anyway—thank you. Not every girl would have said yes."

I couldn't speak, couldn't even catch my breath. I pressed my hand to where the child was growing, still too small to feel, to be anything other than a hope. Just then we rounded a bend into a labyrinth of downed tree branches, and it took all of Albertine's attention to navigate around them. By the time we reached a clear stretch, the stately gray house visible in front of us, I'd composed myself.

"There," she said. "Almost home. And I didn't dump us out once."

I had to consider the source: Albertine routinely made her

headaches sound life-threatening. "What was the original prognosis?" I said. "When the doctor sent him to Deauville? I've wanted to ask Pierre, but he doesn't like to talk about it."

Albertine held the oars out of the water and we floated in place. There was silence except for the birds, which sounded far away now, back where the garden cover was thicker. "Not good," she said finally. "But as I said, there's every reason to think it's all behind him."

I nodded, unable to do or say anything more. I thought of Madeleine, shrieking with horror about bicycles and weather, and of how much I hadn't understood.

"We're just grateful you saw the real him," Albertine said. "All of him, more than just the consumption."

I felt like I'd never seen him at all. And what had he seen when he'd looked at me and lied?

After Albertine and I returned to the house, I pleaded nausea and retreated to my rooms. She sent Cannu for a consult, but he was as relieved to be sent away as I was to send him. Pierre was in Saint-Côme-du-Mont for a rare day of work, consultations the old village doctor had requested; on his parents' insistence he'd taken the carriage, and now I was glad for the protection it offered him from the weather, even though it was a warm day. In the space of half an hour my husband had become both fragile and a liar, and I wanted to swaddle him in cotton wool and dash him against a rock in equal measure.

"I never lied to you. Never," Pierre insisted when he returned to our room.

"How can you say that?"

"I didn't *deny* that I'd been ill."

"How could I have known to *ask*?" I said. "Was I supposed to have a questionnaire?" That seemed like the sort of thing Fortin might have done, and I had a new, terrible thought. "Did you tell my great-uncle? Did he know and keep that from me, too?"

"There was nothing to tell him. Nothing to tell either of you. I was ill, I recovered."

"Consumption isn't—you're not...It can come back."

"So you would have refused me? If you'd known?"

"Of course not."

"Then why does it matter?"

"You should have told me."

"I'm fine. Everything's going to be fine."

"You sound like your father."

I hadn't realized the blow I was landing until Pierre turned bright red. "So you think I'm fooling myself? That's why we should have discussed it? Because you think I'm going to die?"

I shook my head, but his death was all I'd been able to think about. Imagining it, fearing it, wondering what might happen to me and our child without him. I'd assumed we would grow old together, baggy and wrinkled and content. I'd envisioned us on the far side of a lifetime of lovemaking. It embarrassed me, how much I kept thinking of his body, now that I knew it was vulnerable, had been vulnerable since I'd met him. In the weeks before my pregnancy I had not lost my awe of the act itself, the profound strangeness of being touched and entered. The strangeness had a sweetness, but I had looked forward to learning what came after. Now that we might not have more time, I wanted us to have made more of the time we'd had. Frankly I wished we had rutted in every room at Bellenau, in the garden grottoes and the outbuildings, under the trees and on blankets in the park. But that was not who we thought we were. Or that was the couple we thought we had time to later become.

"You're not a doctor. I am, and I'm telling you I'm fine."

He came close and kissed me, hard, as if trying to convince us both. When I didn't stop him, he began to unbutton my dress, as if he'd somehow heard my thoughts, or been thinking the same. He was rather hasty, ungentle, but I didn't say anything, lest he stop altogether. I wanted us both to believe him for as long as we could. He hadn't been laughing at or deliberately deceiving me during our courtship, I decided, just hoping that there was nothing to tell. I tried to trust him, but I couldn't help thinking of all the things I had wanted ferociously as a child, to no avail.

Wednesday afternoons: Alejandro, Jacob, Fleur, Serge, Diego. The only way I can pull it off is that Alejandro and Jacob both live in the same building, and Serge is only one stop farther on the same bus line from Fleur. Alejandro's family has a terrible piano, Alejandro has a terrible ear, not sure why they bother. Jacob's apartment always smells like soup. Fleur's mother is always desperate for chitchat in French, but Serge's parents speak only Russian, so if I've gotten behind and need to make up some time, I can usually exit quickly there. I have no idea what Serge tells them about our lessons, but they pay every week and seem happy enough. The poor child is supposed to be speaking English with me, but the family arrived only six months ago and he's got his head full trying to learn Spanish. It's a service I offer — piano lessons in French, Spanish, or English — but usually I just reply in whatever the child speaks to me. Argentina is a mongrel nation, myself included.

Diego lives out by the Morón Cemetery, and I'm usually running late by the time I arrive. I never want to cut into the time his family has paid for, but then I also hate to cut into their dinner hour. If we don't finish on time his mother seems to feel she has to invite me to stay, and Diego flames with embarrassment, his piano teacher sitting at the family table, worlds colliding. Maybe that's why he keeps his hair so long and falling forward, trying to hide a face that turns red so easily. How he peers through all the hair to see his sheet music and fingers, I don't know.

This week he answers the door himself, and even as the lesson winds down there are no cooking smells, no sign of anyone else in the apartment. The front door opens as he plays the final page of a Clementi sonatina. I've never seen the man who eventually shuffles in, but he looks too much like Diego and his father to be anyone but family. Standing together they're a before-and-after photograph, and I wonder if it is comforting or dismaying to know with such accuracy what will happen to one's face. They all have very round dark eyes, the grandfather's shadowed under eyebrow hairs long enough to tangle. With a comb and a trim he would look kindly, but perhaps that is not how he wants to look. Perhaps as an old man he clings to any ability to intimidate, wherever it comes from. He is tall, and his jacket fits him as if he were once a broader man.

"He sounded all right?" he asks me, and Diego looks up, curious for the answer.

The parents and I don't often discuss the children's progress unless there is either an egregious lack thereof or a great leap that necessitates some decision: additional or longer lessons, or a move to another teacher altogether, one who can drive them harder, challenge them more. I give up the ones who might be great and send them on to someone who can help them become whatever they're meant to become.

"He played well today," I say, although in truth he played indifferently, and it was clear that he had practiced only his songs and not his finger exercises. But he practiced, which is more than some, and I will not betray him to a stranger. I reach down and touch the boy's shoulder and he relaxes a little. I hope it is only his own anxiousness that makes him tense, and that his grandfather is not a taskmaster or an ogre. Diego's shoulder is narrow and bony, as I suppose most boys' shoulders are, but he feels so specific and familiar that I squeeze too hard, as if he is mine and I can hold on to this moment, keep him from slipping away and belonging again to his family.

Mr. Valera sends Diego to the bakery downstairs to break a bill for the lesson fee and tells him to pick up bread for dinner and a treat for dessert while he's at it. At first I'm annoyed by the delay—my own dinner is waiting at the boardinghouse, and Diego seems the kind of child who will agonize over choosing his treat. But once Diego is gone Mr. Valera clears his throat and I realize he's done this on purpose.

"I wanted to let you know that my daughter-in-law isn't well."

"I'm sorry to hear that."

"I'm helping out a bit while she's in the hospital. Not that I'm much of a help. But she's got no family, and my wife's passed."

"Which hospital?" I don't know her well enough to visit, but I have it in mind to send a card.

He pauses, then says, with a guardedness, "Hospicio de las Mercedes."

This is a massive building on the Calle Ramón Carrillo, but it still takes me a moment to place it, as it is referred to less often as a hospital than as an asylum, and less often as an asylum than as *el loquero*, the madhouse.

"I'm sorry. I didn't mean to pry." I shuffle through what I've seen of Diego's mother. Is there something I should have noticed, a madwoman under my nose? But that is uncharitable. I know nothing of her life. Perhaps she has some very excellent reason for running mad and she can tell me later what it was, and whether it's better to fall completely to pieces rather than scraping along. Maybe they can put you back together more solidly then, and you don't have to limp along the rest of your life cracked through. Of course, assuming I ever see Diego's mother again, we probably won't talk about any such thing. We'll nod and she'll hand over my money and we'll exit each other's lives until the next week.

"If you could go easy on the boy, it would be appreciated. His mother can have visitors on the weekends, and he likes to see her, but then that's time lost for schoolwork and practice."

"Of course. I haven't meant to be harsh. I didn't know."

"You haven't been harsh at all, not that Diego's mentioned. I just wanted to get out in front of the thing."

I'm not sure what to say next, and feel relieved when Mr. Valera changes the subject.

"My wife taught singing," he says.

"So you know the business."

"I know I didn't get a hot meal on a weeknight for the first ten years we were married," he says with a scowl.

In the privacy of my own imagination I roll my eyes, then ask, brightly, what changed in the eleventh year.

They finally had the money to hire help, Mr. Valera says, a woman from Extremadura, in Spain, straight off the boat. "All she knew how to do was scorch potatoes, but she trained up all right. We sent her on a cooking course at the French Institute."

"I teach there sometimes."

"Cookery?"

"Lord, no," I say, laughing, although he doesn't know me well enough to know what's funny. I tell him that I'm from France, originally, and teach French-language classes. Was his family from here? I ask.

"Is anybody really from here? My wife and I came over from Spain. Altafulla. On the southern coast, near Tarragona."

"Really? I used to know someone from Tarragona. Not here—back in Paris. More than forty years ago now. Any chance you'd know him?"

"The place wasn't that small," he says. "But what was his name?"

"I—I suppose I don't know what it would have been in Spain," I admit, realizing that I don't. I know only the pseudonyms and pen names that Philippe had settled into by the time I met him. He wore them comfortably, like tailored clothes, without the impression of ungainly false glasses or mustaches.

Mr. Valera crooks an eyebrow. He thought I was only a piano teacher, and now I'm someone who once consorted with people employing aliases. He seems to be wondering what else about me he doesn't know.

*　　*　　*

I wasn't by nature superstitious, but it was as if Albertine naming Pierre's illness had unlocked a Pandora's box, and alongside my humiliation and fear, out flew the sickness itself. Within a month of her departure he started coughing more. Within another he stopped arguing about the horses or haranguing the bicycle company. He pottered in the library and even in the little garden workshop, with its bones and branches and pinned insects. He woke us both coughing every night, and the dark circles under his eyes grew darker. He insisted on moving me to a different room—so that I could get enough sleep for the baby to develop healthily, he claimed. He would say nothing of contagion. He was merely under the weather, he insisted. Just a bit under the weather.

His parents urged him to see a doctor.

"Who?" he said. "The old fart who's been stringing me along? Useless."

It was obvious to everyone that it was a relapse, but this time there was no hospital to blame it on, no city air. We were spooked: if it had followed him here, it could follow him anywhere. But of course it hadn't followed him at all. He'd brought it with him to Bellenau, tucked inside, the way I'd brought our baby. It had been a guest at our wedding, a guest at Fortin's house, a guest at the fireworks. The consumption had already chewed up his lungs, and when its jaws started again to work, his body offered little resistance. There had probably been more damage than they realized before his remission in Deauville, the doctors said, once he finally agreed to see some. Pierre had been right about them being useless. There was little to be done, they said. He'd get better or he wouldn't, and if he got better it would probably be only a matter of time before he got worse again.

I tried not to be angry with Pierre, either for being ill, which was not his fault, or for not having warned me, which was.

Knowing wouldn't have changed anything, I told myself. I wouldn't have refused him. Knowing might have put the same dark veil over him that he had tried to fling over Bellenau, and wasn't it better to have had him as a prince, whisking me off to a happily-ever-after? Yet if I had known, I argued with myself, perhaps I could have better prepared myself.

But there was no preparing for it, not really. Not once Pierre stopped being simply ill and began actively to die. There is no describing it, no metaphor to take refuge in. Picture the garden destroyed, silted up and broken as a man's dissolving lungs. That won't do it. Nor will any music you can listen to capture it. I nursed him until Madeleine grew worried about the strain on the baby and hired a nurse, who kept me at a distance. That was no better. I made myself a maternity apron and washed my husband's blood out of it.

The bicycle finally arrived. I remember that. No one said anything to him, but three days later, out of nowhere, he asked after it.

"Yes," the nurse said, surprised. "It came."

"No," I said. "She's mistaken."

I didn't want him asking to ride it and having to be refused, nor did I want to watch him try to lurch out of bed and discover for himself that he couldn't. I didn't know whether he understood what was happening to him, and I didn't know which would be better, that he understand or that he not. There were so many conversations we should have had, and didn't, because neither of us wanted to name what was happening. Practical words and grand ones, legal wills or our child's future: we replaced them all with silence, with the great unspoken lie that Pierre would somehow recover.

The bargains I offered to God were ugly and desperate: my father's life and Eugénie's, Estelle's and Fortin's. I offered up Eric, said I wished I'd never tended him, never helped him, in whatever small way I had, to turn around on the road Pierre was now traveling. I even offered up Conrad's life, as if it were mine to offer, and not because I thought Pierre was more deserving but because of how lonely I'd been before him, a kind of loneliness I didn't know how to survive again. The only life I didn't offer was my own, which means I also offered the baby. I didn't ask that Pierre be spared long enough to meet his child. It was unthinkable that he wouldn't, that his life could end before the baby's began.

But unthinkable to whom? Only to me. Not to God, who took Pierre in my seventh month of pregnancy, and whom I still have not entirely forgiven. I understand that that is my failing and not His, but then perhaps He should have made my heart larger, or my faith stronger, or simply not snatched back every goddamned thing He ever gave me.

After Diego's lesson, not feeling like making conversation in the boardinghouse dining room, I stopped at the market and took an antisocial little dinner upstairs. I ate two bites and then looked down at the scratched white plate and the hardboiled egg and tinned tuna and bread, and was enraged. It was awful and pathetic and I couldn't breathe. I couldn't breathe. I could jump out the window, but was it high enough? Not quite, not enough to be sure, I'd have to find somewhere taller and I didn't want it that badly. I didn't want it at all, not really. I carried my dinner to the window that overlooked the alley. I opened the sash and stuck my head out, breathed deep. I carefully dropped the quartered egg out the window, piece by piece, and watched the bits disappear in the darkness, only to re-emerge in the orange glow of the sodium streetlights and plop onto the pavement. I was already feeling calmer, but not enough to eat, so I sent the bread and tuna out the window too. Rats would be happy enough to dispose of the evidence.

I hurried to brush my teeth and put on my nightgown while I still felt empty and peaceful. I wanted to go to sleep before my mind could start skipping again like a bad phonograph disk.

The next morning I awoke out of a dream that vanished immediately but ambushed me later in the day as I stood on the bus, headed to the first of that day's lessons. The top handrail was too high for me to grip, and I lurched back and forth as we rounded corners, remembering that Diego's mother had been there outlined by a window frame. In real life I could barely remember what she looked like, but in the dream I knew it was her. I was standing far beneath her, in an orange pool of light from a street lamp. She was looking down at me, and I was supposed to tell her not to do it.

"Go ahead," I said, "jump," and she did.

"We never have to do that again," I told my son. It was the first thing I said to him after he was born.

"True enough," the midwife said. "We're only ever born the once."

But I think she was wrong. Humans are born over and over, as inconstant as caterpillars. A ferry can be a cocoon, a garden an egg. A train car a chrysalis, with a woman emerging from it a wet-winged butterfly.

The second thing I said to the baby was "I'm sorry."

"For what?" the midwife asked.

"I'm not sure," I said, hazy with exhaustion and—not quite pain anymore, by that point, but perhaps shock that there had been so much pain and I had somehow endured it. How had my mother ever steeled herself to do this more than once? "That his father isn't here, I suppose."

"That's hardly your fault. It's just a thing that's happened to you," she said, with the practicality of her profession. "And you'll survive it. You both will."

The baby needed so much, so constantly, that survival became the extent of my ambitions. I looked for his father in every inch, every crease, every expression. But for weeks there were few expressions: even at his most genial, the baby exuded a surly distrust of the world and everything in it. Most of the time he was a crumple-faced meteor of outrage, shrieking his way finally into fits of blank, unconscious sleep. He was not his father's gentlemanly son. He screamed like he was no one's son, like he was a changeling made of furious noise.

Madeleine was thrilled with him. "After what you've been through," she said. "That he turned out healthy. Listen to that racket." She said I'd love him better if I'd consent to receive a little help, at least a night nurse to assist with the wakings.

But I already loved him so much it terrified me. He was mine, and there were so few things I'd ever been able to say that about. I wanted to be his everything, the hands that held him when he woke, day or night.

"You'd *like* him better, if you'd accept help," she amended. "I know you love him."

Becoming a mother had peeled the scabs off my childhood abandonment, and in the hours of darkness, with the baby nursing constantly and sleeping too fitfully in my arms to allow me any sleep myself, I'd begun writing letters. Stupid, angry letters, to people both living and dead, to God, once to the Atlantic Ocean, for reasons that made no sense to me as soon as the sun was up. My father's was the only one I had the nerve to send. I thought there was nothing else he could do to hurt me.

There had been no question that I would name the baby Pierre, as there wouldn't have been even if Pierre was alive, but after he was christened I found that I couldn't say the name aloud, neither about nor to him. "The baby," I called him, to anyone else. To his face I said only "you."

His screaming cleared out a train compartment on the way to the district courthouse. There had to be a hearing, before a justice of the peace, so that I might be assigned guardianship of my own child. If Pierre had survived and I had died in childbirth, the baby would have been his without question. But without Pierre the law would not call the baby mine until the law had approved it. This meant convening a Family Council, composed of the child's nearest of kin on both sides. On Pierre's side stood his parents plus Cannu, given that women other than mothers and grandmothers were ineligible. On the other stood me, Fortin (Estelle had accompanied him from Le Havre but couldn't enter the chamber), and Eric, who had shown up in place of the man who was supposed to be there, Alfred. "He said he didn't want to upset you further," Eric said. "After the letter you sent. I haven't read it. But he said he thought he'd do more harm than good by coming."

"He's such a coward," I said.

Eric shrugged, unwilling or unable to disagree.

The hearing, which would end in a vote, was short but humiliating, consisting of questions the justice put to the Council members: was there any reason to suppose that Pierre was not the natural father of the child? Or that my behavior or morality in any other way disqualified me from motherhood? Could I be trusted to assume both physical guardianship and conservatorship of the child's financial assets? Since the child had no assets, the latter was a simple matter. The grandson of a rich man is still penniless as long as the rich man holds possession of the entire estate. Considering our mutual lack of assets, the justice inquired, could the mother provide the child with the necessities of life?

"She can return to Le Havre," Fortin said. "She and the baby will always have a home there."

"That's . . . terribly kind," Madeleine said, "but we assumed she would stay at Bellenau. It's Pierre's baby."

"It's Louise's baby as well," Fortin said, and it was so strange to hear my name aloud. Who was this person who'd gone and married a dying man and had a baby she couldn't care for? I had nothing: no income and no home and no employable skills. The fact that I had family on both sides brandishing their charity was my only recommendation. In which case why not just give the baby to them, to Madeleine or Fortin, to someone who could care for him better? For a moment I thought of my father not with anger but recognition. Then the baby shifted his weight in my arms, fought a small fist free of the blanket, and I wrapped my arms around him tighter.

"Bellenau," I said. "I'm so grateful, for everyone's help. But as long as we're welcome we'll stay at Bellenau."

"Of course you're welcome," Madeleine whispered. I was too afraid to do more than glance up at Fortin. His face was strange to me. Mixed with his disapproval, which I had seen a thousand times, was hurt.

"Then this seems to me a routine proceeding," the justice said. "The state is not in the habit of snatching nurslings from qualified mothers."

From the way he said it I could tell I was supposed to be flattered. But flattery was fragile: if the law could deem me qualified, it could also deem me unqualified.

"That's not going to happen," Eric said afterward, when I shared my concern. "There's no question you're fit."

"For now. 'A Family Council can be reconvened at any time, by any member,'" I parroted. I hadn't known, until the justice announced it at the end of the hearing, that my guardianship was contingent rather than permanent.

"Any other hearing would go the exact same way," he assured me.

"But there's no guarantee. He's *my* child, and there's still no guarantee."

"I think you've had troubles enough. Do you really need to borrow more?"

He said this gently, and I wanted to believe him more than I wanted to be irate. I'd had enough indignation. I'd been burning up with it, mostly at God but sometimes at Pierre himself, which made me feel terrible, and sometimes at the baby, for all his howling, which felt worse.

After the Council we all traveled back to Bellenau. Lunch was nearly pleasant. It was by far the most company hosted since Pierre had died, and the cook, perhaps pleased to be busy, outdid herself. Eric was too stunned by the surroundings to say anything inappropriate, and Fortin and Cannu conversed with each other instead of boring the rest of the company.

I tried to apologize to Estelle and Fortin, to tell them how grateful I was that they would open their home to me again. Estelle waved a hand dismissively. "Oh pooh. Just look at this place. Of course you should stay." Fortin looked like he had more to say, but swallowed it back: whatever mistake he thought I was making, he would let me make it without a lecture.

After lunch I wanted to show Eric the garden, but Pierre-Joseph said he was feeling poorly—too much rich food, when he'd barely been eating since Pierre's death. He offered to enlist the head gardener for a tour but we refused. I could get us in and out without getting lost, and I didn't think Eric would have the patience for the horticultural details anyway. I left Madeleine and Estelle dandling the baby.

I tried not to watch Eric's face too nakedly as we walked. Did he find the garden as miraculous as I did? Did he find it miraculous in a way he could use? What did inspiration look like, igniting on someone's face? It was February, which I'd somehow forgotten. I'd been almost entirely indoors since September, tending Pierre and then the baby, and still pictured the summer garden. In winter the palms remained green, but little else. Nothing was flowering.

Eric seemed indifferent to everything except the chapel. The door had been left open or blown open, and eddies of leaves had heaped around the legs of the half-dozen pews. Birds had been trapped inside or chosen to nest there, and our arrival startled them into a frenzy. Owing to the cloudy day, the stained-glass windows were subdued. Bright white bird droppings glowed on the floor, the pews, even the altar. The place wouldn't have looked like this if grief hadn't been keeping Pierre-Joseph from his work, and it was sobering how quickly the garden was defiled without him. I had no desire to linger, nor to collect bird droppings on my head or cape, but Eric shuffled to the altar and knelt to pray. Was this for my benefit? Was his solemnity in the garden really a lack of enthusiasm, or the way he thought he was supposed to act, given the cataclysm that had brought him here? Was I supposed to join him at the altar rail? I didn't have it in me, not that day or for a long time afterward. Any prayer I might have made would have been just another angry, unhinged letter. I simply waited for Eric to finish, and after he rose we exited the chapel in silence. I wouldn't have wanted my own prayers questioned, so I didn't say anything, and he didn't offer any explanation.

I was ready to turn us toward home, but he spotted the studio building and asked about it. I hadn't been inside since Pierre had stopped going, and I feared what might be there, whether feral invasion or homely still life, perhaps Pierre's handwriting on unfinished specimen cards. But I decided that entering with Eric would be easier than walking in later alone. I needn't have worried, it turned out—the door was unlocked but tightly closed, and the interior remained undisturbed. Pierre had put everything away neatly, as if he knew he wouldn't be back to continue his work. The skulls had been moved to an upper shelf, replaced by a selection of books that Pierre had either brought from Le Havre or removed from the library in the main house.

"May I?" Eric asked.

I gestured in invitation at the skulls, but he reached for the books, and I gave up predicting what he would or wouldn't find interesting. I stared out the lead-glass windows while he read. My breasts were growing heavy with milk and I said I needed to get back to nurse the baby. Eric nodded distractedly, absorbed in a book full of anatomical sketches of sea life. I had no idea why it was here, sea life being nearly the only kind of life not found in the garden, and I suggested he keep it. I didn't know if the books belonged to Pierre, or Pierre-Joseph, or the estate, or what the difference might be. But I knew I would never read them, not as a scholar or a scientist, and they would only remind me of Pierre. Eric wouldn't read them as a scientist either, but he might be able to make something out of them, and I thought Pierre would like that, his book escaping from this place he'd resented.

When we got back to the house a carriage was already waiting to take Estelle and Fortin to the train station, but Albertine, Cannu, and Eric were all staying until the morning, and we lingered awake together. Albertine told stories about Pierre as a boy, and the baby fell so peacefully asleep in my arms that I was loath to move and risk waking him. Eventually Albertine and Cannu retired.

"You should go to bed as well," I told Eric. "You've got an early train."

"I'll keep you company. I could show you what I'm working on," he said, admiring the fine piano, "but I don't want to wake him."

"When he's this asleep, nothing wakes him," I said. "It should be fine, unless you're planning something Wagnerian."

Eric gave a mock shudder and sat at the piano.

The music was spare but slowly stomping, a march falling asleep on its feet. It was finely filigreed at best and droning at worst. Not at all what I'd expected. I wanted to ask him to play again the piece I'd heard at the Mirliton, but I didn't want to hurt his feelings.

"Shall I play the next one?" he asked. "That was 'Air of the Order.' Then comes 'Air of the Grand-Master' and 'Air of the Grand-Prior.'"

"The Grand-Prior?"

He looked at me, confused. "I really don't ever tell you anything, do I?" He explained that he'd been appointed resident composer for a Rosicrucian religious order led by Sâr Joséphin

Péladan, someone Eric clearly thought I should have heard of, though I hadn't.

Fortin had once ranted that the only thing preventing Rosicrucians from being heretics was that they were firstly fools, so steeped in occult mysticism they were worthier of pity than of excommunication. "Do you believe in the teachings?" I asked. "Or is it just a job?"

"How could I have 'just a job' writing ceremonial music if I didn't believe in the ceremony?"

Perfectly easily, I thought. Even I could say one thing ("Albertine, what a lovely new hat!") and believe another ("Albertine, it looks like a bird fell into a tar pit and died on your head!"). Let alone Eric. But I supposed his lingering prayer in the chapel was explained, and sincere.

"I used the Golden Ratio in planning the development. I got the idea from Claude Debussy, but don't tell anyone."

"Who would I tell? I don't even know who that is."

"I suppose you wouldn't."

"Should I? Is he famous?"

"Not *yet*," Eric said, and I had a glimpse of his life, how he and Claude and their friends lived in the *yet*: not now, but soon. The world was going to come to them, and it would lie down at their feet.

"Are *you* famous yet? Did the Académie des Beaux-Arts select you after all?" I hadn't planned on saying anything like it, but it felt like he'd opened the door on a way to ask, lightheartedly, how Greatness was proceeding.

"The fools turned me down," he said airily. "But Sâr Péladan should be able to open some doors."

"I thought you were composing the music for God."

"The music is an aid to mystic contemplation. If me becoming known means more people will hear it, then I think God will be entirely in favor."

My brother might have joined a cult, but he hadn't surrendered the devotion to his original gods: art and fame and cleverness. I suspected they would win out over the mystics eventually.

"I'm not ignoring it," he said, after a pause. "What's happened. I just don't know what to say."

I rose and sat beside him on the piano bench, although the baby shifted restlessly at the movement. I leaned into Eric's side, and thought about how I hadn't been this near anyone other than the baby since Pierre's death, and wasn't sure when I would be again. Eric didn't lean back into me, but he didn't move away. "There's nothing to say," I said. "But thank you."

"Shall we put the baby on the lid and play a duet?"

"Then he'd definitely wake. Besides, I don't know any duets."

As if he knew we were speaking about him, the baby opened his eyes. There was a moment of breathless stillness, as Eric and I looked down at him, hoping he might fall back asleep. Then, of course, he tugged air into his lungs and screamed.

I waited for the garden to show up in Eric's music, hoped that something good might yet come out of my personal disaster. For the first years I told myself that inspiration must be allowed to take its sweet time; beyond that I assumed the garden hadn't provided any inspiration at all. But then twenty-odd years later, plus the months it took for Conrad to send me a copy, Eric wrote a trio of pieces about sea creatures, titled with their scientific names, introduced with made-up facts and false descriptions. Beneath the lines of music there were little exhortations supposedly from the crustaceans themselves: *It was a really pretty boulder! Nice and sticky!* or *I have no tobacco. Good thing I don't smoke.*

The pieces were collages, with phrases shamelessly lifted from Chopin and music-hall numbers, not particularly crustacean-like, but twirling like sea foam in a shallow tidal pool. Conrad thought they were some of Eric's best work, and I tried to hear them that way—to separate them from the page of biological sketches I'd seen him admire in the book of Pierre's that I'd given him. If I hadn't known where the seed had come from, maybe I could have heard the humor or delight. But for me the pieces were muffled in the circumstances of their making, and all I could think was that he'd picked through the wreckage of my life and made of it only these three little cartoons. Why had I thought I could show a composer something and dictate what he made of it? Was I angry because the pieces were funny, or because they were so *small*? Did I want to think my life was an opera, a symphony?

One of the great lies of tragedy is that it means more than comedy, when its greatest lie is that it means anything at all.

Philippe

— 9 —

Haggard in your body

COPYEDITS TO TWO SEPARATE TRAVEL GUIDES (MUSEUMS OF Madrid; walking routes of Catalonia) were due by the end of the week, but Erik wouldn't leave him alone about *Uspud,* for which he was demanding a final act so that he could offer it to Tomaschet for a slot in the shadow theater the following month.

"I have no idea how it ends," Erik groused. When Philippe promised he'd get it to him in a week, Erik insisted that wasn't nearly enough time.

"You always do everything at the last minute anyway," Philippe said. "I know you."

"If I'd realized you were going to get so boring, I'd never have sent you to wait in line at the Mirliton."

Given how the night had gone, Erik had multiple reasons to rue that particular plan. But Philippe's launch into occasional paid employment had been, oddly, the most enduring of Erik's complaints. Philippe had met more money in front of the Mirliton than he'd met in Paris in the previous four years combined. Standing there in his semi-decent shared suit, apparently a man who could afford Saturday night at the Mirliton, he looked the part of someone to whom the money might deign to talk. The money asked him to hold a spot so it could run to the tobacconist's down the street, and then the money passed him a cigarette. The money asked him what he did. A writer, he said, since that sounded marginally more respectable than "a poet." The money asked him where he was from. Did he do any translation work? Some of the money worked for a publishing house that was partnering with a Spanish press to translate a series of travel guides. Absolutely, Philippe said. He did translation work. He did any kind of work. Well, in that case, other money that edited a political journal chimed in, perhaps Philippe would like to query sometime, an outsider's perspective on French affairs? The other money's wife even read poetry, and she and Philippe chatted about Mallarmé.

Philippe had run into the nearly-as-famous Verlaine a few weeks earlier but didn't know if the man was considered too disreputable to bring up in polite society, whatever his past renown. They had literally run into each other, as Verlaine was drunk and head-butting people at the Café François I for no apparent reason. Verlaine had a famous head, stupendously round and hairless, with a cramped little face, and in the end Philippe couldn't resist recounting the way it had smashed into his skinny midsection. The story was a hit—a relief—either because the crowd saw itself as too fashionable to be scandalized or because Verlaine had passed beyond mere scandal into legend.

When Philippe contacted the travel publisher the very next day, he'd tried not to assume the man would remember him. But the response came right away: *Of course I remember you. How many people do I meet who've been head-butted by Verlaine?* Then the publisher offered several hundred pages of translation work, paid by the page.

Had he been doing Paris wrong this entire time? Philippe wondered aloud later, sitting at a celebratory meal with Erik and a couple of other friends. He didn't regret his single-minded march across the city into the chaotic embrace of the Chat Noir. And drinking in the same café where Verlaine was slowly killing himself was what had clinched his good fortune. But where had

194

all *these* people been? How had he never spoken with them until the Mirliton?

"You weren't looking for them, and your clothes were too awful," Erik answered, though Philippe had been posing the question only rhetorically. "So you managed to meet a bunch of boring people, and they offered you boring work. Why are we celebrating?"

Philippe had invited Erik and their friends Alphonse and Narcisse out to dinner and offered to pay, in honor of the simple fact that he was capable of paying. A language textbook for which he'd helped to write exercises the previous year was going to have a second edition. They were at the Taverne du Coq d'Or, on the Rue Montmartre, where the food was good enough that respectable people came to eat it. Philippe was wearing the shared suit plus decent black shoes he'd bought with his first paycheck, and was feeling nearly as if he belonged.

But Erik wouldn't stop complaining about the food, a prix fixe menu where every course was apparently something he hated. "Snails? Eating them is like chewing pencil erasers. No one really likes snails."

Philippe didn't care for snails himself, but he didn't understand why Erik was being quite so petulant. He kept needling the table, then the tables next to them, about snails. Was any creature fouler? If snails were fit food for humans, why not eat bees? Earthworms? Why not dogs and cats? They both had to be tastier than snails, yes?

"No!" someone at another table shouted. "No, they're not!"

The tables were very close together. Everywhere in Paris the tables were close together, and the chairs, and the plates and the bowls, and Philippe was always getting jabbed by somebody's elbows.

"An expert!" Erik shouted. "We've found an expert!"

"Why don't you shut up?" The man was older than most of the dinner crowd, not really old, but of their parents' generation.

He had steely hair and crow's-feet around his eyes, deep furrows in his forehead and around his mouth, a nearly worn-through handsomeness. He was alone at his table and didn't look as if he was expecting anyone else. He looked like he was done expecting anything or anybody.

"I'm just chatting with my friends here," Erik said. "Sorry if we've disturbed your dull supper."

Rather than the prix fixe, the man had a carafe of wine and a single serving of fish in front of him, nearly demolished, with a pile of pinbones heaped at the side of the plate. He picked one up and bent it between his thumb and forefinger. "You chat very loudly."

"We'll keep it down," Philippe said.

"We'll keep *him* down," Alphonse said.

Erik's response was to climb on top of his chair. This would play just fine after midnight at the Chat Noir or the Auberge, or a dozen other places, but dinner hour at the Coq d'Or?

Philippe didn't want to get kicked out, at least until the cheese course. After that, maybe. But he was very much looking forward to good cheese. "This isn't a show," he hissed. "It's just dinner."

"It's always a show," Erik hissed back in an incredibly loud stage whisper meant to be heard by both their table and the curmudgeon next to them.

"You should listen to your friends," the older man said.

"You should enlighten us on the subject of dogs and cats," Erik said.

"What about them?" the man asked.

"Between snails, dogs, and cats, which would you eat?"

"Are we considering personality, or purely taste?" Narcisse jumped in. "Because I'd rather kill a snail than a dog any day."

"Speaking only to taste, dog's the one you want," the man said. "Tastes like mutton. Cat's dry. Like sucking on a wire."

Alphonse, several years older than the others, shifted uncomfortably, with recognition, and touched Erik's elbow.

Erik didn't notice. "A taste for the exotic, eh? What else have you eaten? Can you enlighten us on giraffes?"

"You'd have to find someone richer," the man said. "The zoo meat was too dear. The rest of us ate whatever we could. Sawdust bread and rats, when we could get them."

"The siege," Alphonse said.

"You are such fucking *children*," the man spat. "All of you." He considered the fish bone, laid it back down, picked up another.

"Yet you've come here to drink with us," Erik said. This would have been reasonably accurate at the Chat Noir, but most people ate at the Coq d'Or for the food, not the atmosphere.

"I come here and wonder if my boy would have ended up like you. I try to decide which is worse—to think that he would have, or that he would have been a better man than the whole worthless lot of you. And yet here you all are instead."

"I'm sorry about your son," Alphonse said, giving Philippe a plaintive look, a plea for help.

Good Lord, Philippe thought: *I'm* the second most responsible person at this table? "Please," he told Erik, who was squatting on his chair seat, chastened into no longer standing but not ready to sit back down. "Please don't get us kicked out before the cheese comes."

Alphonse appeared unimpressed with this reasoning, but Erik sat back down.

The older man gulped the last of his wine directly from the carafe, then banged it back down on the table. Philippe wondered if he had watched his son starve to death, or lost him to the shelling, or the street violence afterward. The man sucked one of the fish bones clean, put it in his jacket pocket, and patted it. He took his strange souvenir and left. Philippe, along with the others, slowly let out his breath. He felt shame, but also annoyance at having been made to feel shame, a grievance that seemed to be shared around the table.

Narcisse was first to recover. "It's settled, then. Dogs win on taste, but cats or snails on lesser personality. So it's really a question of the heart versus the stomach."

"That's the only choice there ever is," Erik said sourly. "The heart or the stomach." He glared at Philippe, an accusation.

Philippe pictured himself as a giant walking stomach squirting acids, an image both unpleasant and, he thought, undeserved. He rejected the premise: why did there have to be a choice? This was one more of Erik's aphorisms that sounded less wise the longer you actually thought about it.

"This one's true," Erik responded when Philippe tried to argue. "You just wish it weren't."

When the cheese course came, the waiter was very proud of the Livarot, a regional specialty brought in from Normandy, and Erik and Alphonse toasted to it. Philippe found it toxically smelly, like a dead animal pulled from the insides of a cow.

"Look," Erik said, "if you can't get me the full libretto for *Uspud*, at least tell me what happens at the end so I can sketch it out."

"He dies. Everyone dies."

"Is that really what happens, or are you foisting me off?"

"That's the way everything ends, if you wait long enough."

Erik rolled his eyes. "If I could afford to pay you by the page I bet I'd have it by now."

"I bet you would," Philippe agreed.

"How about I just finish it myself?"

Philippe could tell this was meant to shock him into possessiveness. But the prospect didn't alarm him. It didn't make him feel anything. He had only vague memories of dreaming up long lists of fictional saints and gruesome deaths very late one night at the Auberge as they sorted through the pile of leftover puppets from *The Temptation of Saint Anthony* that hadn't already been mutilated for use in *Pierrot Pornographe*. He didn't feel any more loyal to *Uspud* than he did to the travel guides or political analyses or the language textbook. It was neither a chef d'oeuvre nor his heart's desire. What was the last project he'd really loved? Certainly not *Pierrot Pornographe*, although it had debuted to a certain kind of acclaim.

His siege play, he realized, and his face burned, thinking of the man at the next table. Tomaschet had been right all along. Just as well Philippe hadn't managed to finish it. "Go ahead," Philippe said. "You're welcome to end *Uspud*."

Erik sullenly ate through the rest of the cheese.

As they left the restaurant, Philippe caught sight of the fish-bone man. He hadn't left, just moved to the bar area, where he was bent heavily over another carafe of wine, now empty. Philippe shooed his friends on and stayed behind. The bar had the same mixed clientele as the main dining room, bohemians and businessmen, though with more single women. Or at least unaccompanied women. No way of knowing who was genuinely single.

Philippe sat at the bar, next to the man, and ordered two glasses of wine. "For you," he said, sliding one over on the marble counter. "I wanted to apologize. For my friends," he added, cowardly, because although he hadn't said anything offensive in the restaurant, his shadow play, if he had finished it, would have been worse than anything Erik or Narcisse had said.

The man slid the glass back without drinking.

"I'd like you to have it," Philippe insisted.

The man took the little fish bone out of his pocket and pushed it under his left thumbnail, as if he was scraping dirt. The nail was clean, but the man kept pushing. "You want me to tell you I was wrong about you."

"I don't want anything."

"I don't have it in me, all right? I don't know you from Adam, and I don't have it in me tonight."

"I was sitting here," a girl said, from behind them. "If you don't mind. I just slipped out for a moment. That's my shawl on the peg."

Philippe slid off the stool with relief. She was dark-haired and very young, with an accent he couldn't place. Short, only up to his shoulders, until she climbed onto the seat and looked him directly in the face.

"This yours?" she said, of the wineglass.

"You can have it."

She eyed it suspiciously.

"It just arrived," Philippe said. "He can tell you."

He gestured at the man, who was standing now, buttoning his jacket.

The man nodded to Philippe and the girl, a stiff farewell. "I'm going to leave you two to it," he said.

Philippe and the girl looked at each other, and Philippe wondered if she was as perplexed as he was by what "it" they were meant to be getting to. The girl shrugged and Philippe sat down. Along with the untouched wine, the man had left the fish bone, its tip pink with blood.

She turned out to be from Gipuzkoa, Basque country, which explained the accent. They switched to Spanish, which she knew much better than French, although Philippe, with a mixture of fascination and alarm, found himself stumbling over phrases, groping for words that came to him first in French. Five years. Was that how little time it took for his old self to disappear? Could his family tell, even through his short, uninformative notes, how his grasp on his own language had loosened? No wonder their disappointment in him was undimmed. His freelance work had been enough to keep him clothed and fed, but he still lived close to the bone. The little money he'd sent back had not impressed them.

Philippe and the girl—Alazne—commiserated about this, about their families back home, the unreasonable expectations, the uncertainty as to what "home" meant anymore. He bought them more rounds of drinks, after which she suggested they go together to her room.

So easy? But so little else had been. Philippe had earned something easy, he thought, a night with a girl who fancied him, and didn't bother to make a show of waiting, didn't bother with questions about the future. Didn't bother about the future at all. The sex itself was easy, Alazne reading him so well he knew he would once have been discomfited with her apparent experience. But why? What good did keeping girls in the dark do for anybody? All hail Montmartre, where a girl could learn what a man liked without being married to him.

The sex was not tender, exactly, but it did not feel transactional, so he was confused and a bit hurt when she began to dress immediately afterward. Confusion that turned to horror when she asked him for payment. He had not understood that this would happen, had thought the interest, and the pleasure, were mutual. He burned with shame, both for the misunderstanding and for the fact that he had no money to give her. He'd brought enough cash to pay for the dinner and had planned to go home straight afterward. He'd barely had enough left for their drinks at the bar.

Alazne glared at him with a contempt that tipped over into rage. He could tell she didn't believe him and thought he'd deliberately cheated her. She slapped him, then cowered, and he saw in her eyes a blunt appraisal of her odds. Could she hurt him worse than he was capable of hurting her? No, she would not make that wager.

A door slid shut across her eyes. "Get out," she said.

Upon realizing the misunderstanding, he'd wanted to make arrangements to send the money to her somehow—he was a fool but not a cheat—yet once she was afraid of him all he could think of was to get out of the room as quickly as possible. Not to spare Alazne her fear, but so he could stop being a man that a woman was afraid of.

He replayed their flirtation at the Coq d'Or over and over, trying to figure out how he was supposed to have known. Montmartre prided itself on being a place where all the usual rules were suspended, but Philippe could see how a few more rules would be useful. When nobody was respectable, how did one tell the free spirits from the working girls? She'd thought he was a bourgeois, working for a publisher, an immigrant made good. Would she have seen him differently if she'd known he was a poet? Sure, Philippe thought: she would never have willingly taken him to bed.

Of course he tried to write a poem about it. But he was so ashamed of what had happened in her room that he could barely stand to think about it, much less write about it. The poem he came up with was nothing but an opaque blur of abstractions. All scrim, all puppets, no flame.

He wrote another postcard to Miguel, who had not written him back a second time. He felt as if he were waiting for lightning, standing in a clear field and willing the wind to rise. *I met Verlaine,* he wrote. *He says his current project is a series of essays about "cursed poets." He means the tortures of genius, but perhaps I can still qualify via gross incompetence.*

This time Miguel bit: *Verlaine? Have him sign something for me. (Though if you're really that miserable, why not leave?)*

One afternoon Erik finally invited Philippe to join him and Claude at the Librairie de l'Art Indépendant. The Librairie was both a bookshop and a boutique publisher specializing in elegantly produced books by obscure poets and foreign writers. Philippe had had his eye on the place since moving to Paris, although the longer he went without his work appearing on its shelves or in its catalog, the wider the berth he'd given it, until he sometimes avoided the street entirely. But the chance to meet Claude, whom he'd heard so much about, lured him past the elegant wooden tables piled with books for sale and into a plush seating area where the owner held salons and invited select artists to linger and work.

Claude turned out to be a mop of dark hair and a rather elfin beard, with no hint of competition or possessiveness over Erik. He was friendly and self-assured, and according to Erik did very well with the ladies. Claude had bedded a married woman when he was only sixteen, Erik had once confided, and was currently living with the pretty daughter of a tailor without having bothered to propose.

"So the two of you aren't...?" Philippe had trailed off.

"Aren't what?" Erik said, and if his innocence was a con it was perfect, without cracks or clues.

"Never mind," Philippe said. Erik's heart remained as mysterious to him as ever.

At the Librairie de l'Art Indépendant, Erik introduced Philippe as "an occasional poet."

"As in, you write poems for special occasions," Claude said, "or you write only occasionally?"

"Neither's true," Philippe said. "But I assume he meant the second."

"It is true," Erik said.

"I write all the time."

"The first is a rather good idea, though," Erik said. "Poet for Special Occasions. I should take an ad out in the papers."

Likely no one who would hire a poet out of a café paper would have the money to pay one, but otherwise it wasn't a bad idea. Erik was writing nearly as much as Philippe did these days, humor columns and treatises on music that might or might not be meant as humor pieces. He'd broken with the Rosicrucians and gotten so much attention for his scathing open letters to Sâr Péladan that Philippe wondered if that hadn't been the plan all along. Erik's primary complaint, rather than anything about the group's mystical beliefs, seemed to be that Péladan hadn't given his compositions enough attention.

Whatever his complaint with Péladan, most of Erik's new pieces still had the sound of his Rosicrucian ceremonial music:

spare, slow, everything played at the same volume. Philippe found himself longing for a story—for a dramatic, swelling crescendo, a dewy-eyed melody, or the palpable melancholy of the *Gymnopédies* as some clue to what he was supposed to feel, or as a prompt to feel anything at all.

His current, half-finished libretto for *Uspud* was overcompensating. If Erik wanted to explore what happened when music and words were at odds with each other, well, Philippe could certainly play along. Shadow plays often used spoken narration, and he'd filled the slow silences in Erik's score with gore and mayhem. It was hard to top the travails of actual Catholic saints, but he'd invented some saints of his own, then obliterated them one by one. Of course Uspud was meant to die at the end—had Erik even needed to ask? Uspud was the only character standing after the second act, a lamb to the slaughter.

Listening to Claude and Erik talk about music, Philippe was lost within minutes. He thought of Erik's face the one time he'd ever heard Philippe speak anything other than French, to a Catalan dancer they'd run into at the Moulin Rouge. "You turned into somebody else," Erik had said. "I looked for you but you were gone." With Claude, Erik became somebody Philippe only partially recognized. Both of the composers blossomed in the easy conversation. Claude had won the Prix de Rome several years earlier, making him permanently suspicious in certain quarters of Montmartre. Surely one of the Conservatory's golden boys couldn't also be one of their own tribe. Why not? said Erik, whose own dismal time at the Conservatory had been forgiven. Why not, when Claude made music like this?

Claude played a work in progress for them, asking for feedback, but the piece sounded finished to Philippe. It was pretty in the way some of Erik's music was, but denser, shimmering. He thought of the paintings that looked simply like a landscape from ten paces, but once you got up close the blue of a river or the green of a field was made up of ten other colors and a thousand individual brushstrokes, a disorienting dazzle of lines that both did and did not fit together. Claude's music made Erik's sound like line drawings or prints. Still pretty, but the same saturated blue all the way across the page.

Claude asked Philippe for recommendations of poems to set to music. Philippe knew Claude had already done Baudelaire, because he'd dedicated a copy of the suite of five poems to Erik, who'd shown it around to everyone, as giddy as a boy with a long-desired birthday gift.

Philippe suggested Verlaine. His second book, *Fêtes Galantes,* rather than anything newer.

"Why didn't you recommend yourself?" Erik asked him later, after Claude had left to go home to his not-wife. "You should've offered him your own poems."

It hadn't even occurred to Philippe. "If he'd been interested in my work he could have asked. It would have been pushy to bring it up myself."

"So push! No wonder you aren't getting anywhere." When he got no rejoinder but an aggrieved stare, Erik mentioned that he'd finished *Uspud* but that Salis and Tomaschet hadn't gone for it.

"That's too bad," Philippe said, and meant it, but the last five years had been such a constant stream of rejection that this one didn't even dent him.

When Erik said he'd asked the Paris Opéra for a meeting, Philippe thought he was joking, but Erik insisted he'd demanded an audience with Director Bertrand.

"But it was written for puppets. It was never a ballet."

"Dancers can't be that different. I told the director if he refuses to meet I'll report him to the Minister for Education for failure to foster new work. We're never going to get ahead of Germany if the only music anyone gets to hear is a century old. At least. And sung in Italian." Erik thumped the piano self-importantly.

Maybe Erik had managed to do the impossible and transform

Uspud into a brilliant full-length ballet. Or it was still the violent, semi-incoherent shadow play that Philippe remembered.

Since there was no way the director of the Paris Opéra would look at it either way, Philippe supposed it didn't really matter.

Two weeks later Erik was pounding on Philippe's apartment door in the middle of the night. After subbing at the Divan Japonais, Erik explained, he'd arrived home to find a note from Director Bertrand. They had an appointment! It had taken threats, but finally something had worked!

The mention of a threat jerked Philippe fully awake.

"A duel's not a proper threat, really," Erik reassured him. "Especially since I don't know how to duel. Not that he's likely to know how either, the coward, but it's just as well he didn't take me up on it."

"You challenged the director of the Paris Opéra to a *duel* because he wouldn't look at your score?"

"Our score. You could be more grateful."

"I could be deported."

"I did everything on the up-and-up. If he wanted to have me arrested, he'd already have done so. You're wasting time. Our audience with him is first thing in the morning. So, six hours."

"We can't show him *that*." Philippe pointed at the score stuffed under Erik's arm. It was a battered sheaf of papers covered in corrections in both pencil and pen, strike-throughs and arrows and rearrangements. The libretto and the music alike were barely legible. To Bertrand it would resemble a madman's scribblings.

"We're going to recopy it," Erik said. "I've brought fresh paper."

But he hadn't brought any light. And how could they both work on Philippe's single small table when he had only one chair? (Although he'd moved to a marginally better room in the same building, he still didn't spend enough time there to justify furniture.) Together they dragged the table over to the bed, where Philippe sat, trying to write from an uncomfortably low level, his elbows cocked, while Erik took the chair. A café would have been more comfortable than this cramped table by candle-light, but it was so late that even the Butte was asleep.

Philippe forced his attention to the blank sheets of heavy, crisp, cream-colored paper. Erik had beautiful handwriting and serious taste in stationery, and Philippe didn't want to let him down. The copying went more quickly than he'd expected—in addition to being gorier than he'd remembered, *Uspud* was much shorter. Nowhere close to a full-length ballet. Bertrand wouldn't even have to open the folder to know they were frauds; he'd see the skinny stack of paper and roll his eyes.

Erik was writing furiously on staff paper. Philippe still didn't really read music, but he didn't see how the tower of treble lines could be correct.

"I'm orchestrating," Erik explained.

"Now?"

"Only for harp, strings, and flute. There's time."

Philippe looked where Erik was pointing for the flute line. He was pretty sure a flute could make only one sound at a time, not the several simultaneous notes on the page. His stomach hurt. Then he remembered that he didn't know how Erik had chosen to end the play.

He flipped to the back of the libretto. Uspud did indeed die, but not before tearing a basket of puppies apart with his bare hands and watering the ground with their blood. Presumably the puppies were meant to be disguised demons and not actual pup-pies? Then another pack of demons in monstrous form—dogs stitched to fish stitched to bird wings stitched to bull heads, snorting fire through their nostrils—took their revenge and tore Uspud limb from limb. It was disgusting and unstageable but not, Philippe saw as he read the whole thing backward, any more so than the rest of the play. Even Uspud's Act II conversion was symbolized by a woman taking out a knife and stabbing him through the heart: the Holy Spirit penetrates. The whole thing was ridiculous, and copying it out cleanly on expensive paper just made it look worse, too sincere and self-important to be passed off as a joke.

"What are you doing?" Erik said. "There's no time for new text. Copy!"

"I have to fix the puppies. The puppies at least. I'm drafting out a new third act and then I'll copy it all down neatly."

"I like the puppies. You said I could finish it."

"What is *this*? 'It rains blood, severed heads, and shreds of burnt flesh, for a very long time.' How is the Opéra supposed to stage that? How were *we* ever going to stage it, even for shadow theater?"

"Why are you worrying about this *now*?"

"Because someone else is going to see it!"

A lot of people had seen it already, Erik assured Philippe. He'd done play-throughs for both Salis and Tomaschet, with Narcisse reading the narration aloud. Philippe was not assured. Narcisse and Salis and whoever else had been hanging around on an off night had seen stranger things—perhaps not bloodier, but stranger—and they would have recognized the piece for the bit of frippery that it was. Putting this in front of Bertrand, however, would imply they believed in its alchemy, that their game had magically turned into a ballet, and that this was the best they could do.

"Honestly?" Philippe said carefully. "The third act as it reads right now is ridiculous."

"Honestly? It's no worse than the first two."

They looked at each other in the dim light of the candle. Philippe didn't disagree, but still felt as if Erik had punched him. If he thought the whole play was ridiculous, why challenge Bertrand to a duel just to show it to him?

So he could say he'd challenged Bertrand to a duel, of course.

The third act didn't matter because *this* was the fourth act, Erik's threat of violence against the Paris establishment, with Philippe his unwilling second. But how far did Erik plan to take it?

"You don't own a gun, do you?" Philippe asked, the edge of worry plain in his voice.

"Of course not. You mean for the duel? I suppose I pictured us with swords."

"You own a sword?"

Erik admitted he did not.

"You were going to—what?—poke him with a walking stick?"

"We've got an appointment with him, so it's moot. Nobody has to be stabbed."

Just humiliated, Philippe thought. They'd all live to see another day, but they'd have to leave their careers for dead on the steps of the Palais Garnier.

"I thought your 'career' was translating travel guides."

"That's not fair." Was this whole stunt meant to punish him? Philippe wondered. But what for?

He recopied the libretto, with some judicious edits to the third act, aware even as he made them that he was touching up the paint on a burning building. Erik was still working when Philippe finished. He felt guilty for stopping, but realistically there was nothing else for him to do, and he crawled into bed for an hour.

Erik woke him, looking as though he hadn't slept at all. It wasn't a long walk to the Palais Garnier, half an hour along the Rue des Martyrs, and Philippe wished it were longer. It took them forever to find the side business entrance, and the golden angels and white columns at the front seemed to mock them every time they circled the building without success.

"The siege of the Opéra," Erik said, and Philippe winced. "We're testing for a break in the walls."

They finally found an unlocked door and asked the man in the nearest office for directions to Director Bertrand's office.

"I know he's expecting you," the man said, and smirked.

Bertrand's secretary showed them into a room with groaning shelves and a massive desk covered in stacks of correspondence, bound scores, and piles of loose paper. Philippe realized he'd been expecting a stage set of an office, some gentleman's velvety redoubt. Bertrand might not have been promoting French youth, but clearly he didn't spend all day sipping wine and cackling about wrecking their hopes, either. This was a real office, for a real person with a real job. Philippe wondered what it would be like to have one.

Bertrand's gaze flicked over them, perhaps checking for weapons. "Gentlemen," he said. "My apologies that you had to ask so . . . strenuously for an appointment. I'd written you earlier, but apparently my first letter went to the wrong address. It just came back to me yesterday."

"Oh," Erik said, already deflating.

"Now—you said you had a ballet you wanted me to look at?"

Bertrand cleared a channel in the middle of his desk, sat down, and gestured at two chairs. Philippe sat but Erik hovered, clutching the score to his chest. Were his fingers shaking a bit as he finally lowered himself into the chair and put the music down on the desk?

When Bertrand reached for it, Erik laid his hands flat on top of the folder. "Just to warn you," he interjected. Followed by nothing.

"Yes?" Bertrand asked, still leaning forward.

"This work is not for the masses. In fact, we can say with great confidence that this will make no money at all."

Bertrand leaned back in his chair. "While of course we have staged some challenging material, I can't say I've ever knowingly programmed a work that can't pay for itself."

"It's not only a matter of not paying for itself," Erik amended. "This will almost certainly lose you a great deal of money."

Bertrand glanced at Philippe, who kept his face blank and serious. Bertrand appeared to suppress a small smile. If this was the game Erik wanted to play, his air suggested, it was an easy one for Bertrand to go along with. "Why is that?"

"The needs of this particular show are extravagant," Erik said, stumbling over the word "show," aware that it was wrong as soon as he'd said it. "Ballet," he corrected. "This ballet requires formidable stagecraft."

"Then there is of course no company in the country better qualified to stage it than we." Bertrand reached again for the score, and Erik pulled it back toward himself.

"Yes, but we are also unwilling to give up artistic control of such a masterpiece. We would demand final say over everything: casting, costumes, scenery. I would conduct the orchestra myself."

"That, gentlemen, is an absolute impossibility. As I'm sure you know."

Philippe could have sworn the man winked at them, but it happened too quickly for him to be sure.

"Well, if you are going to be so totally unreasonable," Erik said, "I suppose we have no reason to take up more of your time."

"And I wouldn't want to take up more of yours. But if you arrive at a more conventional proposition, please feel free to try me again."

"Do you mean that?" Erik asked without bluster, with a hopefulness so naked it made Philippe uncomfortable.

Bertand was agreeable and seemingly sincere, although he recommended against further threats of violence. He walked them as far as his secretary's outer door and shook their hands gravely.

Philippe felt both mocked and relieved. They got lost in a warren of hallways trying to find the exit and crossed paths with dancers arriving for a rehearsal. The dancers were in street clothes, but too lean and graceful to be anything else.

Try to enjoy this, Philippe told himself, *because this is as close as you are ever going to get to premiering a work at the Paris*

Opéra. He couldn't decide what if anything to say to Erik once they finally made it outside and beyond earshot of any Opéra employees, but Erik spoke first, as if knowing exactly what Philippe was thinking.

"We couldn't leave it there. He might really read it."

The obvious next question was why spend all night copying it out if they weren't going to show it to anybody, but Philippe could guess the answer. He knew how it felt to read back over something you'd cared about and see it all gone to ashes, to rags and blood and fart jokes. Or worse, to see that the idea was still sound and that it was one's words that were lacking. He wondered what kind of dark night of the soul Erik had endured while Philippe had taken his hour of sleep.

"Don't laugh, but I might need Bertrand someday. And you can't tell anyone I said that."

"I won't."

"Definitely not Salis. Or Tinchant. Or Narcisse. Or—anyone, really. Absolutely not my stepmother."

"Your stepmother thinks I'm a thief, remember? We don't chat."

Erik gave him a quizzical glance that suggested he did not in fact remember. "It might have turned out all right for you, showing him, but I couldn't chance it."

"What do you mean, 'all right for me'?"

"Oh, you know."

"I don't." But he could narrow it down to two possibilities. There was Erik's opinion of Philippe's distractedness, the way he thought a foot in the door of travel publishing was a foot out the door of Art. And there was the possibility that Erik had come to believe Philippe had never had any business inside the door of Art at all. He'd shown Erik hundreds of lines by now, and the only words his friend had ever wanted were for cheap love songs, shadow plays, or jokes.

"I'm going to miss you," Erik said.

"I'm not going anywhere."

"Yes you are. Maybe I am too. I'm not sure."

"We'd still be friends. Even if I quit the shadow theater."

"I suppose," Erik said, in a voice that lacked all conviction. Clearly not wanting to talk anymore, he started humming with gusto.

Philippe recognized the song Claude had played, the work in progress. He tried to join in, but couldn't remember it well enough, not the way Erik apparently did. The music darted ahead of him like a fish, glittering beyond his reach. Was that why he hadn't suggested his own poetry to Claude? Because he could hear how far beyond him the music was? Existing in a whole different element, when all he could breathe was air?

He mourned the person he'd been when he'd offered his poems to Erik, blissfully unaware of any possible divergence between the two of them, in either sensibility or ability No, he corrected himself, remembering. He hadn't offered his poems to Erik. Erik had asked for his work. It was Erik who with that invitation had either overestimated Philippe or underestimated himself. Maybe the sooner Philippe quit the shadow theater, the sooner he'd be setting Erik free.

Erik paused in his humming. "You can keep the suit."

Philippe thanked him.

"It always looked better on you," Erik said.

"Liar."

Suzanne

— 10 —

From the top of yourself

SUZANNE WAS WEARING A CORSAGE OF CARROTS. SHE'D bought them that morning, washed them clean in a Wallace fountain in the Place Émile-Goudeau, tied the three ends together with a ribbon, and pinned the bow above her heart. Now, nearing midnight, the shorn yellow stubs of the carrot tops had begun to shed, falling and sticking to her dress. Adrien, the only one of her crowd still left at the table, reached to pick them off her. She was comfortable with most of her old lovers this way. They continued hiring her for modeling jobs, continued painting her unlaced with her hair down, and sometimes that led to something more, and sometimes it didn't.

The orange of the carrots was bright in the sooty cabaret. With wood so expensive in the city, most winter fires burned foully from bricks of compressed coal dust. There was none of the cheerful crackle she still remembered from her childhood village. She hadn't returned since her mother had brought her to Paris, hoping for more lucrative work than her position as a linen maid in Bessines-sur-Gartempe. Her mother had failed utterly at this mission, but Suzanne had eventually been hired by a circus. She loved that she could tell people that she'd joined a circus and it would always be true.

"The only thing more fun than a good lie," the ringmaster had once told her, "is a truth so fantastic people assume you're lying." She hadn't been sure this was true, or even what it meant, but she'd nodded along. Her most vivid memory of him was of how stiffly he waxed his mustache. She still remembered that poke of little sword points of hair on her cheeks, her hands, her stomach, her thighs. She'd been fifteen years old.

Only later, after a career-ending fall from the trapeze, after the ringmaster had started spending nights with one of the high-wire girls, did she start to understand how he might be right about the most delicious lies being the true ones. The truths of her childhood had ranged from the ordinary to the embarrassing (charwoman mother; absent father; jobs as a dishwasher, seamstress, fruit seller, and factory worker weaving funeral wreaths, all before the age of fourteen). Her circus life was, in its own way, just as ordinary: when you were a trapeze girl, you were merely one trapeze girl in the company of other trapeze girls, high-wire girls, tumbler girls, cigarette and beer girls, all of them there to earn a living. But if you left the circus for the outside world, you became a *former* trapeze girl, a fact that was, Suzanne thought, the single most valuable thing she might ever own. The story had won her drinks and meals and nights in warm apartments. It had allowed her to choose which warm beds she took her sleep in, or her pleasure. It had allowed her to demand pleasure, which she did forcefully enough that this became the third or fourth thing many men learned about her in Montmartre: artist's model, sometime artist, former trapeze girl, serious inquiries only.

She generally preferred brasseries to cabarets, but she and Adrien had run out of things to say to each other years earlier. Tonight she was content to sit back and watch the acts. Adrien kept her glass filled.

"Are you coming to the studio again this week?" he asked, between songs. "I have to send the curtains back soon."

He was in the midst of painting her as an odalisque, beneath a ridiculous set of canopied bed curtains in damask and gold that he'd seen in a painting at the last Salon and tracked down to a studio rental office. She'd seen the work taking shape on the canvas: the incredibly ornate curtains, then the curve of her bare body, at present just a few penciled lines, an afterthought on the bed. Adrien had never sold a painting, but he had family money and was always renting exotic props and people, gold platters loaded with imitation grapes, buxom girls to pretend to eat them. Suzanne was bartering her own buxomness in exchange for the opportunity to paint—to use Adrien's paints and brushes and try her hand at replicating the particular drape and nap of the curtains herself.

This was much of the difficulty of becoming a painter, the learning not only of brushstroke and blending but also simply of seeing, of being able to look long and hard and purposefully. What she saw when she sat in her apartment with a pad of drawing paper was her son demanding her attention, the sideboard with last night's carrots wrinkling, the lump of burnt candle she'd warned Maurice not to light, worrying he would either fall asleep and set himself on fire or fall asleep and waste the light.

"I'll be there tomorrow," she told Adrien. "But I should probably be getting home for now."

"The show's almost over," he protested.

A professional farter took the stage and launched immediately into a rendition of "Les anges dans nos campagnes," followed by a version of "La Marseillaise" that had the government censor in the corner scribbling furiously. Then the flatulist blew out a candle, not with his mouth. The flatulist and the accompanist got into a silent quarrel over who was responsible for relighting the candle so that the flatulist could do the trick again, from a greater distance, by shooting a jet of water sucked up from a bucket. The accompanist reluctantly performed the honors at arm's length, match held with the tips of his fingers. Then he returned to the piano and resumed the jaunty background music, his body bobbing. His hair, nearly to his shoulders, brown and very straight, swung with the rhythm of the song. His face was a strange mix of concentration and absence. He was swinging a hammer, digging a hole. This was hard work, the playing, and it required a portion of him. But the portion it did not require seemed somewhere else altogether.

No one wanted to follow a flatulist onstage, which meant this act was by default the finale. For the last number the accompanist and the flatulist led a sing-along of a particularly off-color song: a roomful of people could not be held responsible by the censors the way an individual performer could. Everyone joined in, voices raised in out-of-tune exultation, an agreement for all to be equally guilty. The flatulist, unaccustomed to having to remember lyrics, flubbed one of the verses, and the accompanist sang out the words. He didn't have much of a voice, but his enunciation was clean and proper, even fussy, like a teacher delivering a strangely profane lesson.

Both men stepped off the stage to applause, and Adrien waved the accompanist over to their table. Suzanne hadn't been aware that they knew each other, but Adrien knew a lot of people. Anyone with money who was willing to spend it knew a lot of people. Adrien introduced Erik, and Suzanne complimented him on the sing-along.

"I like your carrots," he said, pointing at her corsage.

She thanked him and said she had to go, and an expression of wounded surprise flashed across his face. She had a son, she explained. Nine years old. "I should make sure he hasn't burned the building down."

"How old are you?" Erik asked.

It was a forward question, but avoiding a response might make it seem like she was embarrassed by the answer. She wasn't. Was she? "Twenty-seven."

"Oh. You must've had him terribly young."

She nodded. Shame was a wasted emotion, and Suzanne had pledged to rid herself of it.

"I'm almost twenty-seven myself," Erik said. "A few more months. Then we'll be the same age. Unless your birthday is before May."

"September."

"Perfect. So we'll be the same age for a bit, and then in the fall you can go ahead and report back to tell me what's coming."

"Sevens are rather pointy. More savage than sixes. I think that's all I have to report."

She supposed she was flirting, but it felt more like playing along with a child, entertaining Maurice's latest conviction about fairies or teleportation. He'd recently become obsessed with the pneumatique system, which whisked messages sealed in capsules through narrow tubes underground. It was faster than the regular post but more expensive, so she hadn't ever used it and was baffled by Maurice's fascination.

"Did you know you can send a message by tube?" she said. "There are kilometers of underground tunnels, just for letters, right under our feet." It seemed the kind of thing this Erik person might find charming, and charm was a mode she assumed nearly automatically. One never knew when things might go in a useful direction.

"The pneumatique? Sure. I don't think the lines run up here, though."

"Water barely runs up here," she scoffed, trying to sound cynical and expert.

He scrunched his face in commiseration. The woes of water pressure united everyone on the Butte. You could sell a painting or land a dance gig, but you'd still be standing the next day in the same long line with all your neighbors to fill a bucket at the sluggish public fountain or apartment spigot.

Suzanne asked Erik if he'd ever used the pneumatique.

Of course, he said. It was very useful for canceling things. You could let someone think you'd be there right up until a few hours beforehand, and then when they received the pneu there would be no time left to scold you. "Letters come too early or too late," he said, "and if it's too late then you've been unforgivably rude."

"As opposed to an acceptable amount of rude."

"Exactly."

As Suzanne pulled her coat and hat on, Adrien and Erik discussed whether they wanted to stay for a nightcap or go elsewhere. "I wouldn't mind a bite to eat," Erik said.

Suzanne unpinned her carrots, untied the ribbon, and pulled apart the corsage. "Here," she said, holding out the smallest one.

Erik grinned and bit into it, chewed like a horse. He had good teeth, she noticed. A wholesome face, although he dressed like he was trying to hide it, in an old-fashioned frock coat and battered hat, with pince-nez glasses on a long velvet ribbon.

"Always prepared," Adrien joked. "Whether it's a midnight snack or breakfast the next morning."

Suzanne supposed this was meant to be racy—she could remember once sharing a radish crown with Adrien, unraveling it slowly in his bed while he stirred sugar into the coffee. Those months pricking her fingers on funeral wreaths had been good for something: she could weave nearly any kind of vegetation into nearly any accessory—edible wristlets, necklaces, brooches. She enjoyed having a look, a signature eccentricity, and it kept men from trying to ply her with jewelry. She could ask for gifts of art supplies instead. Or cash.

"Am I stealing your breakfast?" Erik asked, appearing concerned rather than amused.

He was, but she certainly wasn't going to tell him. Maurice would get the remaining carrots, and if she made it to Adrien's studio early enough he'd probably offer her something. If not, well, it wouldn't kill her to go without for a morning. Now that she was a painter instead of a trapeze girl she worried sometimes about her muscular body running to fat.

Suzanne leaned very close to Erik, who was holding what was left of the carrot dumbly upright, like a scepter. She tilted her head and scraped her teeth along the side, a shallow bite. "You're not stealing anything. I gave it to you," she said, and left with shreds of carrot in her teeth.

It was a nearly full moon, an easy walk home and so much light in the apartment through the ragged curtains that she decided to stay up to sketch her son, sleeping in their bed. At nine years old Maurice was becoming self-conscious, or perhaps just contrary. He rarely permitted her to draw him. "Stop staring at me," he would complain.

When she'd first started learning to draw, she'd gone dutifully to one of the free-entry days at the Salon to examine the paintings. She laughed aloud at the absurdity of the still lifes—golden bowls of jewel-like fruit—or the portraits of ladies in silk gowns, posed on upholstered chairs in chinoiserie interiors. She had never seen any of these things in real life, would never be able to observe any of them long enough to paint them. In the crush of people on a free-entry day there was no chance of pausing even to make a sketch. She went home and drew Maurice, used his elbows to teach herself elbows, his feet to learn feet; she labored over the curve of his back as he played with pebbles on the ground, or his hand around a stub of pencil as he made his own drawings, scribbled on the pamphlets the local Benevolent Society slipped under the doors in her building.

The society offered fresh milk once a week at the local dispensary, watered down and tinged blue, but mostly they offered advice: against the demons of beer and absinthe; in favor of the virtues of factory work; partial to the conception of children in June and birth in March, to give them a long head start on the following winter. Maurice had been born on December 26, 1883. He had turned nine a few weeks ago, her miracle.

After the birth, Suzanne's mother had quit her job to care for Maurice so Suzanne could return to modeling. Maurice had been a difficult baby, then a difficult child, and Suzanne's mother grew increasingly bitter about the village job she'd given up long ago, as a maid at a large country inn. How had she come to Paris and ended up with even less to call her own? She fought with Suzanne constantly, and no one was surprised when, on Maurice's eighth birthday, she announced that she'd found herself a job as a domestic. It was live-in, she said, but Maurice was eight now, and mother and son could manage without her. In Bessines, children were often sent out to work by the age of eight. If they could survive a blacksmith's forge or a laundress's scalding water, Maurice could survive aloneness.

The blankets were up to his chin, so she drew only his face, dark eyebrows and hair, soft as duck's down. The boy was her shadow, inky and forbidding, thin as a sheet of newsprint. He had her surname, which had shocked even the usually unshockable among her employers and fellow models. There were plenty of boys in Paris being raised by their mothers, but most of them had at least some man's name, even if it wasn't the right man. People looked to paintings for clues: Suzanne was especially beautiful in Renoir's and in Puvis de Chavannes's, but not in the work of Toulouse-Lautrec or Degas, who were therefore suspected less. She was not beautiful in Adrien's paintings either, but because his lack of skill made everyone look unattractive, he could not be ruled out.

Suzanne finished and hid her sketch, so as not to be scolded by Maurice in the morning. When she climbed into bed his skinny limbs wound around her. She caught a whiff of her own rank, fermented breath—she must have been drunker than she realized—and turned away to spare Maurice, who burrowed into her back.

The next morning, a knock on the door: a uniformed deliveryman from the nearest pneumatique office, hand-carrying messages to their final destination. He handed her the card, postal stationery with elegant handwriting, her very first pneu. The card didn't look special, only a bit curled at the ends, like a mustache, from having been rolled in the canister. The return address was on the Rue Cortot, less than a five-minute walk from her apartment on the Rue Girardon. The sender would have had to travel considerably farther to post the pneu than to drop it off by hand. In place of a message was a drawing of a bunch of carrots, one with a perfect crescent-shaped bite taken out of it, a tiny scalloping of teeth. *Thank you*, she read beneath the carrots. *From Erik*. She couldn't help critiquing the drawing: as a cartoon, it was neatly done. But it was only a cartoon, no attempt at shading or texture. A prepaid reply card was enclosed, but she didn't know what to reply. The pneu was a novelty, but too small and odd for her to discern either what Erik hoped she'd do or what she herself wanted to do in response.

She had a flash of guilt that she hadn't waited to open the pneu with Maurice. He'd somehow managed to sleep through the deliveryman. What time was it, anyway? She checked the sun outside the window.

"Ah hell," she said, and shook Maurice awake. "School. You're late again."

In any other season she would have been late for work as well, but in winter the light was so short that the two or three daily sittings shrank to one, when the sun was at its feeble highest. Suzanne had managed to work steadily ever since her circus résumé had first won her jobs modeling for dancing paintings, or the ancient Olympics, holding action poses until her arms trembled and her bad shoulder, injured in the trapeze accident, ached. Her face at rest was surly, but she could strike her charm like a match. Her body was already electric. She was popular with both the denizens of the major old-fashioned ateliers and the lone artists in their grotty upstairs studios. She'd posed for whole rows of apprentices, all churning away on drapery in the hope of impressing a master enough to be tapped as a contributor to the massive history paintings the studio produced. Some of them intended to make a career out of a single specialty—lace or horses or human hands. In spring there were sometimes train rides outside the city to be painted en plein air by men who had either gotten fed up with history paintings or avoided the ateliers altogether. They had barely enough money for paint, most of them, but they could paint what they liked. They painted Suzanne, over and over.

Her real name was Marie-Clémentine, but people had begun calling her Suzanne after she was hired for three separate paintings of Susanna and the Elders. She'd perfected a look of coy alarm, learned how to direct it at both the old leches inside the painting and the viewers outside it, lecherous in their own way. She posed as Artemis and Mary Magdalene; as nameless nymphs and wives; as ruddy young mothers, until it became too obvious that she was soon to be an actual mother and she was fired from a picture of the warrior mothers of Sparta. Somebody must have birthed all those warrior sons of Sparta, she pointed out, but the casting director wouldn't yield. The studios wouldn't touch her. Neither would any of the supposedly adventurous artists who had painted her as a morphine addict or whore. Nobody wanted to paint a pregnant woman.

She'd tried the model market in the Place de Pigalle, but she ended up sitting in the cafés afterward with the other leftovers. One afternoon an older woman attacked a man for sketching her without permission. There were no people at all in his picture, he insisted, but she kept shrieking for money. He was vindicated by his sketchpad: an empty geometry of tables and chairs, smoke curling from a cigarette abandoned in an ashtray.

"That's my cigarette," she said.

Exasperated, the young man erased the ashtray, a gray smudge left on the page like a phantom.

"You've burnt me up," the woman said. "You've looked and burnt me all up." She cast around for allies, sure Suzanne would take her part.

Instead Suzanne complimented the man on how the rattan seat backs he'd drawn broke the light into curls like hair fallen beneath a barber's chair. That was how she met Adrien—after she was pregnant, not before. He was still terrible at drawing people. He avoided it as much as possible, but still lifes were rather out of fashion.

When she arrived back at her building that afternoon, her hair still elaborately curled and piled high from modeling as an elegant ball guest, she went first to the back garden. She was looking for her goat, but found Erik. He was wearing the frock coat from the previous night, the length so out of date she'd assumed it was a stage costume. The coat lessened her interest, which allowed her to recognize that she was, in fact, interested.

He looked on in satisfaction at the brown-and-cream-colored goat, who was gnawing at a globe of celery root with a blissful look on its face. "I've seen it around the neighborhood," he said, "but didn't realize it was yours. One of the neighbors told me."

"You were looking for me?"

"I wanted to make sure you got the pneu."

"I haven't had a chance to write back."

Erik asked if the goat had a name and she said it didn't. He frowned a little, but she couldn't tell whether that was because he thought the goat ought to have a name or because he'd accidentally driven the conversation into a hole. He'd hoped to get celery tops, he said, so that she could make something out of them, but it was the wrong time of year.

"That was kind of you," she said.

He'd bought the root anyway, he said, even though it seemed too ugly to do anything with, and when the goat tried to eat his coat, he'd distracted it with the celeriac to escape.

"I'm sure it's grateful. Since the weather turned, the poor thing has been subsisting on paper. First drafts—all my bad ideas."

The goat had been a gift last spring from Puvis de Chavannes, left over from a sitting for a country picture. The animal hadn't been docile enough to pose, and the painter had offered it to her after it chewed the pocket off a jacket he'd left hanging on a chair. There was enough left of the little hill village which Montmartre had once been that a goat could survive. Suzanne's own apartment building, hacked into artist apartments with large windows that boiled or froze the inhabitants, depending on the season, still had a grassy back garden. Other buildings retained courtyards, farm plots, stables, and sheds overgrown with weeds and vines. There were windmills, real windmills, not just oversize toys like the sign over the Moulin Rouge. The goat had had plenty of forage, and for the first time in his life since he'd been weaned, Maurice had good milk to drink. Since winter had fallen, though, the goat had been subsisting largely on trash and paper, plus the beer and stale bread that carousers thought it was amusing to feed it late at night. The goat had twice eaten all the squares of newsprint out of the building's latrine, and her neighbors complained. Suzanne bought hay when she could, but the animal's milk had nearly dried up. On especially cold nights Maurice tried to bring the goat inside to bed with him. The building concierge had heard hooves on the stairs and threatened to evict her.

Erik offered to donate some potatoes to the goat, leftovers from a Sunday family dinner. "I still need to get you something, though," he added.

"You don't need to get me anything," she said, although she wouldn't stop him.

The next day, in the studio, Suzanne persuaded Adrien to lay some pillows on the bed in the vague shape of a woman. "I can tell you're not even looking at me," she said. "You're concentrating on the curtains." She could always tell when men were looking.

Her freedom thus procured, she sat side by side with Adrien, painting the same set of bed curtains—tricky delineations where the gold velvet met the red silk, the snaky braid and tassels. She'd promised herself that she would look as hard as she could, capture as much as she could. But her fleurs-de-lis came out spindly, their curves swelling and shrinking out of sync with the movement of the drapery. She took a break, painted a cat in the middle of the bed, a marmalade with cool green eyes.

Adrien glanced over and snorted. "That's a fancy bed for a cat."

"That's a fancy bed for an invisible woman."

"I gave him your address. Erik, from last night. I hope that's all right. He was very taken with your carrots. He's harmless, or I wouldn't have told him anything."

"I know," she said, and mentioned the pneu and the celeriac. "'Harmless' doesn't sound terribly exciting."

"Is that what you want? Exciting?"

She listened beneath the words, to whether he was saying them with mockery or private longing, or whether he had other friends to set her up with, depending on what she wanted.

"He's a composer, if that makes a difference," Adrien added. "He isn't just an accompanist."

"Is he any good?"

"I don't know, honestly."

"Do you have anything else to sketch?" Suzanne asked, changing the subject. "Anything other than carrots, nine-year-old boys, or goats. I could sketch you," she added. "You wouldn't even have to stop painting. I'll just do *The Artist at Work*."

Why did he look so surprised? After all, how many times had he drawn or painted her? She needed the practice, because although she could have a career without being able to paint fancy curtains, she doubted she could have one without being able to paint men, something she currently didn't do well. Maurice had once told her, in tears, that a canvas in their apartment was giving him nightmares, the way the men's arms sprang from their shoulders at graceless angles, their buttocks thrust backward, their necks long and columnar. In the few biblical scenes she'd tried, it was Adam who wore a fig leaf and Eve who was unashamed.

"I suppose I could use a break," Adrien said. "I'm going cross-eyed trying to get this gold right. Where do you want me?"

"On the bed?"

Adrien laughed. "Are you serious?"

"Why not?"

"Men don't really lounge about seductively on beds."

"You think women do?"

"Fair point. Am I being seductive, or just sleepy? Or perhaps I'm tragically ill."

"I am curious to see you attempt 'seductive,'" she said.

More game than she'd dared to hope, Adrien started to strip his clothes off. Shoes first, then painter's smock, then collar and waistcoat, then shirt and socks and trousers. In a burst of bravado he whipped off his long underwear and jumped backward onto the bed. The frame creaked. He sprawled unashamedly for all of a moment before he started rearranging himself.

"What about the classic smirk over the shoulder?" he asked, pulling up his knees and turning his back toward her.

"You had me facing forward."

"I also had the stove roaring. It's freezing in here now."

She offered to build the fire back up.

"Don't bother," he said, and wormed his way under the top coverlet.

"That's hardly fair."

He relented, slightly, turned toward her and leaned his head on one arm and pushed the coverlet down to his hips with the other. His skin was nearly as pale as the sheets. Dark hair stretched across his chest and in a line down his stomach. He had no idea what to do with his face, but the pose itself wasn't awful. In fact it was so ordinary it looked bizarre, a position she'd seen often in real life and never, not once, on a canvas.

She sketched as quickly as she could, not sure how long he'd play along. As she drew, his expression got more and more strained. He shivered, and she could tell from his gooseflesh that he wasn't just whining. But if she stopped drawing long enough to feed the fire, she knew he'd get up.

"I'm bored," he whined.

"No fortitude. Clearly not cut out for this line of work."

"I'm not cut out for any line of work. You know that." He grabbed the edge of the sheet and flicked it at her.

"You're moving," she complained.

"It would be warmer in here with two. Aren't you finished yet?"

She wasn't, but felt she was pressing her luck. She put the pad down. She didn't owe him anything, she thought. But he was a friend. Adrien had never laughed at any of her paintings, even her worst beginner's efforts. He'd never made fun of her wanting to learn how to paint in the first place. Maurice wasn't his, but she wouldn't have minded if he had been. Besides, Adrien had always shown her a good time.

"I suppose it is a little cold in here," she said.

She took off her shoes and smock, crawled into the bed fully dressed. Adrien reached for the buttons on her dress, but she caught his hands and held them. She wanted to see what it felt like, to be clothed with a naked model. It hadn't ever happened before, probably wouldn't happen again.

"Only with a sheath," she warned him. She kept track of the days of the month, and this should be a safe one, but after Maurice she didn't take chances. She loved him, but that didn't mean she wanted another.

Erik showed up yawning and disheveled for the breakfast date they'd planned. This was early for him, he apologized—cabaret work had turned him semi-nocturnal. "I'm an owl," he said, "except not at all wise. I suppose you're the lark."

"Painters live and die by the light," she said. "You can go back to bed and we'll try another time, if you like."

Erik wouldn't hear of it, especially now that he'd kept her waiting. He was determined to give back the minutes he'd been late. He led them east, behind Sacré-Coeur. Parts of the basilica were still hunched under a tortoiseshell of scaffolding, but the interior had finally opened for services, and the snowfall of white construction dust that had coated her early years in the neighborhood had slowed to flurries. She was gradually getting used to the church, however strange the shape. Some people described it as a giant white pope's hat. Others, who had been here during the Commune, said it was a bulbous fat cock pointing straight up into the sky, the government's hard-on for God.

She had no idea where Erik was leading them. Breakfast in Paris was not usually a formal or substantial affair. Suzanne had spent a handful of nights in beautiful hotels, and the morning tray still held only breads and jam, coffee and hot chocolate. Each time, the man had ordered her hot chocolate without asking and had drunk the coffee himself. How determined he must have been to look at her and see nothing but sweetness.

They crossed over Clignancourt, then Boulevard Barbès. It wasn't a long walk, but it seemed unnecessarily far to travel for a bread roll.

Erik was still striding purposefully just ahead of her, so there was no conversation between them. "Nearly there," he said, and turned alongside the Hôpital Lariboisière.

On the other side of the street, train tracks splayed like finger bones, a hand laid flat behind the Gare du Nord. She still didn't expect it when he led them through the front doors of the train station. The morning rush had slowed, but trains still screeched and puffed at the platforms, disgorging dark wool coats and hats. He picked a table at a traveler's café near the front doors, utilitarian and grimy, and ordered them each the same thing. The bread was tasteless. The coffee had a bitter bite that was not un-pleasant but did nothing to explain the venue.

"Station time," Erik said. "I brought us here so we'd be on sta-tion time." He gestured at the enormous clock, deliberately set, like all station clocks in France, five minutes slow. Station time was permanently five minutes behind the time in the outside world. A grace period to allow travelers to buy their tickets, find their platform, say their goodbyes. Trains arrived and departed from a special realm, he said, a land where everyone had just enough time to buy a newspaper, read the signage, get lost and unlost. There were always people rushing, of course, counting on the extra five minutes and then some. But in train stations you could feel as though there might be just enough time for everything. "Time travel," he concluded. "I'm making up for my lateness."

"But don't we just leap five minutes forward again when we leave?" Suzanne asked, then stopped herself. She hadn't been playing dumb, that time-honored way to keep a man talking. Erik's rhapsody about station time had actually caught her off guard, briefly confusing her into wonder. It had seemed possible, for an instant, that there were folds in time, seams engineered into the fabric of her life that she'd never noticed. Now she scolded herself, and played along. "We have to stay inside, then," she said. "Until breakfast is over."

Breakfast was technically already concluded—she'd finished hers while Erik lectured, and Erik had inhaled his the moment he'd stopped talking, seeming barely to chew. He looked at their empty cups and plates, then cast about the station for what else they might do. They ended up at a newsstand, where he trans-lated the English papers for her—every story ended with a sea monster rising out of the Thames. Sometimes it wiped Lon-don off the map, and sometimes it simply demanded a ticket to *Charley's Aunt*, which was breaking sales records at the Royalty Theatre.

A rail-sea-rail London–Paris service arrived on platform 10, and as the people streamed out of the carriages, Suzanne said they must be refugees, fleeing the monster.

"You'll be safe here," Erik reassured them, in French and crooked English, standing at the platform exit with his arms outstretched in welcome. "Though you'll need to mind the were-wolves."

At the expressions on the passengers' faces, Suzanne laughed harder than she had in a long time.

The conductor of the London service walked over to ask Erik what he was thinking, frightening good fare-paying passengers.

"I know you've had a narrow escape," Erik said. "Please just take a few deep breaths and you might not feel so unreasonable."

"Do you have a ticket?" the conductor asked.

"To London? God, no, not with a rampaging monster on the loose."

"To anywhere."

Erik insisted he wasn't trying to board the train, wasn't even properly on the platform, and had every right to stand there.

The conductor was unamused, and Suzanne bent down and raked her fingers along the floor. There were discarded tickets everywhere. "To Dunkirk," she announced, holding one up like a trophy. "We're newlyweds. On our honeymoon."

"You're honeymooning in Dunkirk?" the conductor asked, and grabbed the ticket.

"We are people of unusual tastes," Erik said.

"You must be time travelers as well. This ticket is for yesterday."

"We are," Suzanne said. "That's exactly right. We're time travelers." She reached for Erik's hand and took it in hers, startling him, and she felt both the moment he started to pull away and the moment he stopped himself, clumsily threading his fingers through hers.

*   *   *

They had the regular sort of dates—dinners, drinks—and some stranger ones: a pet store and a cemetery and the Luxembourg Gardens, where Erik rented two small toy sailing boats. In the slack breeze, they used long sticks to nudge their ships around the duck pond.

"My family came here once, when I was a child," he said, and she thought she could hear in his voice how it had only ever been the once.

One Sunday he escorted both her and Maurice to Notre-Dame de Paris, which made her suspicious: she did not need a missionary in her life. As they stood outside the soaring facade, the towers and saints and the enormous rose window, she asked why they'd come.

He looked at her like he didn't understand the question. "Because it's beautiful," he said, and she took his hand again as they went inside.

He never reached for hers, which was strange to her but not unpleasant. A gentleman, she thought. A novelty. He was in every other way so obviously besotted with her that they became a very public item very quickly. He dedicated songs to her from the stage, published drawings of her in the café papers. They were caricatures, like everything else he drew, giving her a serious face and a high helmet of hair, puffed sleeves like little epaulets. He took out ads in the café papers touting their imaginary business partnerships: FORTUNES TOLD, read one, BY THOSE WHO HAVE BEEN TO THE FUTURE AND SEEN IT ALL.

One warm weekend in early spring, Suzanne, Maurice, and Erik took a train outside the city to a fête foraine. It was early in the season and most of the fair's caravans and tents were still locked or packed away, but Suzanne thought Maurice had been looking even paler than usual and wanted to get him some fresh air. The carnival exhibitors would shake off the last of the winter mud soon enough, set up for a month or so here outside Paris, then tour through France the rest of the summer, returning to the city in autumn. At least the carousel was operating, and Maurice enjoyed it so much she bought him three straight rides. They strolled then through the overpriced game booths, and Maurice and Erik both proved terrible at chucking balls into a distant row of tin pails.

The game operator handed Erik a consolation prize, a printed cartoon of a dog that was really just an advertisement for the booth. "For your boy," he said.

The three had spent very little time together as a group, let alone a family, but Suzanne noted that Erik didn't correct the operator, and that Maurice didn't protest.

Farther down the midway they found the animal exhibitors. Many of the caged beasts had bald spots or rheumy eyes, but one enclosure in particular contained two bears so skinny and forlorn that Suzanne wanted to whisk Maurice and his soft heart away as quickly as possible. The keeper limped down the steps of her shabby caravan and offered to prod the bears into tricks. Suzanne declined, in an effort to hurry their group along, but Erik lingered, staring at the keeper. Suzanne looked at her more closely now. Though she was worn, her eyes dark with hunger, the woman was very beautiful under the mishmash of shawls she'd wrapped around herself.

If the bears didn't interest them, the keeper said, she had a hyena around the back.

Erik paid her the fee, but Maurice didn't want to see the hyena and couldn't be coaxed. The keeper grudgingly offered their money back but Erik told her to keep it.

Suzanne had a flare of jealousy. Was this pity or desire? If it was the former, fine, but if it was the latter, she didn't understand. Why the keeper and not her? Her confusion at Erik's gentlemanly restraint had passed from admiration to impatience and was now a source of growing frustration.

"Have we met before?" Erik asked the keeper. She shook her head and scurried inside with his money.

That night, after Maurice had fallen asleep, Suzanne walked to Erik's apartment carrying a candle in a saucer to light the way. The front door to the building was propped open, either by a resident or by a concierge sick of being woken by a hodgepodge of tenants who kept odd hours and constantly lost their keys. Erik had told Suzanne he had the night off, but when she knocked, no one answered. She waited, knocked again, pressed her ear to the door. Perhaps she'd misunderstood him, or he could be out with friends, of course. But she thought she heard the faintest of noises, a floorboard creaking under the foot of someone trying very hard to be still.

She shouldn't have to stoop to it, Suzanne thought, but she plotted. She asked Adrien if she could use his studio for an afternoon, uninterrupted. With its stove and soft bed, it was so much nicer than her apartment. He agreed, but with an expression that made her wonder, reluctantly, if she might be cracking his heart a little.

She told Erik she wanted to paint him. Not just a sketch, a real sitting, with good light and the supplies she needed. She bought a bottle of wine. On the way to the studio she bought another, in case it was needed. They could both drink heroically. The fancy curtains had been returned to the rental office, but the bed was made neatly, with crisp white sheets and a woolen blanket. When Erik arrived he ignored the bed, sat squarely on a bare wooden chair in the middle of the floor.

The day was balmy, the stove unlit, the sun warm through the windows, but he wouldn't remove so much as his hat. "You said you wanted to paint me, and this is the way I dress."

"Indoors?"

"When I'm working, I do."

"This isn't your official state portrait. We're not recording you for posterity."

She was joking, but Erik was miffed. "Then what are we doing?"

Good question, Suzanne thought. Fine, she said, leave the hat and jacket and glasses on. "You couldn't have worn a brighter waistcoat?" she complained. His entire torso was lost in an expanse of faded black. He sat there combing through his beard with his fingers.

She folded blue into the dark of his waistcoat, red into the dark of his suit jacket, so the fabric came alive. She thought of Renoir while she did it. She thought of Puvis de Chavannes, which made her think of the goat. The trees were budding. If the goat could hold out just a little bit longer, it would make it through the summer at least. And next fall? She couldn't think that far ahead. The midwife hadn't thought Maurice would make it through the night, and he had nearly made it through the decade. He would be sixteen when the new century came, a man at the edge of something extraordinary.

While choosing colors for the face, she noticed how pink Erik's lips were, almost red. There was pink in his cheeks too, and while it might have been the wine she guessed he was getting hot. "Aren't you warm?" she asked. "Don't you want to take your jacket off?" How many times had artists invited her to relax, unpin her hair, unbutton her costume, make herself more comfortable? She felt like an understudy in an old melodrama, taking on an unfamiliar role. Everything was a struggle: persuading him to take his jacket off, convincing him to sit on the bed. She had to tell him that the sun had moved, that the light would be better if they repositioned. Then he tried to drag the chair with him. "Just sit on the bed," she barked.

He sighed but kept up his chatter. They should mount a gallery show together, he said, paintings and music specially written to go with them. He'd tell the audience not to listen, not to sit and watch the musicians, but to keep standing and looking at the pictures. "So your paintings would be the most important thing," he said. The music would worm into the ears of the audience sideways. He liked the idea of music that no one was quite listening to but that they heard all the same. "Furniture music," he said.

"I think that's plenty for today," she said finally. Her bad shoulder was aching, and enough of the picture was done that she would be able to remember where she wanted to go when she picked it up again.

Erik asked if she wanted to eat dinner somewhere. Maurice could join them, he offered.

Suzanne had had lovers who couldn't remember she had a son, or whom she'd never even told. She was touched at how carefully Erik considered Maurice, his needs. But no, she didn't want to take her son to dinner right now. "We can stay here a while longer," she said.

"What is this place, anyway? Whose is it?"

"A friend's."

She poured them each more wine and sat beside Erik on the bed. She kissed him. He let himself be kissed. His beard and mustache were very soft. He let her unbutton his waistcoat, and his shirt. His hands lay beside him on the bed. He kissed her back once, hesitantly, and she put her hand on his waist. His skin was clammy. She started to move her hand lower.

"Do we have to do this?" he asked quietly.

"What do you mean?"

He repeated himself, asking it as a real question, and waited for her answer.

She pulled her hands back into her own lap, feeling a little sick. She had convinced herself, every time, that she wanted it, or that she was at least willing. Mostly she was. The ringmaster? Her body had been still a girl's body, narrow limbs exhausted from training. But all right, yes, why not. Why remember it differently now, when she didn't have to? Why remember it at all? Twelve years later and here was a lover in her bed asking if he had to. "No, we don't have to," she said. "Of course we don't *have to*."

"But you want to."

"You don't?"

He thought about it, looking as if he'd thought about it before, as if he kept checking back with the question, hoping to arrive at a different answer. He shook his head.

"I see," she said, although she didn't. "Is there someone else?" she asked, although she knew there wasn't. It just seemed like the question to ask at a moment like this, to try to turn it into the kind of moment that she could recognize.

"Of course not," he said. "I love you." It was the first time he'd ever said it plainly, directly.

"But you don't want to. . . . Not now? Or not ever?"

"If we have to, I could—"

"Please stop saying *have to*. I'm not a monster."

"I don't know what you want me to say. I don't know what you want."

"I think it's obvious." It was humiliatingly obvious—to have wanted and not been wanted in return. She had never in her life not been wanted. She had built her whole life on being wanted, and built it well, so that she could do the work she wished.

"I want you, I just don't want—" He cut himself off, then tried again. "I love you. I love your carrots. I love your paintings." He said this tenderly, trying to offer her something precious. And it *was* precious—but not in the way that he wanted it to be.

She understood that she could say she liked his music and he would take more pleasure in that than in anything she might do with her hands. He would praise her mouth for the jokes it could tell or the praise it could deliver him, not for any other reason.

"Is that enough?" he asked.

"I don't think so. I don't think it will be," she amended, trying to gentle it with future tense, although it was as true now as it would be later. She didn't want to seem so sex-starved as to end things with him that moment, for that reason, on Adrien's borrowed bed.

*   *   *

They kept trying for a while at—something. She wasn't sure what it was. Many evenings Erik brought armfuls of rotting produce for the goat, now that it was early summer and the pushcarts were laden with more than they could sell. Suzanne couldn't tell if these visits were a pretext to see her or if Erik was really that fond of, or concerned for, the goat. He offered her greenery to weave jewelry from, but she refused.

"You're unhappy," he said to her. "You're different."

"You're unhappy, too," she said, although he shook his head. "We're not going to be able to make each other happy. It's no one's fault, but there it is."

"It's your fault," Erik said, and she sighed.

He told her he wouldn't stop her if she wanted to take her pleasure elsewhere, but when she was seen in public with other men Erik savaged her about it later, either in person or in the papers, where his cartoons of her grew uglier and uglier. He blew up the imaginary businesses he'd created one by one: their fortune-telling enterprise ended when the clairvoyant couple traveled to the future and boarded a rocket to the moon. They sadly wouldn't be returning to Paris, the ads read. They were lost forever, somewhere out in space.

She continued to work on his portrait. At first her frustration twisted it, made his skin sallow and his eyebrows devilish. But in the end she remembered her loyalties. Not just to Erik, but to Renoir, to de Chavannes, even to Adrien, she thought, as she folded colors into each other and made the background glow. To all her teachers, both the generous ones and the accidental ones. To posterity, she thought wryly. Just in case Erik ever did become famous, here would be an accurate portrait. Hat and all. Warm face and full, untouchable lips.

The picture was finished, leaning against a wall in her apartment, when there came a knock at the door one night. In these summer days she'd been working long hours in the long light, as both model and painter. For the first time in her life, a little more of the latter than the former. She'd arrived home to find Maurice missing, but it hadn't been dark long, and she wasn't yet worried.

Erik stood in the hallway, obviously drunk, a candle wavering in his hand. "I've changed my mind," he said urgently. "We should do it." He reached clumsily for her waist.

"You can't even say it."

"Who ever says it? No one really *says* it. I want to."

"I don't think you do."

"Admit it. Admit that you loved me."

Admit? What was an *admission* of love, as if some crime had been committed? "It's not going to work," she said. "We're just not going to work."

"Let me come in," he said, and peered past her.

Without turning she cataloged what he might be able to see. The table and chairs, the edge of the bed, a white canvas on an easel. The pencil lines would be invisible in the dimness, and the piece would appear as nothing more than a giant white rectangle, a portal to some possible future. As he tried to push inside the apartment, she turned and blocked him with her hip. "Please don't. Maurice went to bed early. Don't wake him up."

"He's not here," Erik scoffed.

"Yes he is."

"You're lying. I know you're lying."

His tone of voice made her pause. "Where is he?"

"Same place he goes most nights you're out. Sometimes afternoons. He's got a tab at the Lapin Agile. Most of the drinks he gets for free. People feel sorry for him. Nine years old and cadging beer." Erik swayed.

Her face burned. Was this true, or was Erik taking his revenge? Was it both?

"You're a terrible mother," he said. "You can't even take care of a goat."

She slapped him, then drove a shoulder hard into his ribs. Her good shoulder, with all her strength behind it. He staggered backward across the landing and hit the opposite wall. The candle flew from his hand and guttered out. They stood in the pitch-dark, both breathing hard.

How dare you? How dare you? her heart howled, but she kept her voice flat and calm. "The Lapin Agile, you said? I should fetch him." She reached behind her to pull the door shut. It wasn't locked, but what would Erik take? The wrinkled asparagus on the table? His own portrait? Let him. She didn't want to look at it again. She started down the stairs, leaving him breathing heavily in the darkness.

There was almost no moon, but the Lapin Agile was lit up brilliantly. The famous sign, the cheerful rabbit leaping out of a frying pan, creaked on its iron hooks. She walked in the front door. Adrien was there playing a card game with other men at a large table. She asked if he'd seen Maurice, and the hush that fell over the table gave her her answer. Her son was hunched at a corner of the crowd, thin as a shadow, with a large glass of beer in front of him.

"Come here," she said.

Maurice slowly stood and began circling the table. He wasn't walking straight.

"Which of you bought him the beer?" The men shuffled their cards in strained silence and her eyes burned. "You son of a bitch," she said to Adrien, because if it hadn't been this glass it had been some other, and he'd known and not told her. Maybe she was the reason he'd done it.

At the apartment, Maurice staggered forward, bounced off the edge of the table, caught himself, and sank into a chair. She thought of how he would bruise where the corner of the table had jabbed him, partway up his rib cage; she thought of how small he still was, how the table that fit her at the hollow of her hip came up only to his side. She remembered him even younger than he was now, seated at the table that came up to his chest, with a carrot in his mouth, and his shoulders pushed up around his ears. There should have been some cushion for him to sit on, to raise him up. There should have been milk. There should have been warm curtains that could keep out both the light and the cold. It was an abstract, wistful sort of wishing—not that she could have provided those things, because she'd had no way of doing so, but that the whole world should be different, that it should be the sort of place where a boy could have a cushion to sit on. Even to drink his beer like a man.

"I'm sorry," he whispered.

She thought of all the nights he'd spent in the dark, told not to light even a candle. Of course he'd sought out light and warmth wherever he could find it. She could imagine the men finding it funny, even generous, buying beers for this boy who might, for all anyone knew, have been their son.

"I'm sorry," she said, and she thought there should be more that came after that, but she didn't know what else to say. "Let's get into bed."

Maurice toed off his shoes, then climbed straight in, still in his clothes. She climbed in after him, pressed her nose into his hair, its lank thickness smelling of smoke. She remembered when his hair was a fuzzy halo that smelled only like her. She squeezed him, trying to find, under his clothes, the shape of the body she'd made. He was a language she'd invented but no longer spoke. On his skin she found the scents of cigarettes and cigars and pipes and cigarillos, but no coal soot, no wood smoke. They'd all survived another winter, another cold, rainy spring. She whispered to her son that it was summer now, and everything might be different.

Erik

— 11 —

Apply yourself to renunciation

SUZANNE BEQUEATHS HIM HER GOAT, VIA THE PREPAID REPLY card to the first pneu Erik ever sent her, adding that she doesn't want to see him again. Erik is pleased about the goat, though not the rest of the message. He wants the goat to have a happy life, and perhaps a happier life than Suzanne. Biqui, he names it, which was once his private pet name for Suzanne. He calls the goat loudly in the garden behind her building, on hot days when all the windows are open, and hopes she hears him and is angry. He brushes the goat's hair—glossier, surely, since he took over?—and thinks how he's proving Suzanne wrong. But wrong about what? Arguably, she ended things after they finally saw each other correctly.

Her pneu should no doubt have noted that the goat is pregnant, which Erik learns only when a neighbor, now an acrobat but a shepherd in his boyhood, comments on how unusually late Biqui must have bred, if she hasn't kidded by now. Goats are already so wide, the shape of olives on toothpicks, how was Erik supposed to tell? When her time comes he enlists the help of a midwife (for babies, not goats, she warns him sourly), and the acrobat. Between the two of them Biqui comes safely through, but they lose the kid. No matter, the acrobat says. Her milk's come in all right. And she's got plenty of years left to try again.

247

"How many years?" Erik asks, and is rather dismayed to learn that a doe can breed for a decade.

He tries to picture his own life in a decade, and can't. Or rather, he pictures too many things at once, a ballet at the Paris Opéra, plus tremendous sales for his cabaret compositions, plus election to the Académie des Beaux-Arts, and before the solemn ceremony at the Institut de France there will be a parade down the Butte, with Erik hoisted up in a chair, crowned king of composers, prince of all the reprobates. After the ceremony, Bruant will beg him to accept a commission for a song for the Mirliton, and Eugénie and his old Conservatory teachers will apologize for all their nagging. He'll walk home that night (having turned down a flood of offers for transportation, of course) and hear his music, four different kinds, pouring out of the Salle Érard, the Mirliton, a piano student's family apartment on the Rue Magenta, and an Incoherent Art Exhibition, where he'll be awarded best in show. The reviews will discuss how he's created something utterly and irrefutably *new*. He doesn't know what it is, this new thing he's made ten years from now, and he'd rather not wait ten years to figure it out. He'd like to know now.

In none of these fantasies is he accompanied by a goat, and it seems like one might get in the way. In none of these fantasies is he partnered with anyone, man or woman, and it seems like one might get in the way.

He isn't *opposed* to the idea of company, exactly, but they'd have to part ways on that triumphant walk home, because he can't bear the prospect of anyone moving his things; or throwing out any of his letters, pneus, and newspaper clippings; or speaking to him when he's trying to compose in his head. He doesn't want anybody in his living or working space, and he doesn't want anybody in his bed. He just doesn't. He's not even sure what it's supposed to feel like, that kind of wanting, which has made its absence difficult to fully recognize or explain. Suzanne is as close as he's come, and look at how well that went. He thinks of her as a failed experiment, and he has listened to Conrad natter on about his research often enough to fear the specter of "reproducible results." If the experimental conditions remain unchanged, why repeat the experiment with hope of a different outcome?

She was one of so many people here who used their bodies for work—he thought that perhaps he'd be relieving her of an obligation. He pictured them in adjoining studios, making their art. There were enormous, bright glass windows, and birdsong outside. She and Maurice would knock on his door whenever they needed him and wait for him to emerge, rather than barging inside. He'd visit her studio to examine her latest paintings, with their unsentimental, even ugly, bodies in jarring colors. He'd already started writing furniture music for her gallery shows, compositions with just enough of their own strange, jarring texture to complement her work but also fade behind it. His music would creep along the walls and ceiling like ivy, seep across the floor like fog, until the attendees were breathing it more than listening to it, and he was in their lungs every bit as much as their ears.

That kind of touch is one he might enjoy, he thinks, the way he enjoys the thick velvet corduroy of his suits, a comfortable armor. He bought the baggy suit several years earlier and loved it so much he ordered five more. They now constitute his entire wardrobe, and in summer sweat trickles down his back and sides, his body touching itself. He loves a crisp collar, pushes his throat forward into it just to feel the starched edge of it push back, hard as a fence rail. He loves the smell of the starch, and he loves the way smells touch the inside of his nose. In this way he loves even bitumen and bleach, night soil and soured milk. He steps off a curb and into horse manure, and the smell greets him for hours afterward. He touches the city and the city touches back.

Biqui's coarse hair is a touch he loves, her soft, dry muzzle, her grasping lips and blocky teeth. The gaze of her strange eyes, yellow with black rectangular pupils, vaguely demonic—is that a kind of touch? Erik imagines that he can feel the goat's stare. He is sorry for the loss of her kid, which the acrobat has wrapped in a towel, and says he'll dispose of on his way to work. He's late, he says, and needs to be going.

Erik asks the acrobat whether Biqui is at the start of her decade, or well into it.

The acrobat calls over his shoulder to check her teeth.

But check them for what? It's not as if they have numbers written on them.

Erik and Philippe never touched each other, and Erik wonders if they might have lived the life together he pictured with Suzanne, in side-by-side studios. Has he missed an obvious solution? But probably Philippe wants to be touched, even if he doesn't always seem sure whom he wants to do the touching. Besides, what would Philippe be doing in his studio? His travel books would be a waste of the windows and birdsong. Erik thinks this derisively, but he misses Philippe, who has moved out of the neighborhood into an apartment beyond the Rue Drouot, which both men once considered the edge of the allowable world. Everything with him is less now: less time, less laughing, less drink, less work. Philippe has publishing friends now. He has friends who aren't Erik. Erik wonders, with an uncomfortable mix of jealousy and contempt, if he's happy. If all Philippe wants out of life is a steady paycheck, well, ambition achieved.

Wine is touch, and liquor. On the tongue, in the belly and brain, the slack sponginess in his hands when he's had too much, the slowness in his mouth. The way the bartender at the Auberge sometimes hesitates to slide the glass across the bar, or the way a waiter makes eye contact with Tomaschet for permission to serve him. Erik recognizes that look, and goes to visit Albert Tinchant in Lariboisière, the charity hospital. Erik brings him socks and magazines and handkerchiefs. He knows no other way to care for someone than the ways he would want to be cared for. Tinchant is angry that he didn't bring liquor.

"It isn't good for you," Erik says limply, because Tinchant looks awful, bloated and yellow and as much like a corpse as Erik's ever seen a living man. How much difference can a drink make now?

Biqui and Tinchant together make for an awful lot of caretaking for Erik, who finds it easier to care for no one but himself. How does such a squat little animal eat so much? Why does it need to be milked each morning, when Erik has finally crawled into bed for the night after work? There aren't many children in the neighborhood, and he's trying to avoid Maurice, but he puts together a squad of junior goatherds to tend the animal, invites them to drink whatever milk they can get out of her. He keeps a metal bucket, wooden stool, and tin cup stacked neatly in the garden behind Suzanne's building. There are a handful of articles about his goat in the local papers, none written by either him or Philippe, and he's embarrassed to realize that they're all sincere and approving, celebrating the charity of a local benefactor. He doesn't want to be known as a local benefactor; he wants to be known as a composer. This, as much as the prospective cost of feed once winter comes, is what drives him onto a tram one day in late summer, headed outside the city to the fairgrounds.

She might be out touring, but he hopes to find the familiar sullen bears, the gypsy caravan painted in stripes. It's early in the morning—he's tried to arrive before the crowds—when he finds the closed caravan and bangs on the door. The bear keeper opens it rumpled and blinking. He can't decide what to call her, her real last name, or informal first, or her stage name, which is what everyone called her when they first met. Or maybe he was wrong when he came here with Suzanne and he doesn't know this woman after all.

"La Vorace?" he says, choosing the stage name, and her breath bursts out and in like he's shot her. "Lisette?" he tries again. She still doesn't speak, and he starts explaining how he once accompanied a handful of her performances at the Divan Japonais.

"What do you want?" She cuts him off.

At least she's not going to pretend he's wrong. He tells her he's giving away a goat and that she is the only person he could think of who might want one. He refers to the goat by name, and Lisette hesitates. Does he understand, she asks, that she can't afford to keep a pet?

Biqui can be milked, he says, realizing Lisette is thinking of the goat as prospective bear food.

How old is the goat? How much milk does it give? Lisette rattles off more questions, and it's clear she knows a great deal more about goats than Erik does. La Vorace a country girl? Who knew?

The Voracious, she was called, because she always entered from the back of the house, sashayed her way up to the stage through the tables, stealing sips and swigs from audience members' glasses. The second half of the show Erik had accompanied started with a number called "La Vorace Goes to Bed." There was a halfhearted stage set, painted like a bedroom wall bearing a single nail from which hung a limp cotton nightgown. La Vorace entered bundled in clothing and began removing layers. As she started unbuttoning her dress, the crowd was enraptured. Erik had been told to play a popular waltz tune, but he realized he could play almost anything and it wouldn't matter. Only Lisette seemed to hear the music, swaying her hips as she loosened her stays. When she was nearly naked, her corset gaping open, she reached for the nightgown on the nail and slipped it over her head. It covered her ankle to neck. There were some men in the audience who groaned aloud, as if in agony, and others who found themselves strangely comforted. They were not really going to see a naked woman on the stage. Even in Montmartre, there were still rules.

Erik congratulated La Vorace after the show, knowing he'd seen something special. Maybe not his kind of thing, but he could recognize its genius. Within a month, half the music halls in Paris were doing a striptease: "Clarice Goes to Bed." "Aimée Is Visited by the Physician." "Alice Goes to the Beach," which ended in a swimming costume.

Soon after that La Vorace was performing in theaters with orchestras instead of pianos, and her path and Erik's did not often cross. He assumed she had retired to be a kept woman—some rich man's mistress or, if she'd gotten very lucky indeed, a rich man's wife. A more tactful person would ask this in a different way, or not ask it at all of a woman bundled in moth-eaten shawls beside a bear cage, but Erik says, "What *happened?*"

She invites him in. She pours them each a drink, into dirty glasses. She saved up her money, she says, retired when she had enough to buy a business. But she had a run of bad luck. There were two panthers, originally, but they died of distemper; then a lion with a wonderful mane died of parasites. After that, one of the bears took a swipe at her ankle. It healed badly and now she can't go back to dancing even if she wanted to.

Erik notices her dark brown front teeth and the deep grooves in her face, and suspects she wouldn't be able to go back either way.

There was never as much money as he might have thought, she says. There were only so many numbers she could perform half-clothed, and the theater owner told her she needed new costumes befitting her new celebrity. When her name was famous enough to mean something on a poster, she was asked to pay for the posters. Now she makes ends meet, she says. She gathers herbs in the forest to brew health tonics. She has printed labels with her face on them, smiling, teeth all white. She tells fortunes.

"Are you any good at it?"

"Give me your hand."

He unfolds it slowly. She catches his fingers and draws them toward her. When her index finger traces his palm it tickles, and his hand curls up like a hedgehog. Lisette starts to force the fingers flat and he yanks his hand away.

"No," he says. "No thank you. But I'll buy a tonic."

She offers him several different formulations, and he selects one meant to be rubbed into his scalp, to save his thinning hair.

"You're not giving me the goat, are you? You're buying this to apologize."

"I don't think I can. I'm sorry. Not to kill. Are you angry?"

"I didn't have a goat before, and I don't have one now. I've got other things to be angry about."

He returns to Lariboisière that afternoon with a flask, but the bed is empty and neatly made. Erik walks next to the Chat Noir, both to submit an obituary for the café paper and to ask about funeral arrangements. As far as he knows, Tinchant doesn't have any family. The old regulars at the Chat Noir are probably the closest thing.

Salis comes out to see him and pounds him heartily on the back. "It's been ages," he says. "We miss you."

"No you don't," Erik says. "You never miss anybody."

"Not true."

"Maybe you miss them when they won't work for free anymore."

"You wound me," Salis says lightly.

"You did this," Erik says, with helpless fury. He wants a gun, a sword. The siege of the Chat Noir.

Salis starts laughing. "Tinchant? How do you figure that?"

"You couldn't have just paid him? Instead of keeping him drunk."

"Tinchant made his own choices. You're not a child anymore, Erik. Don't act like one."

Biqui's next kid dies, as does the kid the spring after, and the spring after that. He doesn't know if they're dying because of something he's doing wrong, or because of something wrong with Biqui, or if it's just three years of bad luck. He would consult with Suzanne, but she isn't in the neighborhood anymore; she's living north of the city at a country house in Montmagny with her rich stockbroker husband, to hell with them both. Erik publishes an open letter in a café paper excommunicating her from the Metropolitan Church of Art of Jesus the Conductor, whose address is his apartment, and whose single officiant and congregant is himself. His church exists so that his enemies—Suzanne, then several music critics, then the jurors at the Académie des Beaux-Arts, who have rejected him a second time—can be publicly excommunicated from it, an act he performs with gusto.

He pushes more of Biqui's care onto the neighborhood children, even asking if their parents might have a little something to put toward her upkeep. He's out of money. He can't make rent, and his landlord offers him another room in the same building. With the door opening directly onto the bed and the piano, there isn't a scrap of floor to stand on. The apartment is a literal closet, where the building concierge used to keep maintenance supplies. Erik is at first relieved that the landlord is willing to negotiate, to find him a space he can afford. Then he realizes the landlord is probably thrilled to have a chump willing to sleep in a closet.

Eugénie continues to send him home with leftovers from Sunday dinners, and does not touch him. She kisses only Conrad's cheeks, then regards Erik from a wary, mutually agreed distance. Conrad, near the top of his class, is nearly done with his graduate chemistry degree. Erik listens very dutifully but doesn't understand any of it well enough to retain. He supposes, a little guiltily, that this is what Conrad or Philippe feels, listening to him talk about music. He resolves to blather less, but then there isn't enough left to talk about. Conrad's courting a girl, Mathilde. Erik doesn't know where he found her but he's pretty sure it wasn't in chemistry courses. She's dull as a custard. He made the mistake of telling Conrad that, and now, for possibly the first time in their lives, Louise is the person in his family least annoyed with him.

He sends his sister some of his new music. He wants to know what she thinks, but she writes back that she can't play it. The intervals are too big for her hands to stretch across. *I can manage a ninth if I get the angle right*, her letter says. *Everything else I had to arpeggio, so I know I haven't heard it the way you want it to be heard.* How strange, and accidental, the way he's left traces of his body, his long fingers, on the page. For weeks he doesn't write anything new, unsettled by the idea that the shape of his hands is present in the arrangement of the notes. What else can a person tell about him, just from playing his music?

When he starts writing again, he makes a running commentary along the staff lines, questions or commands or exhortations intended for the player. There is an intimacy in having one's music played, and he would like to control what sort of intimacy it is. If pianists are feeling the shape of his body, he wants at least to have a conversation with them. *Texts are not to be read aloud during performances!!!* he writes. *These performance indications are just for you.* A piece ought to be played, he suggests, *Like a nightingale with a toothache*, or *Like a door opening.* Some of them are comparatively practical: *Peacefully* or *Grandiosely.* Some are trickier: *Hypocritically* or *Learnedly.* Some are threats. Some are... he isn't sure what they are, but often the directions are his favorite part of whatever he's working on. Words come more easily these days than notes, which he doesn't like, hasn't wanted, doesn't know what to do with.

Claude finds the performance indications amusing but gimmicky. He plays through some of Erik's music and they have a fight about whether he's following the instructions.

"Don't tell me that was your best stab at *Obligingly*," Erik says.

"You've got me. I did not attempt *Obligingly* because I have no idea what that means."

"You didn't do *Mysterious and tender,* either."

"Look, the feel of a piece is either mysterious and tender, or it isn't. That isn't something the musician should have to be told."

Erik is rejected a third time for election to the Académie des Beaux-Arts. He thought of the application as a lark, the sort of thing he did only so he could write about it later, but when the rejection letter comes he feels kicked in the gut. He shows up at Philippe's door with a bottle of brandy, wanting to be comforted. He's already knocked when it occurs to him to worry about whether Philippe has other company.

"Are you alone?" he asks, when Philippe opens the door in his shirtsleeves.

"Usually," Philippe says, and lets him in.

He pours brandy into glasses and makes a show of commiseration, but Erik can tell his friend doesn't understand why they're mourning the entirely predictable outcome of a joke. It's the siege of the Opéra all over, but this time they aren't out afterward with friends, aren't drowning their sorrows in the din of some Montmartre hole. Philippe has an obnoxious clock on the mantel (since when does Philippe have enough money for a clock, let alone a mantel, let alone a fireplace for the mantel to sit over?) and the room is so quiet Erik can hear it tick every time either of them stops talking.

"This is awful," he says. "Can we go out?"

"I'm too tired. I have to work in the morning."

"You monster," Erik says.

But he's awfully tired too, and when Philippe suggests they both go to bed, offering him the sofa (Philippe owns a sofa?), Erik wakes up the next morning feeling better than he has in weeks. He credits the sofa, the modestly sized room, so much better than his closet.

"Maybe," Philippe tells him. "But it might also just be sleeping. Turns out it's important. Who knew?"

*   *   *

The way Claude's music feels is a kind of touch, and when he orchestrates Erik's *Gymnopédies*, with Gustave Doret conducting at the Salle Érard in February 1897, Erik could weep. The strings wrapping around him, the draped curtain of the harp, the oboe breathing the melody in and the flutes breathing it out. All of it is touch. The velvety chair and the air full of women's perfume, and the gold leaf winding across the walls and trim and pillars, the twinkling chandelier and the ceiling painted like sky. He's barely been inside a room like this since leaving the Conservatory. Now he's listening to his music fill the air between the glittering walls, and it hugs him, dives into his lungs, the muchness of it hard to breathe through.

Gymnopédies 1 and 3 have been programmed as part of a longer concert, but he can't bear to sit through anything else after hearing them. He is greedy, afraid that the next notes will knock the sounds from his head and he'll never get them back, never have this experience again. The audience thinks him arrogant and ungrateful to leave right after his own piece has been played, but it's fear, not dismissiveness, that has him jumping from his seat and nearly running from the room, tripping over knees and ankles. He has such gratitude that his throat clamps down and his heart closes up. He can't get the words out to thank Claude in the way he knows he should, which is to acknowledge that he couldn't have done this on his own. Orchestration can be a favor or a chore, a playful or ornate twist on someone else's melody; it can even be work for hire, the kind of task a composer might manage himself but doesn't want to bother with. But what Claude has done with the *Gymnopédies* is a gift.

"It was your music," Claude tells him in the lobby afterward, with the kind of magnanimity that comes only from having plenty of music of one's own.

Erik wants to scream so loud that the chandelier falls and crushes them both. That would be a kind of touch too, broken glass and obliterating weight, the opposite of the touch inside the recital hall, where he just experienced one of the most intimate moments of his life, and it was with Claude, and Claude doesn't even know. Erik understands the narcissism in this scenario, namely that as much as he admires Claude's music, what he loved most was listening to his own melodies made grand and expansive.

He goes to the bookshops near the Conservatory, hoping not to be recognized, and researches what texts are being assigned in the composition courses. There he buys an introductory text that includes charts of the capabilities of different instruments, what notes each makes comfortably, which additional ones can be eked out at the top or bottom of the range, depending on the skill of the player.

Later he expresses to Claude a fiendish desire to set everything just there, in the danger areas, barely playable.

"That's not clever, it'll just sound ugly," Claude counsels him, inspecting a draft. "And be monstrous to the poor musicians. Take that high B from the clarinet and give it to the flute. There's no prize for being an asshole."

"But that's a prize I could actually win," Erik mourns.

He waters down his ink to save money and returns to some of his older compositions. He digs out a piece he once started for Suzanne, back in that unbearable, galling summer after she broke things off with him. It's only two lines, four if the player repeats the bass motif between them, and he tries to lengthen it, but he can't get anywhere. He was playing with mirrors and rhymes, writing chords that sounded the exact same way even though they were made with different notation. He was making creeping ivy and fog, but also a compact sort of limerick, once you saw it on the page, and the whole thing is so tightly wound up in itself he can't make it do anything else. *Vexations*, he writes across the top, and wonders how many times you'd have to re-peat it to get through a whole gallery show. Too many, and the attendees would start scratching at their ears, aware something was wrong but not sure what it was.

Then why stop at a gallery show? What would happen if they kept scratching, scratching, scratching, into the third hour and the fourth and beyond? At the top, to the right of the title, he writes out an instruction: *In order to play the theme 840 times in succession, it would be advisable to prepare oneself beforehand, and in the deepest silence, by serious immobilities.*

In order to doesn't mean he imagines anyone bothering to do this—but if anyone did commit to the twenty-four hours he calculates the repetitions would take, that player would in-deed need to prepare himself. With at least a jug of water and a cushion, let alone the recommended deep silence and serious immobility. Erik has no intention of doing it himself either, un-til one night in his closet it feels as if the walls are closing in on him, and he kneels on the mattress by the keys, shuffles through the folder where he files his strangest ideas. The title and per-formance indication for *Vexations* are in brown, not the black of the original notes that were written when he at least had money for undiluted ink. The whole page is a portrait of frustration, of his fear that his art is not just standing still, it's moving back-ward. He decides to play it a few more times—maybe tonight he'll hear a way forward. But then he's just playing it over and over and over and over, no longer sure what he's listening for, or what he's hearing.

He's grateful when the concierge eventually bangs on his door, telling him to knock it off. He almost balls up the page to chuck it into the latrine, but he can't do it. He files it instead into a folder of things he's resolved not to return to. He never throws anything away.

*   *   *

La Vorace's tonics are available at a handful of stores in Paris, and when Erik has the funds (a payment for a cabaret commission, usually, or sometimes a gift from Alfred), he dutifully travels halfway across the city to purchase them. As far as he can tell, they do nothing for his hairline, but he feels good when he buys them. It's something of what he still sometimes feels when he lays down fresh hay for the goat. He is tending something that needs tending. He is helping a creature worse off than he is.

He thinks more and more often of Albert Tinchant. Erik is still playing many of the same pianos that Tinchant played, and he imagines Tinchant's body there, feet on the pedals, hands on the keys. A hard wooden piano bench is a kind of touch, as is the smooth surface of the keys, the thin ledge at the ends of the white ones, the angled fronts of the black. The brass ball of the damper pedal under his right foot. Erik starts wiping the instrument down before he plays every night, regardless of who played before or who's playing after him, and while he comes across as a germophobe, what he's really afraid of is ghosts.

He challenges Salis to a duel, issues the demand in a scroll tied with a long velvet ribbon. Erik has gotten a tarnished military sword from his old friend Alphonse and stuck the hilt awkwardly through his belt. The duel is a righteous cause, he explains to the costumed doorman, not merely for personal satisfaction but for back wages owed to half the neighborhood. Erik represents the cry of the people. The people need more than liquor to survive. The people need food, and sleep. Maybe even sofas.

The doorman, the plumes on his helmet waving, takes the scroll. "No second?" he asks, reading through the declaration. "I thought that was customary."

"I couldn't think of anyone who wouldn't try to talk me out of this."

"Salis is gone," the doorman says, off in the provinces with his touring show, an all-star lineup of Chat Noir chansonniers. Or, he acknowledges, performers whom Salis can pass off to the provincials as his all-stars. Having brought the world to Paris, apparently Salis has decided there's even more money to be made in bringing Paris to the world. "It's just as well for you," the doorman tells Erik. "That's a cavalry saber, my friend. Not the easiest choice for dueling."

"Does Salis know how to fence?" Erik asks, caught off guard.

"If you drew a sword on him, he would probably shoot you."

What will he do, then, when Salis returns? Beat a shameful retreat, or risk getting shot?

But he is spared having to decide when Salis catches ill and dies suddenly in Naintré, in western France. It should have been in Paris, Erik thinks, both relieved and crestfallen on hearing the news. The death doesn't feel real if it hasn't happened in Paris. He can't wrap his head around it. It seems possible that Salis might still come striding through the door, asking Erik what he's done with his life so far. Or Salis might still walk up and shoot him through the chest.

"He's gone and died without giving satisfaction," Erik says to Philippe. "I am without satisfaction."

The two of them raise a glass to their former boss, their matchmaker, the person who made their friendship possible by luring Philippe all the way from Spain to a single, bizarrely decorated building on the Rue Laval. Montmartre is a greenhouse, and Salis seeded and tended so many of the plants. Then he tried to carry them back out into the world, caught a chill, and died. Erik thinks of Louise's garden, the tropical foliage hunched shivering through winter, the eerie impossibility of the place. If even Salis couldn't leave Paris without dying, what did that mean for the rest of them?

"He had a good run, I suppose," Erik says.

"He was forty-five," Philippe says, disagreeing. Now that they are both over thirty, some numbers have started to look different.

* * *

The goat is swollen on its left side. Bloat? Erik has no idea, and the shepherd-turned-acrobat has moved away and can't be asked. Erik ties a rope around the goat's neck, leads it to the tram stop, and is relieved that it can walk up the stairs and into the car. He pays two fares, looks around as if daring anyone to stop him. If he were dressed like a peasant, somebody might, lecturing him on city etiquette. But in his baggy velvet suit, he's betting no one will do anything. They'll see that he knows city etiquette perfectly well and has just made a conscious decision to ignore it.

When they debark, Biqui seems to be struggling on the final walk to the fairgrounds, breathing heavily. It's autumn now, and some of the acts are still touring, still winding their way back to Paris for winter, and Erik is hoping Lisette's there. Those who have already arrived are open for business, and he drags the goat past a rickety carousel, past games of chance and strength and aim, plus two other animal exhibitors. He finds a single skinny bear in the cage beside Lisette's caravan. No sign of customers, but he doesn't know whether that's because it's a weekday morning or because Lisette's encampment has reached the point of no return, too sad to draw spectators, so that it becomes ever sadder, and so on into oblivion.

"Not good," she says, palpating the animal's sides. Bloat, she confirms. Advanced. And by the looks of the teeth and the teats, the animal's old.

She didn't breed the past season, Erik says, and her milk dried up.

"But you kept her?" Lisette asks.

Erik can do nothing but nod.

"Soft heart," she says. "Soft head." They could give baking soda and mineral oil for the bloat, she offers, and puncture the rumen as a last resort.

"Stab her?"

"If you're set on trying to save her. But there's a high risk of infection, and as I said, she's old."

Her practicality is exactly what he's come for, yet he's annoyed. He wants some sympathy out of her. Not for him, but for the goat. No one took La Vorace out behind a gypsy caravan and shot her when she was done with dancing. And what is she good for now? Her tonics don't even work. He's being unfair, he manages to remind himself. Lisette is a person, not a goat. But he likes Biqui as well as or better than he likes most people.

"Do you want a drink?" she asks. "While you decide what to do?"

It's only midmorning. Is she offering because she wants one, or because he's got a look to him, something stamped across his forehead, where his hair no longer hides it? He doesn't care. "Please," he says.

This time, when she offers to tell his fortune, he doesn't refuse. He lets her hold his hand, flat and open, and her fingers are warm as they touch his palm.

"You're searching for something," she starts.

"Isn't everybody?" She isn't going to charge him for this, is she?

"No," she says, seriously. "They aren't."

"Am I going to find it?"

"Are you giving me the goat, or not?"

"Let me guess: if I do, it's all laurels and champagne?"

"And if you don't, you're going to die a shriveled-up old man, bitter and alone." She says these damning words with a wink. *We're playing,* her eyes say. *You know how it is. You're a performer, too, even if you keep your clothes on.*

"How can I trust that fortune when you haven't even said what I'm searching for?"

"You've figured that part out yourself. Not everyone does. But I think you know what you want. You just aren't sure how to get it."

"I think everybody feels that way."

"No, darling. They really don't."

*   *   *

He makes her promise to do it cleanly and to wait until he's well out of the fairgrounds, on a tram headed somewhere else. He's so eager to be somewhere else he takes the first tram that arrives, with no idea where he's going. He debarks at Gentilly out of the same impulsiveness and wanders. He's playing at the Auberge tonight, but there are a number of hours until then, and little to fill them. He should be composing, he supposes. That's what he's meant to be filling the days with.

He walks half an hour and arrives at a small town square: a church and a municipal building and a café with no stage inside, just seating and a long bar, and outside a striped awning sheltering chairs and tables in its shade. He has to ask someone where he is, and is told Arcueil-Cachan. It's an industrial suburb, but the center feels like a little village. He imagines plank tables of fish guts and oyster shells, boats and sails knocking in the wind. He hasn't thought of Honfleur in a long time, and this place, really, is nothing like it. The nearest water is the Bièvre River and the viaduct that crosses it, a march of stone arches across the river valley. No one knows him here. There's no one to scold him or send him back to school or fish him out of the basin. He might look at basic orchestration guides to his heart's content, in public, without being embarrassed—everyone here will still think he is an expert. His idea of the people here is narrow and dismissive: factory workers and the unemployed, people squeezed out of the city proper. Uneducated and uninteresting. In time he'll realize he's wrong, but for now he's right enough: there are no other composers. The only musicians here are the people who play dented instruments in the volunteer brass band on public holidays.

He orders a glass of wine, pulls out his notebook. He has always liked the touch of fine paper, the firm slide of a good ink pen. He loves cracking the leather spine of a new notebook, the weight of the compact pages in his pocket. He taught himself how to cut quills out of cast-off feathers from the plucked birds at Les Halles, to see if the fragile *scritch* might make a difference to the things he wrote. Thus far: no.

The sun is on his knees, the gray fabric stretched tight across his legs, and he begins to cook slowly in the unseasonably warm weather. He shifts, pulls the fabric away from his skin. His cheeks are getting red and tight, as is his scalp where his hair has deserted him. He should retreat, but the tables under the awning are full. He listens halfheartedly to the conversations, shuffles through them for one into which he can insert himself, and either entertain the patrons into generosity or act such a pest that the party will leave and he'll inherit the table. But no one is talking about art, or music, or any of his usual subjects. *No one is talking about art.* It takes him several moments to process this, then he listens with anthropological pleasure. The talk is of local factories, a local sports league. Somebody's wife, somebody's mistress. A new rubbish-collection system, and how angry the ragpickers will be to be cheated out of a living. No one is talking about art. No one is talking about art. Its absence makes a wondrous silence in which he can hear his own breath, his heartbeat. A pack of children roars into the square kicking a rag ball, and he listens to their shouts, the thump of their feet kicking the ball, slapping the ground. Touch and sound. Joyful noise.

He rises, turns around, and carries his glass to the table behind him. "I'm looking for a room," he announces.

Louise

— 12 —

Outward, painfully

I FINALLY SETTLED ON CALLING HIM JOSEPH, PLUCKED FROM THE clutter of Lafosse family legacies that constituted my son's name. It would have annoyed Pierre: it was too close to his father's name, too unvarnished a tribute. But his father had failed everyone *except* me. He had owed me nothing and given me great kindness. He provided me and my son a life in an extraordinary place and held the gates against the wolves. Occasionally I remembered they were out there, waiting, but I did not have to look them in the eye. I was a kept woman, and no one asked me for any kind of payment.

I knew it was for Joseph's sake more than mine. We all fed off what seemed to be his unshakable happiness. As far as I could tell, he had wants but no longings. He shrieked for desserts but not for a father, because he had neither memory nor context for one. He had a mother and two grandparents. He had sturdy legs, large feet, long-fingered hands. He had our features, mine and Pierre's mingled, but he always looked so happy that he never looked quite like either of us. He had endless hallways and pathways and rooms and garden grottoes. In choosing the largesse of Bellenau over the privations of Fortin and Estelle, I felt I had done something good for my son, although none of what I had thereby given him had been mine to bestow. Having granted it,

269

though, I couldn't do anything else without taking it away, since to remarry would be to disinherit Joseph.

When Fortin and Estelle came to visit, Estelle would wring her hands about my isolation. At first she asked only whether I had enough company. But after a party for Joseph's third birthday, she wondered aloud where and how I might ever meet someone else. "You may not be ready now, but someday you'll want to marry again."

"Lightning doesn't usually strike the same place twice," Fortin said. He meant nothing of love, but money. "Unless you've got a duke in your coat pocket, it would be a mistake. You'd be cheating Joseph."

However steeply Fortin looked down his nose at luxury, he would never countenance the whims of my heart, or any heart, overriding the security of a son's inheritance. Anyone who was apt to marry me was not likely to be able to provide us with a life remotely as good as the one we enjoyed here. I was trapped, and I knew I was trapped, but the cage was very beautiful. Besides Estelle's and Fortin's visits, I corresponded with a few school friends in Le Havre and received occasional letters from Eugénie or my brothers. Sundays I went with Joseph to the church in Saint-Côme-du-Mont. But the longer I lived at Bellenau, the more the rest of the world receded. The slower I was to write back, the more slowly the letters arrived. I kept reminding myself I was providing for Joseph all the things my childhood had lacked.

When Joseph was five, his grandfather suffered a sudden apoplexy while digging a hole to transplant a greenhouse seedling, an end that I think would have pleased him, had he the opportunity to express an opinion. The aftermath of his death was slow and orderly, like a surgeon's scalpel rather than a ripping of wolf teeth. I suppose Cannu deserves credit for that, though he did it for his and Albertine's sake, not for mine or Joseph's or Madeleine's, and certainly not for the garden's. As soon as Pierre-Joseph was buried, Cannu divvied the estate into parcels and sold off the farthest reaches first, the best farmland and pasturage. He schemed, playing neighboring landowners against each other to drive up the prices. Within the space of a year he transformed the Lafosse family from benefactors to local villains, but he did not line his own pockets. All the proceeds went toward servicing the estate's debts, which turned out to be even more vast than Pierre had once feared. I was ashamed when people turned away from us in Saint-Côme-du-Mont, but since my fortunes were fixed to the Lafosses—since I was, in my own shabby way, one of them—I did not entirely disapprove of Cannu's tactics.

Madeleine drew certain firm lines and held them, to Cannu's exasperation. He couldn't touch the house or the heart of the garden, for example. I didn't know if this was out of loyalty to Pierre-Joseph the visionary, or to Pierre-Joseph her husband, or to the vision itself. Maybe it was loyalty to her own desires; perhaps what had looked like long-suffering acquiescence to Pierre-Joseph's eccentricity had really been a kind of ownership this whole time. Every night that he was at dinner, Cannu lectured her on how much better off we'd all be if we sold and left now, rather than sinking the proceeds of the land sales back into an estate that slurped up every franc poured into it and remained thirsty. The rotting château was, in his terms, a "depreciating asset." But the depreciating asset was also Madeleine's home, and she offered Cannu only a blank, agreeable smile that infuriated him, the same expression that had once infuriated Pierre, because it looked so much like stupidity. I think I was the only one who recognized it as strategy: she understood what Cannu wanted as well as she knew that she would not consent to it, and she was choosing the kind of fight they would have. Let him keep lecturing—it was more comfortable than a battle of wills.

Bellenau was like an onion growing smaller and smaller, with Cannu peeling away the outer acres. What was left was woefully understaffed, and as a literal jungle began to close in, I realized that Pierre-Joseph had created only the outline of one, not the real thing. Now the paths grew narrower and narrower as some plants collapsed and died and others ran riot. Joseph, who was five, loved it. As the spaces of the garden shrank, they also became more secret, as if the place, in its dying, was being made over to child-size. Inside the house, Joseph found mushrooms growing in the carpets of distant rooms whose windows were so loose in their frames that rain streamed down the walls. He sank his fingers into the rotted sills, soft as cheese. He collected pieces of different wallpapers as they tattered and made a scrapbook for Madeleine, who cried when she paged through it. This frightened him, as it hadn't been his intention, and he climbed into her lap to try to kiss away her grief.

As Joseph grew, he began to need things for which Cannu had not budgeted. The village school would have been free, but none of the Lafosses could stomach the idea of sending him to be educated alongside the sons of the gardeners. Pierre and Albertine had had governesses and tutors in the house, but there was no longer money for that. A boarding school was the most logical option, Cannu announced. Fortin even suggested the collège in Honfleur, thinking the choice would make me like the idea better. He volunteered to pick Joseph up every weekend to spend Sunday in Le Havre.

Joseph wouldn't be dispatched to boarding school unless it was over my own corpse, I informed them. "Eric *hated* it there. And it just isn't necessary. Joseph can stay here. I'll educate him."

"You're barely educated yourself," Cannu said.

"I think I know more than a six-year-old," I said. *You found me educated enough to court*, I thought, but did not say. Maybe he'd always found me ignorant but had considered it an advantage rather than a drawback.

"At some point he'll need to be prepared for lycée."

That was years off, I said. Either I would keep far enough

ahead of him, or we could figure out something else when the time came.

Cannu clearly thought the second option was more realistic than the first, but grudgingly agreed that, for the time being, I could educate Joseph at home.

I'd spent my years at Bellenau plowing through the library, but my newfound expertise was more in novels than in anything else. I'd read the complete works of Victor Hugo, but the sample exam packets Cannu sent me from a lycée in Cherbourg were far more impenetrable. I received the message he intended: I had some English but no Latin, no advanced math, no science but what Pierre-Joseph had taught me in the garden. I had plenty of Catholic theology, but the state schools no longer tested that. The exam questions made a mountain I had only half realized existed, much less knew how to climb. I began our lessons already dreading the day I would have to admit that Cannu was right, and my anxiety made me a fussy dictator in the schoolroom. When Joseph rebelled, our lessons sometimes devolved into shouting matches, and eventually I surrendered. We went back to reading fairy tales in the library and drawing pictures of the heroes and villains; we found insects in the garden and I let him invent their names, since I rarely knew the right answers. He made up racing games with elaborate rules and we dashed between trees together. I let him play with the sons and daughters of the remaining groundskeepers, and only sometimes tried to scrub his speech of their influence.

Both Fortin and Cannu found me far too soft. Fortin, when he visited, would lob some of the same questions at Joseph that I remembered him lobbing at me. His dismay at Joseph's not knowing the capital of Belgium was palpable. It wasn't just his letters and numbers, Cannu scolded. The real trouble was that I was failing to instill proper habits of mind.

Only at the piano was I a skilled schoolmistress, perhaps because I hoped Joseph would learn to love it. If he learned math by brute force and hated it ever after, well, that was much the way I had been taught math, and I had survived. But I wanted him to feel at home with and in music. I suppose I thought it was the one thing—not the house, the garden, the dwindling Lafosse wealth shielding us from the rest of the world—that was mine to pass down to him. He showed little aptitude or love for music, but he was young still, and I could wait. I felt that way about the entirety of our desultory schooling: he seemed so young and so happy, and I had been so unhappy as a child, that his joy in the world was worth safeguarding to me at nearly any price.

Cannu eventually confined his opinions about Joseph's education to occasional lectures, although I had the impression he was only biding his time until Joseph was older and demanded a wider world for himself, or I was forced to acknowledge my own limitations. *Fine*, I thought, because I was biding my time as well: once Madeleine died, what was left of Bellenau would be sold and the proceeds divided between Albertine and Joseph. He and I would lose our home, but we'd have an income with which to find another one. It would be my son's income, not mine, and I occasionally felt shame about waiting for it: waiting, constantly, for someone I was fond of to die, for a child to inherit money I would then spend. But what else did I have to wait for?

That was how I taught Joseph geography, when I taught him geography: where might he want to live when the gilded-cage door opened? We invented impossible lives—as Eskimos in the frozen north or settlers in the Congo. We swam with penguins in Antarctica and drank tea in China. In South America we herded llamas in the Andes and ran from jaguars in the Brazilian jungle.

The library at Bellenau had enough fuel for these fantasies, but many of the books were out of date, and Cannu sourly offered corrections when he overheard us. "Buenos Aires is perfectly civilized these days," he said. "There aren't cattle roaming the streets."

"Have you been there?" Joseph asked.

"No," he said. "But I've seen pictures. It looks like anywhere. It looks like Paris."

"Paris is hardly *anywhere*," I said.

"It looks like a large, fine city," Cannu said, meeting my pedantry with his own. "Buildings of stone, paved streets with lights. Banks and government buildings and an opera house and so on."

The harshest of Cannu's opinions about Bellenau, or about Madeleine or me or Joseph, he did not express in front of his wife, and I wished Albertine would accompany him more often. But she stayed in Cherbourg for months at a time, even as Cannu's responsibilities at the estate expanded. For years she claimed that Bellenau's growing shabbiness depressed her too much to visit. Then on one visit she asked me again to go rowing with her. It had happened only the one other time, when she informed me of Pierre's illness, and I braced myself for whatever woeful tidings this rendezvous might divulge. The little boats were by now so rotted that water seeped in through the boards and puddled at our feet. As a result we had to curtail our excursion, and she hurried to explain, with the water rising, how hard the past years had been, trying for a baby, and waiting and trying and waiting some more, all the while with a nephew who'd been conceived in the space of a month living in her childhood nursery. She knew this wasn't Joseph's fault, or mine, and she was trying to set it aside, she said, and be warmer toward us.

Sometimes she was, and sometimes she treated me as if I was something unpleasant left behind after Pierre's death, like the debris on a beach after a storm tide has receded. She'd send Joseph funny postcards for no reason, then ignore his birthday and name day. Sometimes she looked at him with the same expression she wore while sorting through Cannu's early winnowings of the estate, the piles of antiques and unfashionable paintings he'd earmarked for sale: *This should have been mine. You should have been mine.*

*　　*　　*

At dinner there's a new guest at the boardinghouse, the poor man like chum in the conversational waters. In the decades since my arrival in Argentina, the country has latched its gates much more tightly, even as the whole world seemed to catch fire. Newcomers are so much rarer these days that the building goes a little wild for them. What news have they brought? What can they tell us, about either their personal sorrows or those of the world we've left?

This guest turns out to be a disappointment: an agricultural consultant from Uruguay, just passing through Buenos Aires on his way to Río Negro province. I imagine the Italian girl sighing with boredom, although she's moved out already, and I don't know where she went. With the situation in France, he says, the vineyards here would be foolish not to maximize production in anticipation.

"In anticipation of what?" I ask from the neighboring table, although I promised myself I wasn't interested in the stranger. I make my accent sound very French, and he shifts uncomfortably.

"It's a thirsty world," he says. "That's all I meant. Maybe more now than ever."

He corners me the next day at breakfast—he didn't mean any offense, he says, but one can't help reading the newspapers.

I tell him I took no offense. "Besides, they don't grow grapes where I'm from. They grow cows."

Do I still have family there? he asks. Are my people all right?

I tell him I don't have any family.

I can sense the man wash his hands of me at that moment. He was only trying to be polite in the first place, and now I've revealed myself to be an old sourpuss with no one left alive who loves her. What is the point of an old woman who hasn't managed to make herself a family? What is she for?

That's all right with me. I don't really want to talk about the war, especially since the débarquement started, with the Allied forces landing on the beaches of Normandy, and the newspapers became a bizarre roll call of the places of my former life, including even tiny Saint-Côme-du-Mont. I don't want to talk about it partly because I have loved and been loved in these places, and their destruction is not·a conversation I wish to have with a Uruguayan viticulture consultant over breakfast. But also because there is a small vicious voice inside me that has read about the German occupation, that now reads about the Allied invasion, and whispers: *Burn. Let them all burn.*

While Madeleine continued to hold on, Estelle passed away when Joseph was eight, the year the century turned. Fortin and I mourned her together, but I didn't know if he would keep coming to Bellenau alone, once the fresh edges of our grief had worn away. I was pleased when he did, even when he seemed to have saved up his bluster to unleash on me and Joseph. He was a man who liked to be listened to, and once Estelle was no longer there to indulge him, we were expected to rise to the occasion. Joseph found him very forbidding, and he was, but he was forbidding in all the same ways he'd been since I was a girl, and I took some comfort in this.

I had regular letters from Conrad and the sporadic ones from old school friends and from Eric (who had ensconced himself, rather inexplicably, in a new apartment in some industrial enclave far south of the city). I had the library, including all those Hugo novels. I was partial to the orphan Cosette's wild swerves of fortune in *Les Misérables*. Only a half orphan, like me: her father abandons her but doesn't die. Unless he dies later in the novel, and I've forgotten? I think he simply disappears, winks out of her mother Fantine's life and the book for good. Félix something-or-other. I suppose I could look it up.

What if Pierre had winked out of mine, before we were ever wed, before he ever brought me to that château, with its orchids and its wolves? What if I'd said yes to Cannu and never earned his wrath, never met Pierre? What would Fantine have wanted if she could see the future? To keep her hair, her teeth, her life, no doubt. But then she would have also had to wish her child out of existence. It's an impossible question, the undoing of entire lives, both mine and my son's.

When Madeleine died, the year after Estelle, Cannu acted much the same as he had following Pierre-Joseph's passing, which is to say that he wasted no time in the apportioning and sale of assets. Nor should he have, in this case—I think all of us were ready, or at least told ourselves we were ready, to let go what was left of Bellenau and see what came next. Joseph was ten by then, and everyone, including me, was beginning to find him slightly feral. He needed other boys, other children. He did not need another mother, I thought sourly, watching Albertine cosset him. She seemed to have finally replaced her stiff distance with a smothering affection that even a much younger boy would not have borne willingly. Joseph let her kiss him, then wiped at his cheeks.

"It hurts Aunt Albertine's feelings when you wipe away her kisses," I told him when she wasn't listening.

He argued with me, insisting he was doing no such thing, but later he paused with his hand raised to his cheek, his eyes widening in realization. He started to lower it, then brushed it through his hair, a clumsy effort at concealment, but an effort. My little gentleman.

I misestimated how hard everything would be on him after Madeleine died. I shouldn't have. It should have been obvious that Bellenau was his entire world, Madeleine and Pierre-Joseph two-thirds of his heart. I'd trusted too much in the fact that he'd still have me, his mother. That was the loss that had unraveled my life, and so I failed to fully understand what Joseph's other losses, including the phantom loss of his father, meant to him. A mother is everything, I'd wanted to believe, but in truth a mother is only a mother.

Cannu and Fortin offered to host us in Cherbourg or Le Havre, to spare us from witnessing the preparations for the estate sale, the stream of buyers haggling over everything from gardening tools to the house itself. I wanted to stay at first to monitor Pierre's things, to make sure Joseph had anything he wanted from his father. But there was very little that meant anything to Joseph. A few books, some specimen cards in his father's handwriting, a monogrammed handkerchief. As the house continued to disgorge an impossible, overwhelming number of possessions—Pierre's old school papers, a great-grandmother's wedding china, clothes that had been out of fashion for seventy years—I had the feeling that Joseph expressed interest in items of his father's only to please me, afraid to say when he did not want something.

Pierre's bicycle appeared suddenly, standing in the courtyard beside piles of old horse tack. It had sat in a hallway for nearly a year after his death. Then Pierre-Joseph had said he was going to throw it in one of the canals, and Madeleine had said she should try to return it to the manufacturer, and I'd said no, I wanted to keep it. I put on a pair of Pierre's trousers and tried to teach myself to ride. I fell off, over and over again, and would like to say I got the hang of it, but I eventually gave up. I limped with the bicycle into the stables and propped it in a corner, and did my best to forget that it existed.

I was relieved now to see that it was in perfectly good repair: one of the groundskeepers, it turned out, had been using it to commute back and forth to his home in the village. I asked Joseph if he knew how to ride a bicycle and he shook his head. Of course he didn't. It had been my responsibility to teach him, or arrange for him to be taught, and I'd neglected to do it.

"Let's have a go," I said.

One of the stablemen lowered the seat for us. I'd still never learned how to ride it myself, and I wasn't dressed for trying, so all I could do was push Joseph from behind while shouting instructions I only half understood. He was game at first, but once it was clear he wasn't going to take to it immediately, he started to complain. Not about his skinned palms, but about the collection of stablemen and other staff who had gathered in the courtyard to watch his progress. No one was mocking him, but his face was bright red with embarrassment, and I let him dismount and took him inside to clean his scrapes.

"You just need to practice," I encouraged him. "It isn't an easy thing to learn."

"Not in front of them," he said, and I saw, more than the embarrassment of a boy, the embarrassment of a lordling. Master of the manor, last of his line.

I'd thought the pain of watching Bellenau dissolve was only (only!) the pain of losing his home, but it was more than that—he was heir to an estate we were dismantling around him, and there was nothing he could do to stop us. "None of this is your fault," I told him. "There is nothing you could have done to change any of this."

"But can I buy it back someday? If I have enough money?"

I had failed to anticipate this conversation, and I picked my startled way through its shoals. "If you have enough money, I suppose. And if whoever owns it then is willing to sell."

"Why wouldn't he be willing?"

"Maybe he'll have fallen in love with the place."

"But it will still be mine," Joseph said. "He'll understand that. He'll understand that it should have been mine."

Who had given him his thwarted sense of responsibility, of ownership? I didn't think it was me, a woman who had never felt like a lady of the manor, who knew I had never been more than an accidental guest. I also couldn't imagine it was Cannu, after his decade-long campaign to keep any of us from getting too comfortable here. Nor Albertine, who still alternated suffocating affection with spasms of resentment, both of Joseph's existence and his claim to Bellenau.

"Your father would be very proud of you," I told him.

"For what? I haven't done anything."

"For you. For who you're becoming."

"I'm not anybody. I'm just a boy."

"Even so."

"How do I make enough money?"

"You're asking the wrong person."

"Who is the right one? Uncle Cannu?"

I groaned, inwardly. "You'll have to be very clever, and work very hard, whatever you choose. So for now, let's make a start by agreeing to be better about your lessons. We'll both work harder."

"I want to go to school," he said.

"Now? Or after we leave?"

"Can we leave now?"

"We can stay here some months yet. We don't have to go."

"I want to," he said. "I don't want to be here any longer."

Diego is late for his lesson, and Mr. Valera offers a gruff apology. "He went out earlier to play with the hooligans downstairs. I told him to be back in time, but he must have lost track."

Both of us feel too old, or at least I do, to go hunt down the hooligans. Besides, it isn't my job. I hope he doesn't think there will be no charge if Diego doesn't turn up. Even if I wanted to be generous, I can't afford not to charge him. My balance sheet is delicately balanced, month by month and week by week. *Fortin, look at me*, I sometimes think, as I make the numbers work. But whatever respect or guilt he might feel would be outweighed by his disapproval of the meagerness of the figures and the precarious match between the column of expenses and my income.

What will you do when you get too frail or ill to work? I imagine him asking me.

I'm never ill, I reply.

You're seventy-six years old, he says. *You'll get ill someday. Some-day soon.*

You're dead, I say. *You don't get an opinion anymore.*

"Did you ever remember it?" Mr. Valera asks, and it takes me a moment to return from the conversation I've been having in my head. "The old friend's name? When he was in Tarragona."

"Oh. No. Alas, it's gone forever," I say, trying to sound casual. But I want to know what happened to Philippe, and I don't, and won't. Eric can't tell me, and I can't look it up, not like trotting to the library to find the surname of Félix-whoever in *Les Mis-érables*. Philippe is lost to me entirely—truly and forever.

"You're very good with Diego," Mr. Valera says. "If he doesn't make it in time, he'll be disappointed to have missed you."

"I don't know about that. Nothing ruins a child's fondness quicker than finger exercises."

"Except for the finger exercises, he likes you. And the memorizing. He complains a blue streak about that."

"Good," I say, smiling. There was a hint of doubt in Mr. Valera's voice—could any teacher too well liked also be effective?—but I wield both the carrot and the stick.

Diego shows up breathless, only ten minutes left in the lesson time, and I still make him start with his exercises before we move on to any of the pieces he likes. Then I feel bad, and stay twenty minutes late to give him a full lesson. The younger Mr. Valera has arrived home by the time we finish, and I overhear him and his father discussing quietly in the kitchen whether or not he's brought enough food for supper to invite me to stay.

"I should be going," I say loudly, and nudge Diego down from the piano bench.

He tears off into the kitchen, then returns with half again as much payment as usual. He hands it to me and leans for an in-stant hard into my side. Startled, I put an arm around him, and we have a strange half-hug until Mr. Valera appears from the kitchen and Diego breaks away.

"For the wait," Mr. Valera says of the money, walking me to the front door.

"You don't have to."

"We'd like to," he says. "Thank you for staying."

I've been avoiding asking about Diego's mother, but as we linger in the doorway I wonder if I'm supposed to, if my reticence seems uncaring.

I am just about to inquire when Mr. Valera asks, "Do you have children of your own?"

My body goes rigid. I've never been electrocuted, but that's the feeling I imagine, the same feeling the question always gives me. No one has asked it of me in a long time. I heard it less often once I began to look more like a grandmother than a mother, which happened many years ago. More recently I've started looking less like a pink-cheeked, tart-baking, robust sort of grandmother and more like the kind of fragile, cobwebby woman you perch on the end of a sofa during social events and hope doesn't tip over. No one wants to get her started with chatter out of fear that she might never hush, about her past joys, her many ailments, all the departed darlings, or enemies, she's survived.

"No," I tell Mr. Valera, and nothing more.

Cherbourg or Le Havre? I didn't want Joseph's first experience of life outside Bellenau to be Cannu's self-important hospitality or Fortin's ascetic welcome. He had been to both places before, as well as on other short excursions, but he'd never spent any extended time away from the estate.

I asked Joseph if he had an opinion. Not about the wild, eventual lives we'd fantasized, but a next move. We needed a place to go while we waited for the inheritance to be settled, I told him.

What about Paris? he asked.

"What do you know of Paris?" We'd been there exactly twice, once for a strained visit with Alfred and Eugénie when he was an infant, which he wouldn't remember, and once for Conrad's wedding to Mathilde, two years earlier.

"Everyone always wants to live in Paris."

"Not everyone," I said, but he'd given me an idea. Were my Paris relatives any worse than our other options?

I wrote to my father and Eugénie, wondering if they might be able to accommodate us for a short stay. Very short, I promised both them and myself—just until Joseph's inheritance was settled. Once I had their invitation, which felt genuinely welcoming and not just polite, I spoke to Cannu in private one evening, after Joseph had gone to bed. I thought he'd be pleased that I was doing my part to hasten the sale and remove us from his care. But his face was instantly stormy.

"It wouldn't be fair to either Joseph or Albertine, to abscond with him like this."

"I'm not 'absconding' with him. He's my son."

"Albertine is very fond of Joseph. He's her only remaining relative," Cannu reminded me.

"He has relatives in Paris, too."

"That you think so little of he's barely met them."

"I'd like to change that."

"Do you? Or do you just want their charity?"

This struck true, and I almost sputtered. Cannu's opposition was a surprise. I'd expected his approval, which I'd hoped would pave the way for a loan to allow us to leave. Now I didn't know how to bring up the money.

I wasn't sure if it was good luck or bad when Cannu then brought it up himself. He supposed I would need money, he said, even if I had secured a place to stay.

A small advance on Joseph's inheritance would be useful, I agreed carefully.

Cannu grunted that he would set up a hearing in Le Havre. "Don't leave before that."

I hadn't envisioned anything so official, but if Cannu wanted to do this through the courts, perhaps that was all to the good. That way there would be a formal record of what we'd already received, and would later be owed.

"It's only Paris," I said, trying to be reassuring. "It's not as if I'm taking him to the far side of the world."

Many of the women at the resettlement center arrive without husbands or working-age sons, and I never know how much to ask about what has happened to their men. Perhaps the women wish to speak and would like to know someone cares enough to ask. But usually their faces are dour, walling off whatever happened to them back in Poland. The resettlement center provides some assistance, and the Argentine government arranges for a handful of nights in one of the designated immigrant hotels. But after those run out the women are left to piddling occupations—often laundry and sewing—that don't generate enough to raise a family. I worry for them, fear they've come from the frying pan to the fire, but they make it clear they are relieved to be here, and I understand that the frying pan was worse than what I am able to imagine. It wasn't like this when I started volunteering at the resettlement center thirty years ago. We served a flood of families, complete with husbands and sons, often only stopping off in Buenos Aires on their way to one of the agricultural colonies.

Because I can give piano lessons only when the children are out of school for the day, I've learned to fill my mornings with other things. Ideally paying things, like teaching classes at the French Institute, but when the priest at San Isidro told me a resettlement center in the parish needed volunteers, I was idle enough and curious enough to pay a visit. Now I teach Spanish there two mornings a week—survival Spanish, nothing fancy. There's a social room where the refugees gather to drink tea and pick through piles of donations. There's a teacher's room where the donations—food, coats, shoes, toiletries—are piled and sorted. We are the most reliable donors to our own campaigns. I'm embarrassed by my contributions of the little gifts my pupils' families give me: the handkerchiefs cross-stitched with music notes, the pair of potholders printed with composers' silhouettes, the three separate ashtrays with golden music notes around the edges. I do not smoke, have never smoked. Everyone can tell which items in the bins are mine, and everyone can see how useless they are. But keeping them turns my room into a stage set full of obvious props, as if I am not so much living my life as playing a role in a pantomime.

The flood of immigrants is a trickle now; no one can get a visa. The refugees who do arrive have traveled long, circuitous routes, sometimes through other South American countries, and I wonder whether they'll find here whatever kept them pressing on to Argentina. They linger longer in the social room than their predecessors did in the years before the war, clutching the cups of weak tea. I used to apologize for the bad tea, but then the women felt obliged to correct me, to say no, no, how good it tastes. How grateful they are. Now I say nothing.

For decades the same wall clock kept time in the social room, but recently I took it down. When the center was quiet I could hear it ticking, and in all the years I've been coming here the room has never been as quiet as it's been since the war began. I had never noticed the ticking of the clock before, but as soon as I did it drove me to distraction.

"How are the women supposed to know what time it is now?" some of the other volunteers asked me.

"They don't care," I said. "They've got nowhere else to be."

A mother comes with a boy, perhaps seven or eight years old, although many of the children who arrive turn out to be older than they look, their bodies stunted by want. He spends an hour folding sheets of newspaper into shapes. Not vehicles or animals, just shapes, squares that get smaller and smaller until he can barely fold the paper anymore, or triangles whose corners he creases with his fingernails to make as sharp as possible. I once found a book about paper-folding at Bellenau, not in the library but on the ratty bookshelf in the old nursery. Joseph and I spent hours with it on rainy days, creating frogs, cranes, horses, dragons, a ball you could puff air into and swat around. I even ordered special paper, an expense at which Cannu rolled his eyes when it showed up on the household ledger.

I pick up a piece of newsprint and try to remember how to make some of the animals. I keep scrambling the steps, and the paper is too thin to hold the necessary creases. But finally, in a kind of muscle memory, my hands take over as if I'm playing a familiar piano piece, and I manage to produce a ball. The boy comes over to sit beside me, a little warily.

I blow up the ball and hand it to him. "For you," I say in Spanish, unsure how much he speaks.

He turns it over and over in his hands, inspecting it from every angle. He swats it up into the air, twice, three times, catches it again. Then he hops off his chair and scoops a new piece of newsprint off the floor and thrusts it at me. "Learn me," he says.

My heart starts splitting—that I have something he wants, and that what he wants is to be able to make paper balls for himself and not need me anymore. I am a mother again for just a moment, at the very crux of motherhood. "What is your name? How old are you?" I ask, as I begin a new ball and he follows my folds.

"Oskar," he says. "Ten."

Joseph's age, when we left Bellenau. The last time my son was mine. The boy is far too small for ten. I can't stop staring at him, and remembering, and my head gets in the way of my hands and I can't make another ball come out right. We wreck an entire newspaper in the effort, and he is gentle in his disappointment. I am one more in a parade of people who have failed him, and he recognizes that this failure is, in the great scheme of things, minor.

"I'll remember again," I say. "I'll practice and remember." I can tell this doesn't quite make sense to him, but he blames his own lack of Spanish. How does one practice remembering?

Like this. Like this:

I would have walked straight into the lion's den completely un-aware were it not for telegrams from both Fortin and my father asking urgently what in the world Cannu intended. Those gave me enough warning to panic, but not enough to prepare. The single wise thing I did was to beg Alfred to bring someone with him who could wait with Joseph outside the courtroom in Le Havre. I knew enough to guess that I didn't want him there listening, and that if Albertine came I wouldn't want Joseph waiting with her.

I was not prepared for how terribly frail my father seemed. He was not young, I reminded myself, but he certainly hadn't looked like this at Conrad's wedding. His suit hung from him, his skin was sallow, his thinning hair lank. He was clearly ill and hadn't told me, nor did he tell me then—not in so many words.

He shrugged off my concern. "We're here for you and Joseph," he said. "Let's see what there is to be done."

He'd brought Eugénie, and as soon as I saw her I realized I had hoped for Conrad or Eric, but I was grateful even so.

Because Cannu was Joseph's only remaining male relative on the Lafosse side, he was able to appoint whomever he wanted to his half of the Family Council. He showed up with two business associates from Cherbourg who had never met Joseph or me. The pretext for convening the Council was the inheritance: I'd been a suitable choice of guardian when Joseph was an infant, needing milk and a loving pair of arms. But now that he was ten, soon to be a man of means? He would need guidance in invest-ment and self-discipline, in shaping his education and habits and in preparing for a profession.

"It may be no fault of her own," Cannu said, "but Madame

Lafosse does not have a suitable degree of experience to adequately advise her son in any of these areas."

"I have a great deal of self-discipline," I said stiffly, and then proved it by saying nearly nothing for the next hour.

My father and Fortin offered testimonials, but it became agonizingly clear that Alfred barely knew me, and still thought of me as the little girl he'd discarded. Fortin said many kind things, but under prompting from the justice of the peace he admitted his disapproval of Joseph's too-casual education and my too-casual discipline, and agreed that under his own guardianship I'd had no opportunity to develop skill in the management of funds.

Deep inside I laughed—a man who hadn't even wanted me to have a purse? He would have taught a boy, I thought bitterly. He would have taught a boy all these things.

I thought the fact that Cannu was married to the recipient of the other half of the Lafosse inheritance posed an obvious conflict of interest, but apparently even this did not concern the justice as much as my personal shortcomings. Everyone in the room could guess the outcome by the time testimony was finished. Even if we split down the middle—and by this time I wasn't at all sure that my own great-uncle intended to vote for me—the justice of the peace, as the tiebreaker, would side with Cannu, who had assured him I would continue to play an "appropriate" role in my son's life. "One suited to her sex and her abilities," he said.

With helpless rage I stared at him, at the triumph bubbling up in his face under its veneer of solemn responsibility.

"Before a vote," Fortin said to the justice, like a man sliding through a door before it closes completely, "may I propose an alternate arrangement for consideration?" He suggested a split in responsibilities, with the financial trusteeship assigned to Cannu and the physical guardianship assigned to himself.

"To *you*?" I said aloud, shocked.

"I think it's appropriate," Fortin said to the justice, not to me, "that our side of the family continue to play some official role in his upbringing. I've been part of the boy's life since he was an infant, and I'd be honored to continue to guide his spiritual and intellectual formation."

The justice called Fortin and Cannu up to confer with him privately. My father put a hand on my shoulder and squeezed, not comfortingly but tightly, almost painfully. *This is the best you'll be able to do*, I imagined him saying. *Don't ruin it.*

The final result was a 4–2 vote stripping me of any legal right to my own child. My father alone voted with me, in favor of my retaining sole guardianship. I wondered if it was love or loyalty or fear of my further disapproval. Did it matter? He would be dead within the year, and I wished later that I'd thanked him better. My father had been his most loving self on one of the worst days of my life, and I had trouble giving him his due.

Cannu, Fortin, and Cannu's two friends all voted for the last-minute arrangement to divide financial and physical guardianship between Cannu and Fortin. Since it wasn't a tie, the justice didn't vote, merely confirmed the Council's decision.

We all filed out of the courtroom. Albertine rose eagerly from her seat across the lobby from where Joseph sat on a bench, playing cards with Eugénie. Albertine and I both started walking toward him. We watched each other, quickened our paces. I nearly ran.

"No," I said, when I got to him first, and squeezed his shoulders tightly, too tightly, just as my father had squeezed mine only minutes before.

"Maman?" Joseph said.

"He isn't yours."

Albertine looked from me to Cannu and back again. Cannu, still walking across the room to join us, shook his head slightly, and Albertine's confusion appeared to deepen. Had she planned on walking him directly out of the courthouse to her home in Cherbourg, without any of his books or toys, without even a change of clothes? I didn't think I could be more afraid than I'd been in the courtroom, but I started to shake.

We all went to lunch together, God help us, because Cannu and Albertine were pretending the day was a completely objective, dispassionate effort to best prepare Joseph for adult life, and I was pretending to be an objective, dispassionately responsible woman who, despite her apparently manifold failings, could be entrusted with her own child. Fortin and I hadn't had an opportunity to speak privately, and I had no idea what he was pretending, or what he planned.

My father picked at his food, and Eugénie hovered over him. Joseph confided to the table his desire to earn back Bellenau someday, and Albertine smiled approvingly.

"You'll need an awful lot of money for that," Cannu said, and I could tell he didn't for an instant think it would be possible, but Joseph nodded solemnly. "You'll need to start taking life much more seriously if you want to be successful."

Joseph nodded again at Cannu's apparent wisdom. It was a look a boy might give a father, and I closed my eyes so as not to see it, then left them closed so long that the table rustled in concern and Joseph asked if I was all right.

Once I had a moment with Fortin in private, much later that day, I slapped him across the face. Neither of us could believe I'd done it. I held the offending hand tight against my stomach, counted the bones of my corset with my fingertips, and tried to stop them trembling.

"I'm not taking him from you," Fortin said. "I did it so you could keep him."

"You couldn't have suggested me?" I asked. "For physical guardianship? I hadn't realized they could be split."

"I did what I thought was best. I know what it's like to lose a child. I was trying to spare you. You can believe that or not."

The slap had reddened his cheek above his gray whiskers, and his skin appeared fragile and thin there, crumpled with age.

Because my great-uncle had seemed old all my life, I had missed just how very old he had gotten. If he was telling the truth, and had been nothing but my protector, what would happen to me when he was gone? He'd already outlived my grandparents, his wife, and daughter. He lived alone in a house full of ghosts.

"You want us to join you in Le Havre?" I asked, and thought that if the answer was yes, it might be so out of loneliness, not punishment.

He sighed. "Where do you want to live?"

"We were going to go to Paris."

"So go to Paris."

"Do you mean that?"

"Why do you always think the worst of people? The worst of me?"

"I don't."

"I think Le Havre would be good for you, and for Joseph. But if you want to go elsewhere, you're free to. I didn't ask for guardianship so that I could snatch Joseph, or become your jailer. I'm granting official permission to you to take him where you wish. Cannu will provide an allowance from the estate."

"What kind of allowance?"

His lips pursed, as if he heard in the question traces of the feeble-minded leech Cannu had tried to paint. But was I supposed to pretend that I could raise Joseph on air? I needed a roof. I needed food. What I really needed was a husband who wasn't dead, I thought, but by now I thought it without ache, without longing, with little more than a weary exasperation.

Philippe

— 13 —

Attaching too much importance

IN HINDSIGHT, PHILIPPE THOUGHT, HE SHOULD NOT HAVE GONE to the funeral. He had very well-developed hindsight, a writer's occupational peril. Lives made much more sense at a distance; they had a shape and an arc. His foresight was less good, and his in-the-moment sight as panicky and poor as anybody else's.

The day Erik told him that Alfred had died had no shape; it wasn't a point on a line. It was just a day, with Erik wringing his hands in Philippe's doorway, truly wringing them, and Philippe putting his own hand on top of them and saying, "Stop. You need those in working order."

Erik laughed like a crow and Philippe realized he was drunk. "It's true, isn't it?" Erik said. "I'm a laborer. Break a finger and I'd be as far into the shit as any poor sod in Arcueil." All those ideas rattling around in his head, and his body was what paid his bills. "No wonder my father was ashamed."

"He wasn't ashamed," Philippe said, though he didn't know for certain. "When is the funeral? I'd like to be there."

In the moment, this wasn't the wrong thing to say, which meant hindsight was just a great pile of useless. Philippe knew he would say the same thing again, show up at the church in the same black suit, hair neatly combed. He'd try to take his place toward the back, with the acquaintances and business associates,

295

but Erik would see him and drag him forward, to sit directly behind the family: Eugénie; Conrad and his wife, Mathilde; Erik; and Louise and her son.

Louise had been living in Paris for over a year by then, but it was the first time Philippe had seen her since her wedding reception. Erik often forgot that he and his sister were finally living, once again, in the same city. "I suppose we could have invited Louise," he said sometimes, with genuine surprise. Philippe understood from Erik that she and Joseph had planned to stay briefly with Alfred and Eugénie while they looked for an apartment. But by the time they arrived Alfred was so ill that Louise felt she couldn't leave. She enrolled Joseph in a neighborhood school and spent her days nursing her father. Philippe had tried to tell from Erik's accounting if there were familial duties that Louise's help was allowing him to shirk, but heard no hint in Erik's voice of guilt or obligation. To be fair, nursing was more properly a daughter's duty than a son's, even a son more suited to it than Erik. He cared about his father, but seemed to have convinced himself that in Louise's capable hands, Alfred would live indefinitely.

In the church Philippe groped for the boy's name, but it didn't come. He kept kicking his legs, and Louise kept laying a hand on his knee, and he'd stop for a moment and then start back up. He was the only child in the family pew, which looked strange to Philippe. His own siblings had kept him apprised of the steadily mounting number of nieces and nephews born back in Tarragona. Philippe hadn't met any of them, but he liked knowing they were there. If his parents had been depending on him to provide grandchildren, in addition to depending on his wire transfers and general report of having made good, he might have crumpled totally under the pressure. He and Camille hadn't been trying, exactly, when things had gone sour between them, but they hadn't not been trying. He still wondered sometimes if a baby would have saved them, but realistically, all they'd have now would be an unhappy toddler and a marriage even unhappier than it had been.

"You're getting divorced already?" Erik had exclaimed, as if what surprised him was the timing and not the fact of it. "I've had warts last longer."

"You've had three-year-old warts? Never mind, I don't want to know anything more about any of your warts."

Erik had made the right noises of sympathy, asked all the right questions, but Philippe, who'd thought he wanted this show of warmth from Erik, had no good answers. Camille was the friend of a secretary at the publishing house where Philippe had taken a full-time job. She was very pretty, with good teeth and glossy hair and a wonderful laugh. In Montmartre they might have gotten it out of their systems and realized quickly that their mutual attraction was nearly the only thing they had in common. But because Camille was a respectable girl, they'd married speedily so they could dive into bed. The first few months were rapturous, the first year tolerable. By the end of the second they were at each other's throats. Camille had quit her job at La Samaritaine department store because, she said, married women did not work, and was lonely and stir-crazy in their small apartment. That seemed to be all she could talk about: the apartment, and her plans for nicer drapes or wallpaper or china. That or the wild Gothic romances she purchased by the stack, the only things she ever read.

Erik had been without mercy. "You wanted an ordinary life, and you got one," he gloated.

It was Philippe who'd suggested the divorce. He'd tried hard to make it exactly that: a suggestion. Divorce had been legal for less than a decade, and if she couldn't stomach the concept, he would stay. It had never been legal in Spain, and his family assumed that his wife must be a nymphomaniac or criminal for the courts to put asunder what God had joined. *We just aren't right for each other*, he wrote to them. *NOT RIGHT??* his father wrote back in bafflement, in the same block capitals he'd once used for *POETRY???*

In truth, even the French courts wouldn't accept "not right." Camille and Philippe were required to sign allegations of either adultery, gross criminality, or "cruelty or insult."

"The third, I suppose?" Philippe said tentatively, looking through the paperwork.

"Which of us is the cruel one?" Camille asked.

Philippe sighed. Chivalry wasn't dead enough not to make certain demands on a man. "It can be me," he said. "I'll be the cruel one."

Camille threw herself into the task of cataloging his alleged cruelty. The pages mounted until she had at least enough for a shadow-play script, maybe the first part of a novel. The two of them had something in common, after all, Philippe thought, and momentarily reconsidered. But then he read the first few pages and abandoned the effort. *Forsoothe*, he'd apparently once told her, with labored spelling. *I am feeling lustily toowards other women than you, uglee hag!*

At the funeral, Erik bent forward in one of his grimy velvet suits, shoulders shaking. Philippe knew his friend didn't have anything else to wear, but it was wrong for the occasion, and he wished Erik had asked to borrow something. He reached forward and touched Erik's shoulder. He meant to be comforting, but Erik started like a frightened horse. His arm came up as he turned, and he accidentally smacked Louise in the side of the head. Once Erik understood there was no one behind him but Philippe, he glared and turned back around, and all three tried to pretend there had been no commotion. Erik had knocked loose a thick strand of Louise's blond hair, and Philippe watched it come slowly unpinned, unwinding down her back. He couldn't tell if she was waiting until the service ended to try to repin it or if she hadn't noticed. He rehearsed in his head how he might tell her if she stood to leave without fixing it. She had seemed, the last time they met, to be someone easily embarrassed, and he didn't want to embarrass her.

He stared at her hair the rest of the service, his mind wandering. She had a very nice neck. Her posture was precise; he imagined he could place a yoke across her shoulders and it would sit perfectly level. Though in truth almost all women had good posture, because of their corsets. They couldn't slouch if they wanted to. He pictured for a moment his ex-wife Camille lounging in their bed, and what a revelation that had been, a slouching woman with a waterfall of loosed golden hair. He pictured Louise's hair, unpinned, cascading down her back.

When the service finally ended, she didn't seem to have noticed the loose piece of hair. Like the colossal idiot he was, Philippe reached out and touched it, held the hank up off her shoulder like something he'd found. She retrieved it from him, gripping it like it wasn't already attached to her head. Did she think he'd try to take it?

"Your hair," Philippe said. "I'm sorry. I just noticed it had come undone."

Her son gave him a look of loathing. Joseph   that was his name, Philippe remembered suddenly.

Philippe tried to sneak off after that, but there was a gathering planned at Eugénie's. Erik insisted he come, and Philippe was still trying to be the right kind of friend. If he couldn't be there for Erik after his father died, of all times, what was left of them? Who else did Erik have?

Vincent, Philippe thought. At least there was Vincent. Had Erik told him yet? Vincent had been a godsend, a breakout star from the Chat Noir, so loyal that he hired Erik to accompany all his bookings, not just cabarets but large music halls and private parties. He commissioned original songs and arrangements too, and liked to write his own lyrics. This was Philippe's favorite thing about Vincent Hyspa: that he had caused Erik to stop asking Philippe for lyrics or scripts, and so Philippe had been able to stop making excuses for why he couldn't or didn't want to write them. As far as he could tell, Vincent had been near single-handedly keeping Erik from starvation, but Alfred had been the other hand, and Philippe didn't know if Erik could manage without his father's support.

Later the two men found themselves alone in a corner of Eugénie's apartment. The room had barely changed, but Philippe didn't see it with the same awe or hunger. It no longer looked like a foreign land of soft carpets and thick drapes. It just looked like a living room.

Philippe asked Erik if Vincent knew about his father.

"He's touring."

Vincent often left Paris for weeks at a time, engaging local accompanists and leaving Erik with no income, though he could hardly be blamed, given that Erik turned down Vincent's offers to tour with him.

"I hate travel," Erik said, every time Philippe urged him to accept one of Vincent's invitations.

"How would you know?" Philippe said. "You never go anywhere."

"Because I hate it."

There'd been more and more of this reasonless rigidity. Philippe had tried to throw Erik a housewarming party when he moved to Arcueil. "To celebrate an apartment that more than one person can fit in," which was the very nicest thing Philippe could find to say about Erik's plan to live in Arcueil and commute, on foot, ten kilometers to Montmartre every night.

But Erik refused. The apartment wasn't simply where he was going to live, he said, it was a studio. "I'm trying to compose music there. I don't need people milling about making the wrong kind of noise."

"They're not moving in. It's just for an evening."

"The noise will still be there." Erik wrinkled his nose like it had a smell, this noise, that his well-wishers would leave behind.

Noise doesn't linger, Philippe thought, but held his tongue. Maybe for Erik it did. Maybe this was one of the things Philippe just wouldn't, and couldn't, understand, either about music or about Erik. Half the things Erik said were like those optical illusions that contained two truths: a duck or a rabbit. A dog or its master.

"You should tell Vincent," Philippe said, in Eugénie's apartment. "As soon as he's back." Philippe didn't want to be alone with whatever Erik was going to need now, financially or otherwise. It was too much responsibility.

"Have you seen Joseph?" Louise asked, appearing suddenly at Erik's shoulder.

Both men shook their heads and she sighed.

"Do you want help looking?" Philippe said.

"You should leave him be," Erik said, and Louise paused, as if weighing Erik's knowledge of feral boys, angry boys, boys with stitched-together families.

"He's run off before. He usually just ends up playing marbles with the boys on the next block. But I'd better find him."

It turned out Joseph was only in Eugénie's bedroom, which Louise had been reluctant to check until the rest of the apartment had been scoured. He was lying on her bed on his stomach, reading a children's magazine.

"You didn't even take your shoes off?" Louise said, and Joseph waggled his feet in the air. "There are people who want to meet you."

"I don't want to meet them."

"I wasn't giving you a choice."

"I don't know any of these people."

"That's why they want to meet you."

"Who's that?" Joseph pointed at Philippe.

"A friend of your uncle Erik's," she said. Having registered his objections to the hunt, Erik was still in the living room. "This is Monsieur—I'm sorry," she trailed off. "I don't think I've ever known your last name."

"Philippe is fine," he said.

"But for Joseph to call you."

"He can call me Philippe, too."

Louise looked disapproving and Joseph unimpressed, but Philippe felt he couldn't stand on ceremony now. Had he wanted Joseph to feel flattered? Why? Was he trying to impress Erik's sister, of all people? Was he that determined to add one more mistake to his long list of romantic failures?

Joseph asked Philippe if he was a musician, too.

No, a translator, Philippe said, since Erik wasn't there. If Erik was in the room, Philippe would still feel he had to say *writer*, to spare himself the worst of Erik's razzing. But translation was most of what he did now, mostly of informational texts, mostly dull. He asked Joseph which comic was his favorite, indicating the magazine, *Le Petit Français illustré*, which published several regular strips.

"Plick and Plock," the boy answered.

This of course meant nothing to Philippe. Where had he thought that conversation could go? "Are *you* a musician?" he tried again.

"No. I'm going to be a doctor, like my father. But also a real estate investor, because I'll need more money than a doctor makes."

When he was eleven, Philippe would have had no idea what an investor was. He almost laughed but looked at Joseph's deadly serious face and bit it back.

"Then go out there and be polite and assume they're all prospective customers," Louise said.

"They aren't. No one out there has any money. Not real money. Eugénie doesn't know people with real money."

"Neither do we," she said. "Not anymore."

"Uncle Cannu has real money."

"He's got your money," she agreed sourly.

"You said he said he was going to come for the funeral," Joseph complained.

"He said he would. I don't know what kept him, but I won't say I'm sorry. And this is a spectacularly gauche conversation to be having in front of company," Louise added, as if only then remembering that Philippe was there.

Joseph gave a dramatic sigh and rolled off the bed, landing somehow feetfirst, then walked out of the room and slammed the door behind him.

Louise closed her eyes for a long moment. Joseph had left the magazine on the bed, and she leaned over to pick it up. "I'm sorry," she said. "It's been a hard year. For both of us. This was his room, briefly, when we moved in. Then my father got sicker and Eugénie needed somewhere else to sleep, so he and I squeezed in together. There was so much space, where we lived before. Not to make excuses for him. He should know how to behave. He does. He just chooses not to."

"It's the age," Philippe commiserated, although he found Joseph a piece of work.

"Eleven?" Louise said, calling his bluff. "If this is what he's like now, what will he be like at eighteen?"

At eighteen Philippe had been making plans to leave behind his country, his town, everyone he'd ever known or loved, possibly forever. At eleven? Comics and café papers in Miguel's bedroom. They'd held everyone around them in contempt, they just hadn't said it outside that room. Maybe there was hope for Joseph yet. He just needed to learn some circumspection.

"Everyone gets set straight eventually," Philippe said. "If he still talks like that at eighteen, someone will come along and punch him in the nose, and he'll start to figure things out."

"That's in part what I'm worried about."

"Life punches everyone in the nose. Not much use trying to avoid it."

"I suppose," she said.

Philippe remembered that he was talking to someone who'd lost her husband, lost her home, lost her father only days ago. He didn't need to explain things to her. "I'm sorry," he offered. "About Alfred. I don't want to pretend I knew him very well, but he came through for me and Erik, more than once. He was very kind. I don't think we ever made him a franc."

"You didn't. I've been helping with the bookkeeping. And I don't want to pretend I knew him very well either. But that's what I'm supposed to do out there." She turned her head toward the closed door, and beyond it the living room.

Philippe didn't know what to say to any of that.

Louise sighed, and rolled the magazine into a tight cylinder. She was hoping Joseph would be better after they moved out, she confided. She'd been looking for an apartment she could afford on his allowance, although Joseph's trustee considered it an unnecessary expenditure. Louise pursed her lips and knit her eyebrows, clearly imitating someone—the trustee, Philippe supposed—and said, in a hectoring voice, "Your father's death just means there's more room available at your stepmother's. Two women each living alone is *complete* foolishness." But Cannu wasn't the one who had to live with Eugénie, Louise said, dropping the imitation. "Besides, I don't want to sleep in any more rooms that people have died in."

Philippe let that hang there, as if such a thing were possible. This was an old city, and the hospitals had only recently become places you might ever choose to go. Like those in Tarragona, the beds of Paris had been full of both the living and the dead for a very long time.

"I don't want to live anywhere I had to watch it happen," Louise amended, as if sensing his objection. "I'm done with that." She shook her head. "I'm sorry. I've been cooped up here for months with Eugénie and Alfred and Joseph and I—" She cut off abruptly. "I've been cooped up."

She put the rolled magazine up to her eye like a telescope and looked around the room: wallpaper patterned with vines, dark wood headboard, a bad painting of a little blond girl peering into a birdbath. Then she turned the telescope toward Philippe. He stood very still. He raised his hand and waved at her, as if she were a sailor and he was standing on the shore, signaling to the passing boats.

"Had life punched you in the nose yet?" she asked him. "The last time we met?"

"I'm not sure." He thought about it, and Louise let him think, held him pinned in the dark circle of her paper telescope. She was no longer someone easily embarrassed, he realized. He'd been wrong to assume she was the girl he remembered. "I think I was still pretending not to feel it."

She put the telescope down and nodded.

"You?" Philippe asked.

"Are we pretending that life punches you only once?"

"No. We don't have to pretend that."

She unrolled the magazine and smoothed it against her skirt. Before she could reply, the door flew open and Joseph ran in. Both of them jumped.

"He came!" Joseph said. "He came after all."

Louise's gaze jerked toward the open door and her face went white.

"I'm sorry to come so late. The trains were all delayed out of Cherbourg. Some fool jumped in front of one. And who is this?" The man's narrow, sallow face pursed, and Philippe recognized how accurate Louise's imitation had been.

"This is Philippe," she said. "A friend of Erik's."

"Monsieur...Philippe?" Cannu asked, making it clear just how much he disapproved of not being given a proper, full name, and how appalled he was to find the two of them using first names behind a closed door.

*　　*　　*

305

At home that night Philippe kept thinking of Louise, and what exactly one *should* say to an unhappy eleven-year-old boy. What had he wanted someone to say to him? Was there some better path someone should have nudged him toward? He couldn't think of one. He was glad he'd come to Paris, glad he had the life he did. Philippe wrote a short letter to Miguel, as he occasionally still did, sometimes with reply and sometimes without.

It had been more than a decade now since he'd sent him the book signed by Verlaine, something that had taken great effort to procure. He'd hoped that would count for more than it seemed to. He told himself it didn't matter, that he hadn't expected any particular reaction from Miguel, but Philippe still wished, of course, to be forgiven, to receive instead of a cryptic reply a long, chatty letter. What Miguel was up to, who he was with. Perhaps even a paean to what their friendship had once meant. None was forthcoming, and as the stretches of time lengthened between Philippe's sporadic missives and Miguel's even more sporadic answers, Philippe told himself that every letter would be his last. Then, months or even years later, he'd send another, reopening the silence between them as if pulling back the dressing on a wound that should have long since healed. He wasn't sure why it kept itching, or why he kept scratching at it. Philippe had the odd feeling sometimes that he'd left a version of himself behind in Tarragona, and that someday some reply of Miguel's might describe not only his own life, but that of this ghost self Philippe had abandoned.

Philippe had known Verlaine was notoriously prickly about his past, but he hadn't thought that would extend to his books. He'd thought the man would be flattered to sign a volume. But it had taken a steady campaign of not just free drinks but gifts of opium and hashish to soften the poet's mood. Then he softened all the way into maudlin stories about his doomed relationship with Arthur Rimbaud, still without signing.

Rumor had it that the younger man hadn't written a word of

poetry since Verlaine had shot him, had moved to Africa and started a coffee-export company instead. Verlaine started weeping, not over the ruin he'd made of his own life or his sins against his wife and child, but that there would be no more poetry in the world by Arthur Rimbaud, and what if that was his fault?

"You give yourself too much credit," Philippe snapped in exasperation, the unsigned book still in his hands. He regretted this as soon as he'd said it, not because he thought it was untrue but because there was no one in the room who would take his side against Verlaine, and he was not keen to get head-butted again.

Verlaine was a neighborhood mascot, both for the poetry he'd written twenty years earlier and for not having written much since—he could be safely celebrated, no competition to anyone. He'd been appointed Prince of Poets in an only half-sarcastic neighborhood election. Philippe had placed twenty-third, and that was with Erik managing to cast fifteen separate ballots.

"But what if?" Verlaine moaned, eyes wide. "What if I—"

"Maybe he'd thank you," Philippe said. "Maybe he's happier. Maybe he's grateful."

"In Africa? Exporting coffee? I can't believe it."

"I can. Why not?"

"Maybe *you* can believe it, whoever the hell you are. But you are no Arthur Rimbaud."

That was true, Philippe thought. That was perfectly true. He was a lot stupider, for one thing. Rimbaud had written his book, his one great book, and then gotten the hell out before he turned twenty-two.

Verlaine eventually, begrudgingly, signed the book: *To you, whoever the hell you are.* Philippe sent it with a note to Miguel saying this was the best he could do and never returned to the Café François I. He'd gone back to the Auberge, of course, plenty of times, and still showed up at the Chat Noir on occasion. His flight had been neither instantaneous nor total. But if he had to choose between Rimbaud's terms of departure and Verlaine's, he was picking Rimbaud's. Even if that meant Rimbaud without a book, Rimbaud the forgettable, Rimbaud the vanishing. No one would have any idea who Philippe was after he died. Well, unless Erik somehow got stupendously famous after all. Then Philippe would be a footnote, the friend of his youth, some foreigner who sealed Uspud in a barrel full of nails and rained down bloody puppies. That was probably his best remaining shot. The odds seemed very long.

Now that Alfred was gone, Philippe reminded himself to check up on Erik more often than he would have otherwise. He thought of it as exactly that: checking up on, rather than checking in or having a drink or saying hello. He usually tried to catch Erik at some point on his journey north through the city to arrive in Montmartre by the time the evening shows started. When Vincent was touring, Erik still picked up substitute shifts, interrupting his commute with stops at various watering holes. If Philippe was free for lunch, he could catch Erik in Saint-Germain. If he couldn't meet until after work, Erik could usually be found in Pigalle, at the base of the Butte, sparing Philippe the climb back up to their old haunts. Philippe aimed for lunch so he could at least be sure Erik was eating. Philippe always paid, and Erik never thanked him—now that Philippe had abdicated as his collaborator, Erik seemed to think he was entitled to Philippe's patronage.

At a lunch one day in Saint-Germain, Philippe asked when Vincent was due back in town, trying to keep any trace of anticipation out of his voice.

"Not till next month. Which reminds me—would you come with me to this?" Erik shoved across the table an elegantly printed invitation to a piano recital. "I'll need someone to elbow me if I start to laugh or fall asleep."

Eugénie had rented a small recital hall for a Thursday-evening performance. "A recital of her pupils?" Philippe said. "Or...?"

"No, her. Solo. Like anyone cares to listen to her play."

"If you don't think you can stop yourself from being awful, you shouldn't go."

"I'm not actually going to laugh in her face. Do you really think you need to tell me not to?"

Philippe stuffed bread into his mouth and scraped his fork against the plate. "Will Louise be there?"

"I assume so. She and Joseph have moved out on their own, but they're still in the neighborhood. Why?"

"No reason."

The recital hall was open to the public, although Eugénie had explained that she didn't expect anyone but friends and family and her music pupils and their families, and that was exactly who attended. She looked a little silly in her fancy evening gown, wearing cosmetics she had no real idea how to apply. But she played like a fury. Sweat stains bloomed under her arms, her chin wobbled, she was breathless when she finished the faster movements. Philippe was awestruck. No one played like this in the cabarets. He'd never heard Erik play like this, although he understood dimly that his friend could, or at least could have when he left the Conservatory. Had he kept it up? If there was a piano duel right now between Erik and his stepmother, who would win?

"She played well, didn't she?" Conrad asked in the lobby afterward. With Mathilde out of town visiting relatives, he was unaccompanied.

Louise and Erik exchanged glances, trying to figure out how much the other was willing to admit. "She played accurately," Erik allowed.

Eugénie, giddy in her sweaty gown, came over to them and they offered their congratulations. "All this time playing alone in the apartment, I thought I was just trying to fill up the quiet. But I realized I'd been practicing like mad. This has been so much fun. It's just what I imagined."

Even Louise smiled for her, but once she'd walked away, Erik stayed icy. "That's pathetic. She shouldn't be happy—she should be embarrassed at not wanting something more interesting."

Eugénie was Conrad's mother in every way but blood, and he stared at Erik, not in disapproval at his having said something inappropriate but in genuine anger. "Have you decided about the course?" he asked his brother, with an obviously false casualness.

"What course?" Louise asked.

"The composition course at the Schola Cantorum," Conrad said.

Louise and Philippe looked at Erik inquiringly.

"Just something I've been considering," he said.

"You'll have to let us know this month," Conrad said. An apartment with a second bedroom had opened up in their building and he and Mathilde were interested, but they needed to know first if they'd be lending Erik the tuition fees.

"Take the apartment," Erik said. "It's fine. I don't need the money."

"You've decided against the course?"

"You really want to have this conversation now?" Erik hissed. His face was blazingly red.

"We're happy to lend the money, if you think you need the extra training. We just have to know sooner rather than later."

"You're making it sound remedial. If I was never trained in the first place, I can hardly need *extra*."

"What do you need?" Philippe asked.

"You've seen me work," Erik spat. "I need a lot of things."

"Everything with Joseph's trustee is like blood from a stone," Louise said, "but I might be able to help. I can try."

"Oh Lord. When I was composing for Sâr Péladan, not one of you gave a shit, but now that I might go back to school, you're all lining up to help. You just like seeing me on my knees. You want me to crawl on my belly."

310

"That's not fair," all three of them said, at slightly different times, in slightly different intonations, but with equal intensity.

"You know I'd be twice as old as everyone else? Twice as old exactly. I did the math."

"That shouldn't matter," said Conrad the wunderkind, the youngest laboratory director ever at the parfumerie Maison Jean-card.

"It would matter to you," Erik said. "You know it would."

"Even so. That's not enough of a reason not to do it," Louise said.

"They'll all recognize me. I've done just enough that every single person there will know exactly who I am and wonder what the hell I'm doing there."

The same problematic level of fame that had plagued him ever since he'd played for Bruant, Philippe thought. Philippe had evaded it—despite his efforts to the contrary—his entire time in Paris, crouched behind a pen, or behind the scrim of a shadow play, or behind Erik. It had maddened him how invisible his slim successes had been, but now he was grateful that his failures were equally anonymous.

"Pretend it's a joke," Philippe said. "The siege of the Schola Cantorum. No one has to know you intend to learn anything."

"The full course takes three years. I think someone will notice when I do the homework."

"You doing homework?" Conrad said. "You must really be serious."

"None of you are funny," Erik said. "I'm the funny one."

"You'll be the odd, old, funny one at the Schola Cantorum," Philippe said. "Schooling all the professors by the time you're done. Imagine you're playing a character."

"You think I should do it?" Now it was a real question. Erik looked round at all three of them.

"If you think you'd benefit from it," Louise said finally. "But you're the only one who can answer that."

"You're all useless," Erik said, but lightly, resignedly. The humiliated flush was fading from his cheeks.

Conrad looked appeased. There was a sound of guests starting to pop corks at a table Eugénie had laid with bottles and glasses for a champagne toast.

Erik darted away. "I'm going to fetch four glasses, but I wouldn't count on any of them making it back over here."

"The second bedroom—congratulations?" Louise asked.

"Not yet," Conrad said. "But Mathilde wants everything ready."

He and Louise started to discuss Joseph, and Philippe was stranded inside a personal conversation to which he had nothing to contribute but felt unable to leave without seeming uninterested in Louise's woes. Joseph had been in such a poisonous mood that she'd left him at home, she explained, worried he might act out and ruin Eugénie's evening. He was supposed to be catching up on homework, another source of strife.

"Cannu has him convinced that his school isn't worth any effort, just because it's public. Says he should enroll at some military academy in Cherbourg."

"Maybe going away to school wouldn't be the worst thing for him," Conrad said carefully.

"I am not getting rid of my son."

Conrad looked like there was more he might say, but chose silence. "I'll see if I can net us some champagne, since Erik's unlikely to come through."

Once he was gone, Louise turned suddenly to Philippe. "Cannu is full of admonishments about the two of us as well."

There was an *us* that encompassed him and Louise? "This is only the third time I've ever seen you."

"You've been counting?"

"Three isn't a very difficult number to keep track of."

She smiled. "Would you like it to be four?"

This was one of the most forward things any woman had ever said to Philippe, and that included prostitutes.

"I'll make you dinner. I've been relearning how to cook, now that I'm on my own. Which perhaps doesn't sound like much of an enticement, but I promise it's all edible."

"All right," Philippe managed. "Do you mean—where do you mean?"

At her apartment, she said—where else? Tomorrow at eight. Joseph would be staying at a friend's house.

Philippe played the conversation over and over in his head that night. Was there any way she'd really said what she seemed to be saying?

"What kind of 'admonishments'?" he asked, almost as soon as Louise opened the front door. "You said Joseph's trustee was admonishing you. About us."

"It was nothing." She guided him to one end of the sofa and poured them glasses of wine. He cataloged the smells coming from the kitchen. A roast? Potatoes? So maybe this really was just dinner? Could a divorcé and a widow have dinner alone in her apartment and have it still be respectable? He hadn't thought Louise would think so, but he knew there wasn't any particularly good reason why not.

The apartment was small—no separate dining room—and sparsely furnished, with a wildly out-of-scale equestrian painting on the wall opposite the window. The sofa was high-backed, ornamented with mahogany scrollwork, and extremely uncomfortable. He assumed both the painting and the couch were relics from Bellenau, whatever was left unsold after the estate had been liquidated. There was no piano, at least that he could see.

Louise did not join him on the sofa. She sat in one of the wooden chairs at the nearby table and turned toward him. She looked at him appraisingly and asked if he had really bricked his wife into a wall and pushed chicken bones through a hole for her supper.

313

He was at first baffled, then asked, "Do you mean the divorce papers? Is that what she wrote?"

"You didn't read them? That was brave. It must be nice not to have to care what anyone thinks."

But he did care what she thought. And he imagined the French authorities might care whether or not he'd bricked his wife into a wall. "I didn't do anything to her. Is this public record? Could anyone read it?"

"I wouldn't be terribly concerned. I believe Cannu put some effort into locating the documents, to find out what kind of influences I am 'so recklessly introducing into young Joseph's life,'" she parroted.

"Is there a private investigator crouched behind the drapery?" he joked.

"He already thinks we're sinning, so to hell with it. To hell with him."

Sinning? That was the word she chose? He didn't want her regretting this, either dinner or whatever else she intended. "I should leave."

"No," she said firmly. "I can't live the rest of my life as if Cannu might jump out from behind the sofa."

"It's—what?—nine years until Joseph comes into his inheritance?"

She looked at him, expressionlessly. "Could you stay afraid for nine straight years?"

"I don't know."

"You couldn't. You haven't even had practice."

"I've been afraid."

"Of what?"

Of himself? His own desires? His own stupidity or cowardice? He thought how privileged that might sound to her, how modern, a man afraid of himself.

She finally took mercy on his silence. "We're only half-done. I can't stay this afraid forever."

"Half-done?"

"With life."

"That's a cheery way to put it. Are you counting down?"

"Not down, exactly. But I can count." She sounded defensive, but he didn't understand why "Besides, we're not doing anything wrong," she said, as if convincing herself. "And if I am to be punished," she added, pouring them each more wine, "I would like it finally to be for something I have actually done."

They ate dinner. It was awkward in places, but no worse than some of his other dates. Most of the evening wasn't awkward at all. They both laughed easily, usually at some story Philippe had about Erik. She kept comparing his anecdotes to scenes from books, rather than experiences of her own, and he supposed this was evidence of how circumscribed her life had been. But gradually all he noticed was how well-read she was. They liked many of the same authors. This wasn't something he'd had before, certainly not with a woman. There might genuinely be something here, he started to think. Not just some obscure maneuver against Joseph's trustee, or against her own loneliness, but a struck match, a lit candle.

It was this feeling that carried him into bed with her, against his better instincts. "I don't want to do anything you'll regret," he said, feebly and awfully late, given that both of them were naked, his body hovering over hers, hard against the softness of her thigh.

"Please," she said.

She'd talked very briefly about Pierre's death at dinner, and it was strange to know, with such precision, how long it had been since she'd made love. At least, he assumed he knew. Louise was full of surprises, but Philippe was pretty sure she hadn't invited a man over for the night before. When would she have had the chance?

He'd been Camille's first. He'd never done exactly this before, been someone's second, and he was as slow and gentle as he knew how. It wasn't like with Camille at all, when he started to move in earnest. Louise knew there was pleasure here to be had, and she wanted it, worked toward it with him. She put her legs around his back and pulled him in harder. This was better than he'd expected it to be. He reached between them to touch her, and after she came he finished into his hand. He almost didn't remember to pull out—he and Camille had been taking their chances. But he had enough presence of mind to avoid unnecessary risks.

The same philosophy should have propelled him out the door that night, but they fell asleep in each other's arms and awoke to the sound of Joseph letting himself into the apartment. He had a stomachache and decided to walk home early, he announced. Louise flew out of bed quickly enough to close the bedroom door, but once they were dressed Philippe still had to walk through the apartment to leave. They both thought briefly of mad plots—rolling him in carpets, having him hide under the bed until Louise could get Joseph out of the apartment. Would Joseph at least go to bed with his stomachache? But then he shouted to complain that he wanted to play with his tin train set at the table, and why were two sets of dirty dinner dishes left out?

"It will look worse if we seem like we're hiding something," Louise said.

Philippe walked at a measured pace into the living room. The boy looked up like a fish pulled from the river, lips gaping silently. Philippe, trying to convey gentlemanly interest to Louise and absolute disinterest to the boy, took Louise's hand, bowed, and let himself out.

After that Louise disappeared, and by the time Philippe heard from Erik what had happened—learned of his own inadvertent role in the subsequent drama—it was too late. He said he wanted to write to her and asked Erik for her address.

"I wouldn't," Erik said. "I don't think she'll want to hear from you, honestly."

"This isn't my fault," Philippe said.

"I know. But I still wouldn't write. Louise tends to stay angry at the wrong people."

There was an air of love, but also of superiority, in the way Erik said this, as if it was his own expansive ability to forgive that allowed him to recognize Louise's faults.

Philippe had let a hundred moments like this go by over the years. For the first time, he didn't. "You cut people off for no reason at all," he said. "You're impossible."

Erik huffed, blew air out and down into his mustache and beard. If his friend held this brief moment of truth against him, Philippe decided, it wouldn't be the worst thing. It might be nice to have a break from looking after him, worrying about him, buying him lunch. Maybe, Philippe admitted to himself, that was why he'd said it.

Philippe's second marriage lasted only slightly longer than his first, but the third one stuck. She wrote about the cinema for a ladies' magazine—reviews and celebrity profiles—and published detective novels under a male pseudonym. When she got the idea for a new series with a recurring protagonist, a dashing Spanish investigator, she asked on a lark if she could publish them under Philippe's original name, since he wasn't using it.

"Why not?" he said, but one of the strangest moments of his life was walking into a bookshop and seeing a book he hadn't written with his old name on the cover. He thought about sending copies to Tarragona and pretending the novel was his. But the prose was, his wife would have been first to say, rather rushed, and the villain revealed rather clunkily. Philippe didn't think he could do better, but he decided to let everyone back home keep thinking he could.

He did write one final letter to Miguel, dropping any pretense of lightness, begging to know what exactly Miguel was up to: who he was with, how his life had turned out. This need to know the ending of the story he'd walked out of—was it the writer in Philippe, or the human, or the old friend? All three?

The image on the card that came in reply was familiar: sun-faded Tarragona, blue water and yellowed stones. At least that was one thing he knew—that Miguel had stayed in their home-town. But then he had a sudden, paranoid suspicion that Miguel had moved away, that he'd hoarded a supply of Tarragona post-cards before leaving and was forwarding his mail just to mislead Philippe, so that the one thing he thought he knew about Miguel's life was wrong.

Philippe turned the postcard over to read the short message, neatly recorded in handwriting as familiar as his own: *Don't you understand by now? I'm not going to tell you. You don't get to find out. You never get to know.*

Louise

— 14 —

So as to make a hollow

FOR WEEKS BEFORE I ASKED PHILIPPE TO DINNER, I HAD dreaded reading the mail. Albertine's letters, which accompanied the remittances from Cannu, informed me that Fortin had grown frail enough to employ both a full-time housekeeper and a part-time nurse at his home. His old business associates checked in on him often, she wrote, but no doubt he would benefit from family attention. His own letters mentioned nothing of this, and when I wrote offering to visit, he dismissed the suggestion. I could tell this was a test, and that I was meant to insist on coming. I could guess what would happen after that. He was too old for us to believe in a meaningful recovery, in the resumption of his solitary life. If he needed help now, he would need it for however much longer he had.

I knew what I owed him. But my heart shriveled at the prospect of traveling from Bellenau to my father's deathbed to Fortin's, in a house that, even on its cheeriest days, had always felt like a mausoleum to me. I simply could not do it. No—I didn't want to. If Fortin had demanded I come, or shamed me for my absence, I think I would have gone, too dutiful or too timid to refuse. But he insisted my presence was unnecessary, pretended that my avoidance did not trouble him, which allowed me to pretend the same.

So I pretended, and pretended. I did not go even for a weekend, because I knew that once I was there our mutual lie would be exposed. It would be obvious that he wanted my help and that he expected me to provide it. I used Joseph as an excuse: I couldn't pull him out of school now that he was, barely, applying himself. In truth, Joseph cared nothing for Paris or for his school, and continued to speak of Cannu as if he were some great mountaineer who had summited Mount Manhood and promised to belay Joseph up the slopes after him. I had hoped that Joseph could learn to look up to his schoolmasters, or the fathers of school friends, or pretty much anybody other than Cannu. The workers who drained our building's septic tank would have pleased me better. But I didn't feel I could speak against Joseph's admiration without his contrariness making him cleave all the closer. If he thought so much of his uncle, perhaps he would think better of me the better I pretended to get along with Cannu.

Fortin's letters were prideful to the end, even as his handwriting grew slanted and spidery. When it was replaced with a feminine hand, the dictation full of misspellings, guilt overpowered me. I began making plans to come, trying to figure out what I might possibly do with Joseph that would meet with both his approval and Cannu's. But first there was Eugénie's concert, with Philippe standing there, looking handsome and, well, available.

I had thought that once Joseph and I were finally on our own, I might have another chance at love. Or, since I am being honest, let us set the bar lower: another chance at romance. A man on my arm. A man who touched a strand of my hair where it came loose. It might have become love, but it wasn't yet, not when I asked Philippe into my home and my bed. I was preparing myself to go to Le Havre, but not without something to fortify me for one more round of nursing. I wanted at least a taste of what my life might look like after this next death vigil was over.

I assumed I would see Philippe again. I hoped to. I assumed I would see Fortin again. I did not expect him to die so suddenly.

Joseph came home from school, unsuspecting, to a storm of grief. "I suppose he was like a father?" he asked, trying to understand.

I shook my head, but struggled to offer another definition. My great-uncle would never have called me "Daughter," but he'd cared for me when no one else had been willing to, and I had not done the same.

Joseph was kind, truly kind, for days, and I was so relieved that underneath the surliness his heart was still one I recognized. He tried to make me dinner that night, although he didn't so much as know how to light the stove. The soup was awful but I ate it ecstatically, and then he washed the dishes.

I left him in Paris, with Conrad and Mathilde, to attend the funeral. At the service in Le Havre, I could feel the judgment, and I thought that I deserved it. Although Fortin had outlived many of the people I'd known as a girl and had never quite been friendly, he'd been esteemed in the town, and the pews were full of people outraged by my callousness. To show up only now? The dead were the dead. They were beyond our respects. I had failed to come when it counted. I could hear the whispers. Not just disapproval but surprise: little Louise, the dutiful orphan? Ran off to Paris and refused her obligations? Had I hid my black soul for all those years, or been devout then and become corrupted since? Or was I simply ordinary, and they had to fear that their own daughters might run away and not return? They decided, of course, that I was a demon.

I slept at the house, in my old room. So little had changed. The rugs and drapes and wallpaper—all the same. Same linens on the beds, threadbare now and smelling of damp. The same pictures in the same places on the walls, only with a few removed, the rectangles where they'd hung much darker than the rest of the sun-faded walls. The house was as haunted as

Bellenau had ever been, except that its ghosts were more modest. No crumbling elegance, just crumble. I found the missing photographs in the master bedroom, where a forest of framed pictures had sprouted on the dresser and the washstand, all of them positioned to be visible from the bed. Estelle and Berthe, mostly. Some townscapes, ones I knew he'd been particularly proud of, for their composition or technical achievement. There was one of Joseph, taken at a photographer's studio in Cherbourg; in front of a silly painted backdrop of a country lane he stood stiffly in suit jacket and short pants, with white knee socks and shoes polished to a high shine. "I could have taken one better than this," Fortin had said when I'd sent him a copy—I hadn't meant any insult, but he'd taken the photograph as a professional slight.

Still, the one photograph of Joseph was one more than I could find of myself. It was true that I'd never liked having my photograph taken; I could count on my fingers every picture that had ever been made. But there had been a wedding portrait, and pictures of Joseph and me together, when he was both an infant and a bit older. And there'd been at least a couple of Estelle and me, one when I was small and one shortly before she died. My great-uncle's bedroom was a purposeful erasure, and I didn't know whether he'd felt this way toward me for years, perhaps the whole of his life, or whether, alone during his final illness, he'd slipped some photograph from its frame to burn it in the stove or close it between the pages of a book. I looked for evidence one way or another, fanned the pages of his small library, flipped through boxes of glass plates, rifled every drawer. What was my place in this house? What had it ever been?

It was in this way, with a snowfall of paper from an opened drawer, that I learned I was not his heir. As with the telegrams before the Family Council, I could think of nothing to do with my advance warning except arrive at the lawyer's office with a stony air of respectability. Cannu all but rubbed his hands together in glee, though I don't think he knew Fortin's intentions before then, at least not for sure. There was more money than anyone had guessed, given how frugally he'd lived, and Fortin had bequeathed it all to Joseph. Because Joseph was a minor, access to the funds would rest with Cannu, as his financial and now, with the death of Fortin, legal guardian. I didn't know whether Fortin had made the bequest before, or after, I'd failed to visit him. Did he think Cannu knew better than I what was best for all of us, or had he known this would be a disaster for me, and relished the thought of my punishment? If he'd somehow been there, I would have slapped him all over again, and as my palm itched I wondered whether I'd been right to distrust him then, or whether striking him had turned him against me. There was no knowing—neither the order of events, nor my own part in them—and there was no comfort to be found in any of the possible scenarios.

Cannu wished to speak with me privately after the lawyer dismissed us. "Lunch?" he proposed.

I laughed, sounding half-unhinged, and told him I already had my train ticket for the next departure and had to get to the station. This wasn't true, but the only tactic I could think of was to run. Half of me worried I might arrive in Paris to find Joseph already snatched away. I knew that refusing to meet with Cannu was probably not a wise strategy, but at the same time I couldn't see how any conversation between the two of us, on our current terms, would go in a favorable direction for me.

"I see," he said. "Busy as ever."

One thing I had rarely been, since marrying Pierre, was busy. How had I spent them, all those hours, at Bellenau and after? I had raised my son and tried to school him. But I had also read books, and taken long walks, and played the piano. During my father's illness I'd taught some of Eugénie's lessons for her, and tried to find some pupils of my own. But I knew no one in the city, had no music diplomas or prizes or references, and had largely failed. After my father's death I'd signed up for a typing course, thinking I might find a secretarial job, but the instructor told me at the end of the session that I was ten times too slow, ten years too old, two-tenths too plain, and still wearing a wedding ring to boot: I'd never be hired. I had done nothing in my life, and the reason I could understand Cannu's contempt for me is that I felt it too. I have hated myself as hard and as often as I have hated Cannu or Albertine, and I have hated them well and long and truly. I thought such hate must eventually burn itself out like an electric bulb, its glass blackened and ghostly. But somehow it kept glowing. Keeps glowing.

In the earliest Spanish classes I taught at the resettlement center I began with what I thought of as the usual questions, the ones I remembered first learning to answer: *How long have you been in Buenos Aires? Why did you come?*

I had already begun preparing my lies on the passage over, writing them out with the help of a Spanish phrase book. That I was traveling alone drew great attention on the ship, all of it bad, and I was awakened several nights by inquiring knocks on my locked door. When we arrived in Buenos Aires, I paid too much for a double room at my first boardinghouse because I explained that I had come to Argentina with a husband, and that he'd taken work in the provinces and would return.

"How soon?" the landlady asked me.

"Soon?" I repeated, trying only to understand, but she took it as an answer. Then when a husband did not appear, soon or otherwise, I cringed at her pity and moved.

Variations of this happened several times. I claimed the protection of an imaginary husband because I felt in need of any protection I could get. The only men who sought me out were those who did not care that I was supposedly married, and thus I did not particularly care for their attentions. I did not care for anyone in those years. I had had my skin flayed in France, and something hard and chitinous had grown over me instead. When I looked out through my new skin the world beyond was glassy and blurred, the faces threatening. It took me years before I told people that my husband was dead, and years after that to see that Buenos Aires is, at least in good weather, rather beautiful.

I've often wondered if the women in my classes are telling their own lies, but now their truths have made me afraid to ask any questions at all. There are no safe inquiries, though I try: "What do you like to eat?"

"I like to eat," Oskar's mother answers me in class.

"What foods do you most like to eat?"

"I am glad to have food," she says, wary, as if I might report her to the Argentine government for insufficient gratitude.

The room next door holds a children's Spanish class, which we overhear through the thin wall whenever I ask a too-difficult question and my own class goes silent. The children are learning colors and animals. "The dog is purple!" a boy shouts, and the children giggle. I think it's Oskar's voice, but when I glance at his mother, she hasn't reacted. She's simply looking at me, waiting to learn the next thing. I try to figure out what the next thing is, what I might be able to offer any of these women.

Corrections feel like obscenities, but the students demand them.

"My most old boy, they taked him," one woman says, then waits for me to respond with either a nod of approval or adjustments to her pronunciation. Instead, I'm frozen.

"Please," she says, "so I can fix."

"Took," I say. "They took him. They took your eldest boy."

"Yes, eldest. Took. Do not look at me—so. Like that."

I can't imagine how I'm looking at her, can't imagine what loss is flooding out of my own face.

"Do not let me say 'taked' because someone took my child," the woman tells me. "Do not be sorry of me."

"For," I say. "Sorry for you."

"Do not be sorry for me. Do not let me make mistakes because you are sorry for me. I did not come here to sound like a fool."

"Teacher, how to conjugate *burn*?"

The house burns.

The house burned.

The house had burned.

The village has burned.

The village will burn.

Is the village burning?

Yes, the village is burning. So we leave. We left.

"Teacher, my cousin takes the Tuesday-morning class. She says they learned *set fire to*."

"That is correct also," I tell the women. "A man can *set fire* to a house; he can also *burn* it. It means the same."

"Teacher, you are French, yes? You are not Argentine?"

It's Oskar's mother again, and I try to remember how she might know this. Did I announce it on the first day of the session? Did I say something to Oskar? She has never spoken of any other children, but then she also hasn't spoken of the father Oskar must at some point have had. I don't know if Oskar is her only child, or only surviving child. I don't know which parts of her story she is keeping for herself or which parts of mine she might want.

Yes, I tell her, I am French.

How long have you been in Buenos Aires? Why did you come?

I needed to start over, I say, speaking slowly to help them understand, though the slowness makes everything sound momentous and dour. I did not starve; I did not burn. I do not wish to compare with them types of fire, to compete in degrees of heat and height.

In my head, I answer their questions like this: *They taked my eldest son. My only son, they taked him. My family, burnt all to nothing.*

328

*   *   *

After Fortin's death, the money stopped coming almost immediately, in response to an official ruling Cannu received from the same justice of the peace who had presided over the last Family Council. Cannu had filed copious evidence, the last twelve years of my life twisted into a story that made me burn. I was accused both of babying Joseph—his haphazard education, the hours we'd spent at play in the garden at Bellenau—and of giving him too much freedom: the truancy, the amount of time he spent roaming the neighborhood in questionable company. No decision was too small to be held up to scrutiny. The evening I'd left him alone while I attended Eugénie's recital was listed as an example of poor judgment, for reasons I didn't even understand. Was the idea that I'd been excluding him from my family, or that I should not have left him alone at all, as if there weren't twelve-year-olds working ten-hour days in factories a few kilometers away?

Cannu complained that I brought in no income, that I had lived first off my in-laws, then my son. While I had never been proud of this, neither had I ever been able to see a remedy. But in Cannu's telling, the worst of it, hovering over and spreading through my supposed greed and incompetence, was my wickedness, my assignation with a divorced lover, my willingness to expose Joseph to sin. The justice forbade any further remittances going to me, making my physical guardianship—which had always been contingent on Cannu's support and Fortin's permission—nothing more than a stray thread that Cannu could snip at any moment. All he needed to do was request that Joseph be delivered into his care, a demand I assumed I would receive any day.

I consulted a lawyer. "I need to dispute a story," I said.

"We can only dispute facts," he answered.

But taken individually, the facts were largely true. It was the portrait they made that was so warped and ugly. I did not recognize the woman in the filing as myself, only barely recognized the boy, so unschooled and wild, so in need of a firm hand.

Widows were often too indulgent, the lawyer clucked. He'd seen it many times. Perhaps I should be grateful that my brother-in-law had decided to intervene?

I stabbed the lawyer through the eye with his own pen. Except not. Rather, I imagined doing this, then scolded myself for fantasizing, and then reconsidered. What more could I possibly lose? Then a stranger, unlikelier thought bubbled up: what would Eric do in this situation? He'd never be in this situation, not even close, but perhaps I could adopt something of the right spirit.

I lifted a little bottle of ink out of its ornate brass holder and poured it across the leather blotter, across the piles of legal papers that represented my biography as written by someone who hated me. The lawyer spluttered—I was a madwoman, a wastrel, I would owe him for his time, the blotter, the silk handkerchiefs he threw into the puddle to soak it up before it could drip on the carpet.

"Go ahead and charge me for them," I said. "I've got nothing." I opened my empty hands at my sides. "You've read for yourself how much nothing I've got."

The papers had been so specific that I briefly wondered on the walk home if Cannu really had been crouched behind the sofa. But no—I realized much of the information in the filing could have come only from Joseph.

His confusion offered my sole consolation.

"I don't hate you," Joseph said, when I confronted him. His face at first was scornful, but not of me. It was my vulnerability, or perhaps what he thought of as my gullibility, that irked him—had I really taken it seriously, all his adolescent sound and fury?

"Do you understand what you've done?"

"I don't even understand what you're talking about."

"All those things you said to Cannu. About me."

"What did I say?"

"Do you really not remember?"

He shrugged. I wanted to shake him. I imagined doing it, and had an echo of the moment in the lawyer's office: should I just go ahead? Do all the things I imagined, nothing left to lose? No. I held my hand, held my tongue.

"Did you want to go live with him? Instead of me?"

"What? No."

This denial was a little slower, a little more shaded. He'd thought of it, at least, but his confusion seemed genuine. I didn't think he'd actively worked against me. Was that to be my prize—that my son didn't hate me, he was merely so naïve that he'd cheerfully handed over the information Cannu needed to destroy my life?

On a Tuesday evening I received Cannu's request that Joseph be delivered to Cherbourg by the end of the week. There was a bedroom awaiting him, a stocked bookshelf, school uniforms already ordered.

Would they be the sort of books he liked? I wondered. The clothing correctly sized? And did I hope Albertine would guess rightly or wrongly?

I wanted to flee with Joseph, but where would we go? Paris had railroads to every corner of Europe, and in all of them we would be penniless. I hadn't saved more than pocket change out of the remittances. Without Cannu's money and consent I had no way to care for Joseph. Not even to feed or clothe him, to say nothing of educating him or setting him up in the world. I might have had enough pride to choke myself on it, but not enough to starve my child. And I did not want to test his love for me against the loss of everything he had been raised to expect from life. When I imagined us holed up in a garret somewhere deeper in the Continent, or maybe in England, I could not quite picture us clinging to each other; in my mind's eye I was clinging to him, and he was cursing how much I'd given up on his behalf. I did not doubt his love for me, but I was afraid of having to acknowledge that it might not be as all-encompassing as mine for him.

I wrung my hands for two more days, somehow both frantic and paralyzed. I couldn't sleep, although by Thursday evening I'd grown so tired I was seeing things that weren't there. I packed and unpacked suitcases and trunks until the apartment looked like a flea market, pots and pans in the living room, piles of clothes on the kitchen counter. I couldn't bring myself to tell Joseph what was happening, although he wasn't an idiot. He knew something was very wrong.

"Where are you going?" he asked, looking at my open trunk, which at that moment contained nothing except a bar of soap, a pair of stockings, and Joseph's old christening gown.

"We. Us. I'm not going anywhere without you."

"Then where are we going?"

"Antarctica. China. I don't know."

"I don't want to go anywhere. I've got a history exam on Friday." After a pause he asked, "Have you talked to Uncle Conrad? Maybe he could help with whatever's wrong. Whatever it is you won't tell me."

Yes, I thought. Conrad. Steady Conrad, loaner of money, fixer of problems. He'd been keeping Eric afloat since our father died. Couldn't it be my turn to climb up out of the waves and onto his shoulders? The good ship SS *Conrad*.

On Friday I waited for Joseph outside his school with two hastily repacked suitcases. "We're going to your uncle Conrad's," I said, although I hadn't warned either Conrad or Mathilde that we were coming.

After her initial surprise, Mathilde met our presence with equanimity, with rote offers of food and drink. I recognized the blankness on her face as the same one I'd so often donned, the face of someone who knows what's expected of her and will continue the performance for however long it's required.

"Will you be needing a place to sleep?" she asked, with a sidelong glance at the suitcases.

"If it isn't a bother," I said. There was a gas leak in the building, I explained, and the tenants had been evacuated until it could be fixed—words that I hadn't realized would come out of my mouth until they did. But I didn't want to confide in Mathilde, not yet. I wanted my brother.

"Are my things going to blow up?" Joseph asked. "Did you pack my comics?"

"Nothing's going to blow up," I said.

"I wish you'd just tell me what's happening," he said.

Mathilde's cup rattled in its saucer, her hands betraying the surprise she was so carefully keeping from her face.

"Go to your room," I snapped. "I'm sure you have homework."

"What room?"

"I'll show you," Mathilde said. "Follow me."

She ushered him into the second bedroom, which was still unfilled. I knew she and Conrad had consulted doctors, but there had been no remedy. Now here was Joseph, occupying her empty room the way he'd occupy the same childless space at Cannu and Albertine's. How had this family made so few children? I pictured all of us adults circling Joseph like vultures, each of our shadows crossing his face from the air. It was a funny image, for a moment, before I pushed it away. Mine, he was mine. Let the scavengers pluck a child from some other nest.

Conrad was late coming home and Mathilde apologized, saying he often worked long hours. I detected the annoyance in her voice, not for me or Joseph so much as for the regularity of his absence. She asked if I'd like to lie down for a bit while she prepared supper, and I declined but understood then that I must look as sleepless and wild as I felt.

When the front door opened, she rushed around the corner to meet Conrad in the hall. There was whispering and then they came into the living room, Conrad still holding his hat and brief-case. "A gas leak?" he said.

While I'd meant to quickly deliver the truth, I felt myself nodding. It sounded true, as if my life since Pierre's death had been one slow, torturous leak and Cannu had finally lit the match. "*Brooooosh*," I said, flowering my fingers like petals, as if I were holding an explosion in my lap and stroking the shrapnel headed for my face.

"You're not all right," he said, with both kindness and matter-of-factness, as if making sure the three of us agreed before proceeding. He put his briefcase and hat on a chair and joined me on the sofa.

"Cannu's requested custody."

"Starting when?"

"Tomorrow."

Conrad's mouth opened slightly but no words emerged, and I knew I'd shocked him. He glanced up at Mathilde, who began walking backward into the kitchen, politeness pushing her from the room but curiosity preventing her from turning.

"I know I should have come earlier. I haven't known what to do."

"Come earlier to...? Forgive me if I'm missing something, but—I didn't think you had any legal standing. To dispute."

"I don't."

"Then how can we help?" He said this gently, too gently, and I felt too stupid to say that I had wanted him to proffer a solution, as if he might have come across this situation somewhere in all his textbooks, his experiments, as if this were some long and complicated chemical reaction he could still balance. I had made the mistake of thinking an education might yet be full of marvels.

"I hate to ask...but if I had a loan. We could go elsewhere. Joseph and I. Somewhere he won't find us."

Conrad looked at me pityingly.

"I don't know if you have it to spare," I said, as if the most impossible part of what I'd said was only the money.

"And what then? What would you do after it ran out?"

"I'll figure something out."

"What?"

"I said I'll figure it out. I can't think now."

"I believe that's correct. That you aren't thinking straight right now."

"I can't just hand him over."

"You can, if you have to. If that's what's best for Joseph."

How could my own brother think that separation might ever be for the best? I stood and looked down at him, my fists clenched. If I'd had a bottle of ink, I would have poured it down his face. Instead I grabbed his hat from the chair and threw it. It sailed unsatisfyingly across the room and landed on a console table as if it had been placed there on purpose. "You don't understand," I snapped. "You don't know what it's like to have a child."

I was not proud of how his face hardened then over something he never let anyone see. I was glad that Mathilde was in the kitchen, that it was at least possible she hadn't overheard, although I imagined she and Joseph were both standing silently in their separate rooms, straining to listen.

Conrad let his breath out slowly. "If he's not in Cherbourg by tomorrow night, you're breaking the law. You're kidnapping."

"How can you dare call it that?"

"I mean that's how the law would see it. And if you're both still here after tomorrow, I'd be harboring fugitives."

"You won't let us stay."

"*You* can stay. You can stay as long as you need. But we have to take Joseph to Cherbourg."

"So you won't help me." I was moving around the room by then, in tight circles that offered me nothing to break, nothing to spill. I pushed his hat from the console table to the floor, as if that might convince him of anything.

"I am helping. I understand why it doesn't feel that way to you, but I am trying to keep this from becoming worse than it has to be."

"Never mind. I'll ask someone else."

"Who?"

"Eric," I said, the first name that came to my lips, and we were both surprised to hear it, although who else could I have said? I had no one. The only other name I'd churned through in the last few days was Philippe's, and I'd already discarded it: I had no claim on him, didn't even know where he lived, and going to him now would seem to confirm everything Cannu had alleged.

"What do you think *Eric's* going to be able to do for you?" Conrad asked.

For the first time I heard the exhaustion I would hear later in his letters, growing larger and heavier, a snowball rolling down through the years, swollen with ice and dirt and vexation. "I have no idea," I admitted. "But if it's more than nothing, he'll be ahead of you." I marched to the front hallway.

"What do you think you're doing?" he called after me.

I left without answering, because there was no answer. I wasn't thinking anything. I walked three blocks south, toward the address I'd only ever written to, never visited, then remembered that it was a Friday night and he'd likely be working. I reversed direction for four blocks before pausing to imagine a night spent wandering into various nightclubs in Montmartre, with no money and the wrong clothes, hoping to stumble upon him. I turned around. I passed again in front of Conrad and Mathilde's apartment, and thought I heard a voice calling to me, or maybe only imagined it. I walked faster.

It was spring and there was at least another hour of light in the sky, but it was a long walk ahead. Eric had bragged about the length of it, about how strong his legs had gotten, his calves like cantaloupes. He'd also talked about the hammer he carried in a belt loop. "There can be shady characters, that time of night," he'd said. "I look shady enough to dissuade most of them, but if someone comes too close, I brandish the hammer."

I hadn't known if that was true, or warranted, or just an affectation, but as the light faded I found myself wishing for a hammer. I'd left Conrad's apartment completely empty-handed, and I wondered if I'd rue the lack of a handbag or if instead I'd be relieved that it might make me less of a target. Obviously I had nothing to steal. I made my face as forbidding as I could anyway, as if it would matter.

The streets I knew gave way to those I did not, but recognized in a more general way—the apartment houses were the same gray stone, styled with the same types of cornices and waterspouts and wrought-iron balconies. There were the same types of shops with the same lettering on the plate-glass windows. Then those gave way to utterly unfamiliar streets. I kept to the largest, brightest avenues I could. For several blocks the only other women I saw stood posed along the roadway in dresses bright as parrots. I rehearsed in my head what I would say or do if a man thought I was for sale, but no one inquired. I tried not to be wounded that even by the time I finally entered Arcueil, finally found Eric's street, then his building, with its dull plaster and shuttered windows, no one had spoken to me at all.

The building was wedge-shaped, filling the space where two angled roads converged. The hour was late and dark had long fallen, but a group of boys were smoking on the corner at the narrow tip of the wedge. I mean boys truly, no older than Joseph.

When I asked if they lived nearby, they did not answer me at first, suspicious. The tallest one finally nodded. I told them who I was searching for. Could they let me into the building and show me to his apartment?

"He won't be there," the tallest boy said. "He's out."

"I'll wait for him. It's important."

"What'll you give me? For showing you?"

"I don't have anything with me. I would pay you if I did. I could give Eric something for you the next time I see him?"

He stood there cracking his knuckles and I guessed he was about to refuse, if for no other reason than because he could, when a smaller boy spoke. "This way," he piped up, and the tallest boy rolled his eyes.

Little Louise, I thought. They'll like you better, little boy, if you learn to be meaner. But not yet. Not till I have what I need.

The boy opened the front door and took my hand to escort me up a staircase. The interior of the building was very dark. The wall felt both greasy and powdery, cheap whitewash with a coating of smut, and I figured it was just as well I couldn't see the rest of the stairwell or hallway. The boy took me to a door identical to all the others, and I knocked. No answer.

"He's working," the boy explained. "He'll be hours yet. Do you not have a key?"

"I forgot it," I lied, and tried the knob, not expecting it to turn. We both stood there, surprised, as the door swung open. Moonlight from the window spilled into the hallway and illuminated the boy's small, round face. "Please don't tell anyone that his door was unlocked. I'm sure he only left it that way because he was expecting me."

He clearly didn't believe me. "Are you his mother?" he asked.

"Do I look that old to you?"

"No. But he doesn't have a wife."

"I'm his sister."

The boy nodded. Finally, something for his trouble. He could at least go back to the other boys and report that the local composer, the neighborhood hermit, had a sister. "Does he have a mother somewhere else?"

"Does he seem like he needs one?"

The boy just stared at me.

338

"We haven't had a mother in a long time," I said. "Do you have a mother?"

I imagined him saying no, and had a passing fantasy of swooping him out of Arcueil, a playmate for Joseph, a helpless urchin graced with sensible moderation and piano lessons, which he would learn to love.

"Of course," he said. "Everyone has a mother."

I told the boy I appreciated his help and offered to look inside Eric's apartment for something to give him.

He peered into the room, calculatingly, then shook his head and was gone.

I went inside and closed the door behind me, locking it lest the little boy come back with bigger ones to ransack the place. But once I'd found and lit a lamp, I could see what the boy had already guessed: there was nothing here to give him—nothing, anyway, that he might care to take. The room was a musical trash heap. An ancient upright piano was drowning in piles of paper. There were folios disgorging loose-leaf papers, plus teetering towers of twenty years' worth of composition notebooks. Where had he put it all when he lived in the closet he'd bragged about? I soon realized the answer was that he owned nearly nothing else. A lumpy, narrow bed. His gray jackets, his only jackets, were piled on two pegs stuck in the wall. His trousers were flung across the back of a chair whose wicker seat was torn. There was no wardrobe. His shirts and collars and underwear lay stacked in broken crates pushed against the wall, somehow brilliantly white and carefully starched, while an enormous paper-wrapped mountain of clean handkerchiefs rose beneath a washstand with a bowl, brush, pumice stone, and pitcher of chill, murky water. A few dirty glasses stretched along the windowsill and on the writing desk, where they were accompanied by a pile of staff paper bubbled with circles of brown and red, all different sizes from a parade of wine carafes, glasses of calvados, small cups of coffee.

In a separate pile I noticed the same work, recopied neatly, in his usual elegant hand, but without doodles or cartoons. The clean copies were titled with exercise numbers, assignments in counterpoint and voice leading. His homework, from the Schola Cantorum. He'd been doing it obediently. Drinking himself silly during, perhaps, but completing the work. I looked for returned assignments with markings from his professors, wanting to know what they'd said. What did they think about the compositions, about Eric's prospects? About Eric? I longed to see him through someone else's eyes, more expert than my own.

I started to jostle open the small drawers of the desk before stopping myself. There was no lie I could tell myself to justify the intrusion. I had no business looking, no business in this whole apartment. The piano bench looked more solid than the single rickety chair by the desk, but even it creaked alarmingly when I sat. I calculated the hour, the likelihood of waking the neighbors, and pressed the keys slowly and gently enough to make no sound, as if I were trying once again to eavesdrop on Estelle and Fortin's conversations about my marriage prospects. Now, with no other sound to overhear, the air was blank and empty of possibilities. Back then I'd had a future. A future whose unknowns terrified me, but a future. And what future was Eric preparing himself for?

I pressed my fingers slightly harder into the keys. The sound was nearly unbearable, so far out of tune I didn't see how the instrument could be useful for anything. How could you compose on this? Every note would be only a guess, an approximation, of how you hoped it might sound later. In the lamplight my finger pads were dark with grime. The piano had gone long unused.

Alone in the dark, I started to cry. I took a handkerchief, trusting their wrapped brightness in the filth of the apartment. Were his linens this well laundered because he wanted to keep people from guessing that he lived like this? Had Conrad known what I would find here? He'd known enough to tell me not to come. *What do you think* Eric's *going to be able to do for you?*

Nothing, I understood now. Nothing.

Would Eric be angry, or embarrassed, to find me here? I thought about leaving, but I feared the walk back to Conrad's this late at night. Besides, I imagined the boys would tell Eric I'd been here, and it would be worse explaining my absence than my presence.

I played silently at the piano until I fell asleep sitting up and jerked forward into the keys with a yowl of notes, not just once but over and over. My body was emptying itself, of wakefulness, of hope. I investigated the bed. The sheets didn't look as clean as the rest of his linen, but they didn't look as foul as the rest of the apartment, either. I doused the light, pulled the blanket back, pushed off my shoes, then lay on the top sheet in my clothes. I fell asleep immediately.

I have no idea what I dreamed that night, but let's pretend it was something prescient, something wise. I have such dreams, sometimes. A few days ago, for instance, I dreamed again about Mrs. Valera. In the dream we were walking together in Palermo Park. We stopped at a café by a stone fountain. She ordered maté and I ordered coffee, but when our cups came they were filled with small stones. A cat wound around our ankles and we offered her the stones, but she had the sense to refuse them. We ate them ourselves, teeth cracking.

Today, because my second-to-last Wednesday student—Serge, the Russian boy—canceled his lesson, I arrive early at Diego's apartment. Mr. Valera opens the door and from the kitchen Mrs. Valera drifts in, back at home. I am irrationally proud, as if my dream has summoned her.

Diego is at a neighbor's, she says, but with strict instructions to be back in time.

"I know I'm early," I apologize.

Mrs. Valera offers coffee and keeps insisting, even after I refuse, as if she's insisting on something larger—on normality, or wellness, or her place in her own house.

You don't have anything to prove to me, I want to tell her. *You don't owe any of us anything.* "Coffee at this hour will keep me up all night, really," I say. "A glass of water, perhaps?"

My brain rattles through things I know I won't say to her, unless she opens a door she has no reason to open to me. I have no idea what she's come through, or what she might still be trying to convince herself she can come through. I might tell her that we can lose what we think is everything, and that there is still a life left after. But then I realize that life—the boardinghouse, the buses, the boy at the resettlement center with his paper ball, the women in my language classes, the people I have not seen in forty years dying an ocean away—will not look like any kind of comfort to Mrs. Valera. Louise the oyster, gullet of sand, pretending she's licked it into pearls.

"It's good to see you," I say, which seems safe enough, and she gives a tight smile.

"Diego's been a mess at this week's practicing," Mr. Valera announces, tossing his grandson into the maw of the silence.

"As in he hasn't done any, or he's struggling with the pieces?"

"He practices," his mother says.

"But there's no way they're supposed to sound like that," Mr. Valera huffs.

"Do you know which ones he's struggled with?" I drain the glass of water quickly because I don't have a surface handy to set it on and I need both hands to brace myself up and out of the armchair I've been slowly sinking into. I tuck the glass by my hip and lurch upright. Once I'm on my feet I move easily enough toward the piano, then shuffle through the music on the stand.

"I think that one's the worst," Mr. Valera says. "The green cover."

I flip through the piece, the doll serenade from Debussy's *Children's Corner Suite*, trying to figure out what has befuddled him.

"What's it supposed to sound like?" Mr. Valera asks.

342

"You'd like me to play it?" One should never assume anyone wants a concert.

"Please," Mrs. Valera says. "It would be useful to know how it ought to go."

Somehow her asking feels less strange to me than Mr. Valera's request, and I sit on the stool. A sudden flurry of nervousness shoots down from my shoulders. Few, if any, of my families know how little I play anymore. I don't own a piano, have never owned a piano, really—the ones in Le Havre, Bellenau, Paris, all belonged to someone else. Here in Buenos Aires I lived for a time in a boardinghouse that had one in the dining room. At the French Institute there's one in the main reception hall, another shoved away in a classroom, often available but rarely tuned. I play sample phrases at my students' homes, of course, sometimes longer passages, but rarely whole pieces.

This piece, I am relieved to feel once I've started, is complicated enough to stymie Diego but simple enough for me. I have the stray thought that I must once have been rather good, if I can let myself get so rusty and still sound pleasant. The thought occurs to me as if it's about someone else, the Louise I left in France, who cared for music in a different way before it became her livelihood. Who had no livelihood then at all.

"You play very well," Mr. Valera says at the end of the lesson, as he walks me to the door. "Now that Carmen's back, I'll be around less."

"A relief, I imagine."

"Yes and no," he says, then pauses a long moment. "I would like to see you again."

It takes several seconds for me to discern what he means (*perhaps he wants piano lessons for himself?*), then to believe he means it.

"And...from your silence," he says, "perhaps I can assume that you don't feel the same."

"No—I—the silence wasn't my answer. The silence was me being...surprised."

"I figured at our age, I might as well be direct. If the silence wasn't it, may I ask if you do have an answer?"

I haven't thought of Mr. Valera as a possibility, but it has been a long time since I have looked at anyone and thought of possibilities. The first emotion I feel after surprise is fear. What price might I be asked to pay for whatever happens next?

"All right," I say. "Yes." Not because I find Mr. Valera particularly appealing, but because there is nothing anybody can do to me anymore.

In the dingy apartment in Arcueil-Cachan, I half awoke to realize Eric was lying beside me, curled close in the narrow bed. He was wearing flannel pajamas, an arm flung across my side. It was cozy, and somewhere under his smell of beer and body and hair tonic was a deeper smell I convinced myself I still recognized. I fell back asleep, into the smell, into his warmth.

When I woke again he was shaking me. "You're really here? Louise?"

I squinted up at him, still confused with sleep.

"When I got home I thought I was seeing things, and I was too tired to do anything but ignore it. But you're really here?"

"I'm really here."

He was reaching for a suit jacket to put over his pajamas, as if they didn't already cover him neck to ankle.

"I'm sorry," I said. "I wasn't trying to make you uncomfortable. I thought I'd wait in the hall, but the door was open. Well, it was unlocked. I opened it. Then I got so tired. I haven't been sleeping."

"You came to see me in the middle of the night, without telling me?"

What to say? Everything sounded foolish. I could see that the sun was well up. *This is the morning of the day that I lose my child,* I thought. "He's taking Joseph. Cannu." Eric waited, expectantly, for how this explained my coming to Arcueil. "I was trying to think of places to take him—" Eric was already shaking his head, and I said, "I know, I know. There's nothing here for him. It was a mad, middle-of-the-night idea." *Him*, I said, because I thought it might sound less harsh than *me*, as if I still expected something from Eric. I didn't. Or I told myself I didn't. I sat up, back against the wall, knees drawn to my chest. I wrapped my arms around my legs like a child.

Eric sat on the edge of the bed, bundled in his jacket on top of his pajamas. "I wish there was something I could do," he said. Out of anyone else's mouth it would have sounded like a platitude, but Eric meant it sincerely. He did wish it, for my sake and for his. He wished he were a man with resources. He wished I had come to his doorstep and encountered something other than what I found.

I'd asked him to promise me that he'd do something with his life, once upon a time, and this was how he lived. I wanted to reassure him that I had deeper wounds now, and I did not care in the same way whatever he did with his life. But then I thought—why was it still my job to reassure him, on this day of all days?

"I do have something," he said. "I mean, it doesn't fix anything. Please don't get your hopes up. I started saying this the wrong way. But I have something I'd like to give you." He was still talking as he backed out of the room, and I heard the drawers of the writing desk jostling open, being rummaged through. "Here," he said, returning, holding out a tarnished pocketknife.

"As much as I might like to stab Cannu," I said, "it wouldn't get me what I want."

"It's the knife. Father's knife, from the train. You left it for me in Honfleur. I knew I was supposed to use it to come get you, but I didn't know how."

The knife was certainly old enough, and of a type our father might have used. But I couldn't remember it. I couldn't remember our father handing me a knife—why ever would he have?—and I couldn't remember hiding it from Agnès, as I must have. And why leave it for Eric rather than spiriting it away when Agnès made me pack my small bag for Le Havre? I didn't think he was lying, but I couldn't remember.

I told him this, and I could see that I was breaking his heart. I'd grown used to his glasses, and without them his blue eyes appeared watery and unhealthy, the whites yellowed. "I was so little. I'm sorry. I remember the licorice, in your school box. You found it before Agnès meant you to and shared it with me."

We went on this way—Agnès's custard, Conrad's toenails—with Eric draping flesh on the bones of what I remembered until I convinced myself that maybe I did, just a little, remember the knife. He said more that I didn't recognize, or even understand, about some mermaid who lived in the Honfleur estuary, a siren that feigned kindness and then lured boys into drowning.

Eric held the knife out to me on his open palm. It hovered at the edge of memory as I closed my fingers around it. I pulled the tarnished blade out of its slot and touched my finger carefully to the edge.

"All this time?" I trailed off. "Thank you. Thank you for wanting to give it back to me."

"I'm sorry it took this long."

I reached out and embraced him, and he put his arms, tentatively, around me.

"I'm sorry it's useless," he added. "I'm sorry I'm useless."

"You're not useless."

He asked where Joseph was now, and I told him at Conrad's. "Should we go there?" he said. "He's the useful one. The Brothers Useless and Useful. You can say it. I know it's true."

"It's not," I said reflexively, then turned away, because I suspected that my face might contradict my words.

It took him longer than I thought it would for a man with only one outfit to dress. I repinned my slept-on hair as best I could. He listened at the door for a moment before we went out, trying to leave while no one else was in the stairwell. Our anonymity lasted only to the front door. On a Saturday morning the children were in school, many of the adults at work, but there were still too many people out in the streets to avoid them all. At every café we passed men called out to greet him, then couldn't conceal their surprise as they noticed that we were walking together, a man and a woman on a Saturday morning. We did not look enough alike to be obviously related, and Eric squirmed. Whenever we moved into single file to fit through a clot of people, he walked a little faster, in no hurry to move back into step with me.

I walked quickly enough to come alongside him and reached out to take his hand. He jerked in surprise but did not remove it. I'd done it out of pique, but it was pleasant walking hand in hand. His was large and warm, and maybe we were both pretending that it could offer a kind of protection. We were still holding hands as we rang the bell for the concierge to let us into Conrad's building, and we knew it was time to break apart, but couldn't quite figure out how. Neither of us wanted to hurt the other.

"The knife," he finally said. He'd been carrying it in his jacket pocket for me and said he didn't want to forget to give it back to me.

During the walk I'd rehearsed in my head what I would say to Joseph and how I'd take him in my arms, this morning and as many times on the train as he'd let me, trying to memorize his shape and warmth. But Conrad was alone in the apartment.

"I waited as long as I could," he said, his voice infuriatingly calm. "You said tonight was the deadline."

I didn't understand what he'd done until he explained, and then I couldn't make myself believe it until he'd said it twice more. Joseph was already gone, placed on a train to Cherbourg half an hour earlier.

"Mathilde's with him," Conrad said. "To see that he arrives safely."

"Without saying goodbye? How could you?"

"I was trying to keep you from facing legal consequences."

"They would have been mine to face. This was mine to do." My disbelief gave way to more rage than I'd ever felt toward anybody, over anything. Even so, I didn't understand that the way I was scrabbling at the knife was something more than frantic fidgeting. I pried at the blade, the knife such a grubby, unexpected little object that I don't think Conrad realized what it was.

"I didn't know *what* you planned to do," he said. "I had no idea when you were coming back. *If* you were coming back."

Eric must have understood my fury better than I did: when the blade came free and I slashed forward with it, he was there at my side. He tried to grab my wrist but misjudged and caught the blade across the back of his hand. Conrad belatedly jumped backward—it had taken Eric's blood to make him realize the possibility of violence. None of us had thought of me as someone capable of performing it. But mother beasts do worse: disembowel, decapitate, dismember. My child was gone, my own brother the one who had separated us. For a moment, there was nothing I would not do. But in the moment just after, I was watching Eric's blood drip down his wrist and bloom in the white of his shirt cuff.

All three of us thought, *His hand.*

There was a flurry of bumbling. We were each of us as bad at triage as we were at violence. I ran for a kitchen towel and water, and Conrad yelled at me not to use the towel—*risk of infection.* He disappeared in search of gauze and bandages that he hoped Mathilde kept in supply. Eric stood there in the middle of the living room, his hand held in the air as blood slid down it and Conrad rummaged in the bathroom. Finally Eric took his own handkerchief out of his pocket and pressed it to the cut. Conrad emerged with handkerchiefs of his own and a beautiful long scarf of Mathilde's.

"Don't," I said. "You've surely got clean towels somewhere."

We sorted ourselves out, slowly, and sat Eric in the kitchen with his hand above his heart. The handkerchief he'd been pressing against it was saturated, but we were all afraid to look. At last Eric lifted the cloth and I rinsed the skin, daubed it with a clean towel. More blood welled from the cut, but I could keep it clear enough to see.

Eric peered down. "It's nothing," he said. "Almost nothing."

He tightened his fist and released it, made quick trilling movements with his first two fingers, flicked his fourth finger over his thumb and folded his thumb under his fingers, reassuring himself that he could still do everything he needed to. He was pumping more blood out of the cut, and Conrad told him to stop, but we were all relieved. The wound was shallow. The knife hadn't severed anything important. Conrad took over from me as both doctor and nurse, and as he fussed at Eric I asked about the nearest place to buy bandages. Conrad rattled off directions, mentioned money on the bedroom dresser.

Once I was outside in the sunshine I started feeling wobbly and exhausted, and I recognized the sensation as what remained after panic had washed over the body. Was this how I would feel for the rest of my life? Joseph was still gone. My mind returned from the flare of the fight to the larger explosion. Suitcase, train ticket, if I hurried I could be in Cherbourg maybe—what?—two hours behind Joseph? *What will that accomplish?* I asked myself. *Nothing,* I answered. But how could I not go?

I did, later that day, for all the useless hell of it, but I bought the bandages first, and brought them back, and rang the bell for Conrad, and when I entered the apartment I was laughing, laughing, because how had this day, this day of all days, turned into a day about Eric?

Suzanne

— 15 —

Do not leave your shadow

"REMIND ME TO TURN THE CLOCKS BACK LATER," ANDRÉ SAID at the breakfast table. There was no urgency to the statement, as he and Suzanne, both painters, had nowhere in particular they needed to be that day. Larger deadlines loomed, however. The Salon des Indépendants was in May, two months hence, and they were both working on paintings that they watched take shape in their shared home studio with a degree of wary competition.

"That's today?" Suzanne asked, and André pushed the newspaper across the table, tapping the relevant article. As of March 9, 1911, all of France and Algeria were adopting Greenwich mean time, though no one willingly called it by the English name. The switch was to PARIS MEAN TIME MINUS 9 MINUTES AND 21 SECONDS, the newspaper explained, which just happened to be exactly GMT. Local time differentials, including the five-minute grace period of train-station time, would be abolished.

Reading about station time, Suzanne thought of Erik, something she hadn't done since renting this apartment on the Rue Cortot a year earlier. The apartment was across the street from the building where Erik had lived back in the nineties, the place where she'd once knocked at a door he couldn't make himself open to her. She hadn't been sure how she felt about living next to him again, if he was still there.

353

When she asked her prospective landlord about Erik, the man knew exactly whom she meant. Yes, he was still about.

"Across the street?"

"Oh no. Ran out of money, moved to the suburbs. But he still plays piano at the cabarets."

Poor bastard, Suzanne had thought. Did he play his own songs, or someone else's? It wouldn't have made much difference to the man she'd known then—Erik would have been bitterly disappointed either way to still be in the cabarets.

There was a knock on the door now, hard and sharp, and the dogs started barking.

Suzanne, having grown accustomed to that kind of knock, prepared herself for bad news, and asked André if he'd heard Maurice come home the previous night. André shook his head. Coco had already run barking to the front door, but Pierrot, coward that he was, nosed into Suzanne's side. She laid her hand on the wolfhound's soft head, steeling herself.

André offered to answer the door, all the more an act of kindness because Suzanne constantly assured him that Maurice wasn't his responsibility. Twenty-seven years old now, Maurice should have been responsible for himself, but that was a pipe dream.

Her previous husband, Paul, had arranged job after job for Maurice, calling in favors only to have Maurice no-show or arrive drunk. "You have no understanding of *reputation*," Paul had told Suzanne when they fought, mostly about Maurice, about the damage the boy—no longer a boy—had done to his stepfather's professional credibility. To which she'd laughed, infuriating him further. But of course she understood *reputation*. What she didn't understand was why so many people aimed for the exact same reputation, dull and uniform. That was the trap. On the marriage-license application, Paul had insisted they list separate addresses, as if they hadn't already been living together. Perhaps she should have known then that it wouldn't last.

At the door, over André's shoulder, Suzanne saw the unmistakable blue caps of two police officers. They mentioned her son's name, asked if André was family. André delayed a moment but nodded. Suzanne invited the policemen inside. One was grizzled and rotund, the other young and tall and skeletally lean. They looked more like a comedy duo than colleagues.

"You don't look anything like your brother," the giraffe-like one told André. "He's sleeping it off now, but he didn't make himself any friends at the station last night."

"You must be the one got all your mother's good lucks," the grizzled one said, and winked at Suzanne, who at forty-five still possessed more than enough good looks to be winked at. André was twenty-one years younger than she, three years younger than Maurice, and with his golden hair looked like he'd leaped out of an advertisement for one of the new aviation clubs. Maurice, even Suzanne would admit, still looked like a walking sheet of dark, smudged newsprint.

"Oh, I think she kept some for herself," André said.

"Decidedly," the grizzled one said. "I suppose your brother's the black sheep. One in every family."

"What's happened?" Suzanne asked impatiently.

As expected, Maurice had been arrested the previous night. Again. Public drunkenness. Again. It took a lavish kind of public drunkenness to be arrested for it in Paris, and Suzanne didn't care to hear the details. She asked which station he was being held at and inwardly cursed when they told her: the tenth arrondissement rather than Montmartre, where people knew the family and made allowances.

"No place for a lady," the grizzled one said to André. "Be a good boy and save your mother the trip."

"He's not my brother, and she isn't my mother," André said, putting an arm around Suzanne and pulling her against his side. The lovers watched the policemen stutter and squirm and let themselves out.

As the sound of their footsteps receded, André offered to fetch Maurice from the jail, or at least accompany her, but Suzanne said she'd go alone. There was no reason for them both to lose a day of painting.

André was not an especially good painter. He was thoroughly outclassed by both Suzanne and Maurice, though the three of them never talked about this. His real strength was as a dealer, a charismatic salesman, which was the only reason his own paintings sold for anything at all. If he got out of the studio and concentrated on the business end of things, he could work marvels for her and for Maurice, Suzanne thought. But she wouldn't ask him to, or even suggest it, because she loved him and didn't want him to resent her, and because after the way she'd come up, she wasn't going to tell anyone else no.

André had been Maurice's friend before he was his stepfather. Under normal circumstances all three of them did an excellent job pretending there was nothing unusual about this, but during or after a bad binge Maurice, like an ill or sulky little boy, tended to want only his mother. After a night in jail he would not have been overjoyed to see André showing up to collect him.

Delaying her departure for the station, Suzanne knocked softly at her mother's bedroom door, down the hall from hers and André's. Silence, and Suzanne cracked the door to peer in. Her mother was sleeping, which she did more and more of, rising late and retiring early and napping in between. She was eighty, and had been living with her daughter and grandson since Suzanne had asked her to return to help with Maurice. That she hadn't really been able to help was not her fault. She'd already been growing frailer as Maurice grew stronger and more capable of refusing whatever checks anyone tried to place on his behavior.

At Montmagny, her mother had been horrified when Suzanne and Paul allowed Maurice to drink wine openly with dinner. It was watered, but still. "Right in front of you? What message is *that* supposed to send?"

"We can't stop him. If we can at least keep him close to home—"

"You've given up, that's what it says."

Suzanne had not given up.

There was more paperwork at the station than she expected. Receipts for the release money, acknowledgment of charges, an upcoming court date.

"He has to appear in court? He didn't before."

"How often do you two do this?" the desk officer asked, and Suzanne clenched her jaw.

"Severity of the charge, madame."

"Public drunkenness?" Was there some stiffer penalty for habitual offenders?

"No, the indecent exposure."

"The *what*?"

The officer pointed her toward the relevant portion of the report. Please let him only have taken a piss somewhere stupid, she thought before reading, but no—he'd stood under a streetlight and systematically stripped his clothes off down to the socks.

"Why?" she asked Maurice, once he'd been released to her care, his clothes rumpled but resumed.

She didn't really expect an answer, and he didn't have one. He shrugged, wincing in the sunshine outside the police station. He never had a reason. For a while after the divorce, when she and André and Maurice and her mother and the dogs had all moved in together, she'd hired nurses simply to sit in a room with Maurice while he painted and keep him from walking out the door. He started jumping out the window instead. Then Suzanne ran out of money to pay the nurses.

Paul's money had always made her feel hopeful for Maurice, even though nothing the money bought ever seemed to do any good. She'd burned it all down anyway by taking up with André. But he was so beautiful. My God, he was beautiful. And the way he looked at her? She'd tried not to do much hand-wringing about the passage of time, but how many more chances did she have for a man that young and that beautiful to look at her the way he did? Was she really going to let them all pass by, still married to Paul?

"That is generally what it means to be married," Paul had said, after he'd found out about André and she'd tried to open a negotiation.

"That isn't what it *has* to mean," she'd said.

"It is what I assumed you meant when you agreed to marry me," Paul said. "I am not interested in changing the terms."

Had he ever sounded more like the banker he was? The *terms* of their marriage, like the terms of a loan he regretted extending. Certainly she couldn't repay it, the money he'd spent on her and Maurice and her mother, even on the dogs. They turned up their noses at the food she offered them now, wanting the diced steaks the cook had prepared for them at the country house in Montmagny.

"Keep waiting if you like, but you'll be waiting forever," she said, and kicked their bowls across the floor when frustration got the best of her. On better days, she hoped this wasn't true. She could have it all again—the steaks, the good wine, the domestic help. No reason to think she couldn't. Well, plenty of reasons. But there was at least one reason to hope for better, and she wanted so badly for that reason to be her, but she knew it was Maurice.

One of the doctors at the first hospital had suggested painting, offhandedly—just a hobby to keep Maurice occupied, a harmless mother-son activity. The doctor was thinking of painting at most as a site for sentimental overspill, telling her to stretch a canvas the same way she'd grown accustomed to putting a bucket by Maurice's bed for him to vomit into. But immediately it was clear that Maurice possessed a fearsome, bewildering talent. They'd started their lessons at the Montmagny house, their easels set up in front of the glass doors that looked out onto the back garden with its neat stamped paths and hedges. She'd meant to deliver a lesson in perspective, the way the geometry of the garden changed as it receded to a stone wall and pastureland beyond. But Maurice had grabbed a palette and started slopping paint.

The picture he made that day didn't have anything to do with the garden, with the hedges or paths or scenery beyond. It was a picture of the Place du Tertre in late autumn. The trees in the middle of the square were barren, their dark branches splayed delicately across the gray sky, a few leaves still clinging. The colors were flat, the trees out of proportion, but for a very first picture it was extraordinary. The most striking part was how much Maurice *remembered*. The placement of the windows, the colors of the awnings, the size of the chimneys—everything was correct.

"Do you remember everything like this?" Suzanne asked him. "So precisely."

"Doesn't everybody?"

"Why would anyone use models? I wouldn't have had a job." Good Lord, she thought, no wonder he drinks.

But that couldn't be the whole reason. She'd known plenty of drunks, but never one like Maurice. His drinking seemed both reasonless and pleasureless, largely involuntary. At Montmagny, he'd leave for the day to paint en plein air with the neck of a bottle sticking out of his rucksack. She'd go out with the dogs to look for him before dark fell and find him sitting, head lolling, too drunk to stand, somehow still painting with the canvas laid in the grass beside him, because he could no longer reach the easel. The paintings would have bits of dirt and grass dried into the paint, and she despaired at the lost sales, but André managed to convince gallery owners the detritus was a selling point—intentional texture, traces of the painting's terroir.

She had wondered, of course, if she was the reason. Lord

knew Maurice's doctors had been ready enough to blame Suzanne: her inattention and her poverty and her "wantonness." She had blamed herself hard enough for the guilt to eat a hole in her stomach, which burned when she drank coffee. But she'd come to question the Mother Theory. She rebelled at the idea that anything her own mother had done or not done explained who Suzanne herself became. She dismissed also the Gift Theory, to which more recent doctors had subscribed, suggesting that Maurice's artistic gifts came naturally bundled with terrible tortures. Maurice was a person, not an equation, and whatever spurred him to drink seemed beyond anyone's understanding, including his. Whatever it was, she didn't know if he even wanted to be rid of it.

Although it was March the weather was still more winter than spring. Outside the police station, Maurice shivered and asked his mother if she'd brought him a coat.

"I assumed you had one when you went out last night," Suzanne said.

"Maybe I did. I don't remember. I don't have one now, though. Where are we? I want to stop and buy a coat."

"We should check at home first. It's probably there," she said, although she had no idea if that was true.

"If it's the money, I'll just make another painting. I can have one done tomorrow."

Among Maurice's gifts was his astonishing speed. He could start a painting in the morning with the goal of finishing it by evening—enough time to drop it by a dealer and receive money for a bender that night. Purely from a business perspective, it drove André and Suzanne crazy. As painters, it drove them even crazier that most of the pictures were still good. "You're saturating the market," André would scold, though the market for pictures like these seemed limitless—Maurice's elegant, moody paintings were all of recognizable streetscapes and landmarks, infused with a palpable sense of place. His weaker paintings lapsed into picture-postcard nostalgia, but his better ones felt both atmospheric and somehow real. At a time when some pranksters at the Lapin Agile had tied a brush to the tail of a donkey and exhibited the results as exemplars of a new school of "excessivism," the easy beauty of Maurice's work was a potential gold mine.

Damn, she'd briefly thought of the donkey, and wished she had put her goat to work all those years ago. But no—excessivism was a joke. She had not come all this way—this long, circuitous way back to the Rue Cortot—to make, or be, a joke.

Maurice, because he'd tied himself into a series of outrageously bad business agreements, was neither a joke nor a gold mine. He'd signed multiple conflicting dealer-exclusivity agreements, putting himself on retainer to one of them for several paintings every month, and for a pitiful lump sum. Compositions he set aside as poor work he later removed from the studio late at night to barter for liquor. Suzanne started hiding both the worst and the very best of his paintings.

Maurice had been livid when he realized his canvases were disappearing. He'd ransacked the apartment looking for them, ripped open the mattresses and knocked books and china off the shelves.

"We need to protect your reputation," André said. "For quality," he added, since Maurice was at least as renowned a drunk as he was a painter.

Maurice threw a vase at his head. André ducked and the vase exploded against a wall.

"We're trying to protect *you*," Suzanne said to Maurice, and glared at André, who wasn't helping matters. *Quality* made Maurice sound like a factory, with André and Suzanne serving as product inspectors.

Maurice pulled a picture off the wall, a sketch of Suzanne that Toulouse-Lautrec had once made, and spat on it. Then he pulled down a Degas, a large oil of a dancer backstage that had been a gift to her from the artist. Maurice started ripping the backing from the frame, and Suzanne didn't know if he thought his own paintings might be hidden inside or if he just wanted to destroy something that mattered to her.

She and André both moved to stop him, but she got there first. "No," she said, "no," and grabbed at him, trying to pin his arms.

He flung her away hard and she landed in the pieces of the broken vase, cutting her legs. André stood frozen, a seeming moment of indecision about whether to go to her or keep his grip on Maurice. Only once Maurice saw the blood seeping through his mother's stockings did he apologize and begin to cry.

Now, standing outside the police station beside her coatless son, Suzanne asked him who owed him the most money.

"Nobody owes me. They're all paid up."

"Who's paid you the least for the largest number of pictures?"

Maurice thought about it. "Libaude. But he's been straight with me. He hasn't violated the retainer agreement."

"Well, it was a terrible agreement," Suzanne insisted, and started walking brusquely up the street.

Maurice followed her like one of the wolfhounds and asked where they were going.

"To Libaude's gallery," she said. "For money."

"For a coat?" he said, incredulously. "I'll just make another painting. Actually, now that we're moving, I think I'll be all right in my jacket."

It wasn't for a coat, Suzanne explained. They needed money for treatment. It was what the officer had recommended, before Maurice appeared in front of a judge. If they could show that Maurice was pursuing treatment, the officer said, they'd have a good chance at a reduced sentence, maybe only a fine.

When he didn't protest, she assumed the plan was acceptable to him. Then they were in Libaude's gallery, asking for money in a horrible little back office that smelled of cologne and armpits, and Maurice asked, "A hospital? Who's ill?"

She and Libaude both looked at him.

"You," Suzanne finally said. "You are."

"Am I?"

"Yes. Yes, my love."

He looked vaguely around the room. He didn't disagree. "Not the first place. I don't want to go back there. The first one was awful."

"I didn't know it would be like that," she said. "We'll find a good place this time."

"First one? What number hospital would this be?" Libaude asked. When Suzanne declined to answer, he said, "No sense throwing good money after bad."

"You've been taking outrageous advantage of him," she said. "You know it. I know it. André knows it. Maurice knows it, deep down." She talked about Maurice as if he wasn't there. "Do your buyers know it? How do you think they'd react, finding out your markup?"

"Are you threatening me?"

"I came here to appeal to your sense of fairness. But if you don't have one, then yes, I'm threatening you."

Libaude looked at her appraisingly. She'd known variations of that look all her life and felt both pride and a little regret in the fact that Libaude was focusing it on her wits and her will, not her appearance. "How long's he likely to go away for?"

"Long enough that you'll run out of his paintings to sell. In a hospital they'll let him keep painting." She hoped this was true. "In jail they won't."

Libaude gave a wicked smile. "Ah. So that's why you're really here. It's hardly *my* problem that you and your toy soldier live off of Maurice."

"André and I earn," she said, indignant.

Libaude looked skeptical.

"If you want security, against a loan..." Suzanne had come here hoping for a grant, not a loan, but things were not going in her favor. She offered up the three pictures she'd accepted for the last Salon d'Automne. "I don't have as much inventory as Maurice—no one paints as quickly as Maurice, you know that—but maybe we could arrange something."

Libaude asked if these were from the same lot that hadn't sold during her show at the Gallerie Laffitte.

They were. It had been such a victory, her first solo show—the first solo show ever by a woman at that gallery. But sales had been poor. *Story of my life,* she thought, meaning only her life as a painter. Sales had been great when she'd been selling her face, her figure, her ability to hold a pose. But her paintings were considered difficult, the colors rather startling, the bodies unsettling, the women's faces harsh and unsentimental. She was so proud of them, and they sold so poorly. She wasn't sure she and André could make rent on the apartment if Maurice went away for any length of time, and she was ashamed of this need, but there it was.

"I don't want your paintings," Libaude said. "No offense intended, I just can't sell them. And I don't want anything else from you that you might have it in mind to offer," he added, with a leer.

Suzanne's jaw went slack. *Libaude?* There had never been a time, ever, when she would have offered this weasel any piece of her. For nearly a decade she'd been with only Paul or André. *Reputation,* she thought bitterly, remembering the fight with Paul. Would people speak to her this way for the rest of her life? How old or accomplished or rich would she have to become before they stopped? She looked at Maurice, embarrassed but also wondering if he would defend her, and saw that he'd fallen asleep slumped in his chair. There was a bubble of drool at the corner of his mustache, which she wiped away with her handkerchief.

"You treat him like a child," Libaude said.

"You treat him like an indentured servant, or an idiot."

"Idiot savant, maybe."

"This isn't funny."

"Maurice told me once that you have extra inventory squirreled away somewhere. His paintings, not yours."

She didn't answer.

"Bring me that. Bring me all of it, and I'll pay to send him away somewhere."

She didn't like that phrase, *send him away*, but she supposed it was accurate. "It needs to be enough for a private hospital," she said. "A good one."

"And what's the going rate on one of those?"

"Three hundred francs a month," she said, and Libaude raised an eyebrow. This was the cost of the priciest facilities she'd researched, and was astronomically more than Maurice's current retainer. She'd started with the figure to leave room to negotiate, but when Libaude didn't immediately refuse, she pressed. "He deserves the best, doesn't he? We'd all benefit." This was true, Suzanne reassured herself. She and André and Libaude would benefit, but Maurice would too—Maurice most of all.

Libaude tapped his fingers rapidly against the desk in some inscrutable pattern that Suzanne guessed was a calculation, a projection of what the best might be worth to him in the long run. "Where is the best? Can paintings be fetched weekly, or did you mean to send him abroad?"

"There's a clinic in Sannois," Maurice said.

Suzanne and Libaude startled. She didn't know if he'd woken or if he'd only been imitating sleep before.

"It's supposed to be the best," Maurice said.

Suzanne had heard of it, but how had Maurice? Had he consulted with someone independently, thought about admitting himself? Did he want to get better? If so, what had stopped him? Only the cost? Or did he feel he couldn't leave her, couldn't stop painting? She felt a fluttering of something inside her that had both wings and claws.

*   *   *

She returned with Maurice back to the apartment, where he peeled off his jacket and shoes, climbed into bed, and fell asleep. He usually slept most of the day after a bad night. She hung his jacket up and put a glass of water on his bedside table. The fact that he had a bedside table, his own room, and a soft bed with white sheets was proof, she felt, that she hadn't made a total mess of things. She kissed him on the forehead and left the door cracked open.

Her mother had risen and made herself lunch, which she shared with Suzanne in near silence. Most of their meals were now silent. They'd once had a steady repertoire of recriminations over Maurice, over how one or the other of them might have prevented his drinking. Then her mother had made several years of threats to move back to Bessines-sur-Gartempe, to which Suzanne was supposed to offer reassurances that her presence was necessary and cherished. She suspected that her mother really did wish, at least sometimes, to return to Bessines, although nearly everyone she knew there had left or died. But there wasn't enough money for either of them to live separately. Now they scraped their forks against the plates like the last two people left inside a dining car, riding together in uneasy companionship to the distant end of the line. The dogs came to beg, but her mother shooed them away and asked if she should make a plate for Maurice.

"He's asleep for now," Suzanne said. After finishing lunch, she delivered a plate to the studio for André, leaving her mother with the dishes.

André questioned the terms of the deal she'd struck with Libaude. "I wish you'd talked to me first."

"We don't have to give him everything. He'll have no idea what we've held back."

André offered to sort through the paintings with her while Maurice was sleeping. Suzanne declined his help, though she wasn't entirely sure why. Was she that determined to protect his studio time, to keep him from resenting Maurice the way Paul had? Why didn't she want him to know where she kept the paintings? She was relieved when André withdrew to his studio.

"Did you turn the clocks back?" she asked, since he'd told her to remind him.

"Not yet. I'll do it later."

She left by the front door but then walked around the block and came through the back garden of the building across the street. She'd known when they moved back to Montmartre that she had to get at least some of Maurice's paintings out of the apartment, ideally out of her building. The clumsiest ones had to be extracted before Maurice, in the grip of a thirst stronger than either his pride or his critical acumen, sold his own mistakes into posterity, and his bad days hung for decades in someone's parlor. The best paintings she worried would be similarly sold for quick cash, when they deserved so much more. It would have proven difficult to remove large canvases to some bank vault off the Butte with any regularity. She'd tried some of the landlords of neighboring buildings, on the hunt for a storage space, however small, to rent.

It was Erik's old landlord who'd finally had something. The man remembered her from her first stint in the neighborhood, nearly twenty years ago now, and even commented on her and Erik having once been a couple.

"Only briefly," Suzanne said. "I'm surprised you'd remember that."

"If I'd ever seen him with anyone else, maybe I wouldn't. But you were the only one."

Suzanne tested the words for blame, as if the landlord might suspect her of doing something fiendish or irrevocable to Erik's heart. But he sounded matter-of-fact; his old tenant's solitude had been merely one eccentricity among many.

He offered to show her a closet, a few feet wide and about the depth of a man lying down. There was a set of shelves on one side with maintenance supplies, but the left-hand wall was clear. The small, high window on the back wall let in so little light that she wouldn't have to worry about any fading of the paintings, and only a little about moisture. This would suit her, she told the landlord, and thanked him.

He should thank *her*, the landlord said. He hadn't gotten any money out of this space since Erik, who was so desperate to stay in the building when he could no longer pay for his upstairs apartment, had agreed to move into this room.

"You had someone *living* here?" Suzanne said, with horror.

The landlord grew defensive. He thought he'd been telling a funny story, not a horrible one. "No one forced him into it," he said. "He got a piano in here and a cot alongside. It was homier than you'd think."

But there was absolutely nothing homey about this oppressive closet. It was hardly fit for a stray dog, let alone a person.

"Didn't do him any harm," the landlord said, squirming under Suzanne's disapproving gaze. "He's a published musician now! For Christmas my niece asked for sheet music of some piece he wrote."

Suzanne took in this information with surprise and dueling sensations of relief, on Erik's behalf, and jealousy on her own. People were paying money for Erik's music, but still weren't paying money for her paintings. "What kind of music?"

"Who knows. I didn't ask her to play it. The point is, he's still at it. He's doing all right."

Remembering this exchange now as she returned to the closet to catalog Maurice's paintings, Suzanne reflected on how someone could be published and not be "all right." You could have a solo show at the Gallerie Laffitte and still be financially dependent on your own son. You could love your son and not have any idea how to help him.

Once in the storage room, she propped open both the window and the door for the afternoon light, but it was still dim. The worst paintings she should probably just destroy. But she couldn't do it. His work, however little value he seemed to place on any of it, belonged to him.

And the best of the pictures? They were so very, very good. So were her paintings, she thought, in their own hard-won and unmarketable way. She believed that. But she also worried that if people knew her name a hundred years from now, it was going to be as Maurice's mother. She loved him and she hated this.

She could destroy his best pictures too. He wouldn't even remember he'd painted them. No one would ever know.

She'd once marveled to Degas about her son's bizarre, only recently discovered gifts.

"He came by them honestly," Degas had told her, surprised at her surprise. "Child of a painter. He's got it in his blood."

Why was Degas so sure he knew who the father was? Suzanne wondered, annoyed, then with a rush of pleasure realized Degas meant her. Artist begetting artist. These paintings belonged to Maurice and to her in a way they didn't to André, which was perhaps why she hadn't wanted him to know where they were. She would never destroy these. She would safeguard these pictures as long and as well as she could, because she didn't trust Maurice to and because she couldn't imagine anyone else willing to put up with Maurice. Even so, she'd unsuccessfully tried to convince a succession of maids at Montmagny that he was fixable, a real catch, if they could look past the obvious. She was so afraid of him outliving her. If he were alone, she could imagine him ending up in a closet exactly like this one, painting picture after picture like an automaton in the near dark while Libaude dropped off bottles and took the empties away. In her imagination he wore an old frock coat like Erik's, threadbare and foul.

It was a vision from a nightmare, and a fear rose up in her so sharp and wild that she put her fist in her mouth to keep from making a sound. She finished her hurried inventory of the paintings, put the small notebook and pencil stub in her pocket, and backed out of the room. She didn't want to avert her eyes, as if in a moment's inattention she might glance back and find Maurice already there, imprisoned.

So distracted and afraid was she that she walked straight out the front door, with no effort at misdirection. She stopped when she realized, and looked up at her apartment windows across the street. A face appeared in the glass at André's end of the studio, but so shadowed she couldn't tell who it was. She desperately hoped it wasn't Maurice, that he wouldn't put two and two together and ransack the closet cache. But even if it was André, or her mother, she felt exposed, as if she'd stepped carelessly from behind an atelier changing screen not realizing she was naked. There was always supposed to be a moment when she removed her robe or sheet. There was always supposed to be a decision.

When she arrived home André was in the kitchen making coffee. He didn't ask her why she might have been inside the building across the street—and wouldn't he, if he'd been the one to see her?

She felt the first flare of a suspiciousness that would come to plague them, although its later incarnations would be about other women: was there someone younger, prettier, less encumbered? For years and years there wasn't, and by the time André admitted there was, he and Suzanne had been together so long that everyone was shocked by the divorce. It had been such a good match, their friends mourned: how rare it was to find someone who suited so well, and to have the strength to choose each other when everyone else thought the pairing must be a mistake.

She declined the coffee André had made and went to Maurice's door. It was cracked open the way she'd left it, and she peered inside. He was still asleep, still in his shirtsleeves and trousers, his breathing slack and slow. The glass of water on the bedside table was still full. Her mother was sitting in the room's only chair. She held a book on her lap, but her gaze, once Suzanne noticed her sitting there, was on her daughter. "Have you been here long?" Suzanne whispered.

Her mother shook her head. "I just sat down."

"You don't have to stay with him."

"I can read here as well as anywhere. And you've got deadlines."

Suzanne nodded, but instead of going to her studio, she sat on the floor by the bed. She wanted so badly to touch and hold some part of Maurice, but she was afraid to wake him. She leaned her head on the edge of the mattress and closed her eyes. The chair creaked, and she wondered what complaint her mother was readying—whether about Maurice, or about her aimless days, or about Suzanne's, full of striving, and how little it had gotten her. But there was only the rustle of her mother's skirts, full and old-fashioned, and the flap of a blanket. Then a weight settled across her shoulders, and when she opened her eyes, her mother was resuming her chair, having risen to wrap the extra coverlet from the foot of the bed around Suzanne. The room wasn't cold, but both of them knew that wasn't the point of the gesture. Pierrot, the wolfhound, nosed into the room and lay down with his head on her thigh.

Everything in this apartment was still taking place nine minutes and twenty-one seconds in the future, she thought, scratching behind the dog's ears. Maybe that had given Maurice enough time to spy on her, dive back into bed, perfectly rearrange himself, and calm his breathing. Or maybe it had given André time to start the coffee. Or maybe the face had been a visitor from some parallel timeline, now collapsed into the ordinary day. She knew this was all nonsense, but she wanted it to be a magical avenue of thinking, a world tucked between worlds, like the morning she'd spent in the train station with Erik so long ago. Time travel. What might be possible in those nine minutes? Not much, she thought. But something.

371

*   *   *

Suzanne would begin following Erik's career in the years ahead, relieved there was enough of a career for her to follow, not so much for Erik's sake as for Maurice's. The only connection between the two was in her head, but she needed them both to stay outside that room, that terrible dim closet, and if Erik could make it, with what Suzanne believed was a mere fraction of Maurice's talent (and *hers*, she thought), then maybe Maurice would be all right. She bought tickets to things like a Metachoric Festival, and a bizarre dance recital in which the star was bedecked in a tiered tulle skirt and midriff-baring top, her face a blank white mask with tiny, sinister eyeholes. *La Belle Excentrique*, it was called, and André agreed to go with her while Maurice stayed home. At least they'd left him at home, and she was hoping he would still be there when they returned.

"Eccentric, yes," André said afterward. "I wouldn't have called it beautiful. Think it was supposed to be about you?"

"I doubt it," Suzanne said. But someone had chosen to stage it, and people had bought tickets, and when they walked out through the lobby, Erik was surrounded by well-wishers. She felt again the flutter in her chest, more wings than claws.

If she could have predicted the plaque that would someday be placed on the little house in Bessines-sur-Gartempe where she was born, complete with a pompous unveiling ceremony, bunting, and speeches, she might have felt the same way about herself. Wings and claws, but mostly wings. The plaque would indeed identify her as Maurice's mother, but it would also call them both painters: Maurice a "famous" one and Suzanne a "great" one.

Erik

— 16 —

With amazement

A PHONE RINGS. CUE TIN CAN. CUE RATTLE OF KNOB. CUE JAR of marbles, rolled across the floor, caught under a stagehand's foot and rolled back again. Cue jar of marbles sliding past the stagehand and tangling in the curtain ropes. Cue cursing. Cue typewriter, even though no one can hear it, the sound buried in the din.

Serge Diaghilev, founder and manager of the Ballets Russes, watches the rehearsal from the middle of the main floor at the Théâtre du Châtelet. He turns to Erik, sitting beside him, and shakes his head. Jean Cocteau, on Erik's other side, leans in, and now both men are in Erik's space, his air. In his way.

"They're drowned out," Diaghilev says. "Your noises."

The noises were Cocteau's idea, originally, and Erik doesn't know whether to defend them or admit to being usurped. "If I remove some of the brass," he says, "perhaps it will clarify the sound."

"Or we could add more typewriters," Cocteau suggests. "You wanted it to sound *modern*."

Erik points out that Stravinsky managed *modern*, managed an honest-to-God *riot*, with the same orchestra instruments everyone else used. This seems the greater glory.

Cocteau stares at him, his words hanging unspoken but deafening between them: *Ah, but you aren't Stravinsky.*

I could be better, Erik thinks, but cannot bring himself to say it aloud. His younger self would have said it. His younger self would have taken out an illustrated ad in a newspaper just to proclaim it and would have been satisfied at being known for the assertion itself: the terms by which he announced his greatness. (Let the greatness itself remain mercifully unexamined.)

This ballet will be examined. Cocteau has seen to that, if not with the typewriter then simply with the scenario itself, a riff on the flashy publicity parades circus performers mounted. Erik first thought that Cocteau must mean the parade was only the opening choral, before the story shifted to some tender pas de deux behind the scenes, perhaps a trapeze girl turned delicate swan. Cocteau laughed. The parade *was* the story, the whole story: he needed Erik to write numbers for a Chinese conjurer, a master of ceremonies, a group of acrobats, an American ragtime dancer, and a horse.

The scenario is nothing like anyone's idea of a ballet, but maybe this explains why Cocteau approached Erik, who has never composed a ballet. No ballets unless one counts *Uspud*, which no one does. After several years' study at the Schola Cantorum, Erik's a walking contradiction, a rigorously trained music-hall composer. He's capable now of so much more than cabaret commissions, but too few people are interested in paying him to do anything else. He's still surviving off a handful of published solo piano pieces, his humor writing, and haphazard patronage: the singer Paulette Darty introduces him to music student Alexis Roland-Manuel, who introduces him to the mezzo-soprano Jane Bathori, who introduces him to the Princesse de Polignac, born Winnaretta Singer the sewing-machine heiress, who gives him a commission for a choral piece about Socrates, a setting of Plato's *Dialogues* for female voices. Such connections form a web that keeps him aloft, but it's a cobweb, not a fishing net. It's vulnerable to wind and moth wings and Erik's weakness for saying rude things to important people. It does not net him enough fish to ever really be sure where his next meal is coming from.

He has also written a one-act play, both words and music, absurd without being absurdist, because there's no -*ist* yet, no school of it, no philosophy, just Erik being Erik. Because no one has done it before, there's equally no word for how he altered the piano to perform the play, inserting sheets of paper between the strings. The musical passages were meant to accompany the dancing of a mechanical monkey, a role inhabited at the debut by the child of the hosts, friends of friends who had agreed to mount the play in their living room. The venue was even more galling than the measure of gratitude he is supposed to continue to feel for Claude's versions of the *Gymnopédies*, which still pop up in programs of new French orchestral works, sending a steady trickle of admirers Erik's way. The pilgrims who manage to track him down in some café or salon (no one ever braves Arcueil, not since Louise) always seem startled, both by him and by his newer compositions. He doesn't know why the person they find comes as such a surprise to them. Is it the bowler hat?

His suits are all proper now, black wool, approximately tailored. He looks stuck between a banker and a clerk, too old to be the clerk, too shoddy to be the banker. "Are you dressed like that to make fun of me?" Philippe asked when Erik debuted the new outfit. He had simply been tired of his filthy gray velvet. He didn't realize that everyone was going to think he was playing some kind of joke.

Maybe the paper in the piano strings was what led Cocteau to think he could stuff Erik's score full of a typewriter, a siren, a pistol shot. Erik has checked through the percussionists' parts, making sure there are pairs of hands available for all the strange additions. A week before the debut the full score is still a work in progress, and now the time spent with the percussion notation is wasted, because Cocteau has gone and hired a separate typewriter operator. Not even a musician but an actual typist, a clerk

from a law office who took piano lessons as a boy. Of all the typ-
ists who would wet themselves over being in the orchestra pit at
the Théâtre du Châtelet, Cocteau has somehow found one who
acts like a humorless older boy in a crèche, putting up with the
infantile play only until some responsible adult can return him
to his real life. Erik doesn't know if Cocteau hired this sort of
person by accident or on purpose. If the latter, is Erik supposed
to convert him? Is that the challenge, that Erik's music be sufficiently sublime to turn the typist into a musician? Or is the
man's sullenness supposed to remain intact, putting its stamp on
the sound?

"I like that," Diaghilev says, after one of the percussionists
bangs a lid onto a wooden box.

It sounds like hooves to Erik. A sound from the past, from
an age so recently departed that he is afraid to look behind him
for fear he has accidentally scored Honfleur: fish slapping against
plank tables, their guts pinging into metal pails. "I'm cutting the
box," Erik says, "and the marbles."

Diaghilev makes two fists, rubs his knuckles into his eye
sockets.

The stage manager calls to him, holding up a pocket watch,
and Diaghilev reluctantly stands to send everyone home for the
night.

"Notes?" Léonide Massine asks from the stage. He's lead
dancer and choreographer, also Diaghilev's lover, which Erik is
grateful Cocteau mentioned to him, so he could remind himself
not to say anything unpleasant to one about the other.

"Notes first thing tomorrow," Diaghilev says. "I have too
many."

Erik rises and stands in the aisle, surveying the hundreds of
empty seats, trying to make them feel familiar instead of intimidating. He's unaccustomed to hearing music played in empty
rooms. An audience changes the acoustics, all those bodies ab-
sorbing sound and making their own, rustling and coughing and

drinking. Wait, no drinking in the main hall at the Châtelet, and Erik's nervous all over again—he's not used to a sober audience.

He's accosted by the typist, who is quite out of order in directly addressing Erik rather than the conductor. "Do you want me to type anything in particular?"

"I hadn't thought about it."

"If it doesn't matter, you should take out the paper and ribbon. It's wasteful, otherwise."

Wasteful? A sheet of paper and a typewriter ribbon? One of Erik's favorite things about *Parade* is that there is finally *enough:* the size of the orchestra, the size of the theater, the opportunity to send sound billowing up to the Châtelet's gilt ceiling. Erik has not come all this way to be parsimonious with paper. "Use as much as you can. Pull out and replace the sheets, over and over. Just keep typing."

"That's not what the other one said to do."

"The other one?"

The typist points across the room at Cocteau.

"You can't even remember his name?" Erik says. Cocteau is twenty-three years younger but significantly more famous than Erik, his reputation as a writer and general provocateur sufficiently earned that Erik is affronted on his behalf. "What about that quote?" Erik asks. "From the book about the lady. The loose one. About bears dancing and banging on pots. You could type that."

"A book about a loose lady who dances with bears? I can't think my wife would have let it in the house."

Was the reference to his wife spontaneous or strategic? Did he say the same to Cocteau?

Erik doesn't often judge, but he supposes the typist is handsome. Cocteau would think so, anyway. This sort of thing makes Erik's head hurt. This is supposed to be *his* ballet, *his* music, but he's had to put too much goddamn time into thinking about whatever Cocteau might be thinking. Erik has arranged his whole life so as not to need to think this much about anybody else. Or did he arrange it that way because he so rarely understood quite what other people were thinking? Failure of consideration, or failure of empathy? The former makes him a hero, Artist Above All; the latter makes him something in need of repair. He is not broken, he tells himself. Just different.

"Only the quote is about bears," he says. "And pots and stars. Not the whole book."

"You're going to add banging pots?"

"You're not listening."

The typist retreats back down the aisle toward the orchestra pit. Erik follows and they consult the remaining string players, who are still packing up their instruments.

"It's a kettle," one of the violinists says. "It's about language being no better than a cracked kettle, only making bears dance when we long to make the stars weep." Gustave Flaubert, he adds, and the loose woman is Bovary.

The cellists nod. They forgot the kettle, but they know the book, at least by reputation.

Erik is jealous. That book is sixty years old, the author dead for nearly forty, and everyone knows his name. It has been living in the dark of their heads like a mushroom.

"Is my typing meant to be the kettle banging, or the stars weeping?" It could be a legitimate question if not for the typist's insolent tone.

A kettle, Erik thinks. Could a stove be installed in the wings, such that the shriek of the boiling is choreographed? He can out-Cocteau Cocteau. He can out-anybody anybody.

Now Cocteau jumps onstage to speak to Massine, who's still in costume. The poet Guillaume Apollinaire is there too, standing on the floor and leaning heavily against the edge of the stage. He's agreed to write the introduction for the printed program, for which he's coined the word "surrealism."

Erik stands next to Apollinaire and calls up to Cocteau that he wants the typist fired.

"Must we do this now?" Cocteau says. "I thought you'd come around on the typewriter."

"I've made my peace with the typewriter. It's the typist I want to replace."

Cocteau surveys what remains of the departing orchestra and spots the typist folding his metal typewriter into a black leather case, as if it really were a musical instrument. "What's your objection?"

"What's the appeal?"

The men regard each other. They've danced around this already—Cocteau's tastes, his assumption that Erik shares them. The more Erik tries to avoid the topic of sex, the more Cocteau seems to see him as a project. He can deliver Erik to the world, the world to Erik; get Erik's music onto the stage of the Théâtre du Châtelet, and a man into Erik's bed.

"His playing not to your taste, Erik?" Cocteau asks.

Erik winces. He doesn't like people using his first name. It's intimate, tongues plucking at him. No thank you. He doesn't even want his *name* in Cocteau's mouth. In anybody's mouth. He shakes his head.

"Suit yourself, Erik." Cocteau mimes the buttoning up of a shirt, all the way under his chin, strangling himself. "Since you have such particular requirements, why don't you hire the replacement? As long as he can be here for tomorrow's rehearsal with a typewriter in hand, it's fine with me."

Dismissed, Erik lurks, wanting to see if anyone says anything about the costumes, which he considers a disaster, but one beyond his purview to mention. Massine is his best hope. Surely he recognizes how ridiculous Picasso's designs are, great conglomerations of cardboard boxes the dancers can barely move in. That's what you get when you hire a Cubist as costume designer, Erik thinks, as contemptuous of the word as of Picasso's costumes. Everyone laps Picasso up, but he's still an -*ist*. There's a word that describes what Picasso does. It's a word he originated, but still. There is no word for Erik.

"Did you have something else to say, Erik?" Cocteau asks.

Erik shakes his head and creeps away. If he didn't owe Cocteau his professional future, he would ask him to stop with the name. The pilgrims who seek out Erik often call him "Maître," or master, and even when they're joking a little they mean it sincerely. There's a small flock of them—mostly men, all of them young—and together they represent a hodgepodge of musical styles and influences and aims. The most flattering article Erik has ever read about himself turned out to have been written by a fourteen-year-old, which he realized only when he arranged to meet the author, and a boy, barely out of short pants, answered the door of his parents' apartment. For a moment Erik crumpled, the universe one vast joke made at his expense. Then he decided that of course, of course! His legacy *should* rest with people barely out of short pants; adults, well, they'd had their chance to discover him and had largely missed out.

Georges Auric, the fourteen-year-old, is going to make a better critic than composer, but Erik plans to let the boy figure that out for himself. Same for Roger Désormière—he's a better conductor than a musician but doesn't seem to know it yet. Ah well. Erik had to figure everything out for himself the long, hard way, and likes the idea of his admirers doing the same. Not that he wants them to suffer, but he's curious which ones will stick with music, and what parts of it they'll stick to. Erik is the maître of stickiness. It's his most extraordinary quality, but the young admirers can't yet appreciate how painful and exhausting it is to beat your head against the same wall for years, even go back to school to learn how to beat it in better. They admire him now for other reasons, but when they're old they'll admire him for this. Assuming they get old. One by one, they've turned eighteen and been called up to the war.

It is May of 1917. Walking home, Erik buys a newspaper, dips into a café to page urgently through it. No major developments at the front, and he breathes a sigh of relief. He doesn't want *Parade* to have to compete with the war news. He wants the city's undivided attention. He knows he should be glad simply that men are not dying, or at least not dying in such vast numbers as they were in April, at the Second Battle of the Aisne. And he *is* glad—he wants Auric safe, Désormière, the other young admirers. He wants the men he conducted as boys in the children's choir in Arcueil to once again sell loose cigarettes on the stoop outside his building. He wants his nephew, Joseph, home from the medical corps, even if the boy's home is Cherbourg, not Paris. And probably not *boy* anymore, Erik corrects himself, doing the math because he hasn't seen Joseph since before Louise left France.

For the last year, Louise's letters have been relentlessly afraid for her son. Erik feels both frustrated and helpless when he reads them, as if Louise is expecting him to do something about Joseph, or about the entire war. He isn't sure what to say, so only occasionally writes back. He's got a letter half-finished on his desk, but his favorite bit has to do with earwax, and although it's meant to be comforting, he isn't sure it will land right. In a winter missive he suggested that Joseph make snow angels, or find a well-meaning sister to lie to the authorities on his behalf. He meant it as gratitude for Louise, perhaps also as mockery of his own lifelong unwillingness to be told what to do. *I've always wished he had a sister,* Louise wrote back, and Erik knew he'd said the wrong thing again.

When the Germans were within bombing distance of the city, early in the war, Erik volunteered with the Home Guard, but nothing much ever happened. The war is a distant performance: overly long, with no interval to stretch your legs, and terrible reviews. Dull costumes, mud backdrop, no applause. He cares about the outcome, but it's gotten harder to care day by day. In the hour by hour he even forgets the whole thing is happening, until he sits to eat breakfast and there's tallow on his bread, a splash of tinned milk swirling in a cup of something brown that everyone's stoically calling *coffee* but is definitely no longer coffee, and newspaper articles straining to make glorious the acquisition of a few more feet of annihilated land.

Cocteau travels regularly to the front to serve as a volunteer ambulance driver, and describes the situation there as much worse than the heavily censored newspapers suggest. Apollinaire hasn't been north since being wounded, the scar still angry across his shaved, shrapnel-laced head. He isn't fully recovered, and everyone is happy when he manages to attend rehearsals, in part because he makes it all right, what they're doing, putting a circus on the stage of the Châtelet while men are dying a few hours to the north. If Apollinaire, with shrapnel in his head, thinks this is worth doing, that gives them license to do it.

"Maybe it's *because* he's got metal in his head that he thinks it's any good," Mathilde said during one Sunday dinner with her and Conrad.

Erik still accepts the dinner invitations, depends on them, even admires what Mathilde can do with margarine now that no one can get hold of butter. But he and Mathilde have dropped any pretense of getting along.

"She's a scrapper," Erik said to Conrad, with Mathilde seated right there. "When you first married her I didn't expect it."

Mathilde rolled her eyes.

Changing the subject, Conrad mentioned Louise, although neither brother had more news than had been in her latest letters. "I know she wishes you'd write more," Conrad said, in a careful tone that did not entirely conceal his chiding.

Erik neither made excuses nor promised to write more often, simply ran his fingers over the back of his hand, where her cut had faded to a long white line.

The brothers talked then of the war, but what was there to say? Their fighting years had come tucked between the siege and the current conflagration. Erik hadn't thought about the army since he was invalided out, but Conrad, self-conscious about how little he'd been doing, mentioned the ages of every colleague or neighbor who'd joined the fight. At forty-seven, he hadn't yet aged off the Reserve rolls.

"If *you're* called up, we'll know things are desperate," Erik joked.

Conrad didn't find it funny. He'd started exercising again, refusing to admit it had anything to do with the war. Rationing had already slimmed him down, and then he'd bought a membership at a neighborhood sports hall. Erik went to watch one practice and couldn't stop laughing. The men with graying hair ran around in little shorts, tossing javelins and heaving shots, baring their pale chicken legs. If they were that concerned with proving themselves manly, Erik thought, they should just go to Belgium and get themselves blown up already.

He'd begun a series of little musical sketches, *Sports et divertissements*, before the war started. Then the magazine that commissioned them went on hiatus, and he made the mistake of showing them to Conrad, wondering if his brother might have any suggestions for what else Erik could do with them.

"Since when do you write about sports?" Conrad said, his voice thick with the suspicion that Erik was poking fun at him.

"I write about anything," Erik objected. "I always have. None of these are about you."

Conrad gave him a skeptical look.

Why, Erik wondered, did everyone always think he was making fun of them?

Erik finishes his drink (despite the food shortages, Paris is never short of alcohol), folds the newspaper, leaves it on the table, resumes his walk home. He's not happy with the balance of the woodwinds in the Chinese conjurer number, and Cocteau has shoved a juddering roulette wheel into the forte passages.

Now Erik has to find a new typist by tomorrow night. Tonight? He looks up at the stars, trying to guess the time. There were nights before the war that they seemed nearly blotted out by streetlights and smog, but tonight the city is crouched dark and still enough that the sky has its old milky sparkle, only a little blurred. Or is that his eyes? He takes his glasses off, cleans them with a handkerchief, puts them back on. No way of telling. His glasses are meant for close work. It would be unfair to expect them to show him the sky as well.

His feet hurt, his back. As plush as the seats at the Châtelet are, it's been a long few nights, with more to come. All this *rehearsing*. Aristide Bruant would just walk on and own the whole place. What poor sod is accompanying him now? Out of professional solidarity, Erik would like to hire a pianist to operate the typewriter. Who does he know who most needs the wage? He so rarely has anything anyone would want. There's a pleasure to it, heavy and satisfying, like the hammer in his belt loop.

Cue footfall on stone, on brick, on brushed gravel. Cue curb. Cue sewer plate. Cue the Arcueil-Cachan aqueduct looming like sturdy lacework against the stars; *mmmmmmmm*, the typist could write, the shape of the aqueduct. Sometimes by the end of his walk it is so late that it's early, and Erik nods to milk carts, oxcarts bringing produce from the farmland around the city, ever farther out. There's train service that didn't exist when he moved here, between the suburbs and Gare de Sceaux. Or he can walk to the Métro at Porte d'Orléans, take line 4 all the way to Clignancourt if he wants, at the northern edge of Paris. Or transfer at Denfert-Rochereau, at Montparnasse, or Barbès-Rochechouart. He can be whisked through the entire city in a box underground, but he almost never takes the Métro. There's the cost, of course, but it's more that he's come to need his long walks, the way his head empties and his body makes its own rhythm—heartbeat, footfall, the filling and emptying of his lungs. The young admirers think he lives in Arcueil as a political statement, Man of the People. When he was conducting the children's choir some of the locals assumed the same, that he was a Communist come to earn his stripes. He would puncture the illusion if he ever revealed that he moved here only to hear himself think.

It didn't do any good. Maybe it did a little good.

Oxcart, milk cart. Someday, he dreams, the world will not even need the words. They will be discarded like hooves, like sackbuts or harpsichords. Like steamships replaced canvas sails. And he remembers, still, the ropes slithering reptilian across the boards and the splash that night he fell off his uncle's boat. Let those sounds perish from the earth and let them not be mourned. He makes a catalog in his head of objects he might score into music if he could decide what they sound like: the flaring of a bulb's filament, a glass egg of light. An umbrella spun open in the rain, a dazzle of dark. Water disappearing down the new drain in his apartment, even if he still has to carry water from the fountain in the street. The street is named after the nearby Église Saint-Denis. In a century it will be named after Erik. This would give him such comfort, such vindication, if he allowed himself to believe it possible.

In the silence certain noises seem garish—a man pissing against a wall, a lover's quarrel from an attic window. A woman stands alone in the dark with lipstick drawn like a laceration across her face. He does not want to look too long, to make her hopeful, but he swears he recognizes her. Did they perform together? Most of the women who ply this territory have long since come to recognize him, and know he never buys. But this one is new and puts a hand on her hip, lifts her skirt with the other, just to the calf. Her stocking is torn, the pale flesh puffing out like a wound. He makes an apologetic half smile, tips his hat, shakes his head. If she happened to own a typewriter, he could offer her the job. A streetwalker in the orchestra pit. That would out-Cocteau Cocteau. Or would it? He imagines

Cocteau retaliating by replacing the corps de ballet with can-can girls.

This gives him an idea, and when he wakes later in the morning he nearly empties his desk looking for the letter. It can't have come so long ago. The newspapers have barely begun to run preview stories on *Parade*. La Vorace saw one and sent him a letter, care of the Châtelet. She'd sold what was left of the animals, married a magician, and eked out a few good years. Now she was a widow and badly off. She was glad to see Erik's star had risen. If there was anything he could see his way to doing for her, she'd be most appreciative. At first he disliked her presumption, then felt doleful that there was nothing at all he was in a position to do for anyone. He can't even offer her *Parade* unless he can procure a typewriter.

Conrad? Usually his source for any and all items, to the point that Mathilde once scolded Erik for treating her apartment like a department store. "Except you think it's all free. Anything you didn't have to pay for yourself, you think it came freely." But Conrad wouldn't own a typewriter. He has the kind of job that comes with secretaries to type things for him.

Erik continues pondering typewriters while he packs a bag with the score for *Parade*, a notebook, and extra paper and pens, then hooks an umbrella over his arm even though the weather is sunny. There won't be time to come home before tonight's rehearsal. But he never comes home except to sleep anyway.

He has breakfast at his regular café, although many of its other patrons have already proceeded to lunch. He smokes a cigar. The bartender puts a good-sized splash of brandy in his coffee without his having to ask. If he ever meant to be a Communist, he took a wrong turn somewhere. Maître d'Arcueil, treated with deference like some lordly old coot.

Several of the young admirers probably have typewriters. Correction: their parents have typewriters, and to borrow one Erik would have to calculate who's been called up, who's still living at home, whose parents are supportive of their sons' musical ambitions, and whose might see Erik as a villain, Pied Piper of wastrels. Why don't the misfit children move out as quickly as possible and starve, as they did in his day? But where would they go?—that's the trouble. Montmartre's over. The real artists are now in Montparnasse, which the young admirers wouldn't be able to afford. Erik can't afford Montparnasse.

Then there's the possibility of accidentally calling on someone who's been killed in action, splashing into a pool of family grief.

Philippe almost certainly owns a typewriter, but he's out of town. Out of the country, actually, and Erik congratulates himself on knowing Philippe's whereabouts, although he found out only by accident when he showed up on Philippe's doorstep one night drunk and unannounced, and Philippe's wife led him into a living room filled with half-packed suitcases. She was the third wife, but Erik called her by the second wife's name and didn't realize his mistake until Philippe corrected him.

"Where are you going?" Erik asked, and scowled.

To Tarragona, Philippe said, and Erik would have been less surprised if he'd said Tahiti. To see family, Philippe explained. His parents were both still living, but a brother had written him to suggest that if Philippe was going to come at all, he should come sooner rather than later.

"And I suppose you have about a hundred nieces and nephews by now."

"Something like that," Philippe said. It would be good to meet them, he added, but he didn't sound like it would be good at all. He sounded terrified at the prospect of showing up after thirty years and inviting his family's definitive appraisal of whether he'd made good use of the time.

Philippe's older daughter came into the room to toss some schoolbooks into one of the suitcases, and Erik realized with a sick feeling that he could not quite remember her name. Neither hers nor her younger sister's. Because he and Philippe had none of the same friends anymore, there was no one he could ask later.

With a meaningful look, Philippe's wife said they would be leaving early in the morning and there was still a lot of packing to do, and Erik took his cue.

At the front door, Philippe asked him why he'd come.

Erik honestly didn't remember. He'd just found himself walking in this direction. "You weren't going to tell me that you were leaving?" he grumbled.

"I didn't know it would matter to you. It's only for a few weeks. We should catch up when I'm back."

"You are coming back, aren't you?"

Philippe laughed, surprised. "My whole life is here, Erik."

Well, that's something, Erik thought. His whole life is in Paris, and I am in Paris, and thus we are still part of each other's lives.

"I'll send you a postcard," Philippe said.

With Philippe still in Spain, Erik decides to send a pneu, mockingly addressed to *Claude D., National Treasure*. Claude lives on the Avenue de Bois du Boulogne now, just west of the Arc de Triomphe. The address is intimidating, let alone the house. Erik starts walking, counting on the pneu to arrive just enough ahead of him that his sudden appearance will be only moderately impolite. Maybe *Parade* will be a smash—not just a succès de scandale, Erik daydreams as he crosses the Seine, but a purer, definitive sort of success, and he'll invite both Philippe and Claude out to a twelve-course dinner, and it will be just like old times except with enough food. He plans the meal, the course of the conversation, as if that's something that can be planned, and this pleasant exercise takes him through the Jardins du Trocadéro and north along the Rue Hamelin.

He's a block from Claude's house when he wonders whether he owes Claude an apology for anything. For a while he was so careful, reminding himself not to say anything he might regret later, but Claude has been ill long enough that Erik can't keep it up, and perhaps he slipped at some point.

Claude has survived procedures barely invented, attempted in part to save him specifically, the calculus of butchery and risk altered by who Claude is and what he might yet create. "Borrowed time," Claude once said, then corrected himself. "Not borrowed, earned. I've earned every wretched minute of this."

He agreed to the knife, to the radium, because he wanted time with his family, his second wife and child, gifts that, after the disaster of his first marriage, he cannot imagine leaving a second sooner than he has to. He didn't do it for music. But he has kept composing. A set of sonatas, sketches for operas. A ballet for Diaghilev, although the reviews were poor. Including one from Erik, published under a pseudonym, but the voice made it obvious. "I didn't say anything negative about the score," Erik protested to Claude later. "Only the staging." At the time the distinction made sense to him. But now he winces, knowing he will be held to account for *Parade*, both for the things he has control over and for the things he doesn't—Picasso's boxy costumes, the dancing horse, the whole lunatic circus in a blood-soaked season of war.

It occurs to him only now, stepping through the iron gates into the front garden, that Diaghilev might have offered *Parade* first to Claude, who turned it down, and that's why Erik received the job.

A maid opens the heavy wooden door, which Erik once teased Claude was big enough to have a smaller door cut inside it, like the entrance to a medieval castle. He had kept the words light but couldn't entirely hide the resentment curled inside them. The maid greets him politely by name and shows him to Claude's study, where light from the tall windows falls on a brilliantly blue carpet. Claude sits in a green armchair like a frog stranded on a lily pad. He doesn't stand to greet Erik, and Erik wonders whether it's because they're friends of so many years that Claude doesn't feel the need, or whether he'd have diffi-culty rising from the chair. He's too thin, but at least there's color in his face. *Don't die*, Erik thinks. *Please.*

Without asking, the maid pours a glass of water for Claude, a calvados for Erik. He may never have his own maid, but Claude's maid knowing him this well might be almost the same thing. Except that it isn't at all the same thing. But this is pleasant, both the glass in his hand and its confirmation that he's welcome here, still a regular guest after all this time.

"Just tell me," Erik says. "I wasn't the first choice, was I? Was it you?"

"Not me," Claude says. Erik prods and he reluctantly adds, "I heard it was Stravinsky. But when he wasn't available they came straight to you."

"Second choice. Not—tenth, or something?"

"A firm second."

"That's all right, then. But would you have taken it if they'd come to you?"

"The circus piece? No, but you'll do beautifully with it."

No doubt Claude has more opportunities than hours in a day, setting aside the calculation at this point of months or years. That he's still composing at all Erik finds quietly heroic, more so than anything the sons of Conrad's neighbors are doing at the front. The calvados is making his heart full and he tries to say this to Claude.

"Stop," Claude says. "Not from you. You're the one person I count on to spare me that kind of nonsense."

"It's not nonsense. I'm always full of nonsense, I should know."

"Seriously. Stop."

"I'm trying to tell you something true. I don't do it often enough." It isn't just that Claude's still writing, it's that he's still experimenting, dragging eighteenth-century styles into the twentieth with his sonata cycle. "I don't know how many people would be able to do it. I don't know that I could."

"Of course you could. You would."

"I'm flattered, but—"

"It's not a compliment, it's a fact. Look at you. Look at your life. If you're still composing now, there's nothing that could make you stop. What else would you do?"

Erik feels warm for a minute. He feels proud, feels seen. Even feels loved. But the longer he savors the comment, the heavier it grows. Does his life look as bad as a cancer diagnosis? His apartment isn't *that* disgusting, even though he's started letting stray dogs sleep cold nights inside. Does Claude imagine him writing into an abyss of futility every bit as dark as death?

With a note of reluctance, Claude asks if he's come for money.

Erik says nothing. He hasn't, but if Claude is going to offer, he won't refuse. They always use the word "loan," but Erik's given up calculating the principal, let alone whatever theoretical interest might have accrued.

"Because I'm afraid I just can't. Not right now," Claude says. "I've barely been composing, and the medical expenses on top of household—well. Don't marry a banker's wife, is all I'm saying. They've got certain expectations."

As a joke, or as advice, it falls flat, since both men know Erik isn't looking for any kind of wife. But as a confidence, a revelation he's sure Claude would not want widely known, Erik catches it and holds it tight, feeling trusted—and, if he's honest, also feeling a hint of satisfaction. It pleases him to think that perhaps even Claude has been forced to pencil columns of numbers in the margins of his composition notebooks.

"I only need to borrow a typewriter," Erik says reassuringly, pleased that the favor he needs might now look like magnanimity.

After Erik explains that the score for *Parade* requires a typewriter, Claude is silent for an excruciatingly long time. When he speaks all he says is "Really?"

Which is less painful? To claim the idea as his, all his, or to blame Cocteau and admit to being bossed about? Cocteau wouldn't have tried to boss Stravinsky. Probably no one's tried to boss Claude in decades. And Erik *has* come around—he decided last night that he liked it. But Claude is making him unsure today, and why does Claude still have the power to make him unsure? "I'll show you," Erik says, and tugs the score out of his bag.

He tells Claude where the typewriter comes in, but Claude starts at the beginning. "Does *roulette wheel* mean an actual roulette wheel?"

"I wasn't sure what the notation should look like. Trill on a sustained open notehead seemed right."

"Diaghilev can find a roulette wheel but not a typewriter?"

"I'm the one who fired Cocteau's typist, so I'm in charge of replacing him."

"May I say something?" Claude asks.

"Say it."

"I think it would be better without the unconventional instruments."

"Still good with them, good only without them, or not good either way, but better without?"

"I think this is the best orchestral work you've done."

It sounds like praise, but most of Erik's other orchestral work has been idiot-proof orchestrations of his popular songs, meant for cabaret ensembles with little or no rehearsing.

"But these sounds are just clutter," Claude elaborates. "They're you, but not quite. They're like somebody else's idea of you."

Arrogant, to say there's some idea of Erik which can be gotten wrong, and that Claude is the one who's got it right. Claude, Cocteau: why do all these people think they get to have *ideas* about him? But Erik says nothing.

"Has he been difficult? Cocteau."

Erik doesn't want to explain the various ways in which Cocteau has been difficult.

He looks out the tall windows. Trees wave at him from the garden and the avenue beyond.

Eventually Claude takes mercy on his silence. "I can have it sent to the theater, so you don't have to carry it. Why a typist, though? Surely one of the percussionists could do it."

"Cocteau's idea," Erik says, and stops there. If Claude thinks the typewriter is gimmicky, what's he going to think about Erik's plan to put an ex-dancer, ex–bear keeper, in the orchestra? It suddenly looks silly to Erik too, this desire to help out an old collaborator who could desperately use the work. He's with the Ballets Russes now, a full orchestra and all the paper he wants. A modern girl might be all right, but a has-been? Lisette is no older than Erik, but he's already the oldest person in every room at the Châtelet. La Vorace would just remind people of that, lurching up out of the nineties, hungry as ever.

"You could ask Désormière," Claude offers. "He'd be pleased for the introduction to Cocteau."

"He's in town?"

"On leave."

"Wounded, or—"

"Just on leave."

"How do you know that?"

"He came for a visit. Have you really been telling your acolytes that I'm 'a composer of the past'?"

"Absolutely not. Who said that?" He aims for an outraged tone but can feel his cheeks flush red at being caught out. He has indeed been telling the young admirers—though *acolytes*, that's nice, that's a delicious word—that Debussy's music is old-fashioned, that they should be looking to Ravel, Roussel, Stravinsky. And to Erik, of course. In truth it's less to do with Claude being old-fashioned than with Claude being too good at what he does. You might be able to out-Cocteau Cocteau, but you cannot out-Claude Claude. He's a dead end. Erik may or may not have explained things that way to the acolytes, though, and if not he should perhaps clarify. No good having them think he's jealous.

Claude reads in silence all the way through *Parade*, which is torturous. Erik wanders the room, drinking too quickly, trying to make the time pass. He refills his own glass and stands at the windows. Wherever else Claude might be economizing, the glass is immaculately clean, and sunlight pours fiercely over the blue carpet. Erik has a tickling sense of déjà vu and thinks suddenly of Philippe rambling around the Auberge du Clou, unable to sit anywhere near Erik whenever Erik was reading his poems. That was the early days, though.

Erik realizes, decades belatedly, that he can trace when Philippe stopped caring about the work. It wasn't when he started editing travel guides, or got married, or moved off the Butte. It was when he could sit beside Erik and drink or read a book or talk with mutual friends while Erik read drafts. Part of him had stopped caring about Erik's reaction, and it was not the same part of him that still cared about Erik, but Erik felt the change, and was so confused, then incensed, when Philippe kept insisting there wasn't one.

So what does it mean now, that Erik can't even make himself turn around while Claude reads, as if the man might be pulling faces behind his back, making fun of his efforts?

"It's good, truly," Claude says, and Erik shifts to see him straightening the pages, so neat they appear unopened. "It's clever. It's..." Claude takes a drink of water. He looks tired. "It's the wrong show, though. You know that, don't you? The wrong show at the wrong time. It's going to make people angry."

"Because of the war?"

Claude apparently considers this too obvious to merit a response.

"Apollinaire thinks it's interesting."

"I know you open in a week, and it is what it is. You're not in a position to change it. I just want you to be prepared. Depending on what you're hoping to hear, you may not hear it."

"I would like to hear that I am a genius beyond all reckoning."

"Erik, you are a genius beyond all reckoning."

"Thank you." Erik raises his glass in a toast. It's full again, somehow. When did that happen? How many times has it been empty, then full again? "Why did Désormière come to visit you? I haven't seen him yet. I didn't even know he was in town."

"Probably to make sure he saw me before I up and died. Or maybe before he did."

"You're not dying, though. Neither is he," Erik says.

"If you can wait a little longer until I'm actually dead, I really will be 'a composer of the past.' Then you can tell your acolytes whatever you want."

"I didn't say that," Erik insists. He's still standing in the sunshine from the window, his face already so hot he can't tell if he's blushing again, giving away the lie.

"I don't want to argue about it, I just want you to admit it," Claude says slowly, as if wondering what exactly he does want out of Erik.

"Look, I drink too much and say all kinds of things. If I *did* say that, I didn't mean it in . . . whatever way you're thinking I did."

"I suppose I don't care," Claude says, like he's figuring something out. "Not now."

Erik knows he's being let off the hook, but it feels like a dismissal. It feels lonely, as if Claude has already floated somewhere far away and Erik is stranded on the far shore of the plush blue carpet.

Erik is right about one of them: Roger Désormière has decades ahead of him. But Claude has only ten months.

And Claude, meanwhile, is right about *Parade*. Audiences are not just mystified but angry. One critic says something anodyne to Erik after the opening performance and then publishes a negative review, and Erik writes him a string of open letters so abusive that Erik is hauled into court for defamation. He's perfectly guilty, but everyone assumes he'll squirm out of it somehow until the judge hands down a colossal fine and eight days in jail. Erik insists to anyone who'll listen that his outrage isn't about the critic's opinion of his music, but about his duplicity. "If he'd had spine enough to tell me he hated it in person, that would have been fine. I wouldn't have cared a bit."

Erik would still have cared. He would have cared a great deal.

At the last moment, after a lengthy appeals process fails to go Erik's way, the Princesse de Polignac intervenes and pays off the fine, buys Erik out of jail. She wants *Socrate* finished, the setting of Plato's *Dialogues* for female voices.

She invites Erik to a dinner party a few months later to check up on her investment. Erik sends word that to put himself in the right frame of mind to complete her commission, he is eating only white foods. She doesn't know if he's serious or not but tells the cook to make sole meunière with turnips. At the party, Erik eats voraciously, both because he's so broke he's been skipping meals and because the more he keeps his mouth full, the less he has to lie about the progress of *Socrate*, which has been minimal. The money he received for it is already gone. So is what he earned for *Parade*. He needs to ask Conrad for another loan, but they're in a quarrel. One step forward and two steps back, his entire goddamn life, he thinks.

During after-dinner drinks in the parlor, a telephone rings and Erik is so startled by the sound he jumps to his feet, then has to sit down again with everyone watching. He has heard the sound as a theatrical effect, but he's never watched anyone take an actual call. He listens to the Princesse with naked curiosity as she converses with an invisible someone. It could be anyone, anywhere in the city, this modern ghost on the other end of the line. Erik could sing into the round black mouthpiece, *Future! Future, you've found me. In a little bedroom by the sea, I dreamed you up.*

But you're still holding out on me, yes? There's still better to come? I keep hoping but you never call.

The Princesse, misunderstanding his attention after she hangs up the call, asks if he wants to use the telephone.

His palms itch with anticipation and anxiety. Who might he know who would have a telephone? He reels silently through everyone he can think of, but for every name there's a reason not to call. The acolytes gone to the war, the patrons to whom he owes work, the performers he's dodging because the kind of work they're offering he no longer wants. Friends, he's always had friends, but he owes them all money. Philippe, but he's long back from Tarragona and still hasn't written, and Erik's too proud to be the one to make plans. Conrad, but there's the quarrel about Mathilde. Louise, but there's an ocean, which the telephone cables can't cross. That's the real problem, Erik tells himself—nothing to do with him and everything to do with telephones. They're terribly new, and the technology is limited, and of course he wouldn't know many people both rich and fashionable enough to have a phone.

Claude, he thinks at last. Claude really would have a telephone. But then he remembers that Claude is dead.

Conrad

— 17 —

Visible for a moment

WHOM HAD HE BOUGHT THE SECOND TICKET FOR? HAD IT merely been habit, buying two, or did he have someone in mind? He remembered worrying whether he could get tickets at all—Erik had always provided him with comps, and he didn't know if ordinary people could simply walk up to the box office and get seats for a world premiere.

"Sure you can. For this show, anyway," the ticket seller had said, and offered Conrad prime seats, orchestra front and center, for the opening night—December 4, 1924. The name of the show was *Relâche*, the word theaters used for "no performance tonight."

"How clever," Conrad imagined Mathilde saying, all deadpan distaste. But it was a major production with the Ballets Suédois, who would debut the work at the Théâtre des Champs-Élysées. It was Erik's first commission with the company, and only his third ballet. *Relâche* might have a jokey name and slow ticket sales, but it was still a triumph. Of course Conrad would attend.

But whom should he ask to go with him, instead of Mathilde? His closest friend was also his boss, which had never been a problem before, but things were not going well at work. Ernest Beaux was doing Chanel No. 5 down in Grasse, and Jacques Guerlain had Shalimar. Maison Jeancard had been in talks with Lanvin to collaborate on a new scent, but the latest rumor was that Lanvin would instead choose Fraysse and Vacher. Parfumerie was a small world. Everyone knew everyone, and everyone knew that Maison Jeancard was chugging along uninspiringly. It was still profitable, which meant that Conrad's job as laboratory director was safe for now, but without any great triumphs that would not stay true.

"I didn't know perfumes were made by chemists," Mathilde had said, back when they were courting.

"What did you picture?" Conrad asked.

"I don't know. Elegant ladies examining flowers."

"It's ugly men examining fractionating columns."

"You're not ugly," she said. And he knew he wasn't, but had managed not to let it go to his head too badly.

He was the coauthor, along with Paul Jeancard, of the *Brief Guide to the Chemistry of Perfumes: A Scientific Encyclopedia and Study Guide.* It had come out twenty years ago and Conrad still kept two copies on the bookshelf in the living room. One of his secret pleasures was to stay up late reading his own book, taking note of what information had become outmoded and how much of the book was still true, or had even anticipated later advances. It was holding up well, all things considered. He dropped this into casual conversation with Paul at work, how fine their book still was, but he couldn't say it too specifically without admitting that he still liked to read it. There was nothing to learn, no second edition in the works. He just liked rereading the words he'd written and knowing he had written them.

He'd given a copy to Erik, but he assumed his brother had never read it. To be fair, very little of it would have made any sense to him. Erik hadn't questioned why his brother was giving him a book he couldn't read. He knew. "Showing off, are you?" he ribbed Conrad.

But Conrad let Erik show off all the time without calling

attention to it. Why couldn't his brother do the same for him?

"Because he's Erik," Mathilde had said. They hadn't been married long then, but she'd already gotten the lay of the land.

Shortly thereafter Erik had invited them to an extraordinary dinner during which he ordered 150 oysters without asking.

"I couldn't possibly eat fifty oysters," Mathilde protested.

"You just do your best," Erik said. "I'll polish off whatever's left. I can eat a hundred, easily."

This turned out to be accurate. The wine came in prodigious amounts, but it wasn't until Erik asked for champagne that Conrad made a plea for moderation.

"Nonsense. I'm flush," Erik explained. An unexpected commission, payment up front. "This is all my treat. Such lucky timing!"

"Lucky how?" Conrad asked. What new crisis was the money that was now being frittered away on oysters meant to alleviate?

"Because of your book. So I can fête you properly."

Conrad, surprised, thanked him, then demurred. "We only assembled it. There's no new research in it."

"Don't pretend it doesn't mean anything to you. That's a silly thing to pretend."

"Hear, hear!" Mathilde said, and she and Erik clinked glasses.

Conrad tried to remember when else they had agreed. Not often. From the beginning Mathilde and Erik had been oil and water, bleach and vinegar.

Bleach + vinegar = chlorine gas. Bleach + ammonia = chloramine vapor, which, similar to chlorine gas, burns the eyes and respiratory system. Bleach + isopropanol alcohol = chloroform. Depending on the reaction, you could also end up with chloroacetone, dichloroacetone, or hydrochloric acid, all of which could cause agonizing chemical burns. Few people appreciated how many ways there were to die using common household chemicals, Conrad thought. After the Germans had deployed their chlorine-gas attacks at Ypres, Conrad had drawn up plans for converting the Jeancard parfumerie to a chemical-weapons lab.

"You can't be serious," Jeancard had said. When Conrad's uncomfortable shuffling made clear that he was, Jeancard added, "I want to help the war effort as much as anyone, but we're not equipped for this kind of work. We'd gas ourselves, and probably half the neighborhood."

Conrad had applied to other jobs, both with the government and with private firms rumored to be working on weapons development. Efforts were sufficiently classified that it wasn't always clear what he was applying for, and in any case no one bit. He was too old and too expert to be a laboratory monkey, one company suggested after interviewing him, and—given that he'd spent his entire career at Maison Jeancard—too narrowly experienced to join the lab as a chemist. He'd come close to begging for the lab-monkey position, pride be damned in the face of existential crisis, but then he'd run the numbers on the salary difference and realized he had to stay put. By then he was not only supporting Mathilde but also sending regular allowances to Erik in Arcueil and Louise in Buenos Aires, to Mathilde's everlasting frustration.

"Devote yourself to a wartime scent," Jeancard said. "It's not meaningless, what we do. We're keeping spirits up."

But between the supply shortages and Conrad's overly literal interpretations of "wartime scent"—muddy heart notes, panicky top notes tangy as air-raid sweat—they couldn't get any traction. Then Maison Caron launched *N'Aimez que moi*, marketed specifically for soldiers to give their sweethearts to keep them faithful. Conrad thought the scent was a cheap wallop of roses in a vague cloud of violet, and found the entire commercial campaign every bit as tasteless as he'd found *Parade*. The name—*Love no one but me*—was downright threatening.

"It's a blockbuster," Jeancard told him. "Get back to the bench."

Conrad had been a steadfast admirer of Erik's music, the most steadfast, and he'd tried mightily to avoid telling Erik what he thought of *Parade*. Their relationship had already been strained after Eugénie died, with Erik so buoyantly griefless that it was hard for Conrad to be around him. But at a dinner with Mathilde and Conrad, Erik had pressed and pressed, and Conrad was unwilling to lie.

"*Parade* is not 'in poor taste,'" Erik lashed back. "You know what's in poor taste? Spending a war making perfume."

"You asked for my opinion," Conrad said stiffly.

"I didn't know your opinion was going to be so warped by your own guilt."

"Guilt?" Mathilde said. "What does he have to be guilty about?"

"Mathilde, please."

"I want to know what's wrong with making perfume," she said, then turned back to Erik. "You've certainly never complained about reaping the proceeds."

"*Mathilde*. I can have my own argument."

"No, actually, you can't. Not with your brother. You never stand up for yourself."

Erik veered into a monologue about an upcoming memorial concert for Claude Debussy, the politics of which was apparently endless: which pieces, played by whom, who would do the speeches and who hated the people doing the speeches, and why weren't there more young composers participating, why all the old battle-axes?

Conrad's eyes were glazing over, but this was safer than being asked for opinions.

"I think that's enough about a concert I'll never go to," Mathilde finally said.

"What? I'm sorry. I can get you tickets. You can come if you want."

"I wouldn't go if you paid me. I haven't listened to a note of his music since the Lilly business. He may have skulked back to France when enough people forgot about it, but that doesn't mean I did."

The Lilly business was Lilly Texier, Claude's first wife, who'd shot herself through the chest in the middle of the Place de la Concorde after Claude left her for another woman.

"He's dead," Erik said, genuinely shocked. "He's dead, and Lilly was ages ago."

"I don't have to forgive him just because he's dead. I know my opinion of Claude Debussy doesn't matter a whit to anybody, but I get to keep it."

"I spent a lot of dinner parties seated next to Lilly," Erik said, "and trust me, she's not worth it. She wasn't worth five minutes of music from Claude. She was even more boring than you are."

Mathilde left the dining room, left the entire apartment, and Erik offered to clear the dishes but Conrad refused the help. Erik tried again to explain just how wrong everyone was about Lilly, how unequal she'd always been to Claude, how worthless it was to mourn what she'd done.

"We're not fighting about Claude Debussy," Conrad said. "We're not fighting about *music*." He clattered dishes into the sink.

"Aren't we?"

Conrad turned on the faucet and Erik stared balefully at the sink, as if he found the water suspicious or maybe presumptuous, simply showing up without needing to be brought from the hall or the street outside.

"Then what are we fighting about?" Erik said.

"You cannot speak that way to my wife."

"We're fighting about *Mathilde*?" Erik said, with intense exasperation, as if unable to imagine who would ever bother to do such a thing, as if Conrad had somehow tricked him into having an argument about Mathilde when he had been trying to have an argument about art. He pulled a glass out of the pile of dishes and held it under the stream from the faucet. He rinsed it once, then filled it and took a drink. "It doesn't taste any different from the water at the fountains," he said.

"It's the same water," Conrad said. "Did you want to take some home?" He held up the carafe that had been on the dining table, now empty.

"Of course not," Erik said, but the subsequent silence grew awkward, because if Mathilde had been here she would have packaged up food for Erik by now, the way Eugénie used to.

Conrad started shoving leftovers into the carafe, pouring in peas and then jamming pieces of mutton through the narrow neck with his fingers. Once they were inside he held the carafe out to Erik.

Erik took it, but asked how he was supposed to get the food back out again. "I mean, to wash and return this. I'm not complaining."

"Go home," Conrad said.

A few days before the premiere of *Relâche*, a letter arrived from Joseph. He was grown now, married and working as a doctor in Picauville, a town almost exactly equidistant between Bellenau and Cherbourg. He had a small practice there that supported him and his wife. He would never buy back Bellenau, but if this bothered him, he'd never said. He mentioned in his letter that he'd be in Paris for a medical conference—would Conrad like to meet? Conrad wrote back that he had tickets for a ballet and asked if Joseph would join him.

After he arrived in Paris, Joseph sent Conrad a pneu, and they made plans to meet directly at the theater. They had last seen each other at Joseph's wedding a few years earlier, but both were at ages when faces changed slowly. They recognized each other easily. Joseph looked a little like Louise, Conrad thought, but probably more like his father. Conrad tried to call up the man's face, but they'd met only the once. That was once more than Joseph had ever met him.

The theater was plastered with signs reading *relâche*. Not posters advertising the performance, but hastily printed cancellation notices. Instead of leaving, however, the crowd just kept growing as people waited for the punch line.

"Is there no show at all?" Joseph asked, confused. "The whole thing is a stunt?"

Finally the house manager emerged to address the crowd: lead dancer Jean Börlin was ill, no understudy, apologies for the inconvenience. The opening was rescheduled for the following night. Still the crowd didn't disperse. "I'm serious," the manager said. "*Relâche* is relâche. We'll be back on tomorrow. Tonight's tickets honored then. This isn't a joke."

People milled about anyway, waiting for something else to happen, perhaps a burst of confetti and dancers pouring out to reward the faithful, but slowly the December cold and the resolutely darkened theater drove everyone off. Joseph and Conrad found a nearby brasserie, occupied a table, and ordered.

"I'll be sorry to miss it," Joseph said.

"You can't stay an extra night?"

Joseph shook his head and explained that Nancey was expecting. She was pretty far along—he'd like to get back as quickly as possible.

"That's wonderful news!" Conrad said, aggressive in his effusiveness, trying to communicate both that it was genuinely wonderful and that it did not bother him to hear it. The pain of his and Mathilde's childlessness, once it had persisted so long that everyone in their lives was aware of it, had become something like a bad knee or hip—he forgot about it for long stretches of time, then stepped wrong and his body was on fire. He knew Mathilde had never forgotten, not even for a day. Probably not for so much as an hour. He asked Joseph about the due date, Nancey's health, nursery arrangements, names.

"Pierre-something, if it's a boy," Joseph said. "No surprises there."

Their food came, veal cutlets with vinegary beans. They'd ordered the exact same thing without noticing.

Joseph seemed to wait until Conrad's mouth was full before speaking again, as if afraid of how he'd respond. "We were thinking Pierre-Conrad, actually, for the baptismal name. Would you mind? I know we haven't had the chance to be terribly close, but we'd like to include this side of the family. We'd use Louise, of course, if it's a girl."

Conrad chewed, swallowed. He was simultaneously confused and close to tears. "Erik's the famous one."

"We prefer Pierre-Conrad," Joseph said simply.

"But I'm the boring one."

Joseph smiled. "I'm not saying I agree. But even if it were true, it seems like a perfectly good legacy. I think yours would be a pretty lucky life for our child to have."

Conrad had not felt lucky since Mathilde's death, ten months earlier, of influenza, but he could step back from this year and understand, from that removed vantage, what his nephew meant. He *had* been lucky, all things considered. He had his work, a comfortable home, plenty of food and light and fuel. Luckiest of all was his marriage to Mathilde. He'd had a great love, Conrad thought, and felt a bit silly at the grandiosity of the sentiment, but it was true. They'd slept in each other's arms, truly in each other's arms, every night. Their bodies had worn a single deep furrow into the center of the mattress, an empty pool Conrad now found himself foundering in at night. But he was grateful to have had her, however it ended.

"Have you heard from your mother?" he asked, changing the subject before he fell apart in front of his nephew.

They compared the dates and contents of recent letters, found that she'd written them on more or less the same schedule, with about the same information: piano students, concerts, an excursion to the Iguazú Falls with two fellow teachers from the French Institute.

411

"I saw an advertisement the other day," Conrad said. "A promotion from the Blue Star line. Discounted sailings out of Boulogne."

Joseph pushed his last forkful of food back and forth across his plate before answering. "It's not just the fare. I can't lose weeks or months of income, plus the practice would fall to pieces. And especially now, with the baby..." He trailed off still staring down at his fork.

"I'm sorry. I didn't mean to make you defend yourself. I understand how difficult it is. I shouldn't have brought it up."

"Someday, maybe," Joseph said.

They'd both finished their food, and Conrad didn't want to end the meal on this note. "The name," he said. "I'd be honored. I can't tell you how honored I'd be."

It was nearly twenty years ago now that he'd had to fetch Louise from Cherbourg. She'd been standing outside Joseph's new school for several days, shouting for him at the windows. The police were called. She'd run from them, managing to lock herself in her hotel room. Who knew Louise was that fast on her feet? The hotel owner had talked the police into leaving—a respectable-looking woman dragged through the lobby would be bad for business. But someone needed to come for her, the telegram read. Someone needed to pay her bill.

When Louise opened the door to Conrad, he didn't think anyone would be surprised to see her dragged through a hotel lobby. She was disheveled, distraught. He'd barely ever seen her with her hair down, and here it was tangled and greasy. She smelled, he was embarrassed to notice. Had the hotel owner meant for them to leave immediately? he wondered. Could she have a bath first? How might he talk her into the bath? And how in the world would *he* talk her into anything, after she'd tried to stab him?

But she was strangely pliable. She seemed to have forgotten about Conrad's betrayal in the face of a fresher one from Joseph;

he'd had a schoolmate smuggle her a note, shoved under the hotel-room door: *Please stop. I love you but you need to stop.* Her hand and voice shook, with outrage or exhaustion or both, as she showed Conrad the note and wondered aloud how her son could betray her, too.

"He isn't betraying you," Conrad said. "He's right." Remember when she'd been sent to Fortin's house? What choice had she had, he urged, beyond to live the life she'd been given?

But this line of argument failed. "I want him to know I care," Louise said. "At least this way he'll know I tried to get him back."

"And he'll understand that you couldn't. That there was nothing more you could do."

He packed her things for her while she bathed. She'd brought a lot for how quickly she'd left Paris. She hadn't come to Cherbourg only for a last goodbye. She'd packed as if to start another life with Joseph, as a fugitive well dressed enough to cross borders unquestioned. There was even a small bottle of perfume, a newer Maison Coty scent, L'Origan. He'd gifted her various Jeancard bottles over the years, and although his nose had already told him she didn't often use them, he would have thought L'Origan (spicy violet, moderate sillage) would be all wrong for her. He would never have picked this out as the bottle she'd pack for a renegade life. But then he'd never thought she would be a renegade. He felt clueless, as both brother and perfumer.

She was subdued through the journey back to Paris, abusive once he told the cabdriver at the train station to deliver them to his apartment. "So *now* you want me to stay with you. Now that it's useless. *You're* useless. What are you even for?"

"I'm not *for* anything. I'm just a person, Louise. I'm a person too."

Having her in the house was like living with an angry ghost. She barely spoke, but every drawer was jerked open, every door slammed. Her rare words were cruel ones, selected and delivered to hurt him. Conrad told himself that she was throwing herself against him like he was a window that might break and prove her right, that she was totally forsaken and could tumble unremarked to the earth. So he ignored her insults. The window held. He was patient. When was he not patient? Good old Conrad. Good old sap.

Mathilde tried to lure her out for walks, meals, diversions, while Conrad was at work.

One day Louise gave her the slip while the two of them were shopping near the Gare du Nord. Mathilde told him that evening that she'd found her inside the station, checking the departure board.

When Conrad chastened her for not keeping a better eye on Louise, Mathilde rebelled. "I am trying to help," she said. "You know I am. But you need to do something."

Conrad had no idea what to do. Not long afterward he came home from work and there was a bandage wrapped around Louise's left wrist. She didn't try to hide it. She was sitting on the sofa, reading a newspaper, while Mathilde prepared dinner. He supposed she'd say she cut herself accidentally, and it might be true and it might be a lie and he'd have no way of knowing. But when he asked she said simply from behind the newspaper, "I changed my mind."

He was quiet for a long time, then asked her if she was going to do it again.

She promised him she wouldn't.

What was he supposed to say now? Was he supposed to believe her? He did, but was that only wishful thinking? "You're welcome to stay here as long as you need," he said finally. "But I think you should get away."

She lowered the newspaper and glared at him. "I did. I'm here, aren't I? I left Cherbourg."

"Farther."

"How much farther?"

"London, perhaps?"

414

She barked an unamused laugh. "You're trying to get me out of the country?"

"I think it would help. Wouldn't it? You need to go somewhere else or you're going to lose your mind."

They left unsaid that she had half lost it already.

"I'd never see him," she said.

"You don't see him now. If you're farther away, it will hurt less. He'll find you when he's able. Once he's of age, Cannu and Albertine won't be able to stop him."

"Twenty-one? He'll be an entirely different person. He'll have forgotten me."

"He won't forget you."

"You don't remember our mother."

"I was two. Joseph is thirteen. It's completely different, and you know that."

She folded the newspaper smaller and smaller, into a tight rectangle. She chewed the inside of her cheek.

"It won't feel as long as you think it will," Conrad said. "Not if you aren't right here, waiting for him. You need some kind of life for yourself."

"Buenos Aires," she said.

He assumed at first that she was making fun of him somehow, and waited politely for the rest of the joke.

"You said *farther*," she finally added, not joking at all.

"Argentina?"

"It looks like Paris."

"Does it?"

"There's an opera house."

She sounded at best like an uninformed tourist planning a trip on the basis of a postcard. Except she was planning the rest of her life based on even less. Conrad insisted she do more research, and Louise dutifully brought home packets of information from the Argentine embassy. Everything she learned made the idea look more feasible, not less. Argentina was desperate for people.

Certain kinds of people, anyway: the government had very specific ideas about the kind of country it was trying to forge, and as long as the descendants of the colonizers remained outnumbered by the descendants of the colonized, that vision was vulnerable. A city couldn't have a European-style opera house, for instance, absent Europeans with the knowledge and desire to quarry and mortar the stones, to string wires for electric lights, to bring their musical instruments and play European music well enough for their new countrymen to buy tickets and fill the seats to listen. Louise met with Argentine consular officials dispatched to France specifically to persuade more French people to come to their country. There would be a guaranteed stay of several weeks in an immigrant hotel, paid for by the Argentine government, to help her get on her feet. Her musical abilities, modest by Parisian standards, might be genuinely marketable.

The cost of emigrating was the major problem. Cannu should have helped, if only to be rid of her, but he refused. On principle, he said, without explaining what that principle might be. Getting Louise halfway around the world with what Conrad considered enough left over to establish herself safely would nearly wipe him out, and he and Mathilde retreated behind their bedroom door for debates that started in whispers and invariably rose in volume, so that Conrad felt doubly trapped, arguing with his wife and performing for his sister, who could no doubt overhear. The worst fights he and Mathilde had had before this, nearly the only fights they'd ever had, had been about Erik. About his neediness, and Conrad's willingness to provide.

Provide and provide and provide, Mathilde hissed, questioning both the sums he'd calculated and his willingness to spend them on his sister.

"She can't live in a hovel," Conrad said.

Well, she *could*, Mathilde's expression seemed to say.

"She isn't going to live in a hovel."

What else was he supposed to do? Louise was a woman, alone,

and Erik was an artist. They seemed equally helpless to Conrad, equally in need. He'd do with his money whatever he wanted. He was the one who earned it.

"It's *our* money," Mathilde countered. "We're husband and wife."

"And we have enough right now. The two of us. There's no one else."

Her face crumpled as if he'd struck her. He felt like he had. Every conversation they'd ever had about children up to then had been flatly optimistic: If not this month, the next. If not the next, the one after. Any time now. But maybe they needed to start talking about *never*, Conrad thought. Maybe it was time at least to think the word.

Mathilde agreed to the expenditure only if it was made clear to Louise that there would be no money available to do this again. "She can't just decide she doesn't like it there and expect you to wire enough to bring her back."

This was a heavy caveat, since it was unlikely Louise would stumble into any employment or a second husband wealthy enough to allow her to return on her own. She'd be stuck, waiting for whenever Joseph could someday come to her.

Conrad wasn't certain Louise would really emigrate under such conditions, but she asked him to book passage for the earliest departure available.

Was she sure? he asked.

She was sure that she couldn't stay here any longer, she said.

"But what if you're running from Scylla into Charybdis?"

Even if she was, she said, anything would be preferable to bashing herself against the same rock until there was nothing left of her.

Cannu allowed a brief farewell with Joseph, in a town halfway between Paris and Cherbourg. Before Louise left, Conrad checked her bag, making sure she wasn't armed. She'd packed a few keepsakes to give Joseph—the booklet of wallpaper samples he'd made at Bellenau, his father's old specimen cards. Conrad continued rummaging and in an interior pocket found the rusty little pocketknife she'd tried to stab him with. He removed it and hid it in his underwear drawer. She didn't ask him about it later, which he hoped meant she hadn't even realized it was gone. At least, Mathilde did not report to him any attempts at violence. Chaperoned by Mathilde and Albertine, respectively, Louise and Joseph had stepped off their trains, drunk hot chocolate at the train-station café, then re-embarked in their opposite directions. Mathilde mentioned to Conrad that Albertine had tried to make small talk with her in the café as they hovered near Louise and Joseph. "I told her I didn't have anything to say to her. I told her I wouldn't pretend what they were doing was normal. I wouldn't pretend it was right." Conrad worried Mathilde might have made more trouble for Louise by offending her in-laws, but mostly he was proud.

A few days later he traveled with Louise all the way to the port at Le Havre, suspicious that she might still leap off the train and go looking for Joseph. Or just leap off the train and allow her body to be churned under the wheels. They played a few hands of cards. He ate an apple. Mostly they sat in silence, looking out the windows at the cow-dotted fields, the gray stone barns, the twisting Seine. It was the same route they'd traveled as children.

"You don't remember anything?" she asked. "From when we all lived together?"

"No."

"Good old Conrad," she said. "Honest to the end."

"The end of what?"

Louise avoided answering, as if he were being obtuse, but he didn't think he was. He and Louise had been siblings at a distance most of their lives. This was what they were. To say they were coming to an end implied they'd achieved something they hadn't, reached some pinnacle of closeness from which they were now plummeting. But they'd spent nearly their entire lives staring at separate horizons.

When Mathilde died, Erik delivered the same poor impression of grief he'd performed after Eugénie's death, and Conrad couldn't take it. Erik even showed up on the first Sunday after Mathilde's funeral at the regular dinner hour, as if there was any food in the house. Conrad couldn't imagine there being food in the house ever again. Or wait, there was something under a tea towel on the kitchen table. Madame Jeancard had brought it. He didn't know what it was, though, or remember when she'd dropped it off.

"I was planning to take you somewhere," Erik said. "I wasn't expecting you to have anything ready."

Conrad wanted to believe him. He mostly did. But it didn't matter. "I can't be around someone who hated her right now," he told Erik.

"Hate her? I never hated her. I just didn't like her very much."

"See, that's . . . the fact you said that. The fact you thought that was worth saying—I can't deal with you right now."

"I wasn't aware I needed to be *dealt with*."

"If that's really true, then you don't pay any fucking attention."

It had happened so quickly. Both he and Mathilde had always been healthy, no complaints beyond the occasional cold or fever—one more reason their childlessness was so maddening. Mathilde had never understood what could possibly be so faulty and yet so invisible. Neither of them had even gotten sick in the pandemic six years earlier.

But one night she went to bed with a fever, coughing, and Conrad slept on the sofa. He almost didn't check on her before he left for work—why risk waking her, when all she needed was some sleep? He found her with a gray face, her forehead slick with sweat, her breathing wet and strained. Downstairs he asked the concierge to hail a cab, then ran back up for her. He had the strength to get her to the street, but began to fade while the cabdriver argued with him about contagion. Hurriedly Conrad agreed to hold his handkerchief over Mathilde's face to reduce the risk of transmission. But once she was lying across his lap in the cab, he couldn't figure out how without making it even harder for her to breathe. In response to the cabdriver's threats, he offered to increase the fare. At the hospital, Mathilde's face went from gray to violet to blue. She never really woke up. He didn't think she'd been afraid, which was some small comfort. But then he realized that whatever fear she'd felt had come earlier, in the night, while they'd lain in separate rooms.

The nurses at the hospital were kind, but at least one of the doctors seemed a little impatient with his shock. Conrad was, or was supposed to be, a man of science. Had he forgotten '18, or never paid attention? Millions of people had died in much this way, and more died this way every year. This was how influenza killed.

"I make perfume," Conrad said helplessly, and in the moment it sounded somehow ridiculous, as if that couldn't possibly be how anyone, let alone him, would ever choose to spend a life.

At work Paul Jeancard was encouraging Conrad to channel his grief into a great scent, something wistful and elegiac. But he kept getting mixed up as to whether he was meant to be making a perfume that smelled like Mathilde, or one that smelled like her absence, or one that smelled like their earliest, bubbly happiness, or the later, comfortable happiness. They'd had happinesses all the way through, hadn't they. *I need to make a perfume*, Conrad thought toward Mathilde, but all his samples so far were too dark: chypre without floral, bergamot and musk with no top notes, heart notes clotted with fatty orris. Paul had always been the artisan, the better nose; Conrad was a technician. He was out of his depth, trying to put a smell to his sorrow.

Conrad decided to go alone to the second opening night for *Relâche*. It wasn't worth the trouble of trying to find someone else. Was he afraid of people at the show thinking he was lonely? Well, he was lonely. Who did it help to pretend? The cuff links he usually wore to the theater were missing, and he remembered that Mathilde might have put them away in her jewelry box. He hadn't been to a performance since her death. He picked up the box from her vanity table and started sifting through it.

I feel like a potato, she said.

He heard the words so clearly that he gaped at the empty seat pushed under the vanity. Nobody there. Still dead. He checked the vanity mirror, looking for ghosts. Just his own face, haggard and anxious. Had he gone ahead and done it, with the bleach and alcohol, and this was what his brain was coughing up as he starved for oxygen? No, he reminded himself. He hadn't. He'd thought about it, but not seriously, and not for long.

He stared at the vanity table until she floated into focus. She was in her corset, stockings, and garters, her dress still hanging from a corner of the mirror. She was powdering her face, which he was so relieved to see was pink, not blue or gray. "We'll be late," Conrad told her. Whatever sort of falling apart this was, it was not unpleasant.

I'm just trying to look presentable, she said. She took the jewelry box back from him, deftly found his cuff links and attached them to his cuffs. Then she plucked out the dangling emerald-and-onyx earrings she always wore to the theater. *I'm going to be the oldest and dumpiest woman there.*

"Dumpy?" Conrad protested. "You're not dumpy, love."

We're not part of the smart set, though, are we? That was more or less true. They were not the type of people who usually attended the Ballets Russes, or the Suédois. The more avant-garde Erik's collaborators became, the more ill at ease Mathilde had felt in the audience. The crowd kept getting younger and edgier as she and Conrad kept getting older. *I look like a potato, whatever I wear.*

"You do not."

You couldn't exchange the seats?

"They're excellent seats."

I know, but everyone will be able to see us. "Who's the potato?" *they'll say. "And what does she think she's doing, coming to a show like this?"*

"I don't think anyone will be able to see you," Conrad said. "*I'm* not really seeing you, am I?"

But that was all right, wasn't it? Erik wasn't the only member of the family allowed to have an imagination. Louise wasn't the only person allowed to grieve. It was his turn, wasn't it? Except that he still had to go to work Monday morning and continue disappointing Paul, continue disappointing himself. Well, all the more reason to enjoy an evening at the theater with his wife. He helped Mathilde fasten the back of her green silk dress.

Why are we going, when you aren't even speaking with him?

"He's still my brother. And I do actually like his music, you know."

What do you actually like? Every piece sounds different.

"That's part of what I like."

On the way to the theater, she vanished from him and he felt a pang. He handed the usher only one of his tickets and took his seat, front and center. The seats must have all sold eventually, because the empty spot beside him stood out like a missing tooth in the gleaming smile of the crowd. He felt conspicuous and closed his eyes, summoned Mathilde back to him.

"You look beautiful," he whispered, eyes still closed, and beside him she huffed a gentle disagreement.

Have you seen Erik yet?

He scanned the audience, the wings of the stage, as much of the orchestra pit as he could glimpse, but didn't see his brother. Then the houselights went down and a projector sparked to life, and there Erik was. The program mentioned two short films by René Clair, one at the beginning and one between the two halves of the ballet, but it didn't mention that Erik made an appearance. He flickered on the screen, somehow both older and younger than Conrad remembered him; his beard was white but smartly trimmed, and his eyes were childishly gleeful behind small, old-fashioned spectacles. He stood on a rooftop, on opposite sides of a cannon with Francis Picabia, the painter. They leaped up and down, in and out of the frame, like demented little boys. Picabia was in shirtsleeves, his wide, short tie flapping as he jumped. Erik's outfit—a high pointed collar, striped dark tie, vest, and jacket—was antique by comparison. He'd held on to the same staid ensemble so long that it had become another costume, even as he insisted it wasn't. The two men took turns loading the cannon, which at the end of the film fired its shell directly into the camera and at the viewer.

I almost ducked, Mathilde whispered, giggling.

Conrad imagined himself on the same rooftop, jumping up and down and firing cannon shells into the city. It seemed like great fun. He wondered which of them, him or Erik, viewers would think the elder. The previous year had aged Conrad—last spring he'd thought the dark hollows under his eyes were from sleeplessness or grief, but then he'd done nothing but sleep and work all summer, and by autumn realized they were part of his face now, as permanent a change as the molar he'd had pulled recently, or his empty bed.

That doesn't have to be permanent, Mathilde whispered, because she knew what he was thinking, because she *was* what he was thinking, almost all he thought about. They'd been married for twenty-five years, nearly half of Conrad's life. Maybe they'd gotten along *too* well, he thought, so satisfied with each other's company that they'd let their lives contract around them. But that damage (if it was damage at all) was done. Their bed had its single furrow, and anyone new would roll straight into it, where Conrad couldn't imagine wanting company.

Conrad barely saw the first part of the dance. But that was all right. The dance didn't make any sense. There was a flapper girl with a long line of men in tailcoats. Someone rode a bicycle onto the stage. Someone popped a red balloon. There was no set to speak of, beyond the massive wall of bare bulbs at the back of the stage. They were dark for now, but Conrad braced himself to be blinded. Someone behind him was arguing about whether the show was an example of Dadaism or Instantaneism.

Oh, who cares? Mathilde said, and he snorted.

After the first act there was another film, and Conrad searched eagerly for Erik. This longer film was still gleeful, but more unsettling: skyscapes turned upside down, dolls with inflating and deflating heads, a dancer spinning on a sheet of glass with the camera underneath her feet. Eventually there emerged a story of a funeral procession, the hearse drawn by a camel. Unless Erik was in the crowd scene, among a long row of top-hatted men running in slow motion after a runaway coffin, Conrad couldn't spot him. The score Erik had composed for the film was relentlessly repetitive, eerie or dramatic phrases pounded out over and over. They were a fistful of earworms wriggling in one after the other. After a lengthy chase, the coffin crashed to the side of the road; a magician leaped out and made the top-hatted men disappear, one by one. Mathilde gasped as the men blinked out of sight, marveling at the effect. Then a giant sheet of paper reading *Fin* appeared, and Picabia clawed his way through it, after which the film reversed, sucking him back through a smooth, unbroken scrim.

At the end of the ballet there were flowers for the lead dancers, the recognition of the orchestra and the conductor, Roger Désormière—all the little rituals Conrad had learned to love about the theater. The crowd acknowledged the choreographer and producer, and the polite applause began to run out of steam. Where was Erik? No one was standing. Apparently he and Picabia had managed to confuse even the smart set.

Then, amid the waning applause, came the sounds of a tooting horn and the hum of an engine. Picabia drove a car onstage, a yellow Peugeot 5CV with the roof down. The dancers scattered before the car like a flock of pigeons. The driver made tight circles around the stage, and Conrad spotted Erik in the passenger's seat. Same outfit as in the film, same outfit he always wore. He was even holding an umbrella. The car paused near the front of the stage and Erik gestured for the conductor to hop in. Désormière climbed out of the orchestra pit and into the cramped seat, and Erik ruffled his hair, as if Désormière was a little boy on whom Erik was conferring his approval. Conrad wished he could hear what they were saying to each other. Erik grinned and waved, grinned and waved and waved to the crowd.

Some of the audience hooted in amused surprise. Others hooted in derision. "Cheap stunt," someone muttered behind Conrad.

Conrad stood, clapping furiously. He didn't know if Erik could see him.

He's loving this, Mathilde said. *Happy as a pig in shit.*

Mathilde never swore, and Conrad winced. But then again it was nice that she could still surprise him after all these years. Even after being dead.

He still isn't, Conrad said. *Happy.* It might have been nearly a year since they'd spoken, but he knew it was true. Some things stayed true. Some people.

Out of the corner of his eye he saw Mathilde stand and turn toward him, open her mouth to disagree, then close it. *You can make up with him if you want to,* she said. *I won't mind.* She reached out and took his fingers. They kept clapping, palms against the backs of their joined hands.

Not yet, Conrad said. *Later, maybe. There's time.*

Louise

— 18 —

End for yourself

OVER THE YEARS THERE HAVE BEEN A HANDFUL OF BOYS WHO were already blazing. Miniature virtuosos, so short I put books on the piano stool, their legs swinging in the air, their fingers jumping like fleas along the keyboard. Wherever they learned this it wasn't from me, but I'm the person who has to decide what to do with them next.

In some ways, the prodigies are easiest: you send them to a conservatory teacher, posthaste. No dithering around with old women who make house calls by bus. But how am I supposed to recognize the Erics? The ordinary extraordinary boy, with a measure of talent but no willingness to practice, the boy who slouches at the door and keeps his hands in his pockets until asked to play. Who balls his fists furiously when I offer correction, nails cutting into his palms. But who has enough talent, or imperiousness, or impetuousness, or—I don't know what to call it. I don't know what it is. And if I find the boy, the Argentine Eric, what am I supposed to do with him? Does he need more training, or less? A taskmaster or a mother? Immersion in counterpoint or jazz?

I wish I could ask Eric—well, Erik, I suppose. I should give him his *K*. I haven't been withholding the *K*, exactly, just holding on to the *C*. I wish I could ask him what he would have wanted someone to do for him, but I'm sure I wouldn't get a straight answer. He'd probably take offense, thinking I was suggesting that someone ought to have done something differently, that he needed to be saved from the life he ended up living. Thin-skinned as an egg, my brother. Plus now he's dead, of course, and I can't ask him anything.

What I know of how it happened I know from letters. One long letter, really, because after Conrad had told me the story, neither of us was sure what was left to say. Erik was famous enough for music magazines and newspapers to carry obituaries, which is how I learned that he was dead. I was furious at Conrad for letting me find out this way, but then it turned out he'd learned the same way. He and Erik hadn't been speaking, and Conrad had no idea Erik was ill.

Cirrhosis of the liver, surprising only in the precipitousness of Erik's decline. He'd been healthy enough to leap around like a maniac for *Relâche*, but a month later he was falling apart, at fifty-eight years old. The acolytes had installed him in a series of hotels, then the hospital. They wouldn't let him go back to his room in Arcueil. Thank God for that, I thought. *He wasn't alone*, Conrad wrote, trying to reassure both of us. The acolytes had taken charge of him, paid his hospital bills, brought him warm socks and fresh handkerchiefs. Probably they were the family, the siblings-in-art, he would have chosen. Maybe it was all for the best, we told ourselves.

Once Conrad read the news and contacted the hospital, it turned out the acolytes had been trying to find him; they knew there was a brother, somewhere, and there were legalities to dispense with.

If they knew Erik had a brother, why hadn't anyone tried to find him *before* Erik died? Conrad had asked Roger Désormière.

They had offered, Désormière told him. They'd even tried to insist. But Erik had told them he and Conrad had quarreled and that his brother wouldn't want to hear from him.

What in the world had Erik been trying to prove? Conrad wondered. Of course he would have wanted to hear from Erik, he told Désormière, still angry, but less upset with the acolytes than with his brother.

Désormière offered his apologies, and his condolences, on behalf of the acolytes. If it was any consolation, he said, they weren't Erik's closest friends, necessarily. They were just the ones he happened to still be speaking to when he fell ill.

Conrad didn't know if that was consolation or not. He and a few of the acolytes set a day and time to go through the apartment. They met in the city and drove down together, in Désormière's bright yellow car. *It was a hot day,* Conrad wrote. *My hair flew straight up in the wind. I had a lion's mane by the time we arrived in Arcueil.*

So Conrad still has hair, then, I thought, because I'd learned from pictures that Erik didn't. Mine has thinned, but if I wear it up, the bun is still round.

Once Désormière saw the neighborhood, he asked someone to wait with the car, so it wouldn't be stolen. Of course that was just the beginning. It sounded as if Erik hadn't cleaned or thrown out anything since I'd been there, just continued adding to the hoard. The acolytes were horrified. Conrad too, although he'd known enough to brace himself.

Once the acolytes realized that Conrad wouldn't fight them for the music manuscripts, they were warmer to him. *They had a whole speech prepared, about "safeguarding Erik's legacy," about how perhaps as a nonmusician I didn't realize what Erik had accomplished, blah blah blah. It was patronizing. I understand what he accomplished. Or, to be fair, I don't <u>understand</u> what he accomplished. But I understand it was something, and they're welcome to be the ones to try and figure out what it is.*

Finally, I need to confess to you that I told them a fib. Legally, half the contents of the apartment were yours, and you needed to make a claim or sign off on a public sale. I said you were unfindable, that you hadn't been in touch with the family in years, so that the sale could proceed quickly. I hope this was all right? The prospect of letting all that garbage fester there for weeks or months, just to have our Ts crossed and Is dotted, felt absurd. I don't imagine the sale will fetch much of anything, but certainly I'll wire you half the proceeds. And if there are any little items you'd like to have, let me know? I've kept a few of his handkerchiefs, some books and sketches, personal effects, etc.

Oh, Conrad. O! *Unfindable?* I'm right here. But I understand why he said it. I have no practical objection, just the sting of having been written out of the family once more. Plus, now all of Erik's remaining friends, or the closest thing he had to friends, think I'm a ghost.

I'd like the knife, I wrote to Conrad. *I'd like the knife you stole from me, when you thought I might try to stab someone with it.* Conrad dutifully obeyed, making no mention of the theft or how I knew he had it. Really, I'd only guessed. It came wrapped in a handkerchief I assumed was Erik's, although it wasn't personalized in any way, then wrapped again in many layers of newsprint from a very leftist local paper, which would not have had a circulation wide enough to ever make it deliberately to Argentina. I smoothed out the sheets and read every article, pretending it was the day's news, happening just down the street, in my own language.

The truth is that I haven't felt properly French since the Great War. Once the scale of it was clear, I knew I'd missed too much, and that even if I were somehow to go back, I would always be a person who'd left before it happened, who'd sat out the whole thing safely at the other end of the world. It was a selfish little grief, the awareness that my exile had become undeniable.

The worst of it had been when Joseph, having graduated medical school, wrote to tell me that he planned to enlist, would have already by the time the letter arrived, no chance to try to talk him out of it, not that he would have heeded me. He was enlisting as a doctor, he wrote, and I hoped this would keep him back from the front lines, but I felt superstitious about my self-pity. I'd been feeling excluded, and voilà: a son in uniform. I'd tempted fate as loudly and stupidly as fate could be tempted.

I started going to Mass again every morning, then sometimes twice a day, if I finished my late lessons in time. I felt better there, praying for Joseph, not because I thought it would really make a difference, but because it felt like I was doing something. I lit the candles. I said the words. I kneeled and I stood. The priest suggested I visit the resettlement center. I clearly had time, and energy. And guilt. He didn't presume to guess over what, and I hadn't told him about Joseph, because then I would have had to offer some explanation for why we were in opposite hemispheres, on opposite sides of an ocean.

After Joseph made it safely home at the end of the war, I didn't feel like I could just stop going to church. God might find some other pretext to take him, as punishment for my self-interest masquerading as piety. My piety *was* self-interest at first, but I spent enough time trying to convince God and the priest otherwise that eventually it became habit, then solace.

I had long ago tried and failed to bargain with God for my husband's life. So when I prayed for Joseph, I prayed modestly, novenas and prayers of intercession to saints who looked after soldiers and doctors. I asked that he be allowed to do his duty, to be protected so that he could protect others, and protect his country. What I wanted most, of course, was for him to be protected long enough to come to me, then to live as nearly to forever as he could.

He survived the war, as so many did not, and came home. He married and worked and had a son. But he did not survive the inheritance of his father's bad lungs, and forty years old is nowhere near forever. When I received the news of his death from his widow, Nancey, I wanted to claw my own steady, strong lungs out of my chest, as if I might still be able to pass them along to him. Or perhaps I wanted only to disassemble myself, to become a heap of parts beyond any longing.

Nancey enclosed the latest photograph of Joseph's son, seven years old then, solemn in a dark suit. I added it to my small stack and thumbed through them like a flipbook, watching my grandson grow from baby to toddler to fatherless boy. This last one was not a happy picture, but in his face I could see Joseph's at the same age, and console myself that at least they'd known each other, father and son. Seven would be old enough for the boy to remember, to carry Joseph with him. Nancey had written his name, Pierre-Conrad, neatly across the back of the photograph. She always did this, and once teased herself in a letter—who else might the photographs be of? I begged her not to stop. I loved reading that name, written out with both parts.

Strangely, with Joseph's death I could at last crawl into the finality of it and find the smallest bit of comfort. I could imagine my son with God, rather than with Albertine and Cannu. I kneeled in church and asked for nothing at all, and in the silence I listened to my own steady breathing. There was no more wondering whether I would see him again. Not in this life. I could set my hopes on another. There was a cleanness to it, a door open and then shut. My motherhood had banged so long on rusty hinges, smashing my fingers in the jamb. Maybe Joseph and Pierre were both waiting for me, somewhere else. I could choose to believe it.

Oskar and I perfect the paper ball, move on to little animals. I found a paper-folding guide in a used-book shop, so battered and cheap that I could justify the purchase. Oskar's mother has found a job in a laundry. She drops him off most mornings at the resettlement center, which is against the rules—we aren't nannies. But Oskar is old enough not to need much attention, and I enjoy giving him what I can.

He's been practicing folding wolves and wants to show me,

lecturing all the while about animals in a jumbled flood of Spanish and Polish. I know I should encourage him, be grateful that he's blossoming, and I manage to smile. But I find lectures hard to take, even from little boys, already so like little men, so sure I do not possess their endless knowledge.

"Do you know wolves?" he asks me, finally pausing, and I have no idea how to answer. "I mean: see them. You see wolves? Seen," he corrects himself.

I tell him I haven't, though I have to think about it. It seems like one might have stalked through Bellenau, slunk through the palms or drawn up on its hind legs and joined us for dinner.

"Wolves will bite their own paws," Oskar declaims, and runs his front teeth over his wrist. His Spanish has come along impressively. "To get out of a trap. All off, no paw."

"Do they live?" I ask. "Once they've gnawed off their foot?"

"Paw," corrects Oskar, little pedant, and I suppose I'm proud.

"Can they run and hunt on only three?"

"There's a three-legged dog that lives by the bus stop. It eats its own poop."

"In a forest, I mean. In the wild."

Oskar is silent, unsure. Then he announces, "Absolutely," with total authority. "They live a very long time."

"Well, that's nice," I say. "That's good to hear."

For our first date Mr. Valera plans a film, with dinner afterward. The film is a romantic comedy, *Mi novia es un fantasma—My Wife Is a Ghost*. It's funny enough, but I'm so quiet at dinner that Mr. Valera worries the newsreels beforehand might have upset me.

"No," I say. "I just need to tell you something. When I said I didn't have children...I'm not used to having the conversation more than once, but if we're going to—I had a son. He died twelve years ago, back in France. I have a grandson. Do you want to see a picture?"

He can't say no, of course. So I show him, and he says good, kind things.

An old woman's billfold, cracking open. Sepia, with a scalloped white edge. I don't know what makes the yellow-brown color rather than the grays; Fortin might have known, or he might not have. No doubt photography has changed mightily since his time. Pierre-Conrad is almost twenty now, strong as an ox. Good lungs, his mother assures me. He's handsome in the way a man is, no longer a boy, so that I feel strange about having his picture in my wallet, as if I might fancy us sweethearts. He's in medical school—like his father, like his grandfather—and it's looking like this war might be over in time for him to be spared it. I feel as though we are all due for a stroke of luck—what's left of the Lafosse line, anyway. Though if you tell a story seventy years long, a lot of people are bound to die. They aren't especially unlucky, just mortal. Let a story go on long enough, and everyone dies.

At dinner, Mr. Valera suggests we switch from the formal to informal "you." I agree, then point out that we also need to exchange first names.

"Olga Louise," I offer. "But I've always preferred just Louise."

"Felipe."

"Really?"

"What's so funny?"

"Nothing, I suppose."

"I have a piano at home," he tells me, so shamelessly it's like an advertising jingle. I'm not for sale, some late-life wife to make his meals for him. If I were I'd charge a steeper price than a piano. But it would be so nice to live in a place with a piano again. Marriages have been made on less.

With all of France closing around me like a rusty steel trap, I was trying to save my life and was willing to gnaw my own hand off to do it. The only future I could envision was one where I ran as far and fast as I could, lurching forward on whatever limbs I had left. Did I know it would be the last time I'd see Joseph, at the train station? I wondered and then refused to think about it any more, which meant it wouldn't have to be true until it was. I could have guessed that I'd never have the money to return, but at the time I didn't want to. My son was planning to be a rich man—he could come to me, or fetch me, or emigrate himself. Conrad and I each proved to be right: a thirteen-year-old doesn't forget his mother, but he makes a life without her that he will be unwilling or unable to give up on her behalf. This is something I might tell Mrs. Valera, if we ever exchange more than pleasantries. If you have to run, run. If you have to go, go. You can survive it. But he'll survive it too, in his own way.

When I follow news of the Allied advance across northern France, I look for the name of the town with the train station. I can't bear to say it, try not to even think it, which makes reading for it difficult, but I look all the same. I don't know what I want: for it to be wiped off the face of the earth, or for monuments to be raised. But what kind of monument? The ones I've seen are all columns or rearing horses or generals, which would of course be all wrong.

It would be a stone mother, a stone child. They're sitting across from each other at a tiny, rickety table. The sculptor would not need to be as talented as one might think, because their faces stayed so still. They were both trying hard to be calm for the sake of the other. There are two white cups. The hot chocolate was terrible, watery and gritty, but I suppose that wouldn't matter for the carving. There is a small stone valise on the floor under the table.

On Cannu's orders, most of Joseph's possessions had already been shipped to Cherbourg after having been packed up, with my permission, by Conrad and Mathilde. On the train I'd brought a few keepsakes, things that had always been at least as much mine as his, like the book of wallpaper samples he'd once given Madeleine. I wanted Joseph to have them, and I'd imagined that lifting out and describing these items for him might be a way for me to survive the half hour we had together, without my voice dissolving completely. But once we were sitting there, I kept thinking about Erik's knife and the forsaken look on his face when I didn't remember it, or at least didn't remember it in the way he'd hoped I would.

I thought that Joseph might handle these objects in a similar fashion, filled more with my memories than his own. I did not want to see his face trying for my sake to remember, or feel, more than he really remembered or felt. He seemed much older than he'd been just a few weeks earlier, though he looked the same, and when I tried to place the change I realized it was his polite kindness, his consideration. After all his whining and raging since leaving Bellenau, I'd become a person to him. I'd become someone with feelings—the kind of feelings that might propel a woman to stand screaming in the street—and this was someone different from a mother. I both grieved and marveled at this solemn, sympathetic boy in front of me. *This is the person who comes next*, I thought. *This is the Joseph you won't get to know.*

In the end we said almost nothing. He stood, and I worried he was going to curtail our meeting for some reason, but then he dragged the little table away from my chair. He was making room to sit in my lap. He didn't fit, of course, his knees sticking out and his toes scraping the floor. But he managed to tuck his head beneath mine, and I pressed my nose into his hair, which smelled of an unfamiliar soap, and put my arms tight around him. We sat like that until the next trains arrived, whistles shrieking, and we had to rise. I pressed the valise into his hand and told him to open it later, or not at all, if he didn't wish to.

Better, then, to imagine the whole place annihilated rather than enshrined. Crush the station, the town, and—why stop there?—the rails all the way north to Cherbourg. I imagine a bomb flattening the stone house with the pharmacy underneath as an elderly Cannu cowers inside. I imagine him shot through the head by the Germans, but then I imagine he's the sort of person—coward or collaborator—to skulk successfully through an occupation. Then I imagine Albertine shot by the Resistance, or by a British or American soldier who offers some pithy insult in English that she can't even understand, so that her last earthly thought is confusion: *Why is this happening to me?*

These are the biggest events on earth, and I can't help making them small. This war, and the last one, but—but—*me!* Always I come back to myself.

I thought for a long time that this made me small-minded and womanly—that men were superior thinkers because they could hold larger ideas in their heads, hold them in a pure way, without the contamination of petty or private concerns. I'd written a letter to Erik, in fact, in which I described the way Fortin had convinced me that great men could hold a big idea like a jeweler, coldly, with calipers, raising it up to the light. Erik's reply was the kindest letter he ever sent me.

But we're all trying to make something small, he wrote back. *It wouldn't fit in people's ears, otherwise. Take a look in the mirror—just a tiny little dark space, full of earwax to boot (speaking in a general way—I'm sure your ears are no waxier than the average, and perhaps considerably less). You can hardly expect to jam something enormous inside it. The only way big ideas get inside is by making them small.*

Once I left France I was a ghost to Erik, invisible except for the occasional moan from the rafters. In the twenty years that I was in Buenos Aires while he was alive, he sent me only a handful of letters. I tried not to be hurt. He'd finally gained the work he wanted. He was very busy, becoming the person he'd wanted to be. The last letter he sent me, which I did not know would be the last when I received it, was mostly about his work. He was composing music to accompany the projection of a silent film (the only kind then), which posed a fearsome set of challenges, he explained. One couldn't anticipate projector speeds, so the whole score had to be constructed out of modular phrases that could be repeated or omitted, the organist or conductor able to speed or slow the score to sync with the images. I read the letter waiting to encounter his affront at the prospect of his notes being chopped up and rearranged. But instead I sensed only pleasure: the satisfaction of having been asked to do it, the excitement of the challenge, the joy of the work. He complained about money but did not mention that his lack of it was owing to an unreconciled quarrel with Conrad.

With the Allied troops closing in on occupied Paris now, I worry sometimes about Conrad before I remember that I don't have to worry about him anymore. He's gone now too, taken six years after Joseph. I had already guessed, from how many letters in a row went unanswered, before I knew for sure. He never remarried, and it took Nancey some time to let me know. I wouldn't have heard about it in any other way. Perhaps there are chemistry trade journals or alumni bulletins that might have carried a mention? I don't know. I don't know what became of the cat he adopted and wrote fondly of, or whether he ever finished the book he often mentioned to me: a new encyclopedia of perfumes that occupied him after he retired. The early retirement came as a surprise, and I got the feeling that it had not been entirely voluntary, although he continued to mention M. Jeancard without bitterness.

I did not wish to pry, but I wondered, selfishly, what might become of his remittances. Without steady earnings, did he have enough for both of us? Or maybe he had far more squirreled away than I guessed, and now that he was no longer working he would ask me to come back to France and keep him company, or decide himself to retire in Argentina. Daydreams, but I tested them out in my mind, wondering what I'd say if he ever suggested either. I realized that I liked the life I'd made, that I was proud of myself for making it, even though I'd had his help, and that Buenos Aires had become much more familiar to me than France would ever feel again. In any case he made no dramatic suggestions, and in time I understood that he could not have, as the sums he sent grew smaller and smaller, until, shortly before his death, they stopped.

Whenever I die, there will likewise be no easy way for anyone in France to know. There will be only my silence. My death will not be news, and I mean this both because I am old and will presumably be dead in some thoroughly ordinary way, and because I will have done nothing extraordinary.

Felipe calls me Luisa. It took seventy-six years, but I've one-upped Erik. My brother changed a single letter. I've changed languages. Though I am called nearly the same in both.

Felipe always pays for our dates, which in the abstract are not extravagant—films, meals, walks in Palermo Park with stops to rest, since neither of us walks as far at a stretch as we used to. But compared with my previous routine our courtship feels dangerously luxurious. Since Conrad's death I have accustomed myself to exactly what I can afford, and no more. But now there are breaks from the monotony of the boardinghouse food, and theater tickets again—good seats, not stuck behind a pillar or squinting from the second balcony. I enjoy myself, but I'm afraid of what will happen if my daily life starts to look too straitened. Not afraid of Felipe losing interest, but of myself coming to want something that might, like so much else in my life, be taken away.

Felipe gifts me a piece of imported cheese, which he does not suggest we share, as if he guesses I want to take it to my room and savor every scrap of it myself until I have licked my scratched white plate clean. I start to think that perhaps he's getting to know me too well, but then he gives me an ashtray printed with music notes along the gold-painted rim, and I think he does not know me at all. Then he gives me a monthly bus pass, and I think, *Well, maybe. Maybe there's hope.*

*   *   *

For years I looked for Osprey, old Uncle Osprey, my father's weird brother, around every corner. He'd emigrated years before me and deliberately disappeared; beyond "America," no one in the family knew where he'd gone, or even whether "America" meant north or south. But when I stepped off the boat in Buenos Aires, he was the only person I knew on this entire side of the ocean. I didn't really expect to stumble across him, of course, but I wondered, and I planned what we might say to each other. "We're the black sheep," I could announce. "Every generation has one. You probably thought it was Erik, but look where I've ended up!" We'd have a meal together, and it would be so much fun, remembering old times, but at some point I'd have to dump my drink on his head for abandoning his wife and daughters. Little Louise, keeper of all the old crimes.

I looked for him more infrequently as the years passed, needing an old familiar face less once the newer ones had become familiar to me. I moved boardinghouses several times in those first years, sometimes for better food or a better room, and sometimes because I was becoming someone more at ease in my own life and I didn't want to live alongside the same people who'd known me as a wraith with no Spanish, afraid of her own shadow, constantly confused by the bus schedule. Wherever Osprey ended up, he'd be a hundred this year, so it seems safe to assume he's dead. One more ghost.

My ghost family is now much larger than my living one. I imagine myself moving through and beyond them, the gathered generations, a little like walking through a closet of fur coats. They brush my cheeks, my arms, they gather round, gather me up. They are soft and heavy, with a smell of something that was once animal and alive, but isn't any longer. Don't tell the priest. I'm sure the notion of souls like fur coats isn't in any encyclical.

But one morning I put on my nicest dress. I go to one of the handful of smart department stores or boutiques here that sell fur coats. It doesn't usually get cold enough for anyone to want one, but I ask them to assemble a rack for me. (I can do this only once in a very great while, or a clerk will escort me out. Kindly, but firmly. *We think you do not really want a coat today, señora. Perhaps we can interest you in something else. Perhaps this is not a good day for shopping.*) I hold my arm up, palm out, and walk along the rack. I should have invited Mrs. Valera, and Oskar's mother. It's silly, but this feels like something I could finally offer them, something more pleasant than words of wisdom or encouraging exhortations. One by one I put the coats on, feel their sleek weight across my bent shoulders, take them off. There has been no one in this country who touches me, although there is someone now who might want to. I press my cheek to the fur. Hello, ghosts. You are so, so soft.

Felipe invites me to his apartment. To play the piano, he says. He's extended the invitation several times, and I've always invented some excuse. But eventually I decide that whether or not "playing the piano" is meant as a euphemism or pretext for something else, I am willing to find out what the something else might be.

On a Sunday afternoon, the weather bright and chilly, I try to decide what music to bring. No Leybach, both because it means too much to me and because it's too nakedly romantic. In trying to conjure the opposite of the Leybach, I think of Erik's "Cold Pieces." They're opposite only in name, though. They're slim ladies in gloves and scarves and interesting hats, not snowmen with stone eyes. But it would feel strange to play them either way, whether mentioning or omitting that I know the composer. That I am, or was, related to the composer. I end up grabbing a book of Mozart's sonatas—not difficult and not at all amorous.

The apartment is small and cluttered, but the clutter is orderly and clean. No foul bachelor's den. Whatever he wants a woman for, he's managing the cleaning on his own. I thought Felipe might only have been offering me the use of the piano, and that he would putter around while I played, doing whatever he normally does on a Sunday afternoon. But he sits and listens attentively. His voice-teacher wife trained him well.

"If I'd known I was giving a concert," I say, "I would have brought more music. Let you choose."

Then he sits beside me on the piano bench and asks me to marry him. The question hangs glowing in the air. Both because of what the question is and because it's a real question. It's a choice I get to make. I can say yes or no, or anything in between. There's no Scylla and no Charybdis, just two plausible options, laid at my feet. When else have I ever truly gotten to make such a decision? Even when I said yes to Pierre, eagerly and wholeheartedly, I knew that Fortin was listening in the next room, awaiting the one answer he considered acceptable. Now no one, except Felipe, is listening.

"May I say maybe?" I ask.

"I'll be hoping it turns into a yes, but certainly—if you aren't ready, I'd rather you say maybe than no."

"Then the answer is maybe. Please don't be hurt, just patient." For now, there is nothing that could feel more delicious than the choice itself.

I've been teaching at the French Institute for over thirty years but suddenly some paperwork is lost, or someone notices it was never filed. I am asked for my work permit, passport, an ancient visa application, both married and maiden names listed.

"Like the composer," the secretary says.

Is she Erik's single fan in Buenos Aires? Or one of thousands? I have no idea.

"He was my brother," I say, and the secretary's eyes nearly fall out of her head. She runs around the administrative office, then up and down the hallway into the classrooms: how have they been working all this time with someone born alongside greatness, and never known?

"Greatness?" I say, not disagreeing, but curious. Is that the consensus?

"Are you musical too?" asks the instructional coordinator, who has come out of his office to see what the commotion is. When I mention that I teach piano lessons, the coordinator expresses dismay that the Institute has only ever had me in the language classroom. Would I be willing to teach a course on Erik's music? he asks.

"I'd have to figure out what to say." The look on his face tells me that this is the wrong answer, and I revise: "Yes. I'd love to. I'd be honored."

He asks me if I have any pictures of the two of us together. Something they can use to market the course. Or even something candid of him, something people won't have already seen?

I tell him I don't, which is true, but would you like one anyway? Let's open the old woman's billfold and see what's inside. Certainly not much in the way of money—a jangle of pesos and centavos and crumpled bills—but so many ghosts. So, so soft. I won't pretend you'd want to see another of my grandson. (Handsome as anything, though, have I mentioned? He's going to live forever. Don't tell me I'm wrong.) Let's assume that you would rather see one more of Erik. We'll go back to the *Gymnopédies*. Not the choice of the connoisseur, but easily the winner of the popular vote. Not the time he played one at the Mirliton, but earlier. When he debuted them at the Chat Noir. I wasn't actually there, but I haven't let that stop me up to now.

Salis is letting Erik have a recital late on a Wednesday night, the three *Gymnopédies*, plus the *Gnossiennes* and *Sarabandes*, everything he's ever written that he can bear to revisit, that he thinks might—just might—hold up. The audience is composed of his friends, plus anyone still trying to sober up enough to stagger home. Even Rodolphe Salis sticks around. "I've been listening to the doorman call you a gymnopédiste since you were a teenager," he says. "Finally, the mystery unraveled."

Erik clutches his sheet music in his hands, his usual painstaking script growing crumpled and sweaty. Surely he's got the music memorized—he wrote it, after all—but he thinks he might be nervous enough to need the handwritten copies. Philippe's never seen him like this, doesn't know whether to buy him a drink to calm his nerves or just be heartened that he has nerves after all. Erik takes the stage to raucous applause. Philippe, who has been publishing poetry as Lord Cheminot, who was never Philippe to begin with, who was born in another country as someone else altogether, claps loudest. All Erik's friends wear their names like hats, ready to be doffed and replaced. Erik-with-a-K born Eric-with-a-C, his pseudonym halfhearted, a bit too honest.

Conrad is across town doing his homework at the dining table. I am in Le Havre, in bed asleep. The hour is late, but Fortin is still awake, worrying about husbands. His great-niece will need one. That will go rather grimly for her, but all that is yet to come.

Erik spreads the pages of the three *Gymnopédies* out along the music rack. He has declined a page-turner, saying he's too anxious to have anyone up onstage with him. He is worried about his breath, his soaked underarms. He doesn't want anyone to come too close. The café piano is a plow horse, but he is used to it by now, knows how to massage the keys. As he plays, the piano becomes another kind of instrument. The sound is quiet and the room quiets with it.

You have heard these songs. You, reading this now, I promise you, you know them. They're going to show up in concert halls and advertisements, children's piano lessons and programs of turn-of-the-century French music. They'll play in the background of film scenes where someone stares mournfully out a rainy window; they'll play while someone else falls in and out of love. They'll be covered by everyone from jazz musicians to drum-and-bugle corps. They'll become so ubiquitous they are nearly white noise, but then they catch your ear and are beautiful all over again. They are wallpaper that can make you cry. If you have heard any songs Erik ever wrote, you have heard these. It is possible, perhaps even probable, that you have heard only these.

Seven and a half minutes of music, and as Erik raises his hands from the keyboard, lifts his foot off the pedal, they are already over. There is only one debut, and it has ended.

Philippe buys Erik a glass of wine. Salis charges full price. The applause is proud, relieved. The people who know Erik, who have been agreeably calling him a gymnopédiste for months, are pleased to have done so, to have believed in him. The few who had been hoping that the pieces would be garbage, or another parody or prank, are chastened.

Erik is twenty-one years old, almost twenty-two. The most popular seven minutes he will ever write are fading away in the sweaty, soot-dark room. A piano note is dying from the moment it is struck, hammer to string. The vibrations slow and the note decays, a birth and a death with every press of the keys. The last sounds of the third *Gymnopédie* hang and dissipate like smoke, and then they are gone. His life is long yet, but the thing people will love best about him is already finished. Let us hope he does not know it. How would he live, otherwise? How would any of us, if we knew all that was to come?

Acknowledgments

In this book I have aimed to color inside the lines, so to speak, of what is known about Erik Satie's life and work, as well as what records remain of his family members and associates. As one would expect, there is a tremendous amount of information available on Claude Debussy, for example, and relatively little about José Maria Patricio Contamine de Latour, the inspiration for Philippe. Where the record stops, I have invented. I have occasionally changed names or made other minor adjustments for the sake of clarity and narrative. The novel is shaped, even governed, by facts, but it is a work of fiction.

The book has involved a great deal of research, and I have consulted more sources than I could possibly list. I am grateful to all the scholars, creators, and fellow travelers who have informed my thinking and answered my questions, either personally or through their published work, particularly Robert Orledge and Andrea Cohen.

For anyone wishing to know more about Erik Satie, I recommend first his music, available in a wide variety of recordings and formats. The Satie family home in Honfleur is now a delightful, unusual museum. You can also visit Château Bellenâu: the current owners are restoring the gardens and rent out rooms and cottages. Many of Satie's stomping grounds in Paris and Arcueil-Cachan can still be seen, at least from the outside.

Some of Satie's prose writings are available in English translation in *A Mammal's Notebook*, or in the French-language *Mémoires d'un amnésique*. Of the many books written about Satie, my personal favorite is *Satie Remembered*, a collection of reminiscences from people who knew him, compiled and edited by Robert Orledge. *Erik Satie: Correspondance presque complète*, edited by Ornella Volta, was another key text. The best (and essentially only) resource on the life of Louise-Olga-Jeannie Satie-Lafosse is the radio documentary *Je suis la sœur d'Erik Satie* by Andrea Cohen and Gaël Gillon. The most comprehensive source on Suzanne Valadon is *Renoir's Dancer: The Secret Life of Suzanne Valadon* by Catherine Hewitt. Édouard Fortin's photographs of Le Havre have been collected by Dominique Rouet in the book *Le Havre: une ville neuve sous l'oeil d'un pionnier*. A special mention goes to *Satie the Bohemian* by Steven Moore Whiting, which I have had out on loan from the Grand Valley State University library since 2011. Thank you to Hazel McClure and the GVSU library for both your research assistance and your generous loan renewal policies.

Archival research at l'Institut Mémoires de l'édition contemporaine (IMEC) and the Bibliothèque nationale de France was supported by a grant from the GVSU Center for Scholarly and Creative Activity. Portions of this book were written at the MacDowell Colony, Can Serrat Centro de Actividades Artisticas, and Bernheim Arboretum and Research Forest, as well as in nearly every coffee shop in Grand Rapids, Michigan, often alongside writing partner extraordinaire Mara Naselli. Portions of this book originally appeared, in altered form, in the literary journals *Gulf Coast*, *Bat City Review*, *Indiana Review*, and *Sonora Review*.

Thanks to Judy Heiblum, Jim Rutman, and Ben George, who believed in this book even before I'd written most of it. Ben, in fact, believed in my work before I'd written much of anything and, once this book was done, paid careful and graceful attention to every single sentence. For both your faith and your rigor: thank you. I am also pleased to be in the good hands of the entire team at Little, Brown, including Reagan Arthur, Craig Young, Pamela Brown, Lena Little, Pamela Marshall, Allan Fallow, and Cynthia Saad.

Wild gratitude to Marian Crotty and Adrianna Jordan, who read the whole damn thing. Thanks to those who read what ultimately became the beginning sections: Elizabeth Weld, Robby Taylor, Beth Staples, Monica McFawn, and Benjamin Drevlow. Thank you to Taryn Tilton, Laurence José, and Molly Jo Rose for lending their expertise, and special thanks to the people at the Norman Mailer Writers Colony in July 2010, who read a terrible short story about Erik Satie and tactfully told me that it would work better as a novel. I've learned a great deal from all the writing communities I've been a part of, including GVSU, the MFA Program for Writers at Warren Wilson College, the *Kenyon Review*, the *Kenyon Review* Writers' Workshop, the Sewanee Writers' Conference, and the Bread Loaf Writers' Conference.

I'm grateful to everyone who supported my first book in myriad ways. It felt like the Little Short Story Collection That Could, and I owe a debt to all the people who helped push that train up the hill. I'm giddy that I get to do this publishing thing all over again.

My husband, W. Todd Kaneko, made this book possible in a thousand different ways. As for Leo, I suspect this book would have been written more quickly if you hadn't come along, but it would have been poorer, as would our lives, without you. Thank you to my sister, Mary Horrocks, for the fortuitous gift one year of Satie's *Gymnopédies, Gnossiennes, and Other Works for Piano*, and to my earliest piano teachers: my mother, Marlee Horrocks; and my grandmother Marjorie Lee Parmiter. My father, David Horrocks, drove me to another decade of piano lessons uncomplainingly. Thanks also to all the teachers, musicians, directors, and conductors I have had the pleasure of making music with over the years, with special appreciation for Margaret Faulkner, who first assigned me Satie's *Gymnopédie No. 3*.

About the Author

CAITLIN HORROCKS is the author of the story collection *This Is Not Your City* and a recipient of the O. Henry Prize, the Pushcart Prize, and the Plimpton Prize. Her fiction has appeared in *The New Yorker*, *The Atlantic*, the *Paris Review*, *Tin House*, *One Story*, and elsewhere and has been included in *The Best American Short Stories*. She lives with her family in Grand Rapids, Michigan.